Garrett Haines

About the Author

KATHRYN MILLER HAINES is an actor,
mystery writer, award-winning playwright,
and artistic director of a Pittsburgh-based
theater company. *The War Against Miss
Winter* is her first novel.

D0051507

THE WAR AGAINST
Miss Winter

HARPER

NEW YORK • LONDON • TORONTO • SYDNEY

THE WAR AGAINST

Miss Winter

KATHRYN MILLER HAINES

HARPER

HarperCollins books may be purchased for educational, business, or sales promotional use. For information please write: Special Markets Department, HarperCollins Publishers, 10 East 53rd Street, New York, NY 10022.

FIRST EDITION

Designed by Justin Dodd

Library of Congress Cataloging-in-Publication Data has been applied for.

ISBN: 978-0-06-113978-9
ISBN-10: 0-06-113978-5

08 09 10 11 ❖/RRD 10 9 8 7 6 5 4 3

For my mother, who always told me I could do anything, my father, who gave me the resources to make it possible, and especially for Garrett, who made sure I never gave up.

THE WAR AGAINST
Miss Winter

1 Death and the Fool

AUDITIONS WERE MURDER.

On New Year's Eve I went to the final casting call of 1942, the last opportunity I'd have to say I was in something that year that didn't involve wearing a mask, a fur suit, or hawking kitchen products at the Lions Convention. I was trying out for a new musical called *You Bet Your Life,* which, thankfully, had nothing to do with the Germans. Unfortunately, judging from the score, it also had very little acquaintance with the Western scale. The audition was a standard cattle call in a room large enough to serve as a field hospital. Hundreds of women with 8 x 10s in hand lined the walls while two men—one big, one small—roamed in a parallel line judging our attributes. I made it through "too old," "too short," and "too fat," before one of the proctors stopped before me.

"Name?" he asked.

"Rosie Winter."

His pencil scratched across his clipboard. "You sing?"

"Like a bird."

"Dance?"

"Better than Pavlova."

He took a gander at gams that had so little muscle it was a wonder I could climb stairs. "What was the last thing you were in?"

"The backseat of a Willys-Knight."

I was dismissed at "too much personality."

I was used to rejection, but my dismissal from *You Bet Your Life* didn't just signify another lost part in another bad show; it meant I'd officially hit rock bottom. I hadn't been cast in anything in six months. Not only was it time to consider another career, I was going to be kicked out of my boardinghouse, an establishment that only offered low cost rooms to *working* actresses. If that wasn't enough to put the sour on my puss, the love of my life had shipped out the month before after deciding the navy had more to offer him than I did.

On the bright side, I had a day job. I worked at McCain & Son, a small detective agency located at Fifth and East Thirty-eighth, a spit from Broadway. I'd found the job courtesy of the Ladies Employment Guild (motto: Girls, get a LEG up on the workforce). When I started, there were only two employees, Jim McCain, owner and operator (and, I assumed, the "& Son" of the title) and his secretary, a well-endowed, well-preserved middle-aged doll I eventually learned was named Agnes, but was usually referred to as honey, baby, or cupcake. As much joy as Agnes brought into Jim's life, at some point he figured out that he couldn't function in an office where the only alphabetical thing was the soup. That's why he hired me.

While Agnes did whatever it was Agnes did, I answered phones, scheduled appointments, filed, and fantasized. I'd grown up reading the pulps, so working for a private investigator was a dream for me. I imagined I was the lithe and lovely sidekick to a dick whose piercing gaze could immediately discern truth from trouble. Together, we'd break into dark warehouses, guarded mansions, and underground lairs, hunting down evil-doers with names like Captain Zero, the Bleeder, and the Domino Lady. Alas, *Dime Detective* got it all wrong. As far as I could tell, *detecting* was a synonym for *waiting* and both were dull work. Jim waited in his office for clients to call. Then he waited for cheating husbands to leave their chippies' houses. Then he waited for his film to develop as proof of the affair. There was nothing glamorous about it.

At least, I think that was the case. There was another side to Jim's business, a side we couldn't see. Through the front door came the cuckolded men and betrayed women with their desperate rheumy eyes, but there was a back entrance too, where clients demanding anonymity entered Jim's office by climbing up the fire escape and through a window. Agnes and I never saw these people, but we could hear the low drone of their voices as they recounted misdoings that never ended up in the notes Jim gave me to type. I gave these mysterious strangers names like the Mumbler and the Lisper and grew capable of identifying who was who based on only a whispered sibilant *s*. As Agnes and I passed our time in the reception area, I spun tales about what was happening in the inner office. Money laundering, numbers running, strike breaking—I attributed all of it to those nameless, faceless individuals who'd been reduced to vocal tics. Agnes silently listened to my musings, a wry smile hinting that she was far more aware of the truth than she'd ever let on.

I liked Agnes. I liked the job. I liked Jim. He was loud and boisterous and so disorganized he could lose things he never knew he had. I didn't know him very well, but I trusted him in some implicit way. He was one of the few bright spots remaining in a world that was rapidly approaching complete darkness.

I walked to McCain & Son and rewarded my failed audition efforts with a consolation cup of joe from Frankie's Diner. As I entered our suite, I stumbled over a mountain of mail that had been pushed through the door slot. Even though Agnes and I had closed the office on Christmas Eve, the reception area had a nasty stench that hinted that Jim had been working in our absence and had been kind enough to leave food to rot over the holidays. As the radiator groaned its welcome, I gathered up the mail, clicked on the lamps, and dumped my purse on one of the reception chairs. Churchill, our office stray, emerged from the potted dieffenbachia and gave me an irritated yowl.

"Daddy not feed you?" I asked. Churchill didn't answer, but then one couldn't expect the devil's minion to bother with such formalities. I retrieved a tin of cat food from a cabinet, dumped it into his bowl, and crushed the can for the local scrap drive. With nary a thank-you, Churchill raced to the dish and buried his face in the unappetizing mash.

I clicked on the Bakelite for company and turned the dial to WJZ, where they were counting down the last hours of 1942 with that year's chart toppers. As Kay Kyser crooned "(There'll Be Bluebirds Over) The White Cliffs of Dover" I sat at my desk and sorted the mail into letters, bills, and anything else. The anything else included several days' worth of newspapers and a pamphlet some kind soul had thought it important enough to slip through the slot. Beneath a crude caricature of FDR the cover announced ROOSEVELT BETRAYS AMERICA in big, bold type. Bund propaganda. Great. I tossed it into the trash bin and glanced at that day's *Times*. The new list of navy casualties was out, conveniently divided by state. For the local boys the *Times* went one step further, including the names of their wives, parents, and mailing addresses. I scanned the dead and wounded, grateful that the name I looked for came early in the alphabet. He wasn't listed. Jack was all right.

Bing Crosby started singing "Be Careful It's My Heart." I turned off the radio.

I set the paper aside and uncovered a gold-trimmed, leather-bound ledger. The IRS had recently notified Jim that businesses were expected to maintain records and the issue was laid at my feet like a disemboweled mouse I was supposed to dispose of despite my delicate stomach. I opened the book and scanned figure after figure that Jim had identified as "miscellaneous" costs. Sunlight escaped his office and illuminated a column of debits. Jim never opened his door beyond what it took for him to exit the room, and here it was not only unlocked but ajar.

"Hello?" I called out. Churchill stopped eating and the two of us froze, waiting for a response. When none came, I walked to the doorway and again listened for signs of activity. Churchill abandoned his meal and joined me at the threshold. "Hello?" We inched into the room. While the outer office had been cozy, Jim's joint was cold enough to hang meat. Bookshelves lined one wall but instead of holding books they were filled with files that never found their way into my hands. A massive oak desk was anchored near a window and covered by enough papers to obliterate its surface. A phone devoid of the cord that joined receiver to base teetered atop a stack of outdated directories. An empty bottle of scotch and two cheap crystal tumblers huddled on the blotter. There were three chairs: one for the man himself and two—unmatching—for whomever he was speaking with. The walls were bare except for a pair of certificates: one from the police academy and another from City College.

The stench I'd caught a whiff of in the reception area mingled with Jim's cigar smoke and Churchill's piss until it brewed a scent I swore I could taste. I pulled up the black-out blinds, hoping to air out the room, and discovered that the windows were already open. I checked the bin for the source of the stink. Empty. I opened up his desk. The only unusual things in there were a .38 and an unopened bottle of gin.

Churchill paced before the desk, exuding all the warmth of a rolling pin. We usually kept to our turfs, and his desire to accompany me could be read only as feline affront.

"Scram," I told him. I pointed a finger toward the reception area and he responded by slinking over to the closet door and rubbing his rump against it. A tortured sound escaped the lower reaches of his belly. Just when I was convinced I'd imagined it, the sound repeated, twice as loud. Churchill's paw—claws extended—rose into the air and made contact with the wood.

"Enough, Churchill. Out. Shoo." I hit my hand against the desk, hoping to startle him, but he never paused in his activity or let his eyes leave mine. "Is there something in the closet? Is that what you're trying to say?" I stepped toward him as he continued his work. When I was close enough to touch wood, he dashed out of sight. I turned the knob and looked inside.

Jim swung from a phone cord that had been bound around his hands and neck before being looped over the clothes rack. His skin was a deep bluish gray and hung from his bones as if the adhesive that had once joined them had begun to fail.

I backed away until I hit the corner of the desk. I'd been to plenty of funerals, seen loads of stiffs, but they were cleaned up, made up, ventriloquist's dummies—not this statue still frozen in a moment of violence. I wanted to scream, but the impulse was swept away by a desire to retch. That too disappeared and all I wanted was to never lay eyes on that thing in the closet again. I was scared, not that whoever had done this still lurked in the office but that Jim would pull free of his noose, step out of the closet, and announce that as a newly inducted creature of the night, he was required to eat my brains.

But this wasn't the one good story in that month's *Tales of Terror*. This was a man I liked and my being afraid wasn't going to release Jim from his predicament and give him the rest he deserved.

The coppers showed up twenty minutes later. By then I'd drained the gin, cried myself dry, and paced a permanent trail in the hardwood floor. Instead of giving me the third, a bull in a too small uniform asked me for my name then told me to take it on the heel and toe. I couldn't bring myself to leave though. I leaned against the doorjamb that separated my office from Jim's and watched through a haze of cigarette smoke as my former boss was examined, photographed, and cut free from his noose.

The leader of the effort was a sour-faced lieutenant named Schmidt who sat in Jim's chair and scratched notes on a pad. From his uninterested look you would've thought he was at the opera fighting to stay awake.

I mopped my face and willed the gin to clear my head. "Anything else I can do?"

"Naw," he said. "I think we got it all, sweetheart."

I nodded but still found myself unwilling to scram. "What do you think?"

Schmidt piled his feet atop Jim's desk, smudging the files with imprints of his heels. "About what?"

"The war," I snapped. My sarcasm was lost on him. "The body. What do you think about the body?"

He shrugged as though to say, *If you've seen one, you've seen them all.*

Flashbulbs went off in the empty closet, momentarily blinding me. I left my post in the doorway and approached the desk. "How long do you think he's been dead?"

He kept his eyes on the notepad. What I'd assumed were notes about the case was actually a grocery list. "The coroner will have to call it, but based on the stink and the bloat I'm guessing the stiff's been here since Christmas."

I drummed my nails on the desktop until he looked up at me. "Is there any sign of who might've done this?"

He flipped the notepad closed and sighed. "It's pretty cut and dried, doll. We see this sort of thing all the time. Lots of people get depressed this time of year, more so since the war."

"Yeah? And do they usually tie their hands first?"

He shifted his feet until the stains on the papers grew into half-moons.

"Lieutenant, were you raised in a barn?" A question entered his eyes and he shook his head. "Then get your feet off my files. They're not a goddamn doormat."

He slid his legs off the desk—causing further disorder—and slammed his size tens into the ground. "You got a mouth on you."

"How else am I going to eat?" I put my hands on the desk and bent down to his level. "Look, I don't know what kind of game you're playing, but Jim McCain isn't some holiday suicide. He was bumped off, plain and simple."

His face lit up with his best baby-took-her-first-steps smile. "What's your name, doll?"

"It's not doll, that's for sure."

"Fair enough, sweetheart. Are you by any chance a police officer or maybe a detective?"

I looked for a lie to show him up and couldn't find one. "You know the answer to that."

He flipped through his pad until he located the statement I'd given to the bull. "No, *Miss Winter*, you're an actress, and I'm sure a damn good one at that. Can't be easy coming in here and finding the man you worked for doing the dance. I'm going to give you the benefit of the doubt and assume you might be a little emotional, your thinking unclear." He pulled a pack of cigarettes from his pocket and offered me one. I declined with a shake of my head. "You're not thinking like a detective, so maybe you don't see what I see. Here's how it is: your man Jim isn't doing so well financially. We've found a few letters from the IRS that make it look like he was in Dutch." He shuffled through his notes and flashed the Bund pamphlet at me. "Seems like he was making new friends too."

"That wasn't his. I found it in the mail."

"Sure, doll. Whatever you say." He tucked the pamphlet into his notebook and scribbled a note. "So what does a man with no money and bad politics do? The cowardly thing, sure, but he does it all the same. Maybe he's thinking twice about it, worried he won't follow through, so he ties his hands to make sure once he's up there, he can't change his mind."

I straightened up. "And how did he get up there? You think he jumped into the noose after he bound his hands? Or maybe he flew?"

The lieutenant stood and smoothed the pleats at the front of his food-stained pants. He was a chubby man and no amount of fussing was ever going to make his pants lay right. "I'm going to be straight with you." He punctured the air with his cigarette. "Jim McCain was a lowlife and everyone who knew him was a lowlife too. As far as my department's concerned, this is a suicide and anyone who wants to challenge that's going to look like a fool."

I tried to meet him eye to eye but came up woefully short. "What did Jim ever do to you?"

He tapped out his ashes on the desk. "He was a crooked cop and a rotten detective. Instead of arguing with me maybe you should be looking more carefully at him."

2 The Lower Depths

I SAT IN A WINDOW booth at Frankie's Diner and watched as the meat wagon came and left. When I was certain the coppers were gone, I returned to the office and locked the door behind me. Churchill greeted me with a quiet murmur and tangled himself about my legs until one of us couldn't move without the other. Jim's door remained open, his lights blazing an eerie gold. I couldn't stomach the thought of going back in there. Instead, I sank into my chair, picked up the blower, and asked for Agnes's exchange.

To say Agnes was devastated was like saying the Germans were stubborn. The woman wailed and keened until her voice disappeared. Then her grief penetrated her breathing, turning each exhale into an extended moan of dismay.

"I'm so, so sorry, Agnes," I said during the rare moments she was silent.

Her voice returned, deep and raspy, with a shake to it that warned she still had enough tears to sink a U-boat. "Why, Rosie? Why?"

"I don't know." Churchill took refuge in the space between my legs. His tail snaked up my calf like the straps of a Roman sandal.

"He was a good man, wasn't he?"

"Sure. A real upstanding guy." I wanted to comfort her, but I was growing increasingly removed from the emotion of what had occurred. I transferred her pain to a stage where Agnes became a Norse queen mourning the loss of her mate. Everything was easier to cope with if you imagined it set afire and adrift at sea.

A rustling on her end signaled that a handkerchief was making its way down her face. "I know he loved me. Just the other day he talked about leaving his wife. We were going to run away and get married in Acapulco. Did I tell you that?"

"Yeah." She'd told me a similar story dozens of times before, with only the geographic location of their nuptials changing. I had no doubt Jim had made these promises, but I also believed Agnes knew in her heart how empty they were.

"He was supposed to come over Christmas night. I made pork chops. I traded my sugar coupons for the extra meat and everything. I was so mad when he didn't show."

My head weighed eighty pounds. The only way I could keep it up was by propping it on my hand. "You couldn't have known that he was dead."

Her voice pitched upward. "I even called his house. I spoke to his wife. I wanted to know if he was there with her instead of with me."

Jim never talked about his wife; I knew he had one only because Agnes had told me. I assumed she was either ill or never existed to begin with, and I preferred the latter because if Agnes had spoken with a living, breathing woman I'd have to too.

"What did his wife say?" I asked.

"That she had company and couldn't be bothered about this right now. I was so upset I hung up on her."

"Do you have any idea why he came into the office on Christmas?" I asked.

"Who knows? A client maybe? You know Jim, he's always willing to work around someone's schedule if money's involved."

I put my thumb and index finger to my nose and pinched away her use of the present tense. "Do you think Jim made someone mad? Somebody who might've put the curse on him?"

Agnes sniffled. "I don't know, Rosie. I—" The word was swallowed whole and I imagined her squeezing her eyes shut as I would press my fingers together to keep a drink of water from leaking from my hand. "There's nothing we can do, is there? Bad things keep happening and we just have to accept them." I didn't respond. The war had taught us that we were powerless. No amount of talking about it could change the situation. "I've got to go."

She disconnected and I stared at the horn. As rough as that call was, the next one was going to be much worse. I didn't want Mrs. McCain to hear the news about Jim from someone like Lieutenant Schmidt, but I had no idea how to tell a total stranger that her husband was dead. I practiced it like a line in a Chekhov play, and when I was able to say it without my lips quivering, I located Jim's home number in the directory and asked the operator to connect us.

"Hello? McCain residence." A woman whose foreign accent reduced the number of syllables in every word she said answered the phone.

"Mrs. McCain?" I asked.

"Mrs. McCain no here. Home soon. Leave message?"

While I hadn't thought Mrs. McCain would be fresh off the boat, I certainly didn't expect Jim to have the bees for servants. "Is this Jim McCain's house? The detective?"

"Mr. McCain no here. Leave message?"

I cleared my throat and put my fingers to my temples. I may not have been Emily Post, but I had a sneaking suspicion you didn't announce a death through a phone message. "This is Rosie Winter. I work for Jim. I need Mrs. McCain to call me at the office as soon as possible."

"Mrs. McCain no home."

I increased the pressure on my skull. "Yeah, I got that, but I need her to call the office. Tell Mrs. McCain to call Mr. McCain at the office."

I had eight phone calls in the next hour. One was a wrong number, three were potential clients, and four were people Jim had been assisting through various legal wrongdoings. To each I explained we were closed until the new year and, no, Jim couldn't be reached until

then. By the time the phone rang for the ninth time I was halfway
into my coat.

"Hello, McCain and Son."

"Jim McCain please." A woman's voice, smooth like porcelain,
erupted on the line.

"Who's this?" I asked.

"Who is this?" she echoed.

"This is Jim's assistant. How can I help you?"

The porcelain turned to barbed wire. "Well, *Jim's assistant*, demanding to know who someone is is not an appropriate way to greet
someone."

"I did say hello." The hair on my neck rose, ready to do battle.
"And might I suggest that when you're hoping to talk to someone, it's
best to try to butter up the person who answers the phone; otherwise
they might accidentally hang up on you."

"How dare you talk to me like that!"

I seized rage and let it submerge my grief. "Look, sister, you're
the one who started it."

"And I'm going to be the one to finish it. Put my husband on the
line and when you're done with that, why don't you use the time to
figure out where you'll be working next?"

The coat sleeve I hadn't put on dropped to my side like a broken
wing. "Mrs. McCain?"

"I'm waiting. Put Jim on the phone."

I sank into my chair and dropped my head until it hit wood. "Actually, I'm the one who called for you, not Jim."

The sound of paper being wadded into a ball rustled across the
line. "I'm not interested in Jim's indiscretions. If you've called to
confess something, you're wasting both of our time."

Try as I might to feel bad for this dame, her attitude made it impossible for me to muster sympathy. What kind of woman could have no
contact with her husband since Christmas without sounding the least
bit panicked? Jim was no saint, but I liked to believe that if this broad
took a powder, he would've at least pretended he was concerned.

She cleared her throat. "Are we done, *Jim's assistant?*"

"No, we're not. In the first place, my name is Rosie Winter, and in the second, I'm not calling to confess anything." I picked up a pencil and squeaked its eraser across the desktop.

She overemphasized each word she said. "Then. Why. Did. You. Call?"

"Jim's dead."

Everything went quiet on the line. Churchill paced the length of my desk, then leaped to its top. He batted at my pencil until I stopped its squeaking, then lay flat on his belly, waiting for his prey to resume its activity.

"Oh," Mrs. McCain said at last. In the distance a bell rang at her house. Frantic footsteps rained across an unseen floor followed by the maid's voice, tinged with hysteria, declaring, "Police, missus. Police." Mrs. McCain cleared her throat again and her voice grew softer, not from emotion but from a greater distance between her and the phone. "Thank you for calling."

I stared into Jim's office and tried to imagine him sitting at his desk, smoking down the remnants of a cigar he'd decided would measure the minutes until it was time for him to dust for the day. "I'm so, so sorry. If you need anything—anything at all—please let me—"

She cut me off. "I think I can manage things from here. Have a pleasant evening."

I left the office at 6:30 and headed toward the IRT at Times Square and Forty-second Street. The dimout had been in effect since September, and already the city's skyline was disappearing as light after light was extinguished from the tall buildings that dominated midtown. The mercury hovered just above zero, making the last night of the year the coldest on record. Early New Year's Eve revelers wearing brightly colored paper hats atop their wool caps prepared the area for that night's big bash while streets made barren by the gas and rubber rations turned white from a light snowfall. Stark signs plastered on shop windows and phone poles ordered us to close our heads for the duration: HE'S WATCHING YOU. THE ENEMY IS LISTENING—KEEP IT TO YOURSELF—HE WANTS TO KNOW WHAT YOU KNOW. THE SOUND THAT KILLS: DON'T MURDER MEN WITH IDLE WORDS. I burrowed deep into my coat and kept my gaze rooted to the sidewalk. The darkness, the events of the day, and the posters combined to turn everything into a threat. An overflowing trash can was the final resting place for a dismembered corpse. A noisemaker spun prematurely was a woman's scream. Even my own footsteps became the frantic footfalls of a hatchetman fast on my heels.

Think of something else, I told myself. I tried to remember a book I'd read recently, but the only stories I could recall were from *Terror Tales* and they made poor companions. I hummed a few bars of a song only to discover that my choice of tunes was "I'll Never Smile Again," which I cut off in mid-verse in case it should prove true. I decided the only safe distraction was the bard and so I plumbed my mind for the little bit of Shakespeare I'd committed to memory. A ditty from *Macbeth* rose to the surface and allowed me to momentarily root around a Scottish castle as I intoned: "Tomorrow, and tomorrow, and tomorrow / Creeps in this petty pace from day to day, / To the last syllable of recorded time; / And all our yesterdays have lighted fools / The way to dusty death."

That did it. I decided to stop thinking altogether.

At last I made it to the station and followed the stairs down to the turnstile. The platform held a handful of people other than me, and from the looks of them they were all recent releases from Bellevue. Incandescent globes illuminated the underground world in a sickly yellow haze while a corroded pipe leaked an irregular stream of water that whispered *pling pling pling*, then paused before resuming its meterless argument. A shadow darted in and out of my periphery. Each time I turned to identify it, it became lost in the pillars.

The Seventh Avenue local arrived ten minutes late. I took a seat at the rear of the last car and spent the bulk of the ride replaying every conversation I'd had with Jim over the past week. He wasn't depressed. Even the IRS thing had been a giggle to him. Clearly there was trouble at home, but Agnes had been the antidote for that. I squeezed my eyes shut and saw Jim hanging from the closet, a breeze swinging his body, his unseeing peepers suddenly registering the person who stood before him. *Bad things keep happening and we just have to accept them.* Boy had Agnes hit it on the nose. I had nothing left, not even the ability to change things. I opened my eyes and found an enormous man half-hidden behind a newspaper, his tiny, close-set eyes boring twin holes into my skull.

3 A Doll's House

I exited the Christopher Street station and disappeared into the growing foot traffic just in case the creep with the petite peepers decided to tail me. He didn't, as far as I could tell, but that didn't stop me from shadowing two merchant marines for a block and a half. By 7:00 I was safely at the George Bernard Shaw House, or, as I called it, the Home for Wayward Actresses. It was a rooming house at West Tenth Street and Hudson in the Village that had once been a popular hotel for seamen and remained a fine example of Civil War architecture, since the current owner was too cheap to bring it up to twentieth-century standards. Some starlet who married well had financially endowed the joint at the turn of the century and made it possible for mugs like me to enjoy a cheap roof over our heads provided we followed her career path.

On any given day you could walk into the house and find singers warming up in the parlor, dancers using the banister as a barre, and a half dozen women talking to the walls as they tried out lines they had to have down for auditions and rehearsals. Evidence of the work we did was everywhere. The parlor table was littered with back issues of *Variety, Radio Stars, Cue,* and *Photoplay.* A bookcase teetered from the weight of scrapbooks filled with reviews. The piano sagged beneath copies of the latest Broadway scores, and the radio blasted programs the twenty women I roomed with prayed would be their big break.

As I entered the building, I passed the wall of shame where our den mother, Belle, had hung past and present residents' 8 x 10s in lieu of wallpaper. While the Shaw House was long on entertainment and short on costs, it did have its downsides. Since our rent was subsidized, we were expected to follow a slate of house rules. In addition to having to work in the theater a certain number of times each year, our comings and goings were monitored more closely than they would be at Attica. And there were so many restrictions regarding what we were allowed to have in our rooms that it was easier to pass around a list of what could be there than what couldn't.

I entered the lobby on my tiptoes and scanned the room for Belle. I had a week left before I reached the six-months-with-no-work mark; after that, I was out on my keister. My plan was to avoid her until I got work or she got religion. Fortunately, it appeared the house had been vacated for the night. Everyone but my best pal and me had taken jobs ringing in the New Year with the troops at the Stork Club, the Stage Door Canteen, and the new Rockefeller Center. The gigs promised cold, hard cash and fleeting romance. While I loved the green stuff, I didn't want to surround myself with men who were ready to ship out and leave everyone else behind. Why spend the end of the old year confronting the thing I was trying to forget about the new one?

"Rosie!" Jayne ran down the stairs, flung her arms around me, and squeezed me so tight I thought she'd dislocated my shoulder. My best pal was a petite blonde with the body of a Parisian vase and the voice of a two-year-old. She was a nice person and a hard worker, which, combined with her looks, made every director who crossed her path want to help her career. The last fellow got her all the way to Broadway and even paid the press to puff about the discovery of the new "it girl." Review after review heralded her comic timing and bombshell good looks, but then one critic who shall remain nameless dubbed her "America's squeakheart" and soon all the others followed suit, forgetting her merits and focusing only on her voice. The truth was, her pipes were pitched too high to carry well in a theater, sentencing Jayne to spend the rest of her career modeling, dancing, and playing children in Texaco Star Theater radio productions.

"Belle around?" I asked in a stage whisper.

Jayne mimicked my attempt at being covert. "She's out for the night."

I gave her a more generous hug. "How was your trip?"

"You tell me." She held up her right hand and wiggled a block of ice that was so large I was surprised she hadn't hired a bellhop to help her drag it around.

I rocked her finger so the light played off the stone. "Will you looky here.... When's the big day?" Jayne was dating one of mob boss Vincent Mangano's lieutenants, a thug named Tony B., who'd taken her to the Adirondacks for a few days. He was a wrong number, but I had to admire his impeccable taste in overpriced gifts. In the last few months he'd showered Jayne with enough shiny baubles to turn her into a constellation.

Jayne freed her hand from mine. "It's not an engagement ring. It's a promise ring."

"And what did you promise him?"

She winked at me. "That I wouldn't lose the ring." She took me by the hand and led me up to our room. Our living space was smaller than a cattle car and dominated by a radiator that, courtesy of the fuel shortage, was there for purely decorative purposes. We both lacked domestic skills and it showed: clothes burst out of cupboards, lingerie peeked out of overstuffed bureau drawers, and a lopsided dime-store Christmas tree winked on the window ledge.

Still, it was home, and I loved it.

Jayne disappeared into her closet and emerged with two overflowing martini glasses we'd won at Dish Night at the Roxy. "Ta-da!"

"Keep 'em coming until I tell you otherwise."

She sat beside me on the radiator and clinked my glass. "Happy New Year."

"That remains to be seen." I tipped a sip of liquid courage. "I decided to go in to work this afternoon and I found Jim McCain dead in his closet." I drained the drink and fished out an olive.

Jayne shot up. "What?"

As I told her about the events of that day, Jayne's face became a tidepool of shifting eyebrows, pursed lips, and bitten cheeks.

"Oh, Rosie," she said when I'd finished, "I don't even know what to say."

"How about this year will be better than last?"

"It has to be. Poor, poor Jim." She put a finger to her kisser and bit her nail.

"Anyway, if I can be completely selfish for a moment, this means I'm unemployed. So if I do get booted out of this place, I won't have enough dough for a new one." Even if I did, there was no guarantee I could find an apartment. Along with its other pleasantries, the war had brought a housing shortage to New York.

"So nothing's come through for you yet?"

I shook my head. "Nope. I'm behind the eight ball." The war was making everything difficult, even acting. Ticket prices had gone up, plays closed faster than predicted, and rationing had just about killed touring productions and the small barn theaters many of us depended on to get through the lean times. The lights on Broadway had even become victims of the dimout. It was a running joke among my friends that if you were lucky enough to get a big break, you had better show up before sundown if you wanted to see your name on the marquee.

I took a deep breath and readied myself to utter the unspeakable. "I think it may be time to accept that my acting career is over."

"Close your head." Jayne pulled a piece of paper from her pocket and waved it at me. "Someone named Peter Sherwood called. He wants you to come to an audition."

"For what?"

She squinted at the scrap and deciphered her hieroglyphics. "It's actually for two shows. A musical revival."

Since the war it had become vogue to bring back shows from twenty years before, as though by resurrecting the past we could collectively forget the present. "And the other show?"

"Something called *The Ghetto*."

"Gee, I wonder what that could be about." When companies weren't reviving junk from two decades prior, they were doing their darnedest to milk the war for all it was worth. Neither option appealed to me. I couldn't muster the smiles for the shows that ignored the war and couldn't find the emotion for those that didn't.

"It could be a great show, a great role," said Jayne.

"Somehow I doubt that. Who the deuce is Peter Sherwood anyway?"

She shrugged. "Who cares? Maybe he saw you in something." Getting a personal invite to an audition was a boon, but it didn't change the fact that it was for a turkey of a play. "Did you see the reviews for Ruby's show?"

"No, and I prefer to keep it that way." Ruby Priest was the house's latest success story. Normally I cheered other actresses' success, but Ruby's personality was such that you couldn't help but hope she'd fall through a trapdoor and never be seen again.

Jayne leaned against the window. "She's going to be unbearable."

"She's already unbearable. Now she'll have reason for it."

Jayne laughed and the laugh turned into a hiccup. She got both expulsions under control and celebrated by finishing her drink. "Don't be mad," she said.

"What am I not being mad about?" I narrowed my gaze. "Was that the last of the booze?"

"No." The hiccup returned and she put a hand to her mouth to suppress it. "I tried out for Bentley's new show."

"I think that's great. You need to aim higher than lousy musical reviews." Lawrence Bentley, an actor turned writer, was the new golden boy of Broadway. His shows were sentimental schlock that usually communicated a highly unsubtle patriotic message or, at the very least, reinforced ethnic and religious stereotypes. Since Pearl Harbor, the public had eaten the stuff up. His scripts were in such demand that on any given night he'd have two shows running, each vying for the same unimaginative audience.

"Thanks," said Jayne. "I just know something good is going to happen for both of us."

"I certainly hope so." A sound I intended to be a laugh came out a squawk. "I've got to tell you, pal, between Jim and not being able to get work . . . I don't think I've ever been this low." My eyes burned as new tears tried to find old exits.

Jayne stood and ceremoniously deposited her glass on the radiator. "That's enough bad for tonight. Get dressed. We're going out."

I mopped at my face. "I'm not up for a night on the town. I want to ring in the new year quietly, just me and some giggle juice."

Jayne took my hand and attempted to pull me to my feet. "Oh no you don't. If you stay in, you'll spend the whole night dwelling. That's no way to end the year."

"I won't dwell. I never dwell."

"Rosie." She tilted her head in a way that recalled every evening I'd spent in our room feeling sorry for myself. It had been a bad year.

I shifted my gaze to the floor. "And besides, tonight might be the night . . ."

"You hear from Jack?"

When thoughts like that went through my head, they seemed rational and wise. When someone else uttered them, I realized my folly. Jack Castlegate—Broadway's favorite leading man and the fellow I once thought would play Romeo to my Juliet—had shipped out right after Thanksgiving and I'd yet to hear a peep from him. Sure, you could blame the war—and I blamed it for a lot these days—but at some point I had to accept that if a man let my birthday, Christmas, and New Year's pass without sending me so much as a hiya through V-mail, there was a very good chance the relationship was over.

"Even if I wanted to go, I can't. I'm on the nut. I'll be lucky to eat this week."

Jayne squeezed my hand. "It'll be my treat."

I took a deep breath and forced a smile. "All right," I said. "I'm yours for the night, but I get to set the rules. Wherever we go better have cheap booze and a big band."

4 The Royal Family

NEW YEAR'S EVE WAS A bust. By the time we hit the streets, so many people were out that we had no choice but to ride the wave and go where they were going. We ended up at Times Square with four hundred thousand of our closest friends. New York's biggest party may have been packed full of people, but the war had muted it as though we'd all come to the silent conclusion that any joy was disrespectful. Instead of the ball dropping at midnight, plane spotter stations filled the night sky with beams of light. The crowd watched in silent awe until the singer Lucy Monroe pierced the quiet with "The Star-Spangled Banner." Everywhere we looked were soldiers with their girls, fiercely embracing, kissing, and dancing as though they had a lifetime of those activities to cram into one evening. As 1942 became 1943 my grief at not being able to kiss Jack at midnight was replaced by the awful fear that I might never kiss him—or anyone else—again.

Everything should've looked brighter the next day, but my hangover and the P.M. papers conspired to ensure otherwise. The first German radio broadcast of 1943 had predicted that the war would last for at least twenty years. If that wasn't enough to wipe the sun from the sky, the year's casualty totals were out, hidden in articles that attempted to downplay their enormity by reminding us that ten times that number of people die every year in accidents.

Jim's obituary was also there, buried between a war bond ad and a public auction notice. The man's life had been reduced to a trio of titles: private investigator, loving husband, former cop. On January 4, the day of the funeral, Jayne had a radio gig, so I called Agnes to see if she was going to pay her respects. After six attempts and fifty-two rings, I decided to go stag.

Jim's festivities were at Lexington and Seventy-fourth Street at Brookside Funeral Home, a joint trapped in turn-of-the-century frou-frou that was as appropriate for Jim as trench knives were for children. Heavy brocade furniture, faded by time, lined garishly papered walls turned dingy by decades of cigarette smoke. Knickknacks dotted every surface while floral arrangements exuding so much scent you would've thought there were midgets with atomizers in them towered above ornate marble-topped tables and delicate stands.

The place was filled with people, none of whom I recognized. One side of the room held a group of uncomfortable-looking tough guys who were probably long acquainted with Jim's fire escape. These men in their chalk-striped suits and pinkie rings hugged one another in greeting and then stood with their folded hands resting in front of their nether regions. On the other side of the room lingered refugees from the *Times* society column. The heavily made up women of this caste greeted one another with kisses that never quite made contact with each other's cheeks. Tailored men exchanged equally sincere handshakes, their voices filled with the sort of exaggerated emotion you'd expect from bad summer stock.

I couldn't decide where I fit in, so I eavesdropped on conversations while feigning interest in a brochure. The tiny pamphlet advised me that as a soldier or the relative of a soldier "you never know when to expect bad news so be prepared and buy a plot."

The thugs didn't talk much, and when they did, it was in low, hushed voices that forced whoever was listening to bend in close to them. Every once in a while they came up for air and remarked on the nice flowers, or good turnout, or some equally innocuous observation they hoped would make their presence seem as natural as the body's. I'd given up trying to determine what their real topics of conversation were when a gentleman whose excessive jewelry branded him the ringleader took a lower-level thug by the arm and moved alarmingly close to me to have a private conversation.

"Have we made arrangements to clean the office?" the boss asked. His voice plucked a nerve. I knew this mug—he was the Lisper!

"Shouldn't be necessary. I was assured no names were used."

The Lisper wrapped his arm around the goon's shoulders. "He was a good man—we drank out of the same bottle—but nobody's perfect. Let's make sure there were no mistakes."

The thug pulled at his cuffs and nodded.

The Lisper looked as if he were about to say more when a bruno with tiny, close-set eyes caught his attention. Wordlessly, the bruno glanced my way. In response the Lisper straightened his tie and gave me a knowing smile.

"How you doing?" he asked me.

I tried to look surprised that I was being addressed; I'm sure it would've read true if I hadn't been staring at him. "I'm hitting all eight," I said through a tight smile.

The Lisper nodded and escorted his companion back to the rest of his group.

While the buttonmen aimed for discretion, the social registry buzzed about FDR's foreign policy and the effect the war was having on both the economy and their vacation plans. The more nervy of the group glanced at the other side of the room and sourly fretted about the inclusion of "those people" in the festivities. When Jim's name came up—and it rarely did—it was only to confirm the deceased's name.

If they didn't know who Jim was, they certainly knew his wife. While my conversation with Mrs. McCain may have yielded a dozen colorful adjectives, the word most frequently used by her friends was *eligible*. Jim's better half was lousy with dough and had so many potential suitors she could've started her own branch of the armed forces.

The question was why a woman like that had married a man like Jim.

I took my place in line before the casket and decided to make use of my time. In front of me stood a man in a gabardine suit. He was sixtyish and balding, with a prominent wine-stain birthmark obscuring the realm between his forehead and nonexistent hairline. This blemish set him apart from the rest of the crowd and I had a feeling that despite his privileged standing, he was constantly battling to be accepted by a world that was rightfully his. This meant he was desperate for conversation with someone who treated him as an equal.

"Good afternoon," I said to him in my best Katharine Hepburn. "Such a tragic loss, isn't it?"

He surveyed me long enough to determine that even if I wasn't someone he knew, I might still be someone. "Good afternoon." He offered me his hand. "How do you know Eloise?"

"From the guild," I said. "And you?"

"The club."

I nodded as though I were familiar with that great institution. "It's lovely that so many people have turned out to support her."

"Yes, yes," said the man.

I leaned into him and lowered my voice. "I was surprised to learn that her husband was a private investigator."

My companion matched my lean and willingly gave up what he knew. "I think we all were. She never mentioned him to anyone."

"Why do you suppose that was?"

"Embarrassment, of course. A Fitzgerald shouldn't mingle with riffraff."

I covered my surprise with a cough. Cromwell Fitzgerald was one of the largest steel manufacturers on the East Coast. The industrial revolution had showered his family with the kind of dough associated with the Rockefellers and the Vanderbilts.

Or at least that's what I'd been told at PS 48.

I kept my eyes on my companion. "Even so, Eloise married *riffraff.* Why go through that embarrassment only to hide your husband away until his death?"

He moved so close to me I could see the hairs lining the inside of his nose. "That, my dear, is the million-dollar question. Perhaps she couldn't bear another scandal."

I raised an eyebrow. "Another one?"

He traced me from top to tail. "My, but you're young. I suppose all of that happened before you were born." He tried on his next words as if they were a set of new dentures. "This isn't the first . . . loss Eloise has suffered. It was so very tragic, especially when the accusations arose. Naturally, Eloise was exonerated of any misdoing, but I'm afraid the memory of all that still lingers."

The body was ready for the next demonstration of grief. "If you'll excuse me."

He took his turn at the casket, slyly glancing at his watch fob to determine if the appropriate amount of time had passed before moving on. I replaced him on the kneeler and stared at the corpse. Dead Jim didn't look anything like Live Jim. His suit was missing its tell-tale wrinkles, his mouth its cigar, and his hand bore a shiny gold ring I'd assumed he'd long ago lost to his weekly poker game. Most distressing was his head. Seeing Jim out of a fedora was like seeing him without a limb.

I closed my eyes and prayed that his end came quick and that his life, despite appearances, had been happy. After that I crossed myself, crossed the room, and searched my pocketbook for something to tip the coat-check girl with.

"You must be Rosie. I'm Eloise McCain." A china doll in a high-end black suit and a hat that looked like a bird in flight blocked my path and offered me her hand. "It was so kind of you to come and pay your respects."

"It was the least I could do." She was unnaturally light, like doll-house furniture made of balsa wood.

Her large blue eyes studied me through the black netting of her hat's veil. "It was so kind of you to call me like you did." There was an artificial sweetness to her voice that made me question her sincerity. Every word she spoke had a duplicitous quality to it.

"It's what I would've wanted someone to do for me." I gawked at her—I couldn't help it. Under her hat was air-spun red hair that twisted, tornado-like, into a pompadour. She barely came up to my chin, but she possessed a magnetism that made me believe I was looking up at her.

She released my hand and her arm gracefully traveled behind her. "This is my son, Edgar." A man in naval dress uniform with a gaze that made it clear he viewed everything as prey emerged and cast a shadow over his mother. He offered me a mitt that resembled the steel claw one operated in hopes of obtaining a prize at a carnival.

"It's nice to meet you," I said. "Jim said a lot of nice things about you. About both of you." I punctuated my lie with a cough and mentally counted the steps to the exit.

Edgar released my hand and gave me the up and down. "How well did you know him?"

I couldn't tell if it was a casual question or tainted with accusation. I decided to give him the benefit of the doubt. "I'd been working for him for only a couple of months. He seemed like a swell guy though."

The interrogation continued. "Are you married?"

I shifted my weight and tried to determine the most polite way to excuse myself. "No."

Edgar raised an eyebrow. "Were you shacking up with him?"

"Edgar!" Eloise's eyes darted about the room, monitoring if anyone else had heard him.

"It's a fair enough question, Mother. We know Jim had his dalliances and she certainly seems the type." From the way he said it, I knew *type* was another word for *cheap*. That may have accurately described my shoes, but I wasn't about to let it describe my person.

I grabbed hold of his wrist and pulled him toward me. "Seems you've forgotten your manners, sailor. Apologize to me and I'll be on my way."

His surprise turned to amusement. Apparently I didn't cut a very threatening figure. "I have nothing to apologize for," he said.

"Then you must be deaf, 'cause I heard a mouthful of rude. Shall we let Mother's guild know or should we keep it between us?"

He fought to hide his smile. "I'm sorry if I was wrong about you."

I swallowed the *if* and released him. I was about to walk away when he snagged the elbow of my dress. He moved in close, until his voice was barely a tickle in my ear.

"You know, Rosie—it could have been to your betterment. What would a girl like you rather be: a whore or an old maid?" The four gold bars that signified his rank winked at me from the wrist of his blue jacket.

I wrenched my arm free and grabbed a fistful of his uniform. Once again I pulled him toward me until he was close enough to kiss. "Look, Edgar, I'm not a day over twenty-two and the only thing I'm about to clean is your clock. Your pop was my boss and my friend so if you're looking for dalliances look somewhere else. I came here to pay my respects, not be insulted."

I let go of his shirt with such force that he wobbled off balance. Before he had another chance to touch me, I pushed through the crowd and made my way to the coatroom counter.

"You must forgive Edgar. He's not himself." Eloise McCain appeared beside me and polluted the air with Chanel No. 5.

I tossed the clerk my number and a little bit of silver. "I have a feeling he's never himself. I don't have time to acquaint myself with his various personalities."

Eloise put her hand on my elbow and gently pulled me away from the coatroom. Her expression changed until it better reflected what I would expect of a grieving widow. It was too careful and studied, though, as if she'd learned grief by watching others go through it. "He's angry at Jim. His death was so sudden, so unexpected." She released my arm and gently took my hand in hers. She glittered with the kind of ice Jim couldn't have afforded and I wondered if she wore it to show the world her status or to remind Jim that her life before him had been much more rewarding. Did she wonder about his death or did she accept suicide as the explanation because she believed it meant he felt responsible for her unhappiness?

Her second hand joined her first, making a sandwich of mine. "He led a double life with us. I think I always knew, but for Edgar it's hard. He idolized Jim and to learn about the mob connections and the other women . . . well, it's a bit like losing him twice, I'm afraid."

I tried to pull my hand free, but she held it fast. *This is a woman who may have killed before,* I reminded myself. *If she wants to touch you, let her.* "I'll forgive him this one time. Grief does bring out the worst in people."

She nodded and forced a smile on her face. "I have a favor to ask you." Polish replaced sorrow. This was the tone she used with her household staff. "We need to close up Jim's office as soon as possible. I'd do it myself, but . . . I don't think I'm ready for that." She tossed a glance over her shoulder. "Obviously Edgar's not a good candidate for the job."

"Have you considered hiring a moving company?"

She laughed the way people did when someone told an off-color joke and the listener had to strike a balance between being polite and being party to unpopular sentiment. "I'll hire a moving company to take things to storage, of course, but first we need someone to organize his files." She moved even closer to me, until I could make out the fine lines interrupting her alabaster forehead. "I must tell you, Rosie: I'm not entirely comfortable with the police's assessment of Jim's death. Perhaps you could go through his things and let me know if there is anything that could confirm or deny the circumstances under which he . . ." She paused and an embroidered handkerchief materialized. She patted at the skin beneath her eyes, where normal people would expect to find tears. "Could you do this for me?"

I hedged; I couldn't help it. "It might be better if you called Agnes. She's been working there a lot longer and I'm sure she'd have a better sense of . . ."

The handkerchief disappeared. "I'd rather have someone who isn't so . . . emotionally involved do it. Would you be willing?"

My hand slid free of hers. "Look, Mrs. McCain, I'd love to help you, but Jim died before I was paid up for December and he still hadn't made good for part of November. I can't afford to keep working for free."

Her lips curved upward. "Free, Rosie? You misunderstood. I would, of course, pay you for this favor and anything else you were owed."

5 The Ghost Sonata

BY NINE THE NEXT MORNING I was at the office packing Jim's files into liquor-store crates Eloise had delivered in my absence. I was miserable from the moment I arrived. The radiators wouldn't stop belching, filling our floor with enough heat to roast a turkey. I tried to adjust the thermometer, but the knob came off in my hand, fell to the floor, and rolled beneath the cast-iron coils. My only option was to prop the office door open and hope the subzero street level weather would rush up the stairs and lower the temperature to somewhere near tropical.

I'd left the bathroom window open to give Churchill access outside, but rather than taking advantage of this liberty, he'd messed all over my desk and turned his still full food and water dishes upside down. I was so put off by his tantrum and the resulting smell that I decided to set aside my fear of Jim's office. I shifted the crates to his desk and did my best to ignore Churchill's whines. He was one minute from getting zotzed.

The office appeared untouched since my last visit. The closet door was open, confirming that the horrors last seen had been purged, and the blinds were up, flooding the room with sunlight. For my piece of mind, I checked the desk drawers and found the .38 and the bottle of gin (now half empty) where I'd left them.

I clicked on the radio for entertainment and spun the dial until I landed on a broad who was more tenor than soprano butchering "He Wears a Pair of Silver Wings" for *The Garry Moore Show*. I sang along with her and turned my attention to the files in the bookcase.

There was little rhyme or reason to what he'd kept there. One folder contained years of correspondence with men whose return addresses were either Attica or Riker's Island. A list of the letter writers was affixed to the inside of the file, with the dates of their incarceration carefully outlined. For those who had been released, there was further notation indicating whether or not Jim had been in contact with them. Other folders held case files, though the cases themselves were remarkably dull—no different from the hundreds we kept track of in the outer office. The only thing that distinguished them was that no client's name appeared anywhere in the files—instead there was a number and a letter used for identification purposes—and the case descriptions lacked Jim's usual detail and instead relied on pithy one-sentence descriptions. I found the system so hinky that as I worked I jotted down the code on a scrap of paper, hoping to unravel a pattern. If there was one, I never found it.

After a few hours of work, I gave up looking at the contents of the folders and decided to put them in numerical order. This helped me increase my pace until several dozen folded half-sheets slid from their containment and scattered across the floor.

"For crying out loud." As I bent down to retrieve them, Churchill promenaded around the desk, stopping in the dead center of the papers. "Off." He didn't move. "Shoo." Still he stood. I snagged one of the folded half-pages and threw it at him. As he breezed from my range, the nerves in my fingers signaled that I'd touched something familiar. The slick paper, the brightly colored covers, the photo inserts: these were theater programs!

I dumped them on the desk and searched for a sign as to why they were being retained. None of the folders was labeled, though the top one bore a cryptic, penciled note asking, "What would shock you?"

"A radio in a bathtub," I told Churchill. "And talking cats." I scanned the programs, looking for some common link between the shows. I assumed Jim was tracking an actor whose wife feared backstage hanky-panky, but as I read cast list upon cast list, no common name emerged. Even the endless list of stage managers, scene designers, carpenters, and electricians progressed with no overlap. If anything, the programs proved there was such a ceaseless number of actors and technicians in New York it was a wonder anybody ever got a second job.

The plays had foreboding, metaphoric names like *Blind Mice, The Pig and the Swine,* and *Franklin's Folly.* I hadn't heard of most of the companies who'd staged them, but that was no surprise; the city was full of theater companies I'd never heard of and would never work for. Still, something was off about these productions: not a single one of them listed a playwright, though two went so far as to claim anonymous authorship. That *was* hinky. The writers I knew would die before they forfeited a byline.

I set the programs aside and took another look at the folder. Jim's scrawl filled the interior, listing the titles of the plays that corresponded with the programs, followed by the dates of the productions. There was additional writing that made no sense in the context of what I'd seen, then a quote written in a more careful hand: "The play's the thing." Finding Shakespeare in Jim's office was like discovering him wearing lacy women's drawers. What was next? An autographed photo of Cary Grant?

I eyeballed the other folders. The file that had been in front of the programs was overflowing with news clippings about the recent Newspaper and Mail Deliverers' Union strike. The file behind it was an extortion case. Jim's sparse prose told the tale of someone who was worried their career would be over if the person in the know followed through on their threats. There was no mention of money. The only detail Jim slipped into his generic description was "Nice gams. Good rack. Bad attitude."

I shook my head at him in memoriam.

As I continued searching, a metallic tapping I assumed was the radiator grew increasingly insistent. I tried to ignore it, but my patience plummeted until all I could think about was that stupid banging. That's when I looked up.

A man stood at the fire escape window, his head framed by the raised blackout blind. When he saw he had my attention, he waved and the tapping ceased. I decided to play it like Dan Turner, Hollywood Detective; I closed the folder, slid my hand into the desk drawer, and withdrew the .38 without being seen. Once I had it safely in hand, I approached the window and lifted the window a sliver.

"We're closed," I said.

He set down an intricately carved walking stick he'd used to bang on the fire escape floor. "I'm here to see Jim McCain."

I gave him the up and down. He was meticulously dressed in a wool coat and black homburg. What I could see of his face bore a well-kept Vandyke beard. I put his age at about sixty, though it was hard to tell for sure since his lid cast a shadow over his face.

"Jim's not here."

"When will he be back?" His voice was low and rich, like a radio announcer's. He removed the homburg, revealing a smooth bald head. His cheeks were carved and ruddy, his schnozzle maroon from the wind.

"It could be a while. Who's asking?"

"My name is Raymond Fielding. Do you think I might be able to come in for a moment? It's quite chilly out here and I've misplaced my gloves." He turned his bare hands palm side up and showed me how red the skin was.

He looked harmless enough. I opened the window to its full height, then dropped the rod into the trash can and covered its landing with a cough. "I guess that would be all right."

He climbed into the office slowly, like a reluctant child, one leg dragging behind the other. "Are you Jim's secretary?"

"Something like that."

"I've offended you." His peepers were blue and faded by age. When he gave me the once-over, it seemed as if every detail was being taken in so it could be reproduced at a moment's notice.

"Why would you say that?" I asked.

"Because you're not a secretary—you just do this for the money.

You have other aspirations." He raised an eyebrow. "Is that correct?"

The only thing I hated more than someone making assumptions about me was someone who made correct assumptions about me. "Isn't everybody trying to be somebody else?"

He cast a shadow over his shoulder. "All the world's a stage, / And all the men and women merely players; / They have their exits and their entrances, / And one man in his time plays many parts."

Jim I could forgive for quoting Shakespeare, but this guy? It pushed him from irritating to insufferable.

"Do you know that line?" he asked, his tone making it clear he assumed I didn't.

"It's from *As You Like It*."

"I'm impressed."

He shouldn't have been; he'd just quoted the play I was named for.

I broke his gaze and pretended to find something interesting in one of the files sitting beside me. "Look, Mr. Fielding, you're in for a long wait."

He nudged a leg of the desk with his cane as though to test the furniture's sturdiness. "Is Jim out of town?"

"In a sense. He's dead."

Fielding blanched and slowly reapplied his hat. "My condolences."

"That'll get me coffee and a doughnut."

"May I ask how it happened?"

While his response seemed genuine, I didn't trust the guy. He was a fire escape client, which meant he had his hands in something dirty. Plus he was rich and my brief acquaintance with people of that ilk told me money and morality were mutually exclusive.

"Heart attack," I said.

"I'm very sorry to hear that. I hadn't known him long, but he seemed like a good man." He traced my figure as if I was a cut of meat and he was a hausfrau trying to figure out if there was enough of me for a meal. "May I sit?"

"It's a free country."

He lowered himself into one of the two chairs in front of the desk. The leg I thought was lazy proved to be counterfeit. It bent somewhere in the middle of his thigh then reclined with the elasticity of a pool cue. "Have you heard my name before?" he asked.

I crossed my arms and did my best to appear annoyed. "No. Should I have?"

He smiled, made a pile of his hands, and set them atop his cane. "No. I just assumed that, as Jim's assistant, you would be familiar with his clients."

"Is that what you were?"

"Yes, I was. A new one." He paused, waiting for my response. I had a feeling this was the point where I was supposed to admit that I did know about him, but since I didn't I couldn't.

"Look, I'm not sure what you want from me. I don't know what Jim promised to do for you and unfortunately he's not going to be stopping in to tell me. He's gone and all accounts are closed. You're going to have to go somewhere else."

He held my gaze and the corners of his mouth tipped upward. "I'm afraid I can't do that."

"Why not?" I asked.

Fielding leaned back in the chair and looked at the floor. "Jim was looking into a private matter for me. He called me before Christmas and told me he had uncovered some important information, but gave no details. I was supposed to meet him today to find out what he had learned."

"So? I don't know what Jim knew. I can't help you. Hire another dick."

He looked up. "You misunderstand, Miss . . . ?"

I slid onto the desktop and crossed my legs. "Winter. Rosie Winter."

"Even if you don't know what Jim discovered, there's a record of it somewhere in this office, presumably among all these things you're packing up to store away. The information Jim was seeking for me was so sensitive that I don't dare go to another detective. The more people involved in this business, the greater risk there is to me. Do you understand?"

I understood he was paranoid, sure. "I guess."

"I would like you to continue the investigation for me. I'm not asking that you do much. Just locate any record of what Jim may have discovered and follow up on any leads he may have made." His hand disappeared into his overcoat and emerged with a roll of bills. I should've stopped him then, but the smell of all that freshly baked dough was too strong to turn down.

"What do you think, Miss Winter?"

"I could be persuaded." Churchill slinked into the room and paused long enough to stretch his hind legs. He continued his path and settled next to Fielding's false limb. "What did you hire Jim to do?" I asked.

"He was helping me track down some . . . missing papers." When he spoke, everything sounded like a euphemism.

I retrieved a pen and stenographer's pad from the desk and tried to look officious. "What are they?"

He checked the room and, once he was assured we were alone, leaned toward me. "I'm afraid I'm not at liberty to say."

I dropped the pen. "Let me get this straight: You want me to find some missing papers, but you don't want to tell me what's on them?" I picked up a stack of stationery and waved it at him. "No problem. Case solved."

"I understand this is unorthodox, but you must trust me—the less you know the better."

I rolled my eyes and prayed for patience. "Where did you store the papers?"

He returned to his earlier position: both hands placed atop the cane. "I kept the only copy in a safe in my house."

"And who had access to the box?"

His expression remained calm as though he'd been through this line of questioning many times before. "Nobody."

"You married? Got kids?"

"Neither. No one should've been able to access it but me." Churchill yowled and pushed his head against Fielding's artificial leg. When the motion didn't get him the pat he believed he deserved, he extended his claws and dug them into Fielding's pants.

"Churchill—no!" I banged the desk but still he clung to his make-shift scratching post.

Fielding looked bewildered at my outburst before realizing that a cat was attached to his limb. "My leg!" he moaned. He jabbed his cane at Churchill and the cat detached and scurried out of the room.

"I'm so sorry," I said.

Fielding examined his pant leg and gradually regained his earlier composure. "It's all right," he said. "I'm not bleeding. No harm done. Where were we?"

What was this guy trying to grift? The only thing that leg of his could bleed was sap. "We were talking about access. So you don't live with anybody else?"

"I have a manservant, but he certainly doesn't know the combination to the safe; nor would he have any reason to be interested in its contents."

I rubbed my eyes, hoping that by doing so everything I was seeing and hearing would start to make sense. "If the papers were locked in a box nobody had the combination to but you and nobody had access to it but you, who, pray tell, do you think took it?"

"That's what I hired Jim for."

I glanced at my watch. It was going on 2:00. Jayne had convinced me to swallow my dignity and go to the audition by invitation at three. "Surely you suspect someone?"

A smile curved across his face, revealing teeth the color of aged pearls. "There's a man named Henry Nussbaum. I think he may be involved."

I located another pen and scribbled the name on the pad. "Did Jim talk to him?"

Fielding stood. "I don't think so. I forgot to tell Jim about him."

I dropped to the floor. "What do you mean *you forgot*?"

"I'm human, Miss Winter. Sometimes things slip my mind." He painstakingly removed a stack of bills from the roll of money. His hands shook, animating the paper until it looked as if it was about to take off in flight.

"That's quite a thing to slip your mind."

Fielding didn't respond. Instead, he dropped the money onto the desk. "I trust this will be sufficient to get you started?"

It would be sufficient for many things, including three months' rent if I got the boot, six months' rent if I didn't. "If it's not, you should consider firing me. How do I reach you?"

"You don't. If I need to reach you, I will."

"I'm closing up the office. I won't be here after tomorrow. " I scribbled my exchange on the back of one of Jim's business cards and handed it to him. "This is my rooming house. Don't call before eight or after nine."

"Don't worry—I won't." Without another word, he hobbled out the front entrance of the office.

I locked the fire escape window and hurriedly went through the files in the outer office, gunning for Fielding's name. There was nothing there. I'd worry about him later. I silenced the radio as a reedy singer insisted we "praise the Lord and pass the ammunition." Before I could switch off the lights Agnes appeared in the doorway.

"I didn't think anybody would be here." She clung to the placard of her coat as though she feared a breeze would blow it open.

"I've been asked to help pack up the office."

"Oh." Agnes shifted her pocketbook from one arm to the other. In a week's time, her laugh lines had turned to crow's feet and her rosy skin had grown sallow. "Are you going out?"

"I have an audition."

She nodded again, though her expression hinted that she had no idea what I'd said. Agnes could be jingle-brained, but even this was strange for her.

"What are you doing here, Agnes?"

She stepped into the room and removed her red wool snood. Slowly, she took stock of the work I'd been doing in her absence. Her eyes lingered on Jim's door before making their way back to me. "I wanted to see if it was real."

I sank into one of the reception chairs. "You should've come to the viewing. It was pretty real there."

She nodded at the floor. Badly chipped red-painted nails bit into her palms. Her hair was unwashed and unkempt. "I was going to go, I even got dressed, but I couldn't stand the thought of being there with all those people and none of them knowing who I was." Her eyes tipped upward to keep tears from tumbling out. "I never minded being his mistress, you know? But now that he's gone I feel like I'm not allowed to be sad because he wasn't really mine." I didn't know what to say so I kept silent. "How was it?"

"They did him up real nice."

She took a deep breath. "I suppose I should clean out my desk."

"When you're ready. There are crates in Jim's . . . in the other office if you need them." I rubbed my hands together and tried to think of something comforting to say. Nothing came to me. "Did you recognize the man you passed on the way up here?"

Agnes made a half-hearted attempt to clean her desktop. Pencils were deposited into a coffee cup. Papers were stacked—whether associated or not—into towers with precise right angles. "What man?"

"An older guy with a cane and a beard. He just left."

"I didn't pass anybody."

Could he still be in the building? Or had he ducked into the shadows when he heard Agnes climbing the stairs and waited until she was in the office before he began his descent?

I clasped my hands in prayer. "Do you know if a Raymond Fielding ever hired Jim?"

She shrugged. "Maybe he was one of the fire escape clients."

"Maybe." I looked at my watch. "I have another question for you, Agnes."

"What's that?"

I pulled on my coat and wrapped my scarf around my neck. "What would shock you?"

She searched the office walls for the answer. "Nothing."

"Nothing?"

She jerked a nod. "Between the war and Jim . . . nothing could shock me."

"Fair enough." I retrieved my pocketbook and put on my gloves. "I'll be back tomorrow to finish the packing. You don't have to worry about your desk today if you don't want to."

Churchill meandered into the room and dove into the potted dieffenbachia. Agnes stared into Jim's office and I knew she was picturing him at his desk, his voice booming that she needed to get her can in there and take a letter. "If it's all right, I'd like a little time alone in here."

"Sure. No problem. Just make sure you lock up." I turned to leave.

"Rosie?"

I turned back. "Yeah?"

Agnes's gloved fingertips danced beneath her eyes, catching tears before they could form. "There's something I need you to take of care and I'm afraid it's not very pleasant. I wouldn't ask you if there were any other option." Her eyes drifted to the dieffenbachia while dread stripped the room of its heat.

That was how I got a cat.

6 Mrs. Warren's Profession

MY AUDITION WAS AT THE National on East Houston and Second Avenue. I bypassed the physical scrutiny and was asked to do a monologue and sing ten bars of an up-tempo song. As Jayne had forewarned me, I was being considered for two shows: a bleak war piece and a bad musical comedy revival. The director for the war drama was an intense man who looked like he hadn't slept in two or three years. The director for the musical was much more jovial and well rested. He was a rotund fellow with such a sustained smile that I wondered if he'd just had dental work done.

"Name?" asked the more somber of the directors upon my entrance.

I clicked my heels together in a regrettably Gestapo fashion and stopped in the center of the stage. "Rosalind Winter." The dramatic director seemed to perk up at the sound of my name, but it was probably just gas.

"I hear you brought a cat to the audition," said Fat and Smiley. Word had spread fast; Churchill was, at that moment, in the lobby terrorizing the other actors.

"You know what they say," I said. "Make 'em remember you."

"What will you be doing for us today?" asked Dull and Dramatic.

"I'll be doing a monologue from *The Duchess of Malfi*." Dull and Dramatic maintained his expression. Fat and Smiley became stout and sulky. He was not a fan of Elizabethan tragedy.

"And what will you be singing?" he asked.

"'Tea for Two' from *No, No, Nannette*." Fat and Smiley earned back his name while Dull and Dramatic sighed at the punishment he was going to have to endure. I waited for a sign they were ready, then plunged into John Webster's poetry. The monologue went off without a hitch. As I looked into my imaginary Antonio's eyes and intoned, "The misery of us that are born great! We are forc'd to woo, because none dare woo us," a single tear slid down my cheek.

I was so feeling the Duchess's pain that when the accompanist started serving up my tea I couldn't shake my somber mood. The song was dangerously approaching funereal, so I decided to pep it up with some fancy footwork. Alas, I forgot where the edge of the stage was. As I bounced along to, "Nobody near us to see us or hear us, No friends or relations on weekend vacations," I lost my footing and fell into the orchestra pit.

I lay immobilized for ten seconds before somebody called out, "Are you all right?" I replied that I was, though, to be square, I would've been much better off if the musicians had taken their instruments home.

"Thank you," I said as I dusted myself off and climbed out of the pit. "Best of luck with your casting decisions."

They didn't ask me to stick around.

I gathered my cat and headed home. In the Shaw House foyer I checked my post box. Instead of V-mail from Jack, I had a note from my ma reminding me that if things didn't work out I could always come home. Since pets were strictly prohibited at the house, before I stepped into the lobby, I shoved Churchill into my bag.

Belle greeted me from the front desk. "Hello, stranger. Long time no see. Why so scarce?"

I froze. It was just my luck she'd be waiting for me. A bottle of Seagram's said she'd been staking out the lobby since noon. "Oh, you know how it is with the holidays."

"Get any work?" Belle was wearing a purple velvet robe trimmed in feathers. She had been half of a vaudeville act twenty years and fifty pounds before and was partial enough to the costumes that she continued to wear them on a daily basis.

"That's a fine how-do."

Belle stuck a pencil in her hair, where it would likely remain until she rolled over in her sleep. "You know the rules, Rosie. I don't make 'em."

"By my reckoning, I still have four days left. It's not going to matter anyhow. I auditioned for two shows today and I fell head over heels trying to get them to cast me. Something's got to come out of that."

Belle nodded and didn't say anything else, which put me on my guard. By this point in the conversation we were usually parrying our razor-sharp wit.

"How's your new year going?" I asked her.

"Fair. The new ration books are out. Mind the expiration dates." Rationing rules were more complicated than chess. Just when I thought I'd figured the darn things out, they changed them on me. "Sign in, will you." Belle passed me a packet of coupons and the house registrar, then receded back into silence. As I scribbled the *R* in Winter, I glommed the reason for her behavior: she pitied me. I'd become like every other girl who was bumped out of the house and never heard from again. I'd entered the path of theatrical failure.

I wasn't going down without a fight.

"Are these new rules?" I asked. Underneath the registrar was a list labeled George Bernard Shaw House Rules, Revised. Twenty-six numbered laws were crammed onto the page.

Belle nodded and continued her pledge to be kind to the dying.

"You misspelled a word in rule three."

That did it. "It never ceases to amaze me how you girls can't remember the rules but you can remember which word I misspelled while typing them."

"You can't blame us, Belle. If you want us to remember something like this, you should consider livening it up with a few pictures and more white space." My bag shifted violently from right to left. I dropped it to the ground.

Belle stabbed the paper with her pudgy index finger. "If you can memorize scripts, you can memorize rules. If you'd read the last set, my revision wouldn't have been necessary."

I put both hands over my heart and feigned shock. "I brought *this* on us?"

"I'm not a fool, Rosie. I do pay attention to what goes on around here."

"Searched my room, did ya?" A yowl of discontent emerged from the floor.

Belle lowered her glasses. "Is your bag meowing?"

"No, but my dogs are barking. I've been hoofing it all over town." I gave my bag a gentle kick. It hissed in return.

Belle produced a second copy of the rules. "Shall I read them to you?"

"What? And spoil the surprise?" I took the list and tucked it into my coat pocket. "I get the gist—no hot plates, no smoking, no alcohol, gentlemen callers are to be received in the lobby, and take to the cellar in the event of an air raid drill. And a happy new year to you, too."

My mewling bag and I ankled upstairs, where Jayne was stationed before her bureau marcelling her blond locks. The stench of roasting hair filled the tiny space. I greeted her by propping open the window.

"Sorry," she said.

"It's not you; it's this place. If the air circulated once in a while you wouldn't even notice the smell." I dropped the bag on the floor and attempted to fan fresh air into the room.

"Did you hear we sank nine Japanese ships?" Since Jack had shipped out, Jayne had fallen into the habit of announcing war victories as though by doing so she could reassure me that Jack was not only safe but had done the right thing by enlisting.

"And how many of ours did we sink in the process?" I asked.

"None that I know of." She read my mood and left the war behind. "How was the audition?"

"The only way it could've gone worse is if I'd accidentally killed somebody."

"Did you meet Peter Sherwood?"

"He either wasn't there or was too embarrassed to admit he'd invited me." The window banged shut, narrowly missing my hand. "In other news, I'm now a detective."

She set the iron in its cradle and gave me her undivided attention. "Do I need a drink for this story?"

"I can't speak for you, but I could certainly use one."

Jayne tipped us martinis while I told her about my day. As I finished, she shook her head and tsk-tsked the contents of her glass.

"You're not seriously going to work for this Raymond Fielding person, are you?"

"I sneezed his dough, so I probably owe it to him to do something. I'll look through the files to see if I can find out what Jim learned, maybe make a few phone calls. After all, the widow McCain asked me to do the same." I chewed my lip. "Besides, I feel like I need to do this. It's not like I have anything else to fill my time."

Jayne nodded solemnly then downed her drink. "Doesn't it seem strange that he'd ask you to follow up on this when he knows you're just a file clerk?"

I fished a bottle from the bottom of her closet and refilled our glasses. "Like I said, his main concern was privacy. He didn't want to start over with another agency."

"But if privacy is so important to him, wouldn't it be better to not say anything to you since you clearly didn't know anything to begin with?"

I was about to ask her to put me wise to what she meant when she squealed. "Rosie! Your bag's moving!" The valise jerked and let out an unholy cry. I opened the clutch and Churchill leaped from his bing and landed with a hiss on the drapes.

"Jayne, meet Churchill. Churchill, meet Jayne." The cat dropped to the floor and prowled about the room, gunning for something to attack. When nothing worthwhile appeared, he dashed beneath my bureau and receded into darkness until he was nothing but a pair of golden almond-shaped eyes.

Barely a minute passed before someone knocked on the door. Before we could tell her to scram, the knob turned and Ruby Priest popped her head into the room. "Hello, girls."

"Hello yourself," I said. Jayne cheesed the glasses under the bed while I braced the door to keep it from opening any wider. Ruby had been at the Shaw House since July and had already worked more than any of us. Worse yet, every project of hers was so visible you couldn't leave your room without being confronted by it. Ruby was on Times Square billboards. Ruby was hawking war bonds with Betty Grable on WNYC. Ruby was modeling dresses in Macy's newspaper ads. It wasn't her success that made me hate her; she was one of those women who got everything they asked for without lifting a finger and rather than being gracious about it, she constantly rubbed her achievements in my face. She'd done it so much that she didn't even have to say anything to make me feel worthless. Like some Pavlovian dog I immediately beefed up my failures in the face of Ruby's accomplishments.

Ruby flashed me a smile worthy of one of her tooth-cream ads and wrapped a glossy black curl around her finger. "How were your holidays?"

"Fine," I said. "Thanks for asking." She was pushing ever so slightly against the door, but I held it steady. "And yours?"

She sighed. "Not much to report. *Night Falls* had its run extended, so I spent a quiet Christmas with Lawrence." Ruby never talked about her family; nor had she ever gotten a phone call or piece of mail that would've verified her ties. It was sad in a way since it was clear Ruby wanted to hear something from someone. She was always the first to the mailbox and the first to the ringing phone. A lesser person might've been intrigued by her family's silence, but I'd assumed her relations were as irritated by her as I was.

I tossed Jayne a look and rolled my peepers. "And how is Lawrence?"

Ruby smiled more delicately and widened her eyes. "Lawrence is wonderful. Naturally he's still riding high on the tail of our resounding success."

"Naturally." I said. "Congratulations, by the way. I heard about your review."

She pushed her hair back from her face with a practiced gesture. "Which one?"

"There was more than one?" I asked.

"I should hope so. Otherwise, why bother acting?"

"There are people who do it for the joy and the art."

"Oh, Rosie *dear*, those people—if they exist—don't live in New York." She flipped her hair and laughed. I gripped the door so tightly I left fingerprints on the paint.

Jayne cleared her throat and feigned interest in our uninvited guest. "So now that the show's closed, what are you going to do, Ruby?"

"I've hardly had a chance to catch my breath, but Lawrence has a new show he's finishing that he wants to open in six weeks. He's offered me the lead."

My mind rumbled with the unfairness of Ruby's getting cast in plays that hadn't even been written yet while I was begging for any theatrical leftover.

As though she heard my thoughts, Ruby turned her attentions back to me. "Did you work over the holidays, Rosie?"

I shifted my sweaty hold on the door. "Not in theater."

She pursed her lips sympathetically. "That's right—you have that little secretarial job. Good for you."

I moved my head closer to hers. "What the deuce does that mean?"

"Just that I know it's been a while since you had an acting job, so it's good you have something to fall back on." She paused and ate up the ire that leached from my body. "I hope you're not offended by my saying that. I'm trying to think positively." Her mood shifted faster than a baby on vaccination day. "Say, I have a famous idea! Why don't I talk to Lawrence about casting you in the new show? I'm sure it wouldn't be a big part, but Belle won't care."

"That's a great idea," said Jayne. I ducked behind the open door and shook my head so fast my ears rang. "That is," said Jayne, "it would be a great idea except Rosie has a job."

"Is that so?" asked Ruby. I gritted my teeth. This wasn't the sort of thing I could get away with lying about. There may have been an endless amount of theater in New York, but it wouldn't take much for Ruby to verify if I had a paying gig.

"Sort of," I said. "Nothing's official yet, but it looks very promising."

"What's the show?"

"I don't want to say yet—don't want to jinx it. You know what, Rube? I'm exhausted and I think I want to call it a night. It was good seeing you." I tried to push the door closed but was interrupted by Ruby's pale well-toned arm.

"I forgot to ask," she said. "Did I hear a cat in here?"

I put my forehead against the door. "No. What you heard was an extraordinary imitation of a cat. Do it again, Jayne."

Jayne's mouth dropped open and her eyes became wide and empty. On cue, Churchill began to cough up whatever he'd devoured in my bag.

"It *is* a cat!" Ruby pushed all of her weight against the door, shoving me out of the way.

"Ruby," I said. "If there is a cat in here—and I'm not saying there is—we'd appreciate it if you kept this between . . ."

She stuck her head into the hallway. "Hey, girls! Rosie and Jayne got a cat." Every door on the second floor burst open and our room filled with ten cooing women intent on coaxing kitty out from under the dresser. When he finally emerged, the women fought for the right to pet him with the same intensity displayed by bridesmaids competing for the bouquet.

"Oh, he's adorable!"

"He's soft as silk."

"Is kitty hungry? Thirsty?"

Churchill lapped up the attention and pretended he was a normal cat. He rubbed his head between bosoms and bellies and stared longingly into ten different sets of eyes. It took fifteen minutes for the excitement to die down. By then Churchill was asleep on Ruby's lap with his head hanging over her arm.

We were strong women, independent women. We lived on our own and we paid our own way. Yet we could be reduced to goo in the presence of a small mammal and we latched on to gossip like it was the air we breathed. Naturally, this could work to my advantage. Churchill and I were sworn enemies, but I didn't have it in me to give him the gate. If, however, someone else snitched, I could lose the cat and keep my conscience.

"Pipe this," I said. "We can't have a cat. Belle can't know about the cat. If one of you says a peep about it, the cat's gone." Everyone nodded and murmured their understanding. Churchill's tail curled into a *J.*

"We won't say a word," said Ruby. And for the first time in the history of the George Bernard Shaw, she was right.

7 The Importance of Being Earnest

I GOT UP EARLY THE next day and went right to the office. All was pretty much as I'd left it except that Agnes had removed Churchill's leavings from my desk and the radiator felt as if it had been upped by ten degrees. The radio and I spent the first hour looking for any evidence of Raymond Fielding. When the only things that turned up were "hillbilly music" and the heat, I decided to grab some breakfast.

Ten minutes later I had a cup of java, a doughnut, and a plan to go back through the files I'd packed. As I returned to the office, I was knocked over by a one-two punch of cheap cologne.

"Hello?" I called out. Jim's door stood open, but instead of being filled with the morning's pale sun, a shadow devoured the light. "Hello?" I followed the shadow to Jim's window and found a man in a black wool flogger and gray derby. He was as big as a skyscraper and weighed at least as much. He walked toward me until he was close enough for me to make out his Neanderthal-like features.

I should've took to the air, but I hated to waste a perfectly good doughnut. "May I help you?"

In his hand was a crude metal appliance that I took for a bean-shooter. He squeezed it as though he were readying the device for action. "Where's the knob for the radiator?" he asked.

On closer examination, the tool appeared to be a well-worn set of pliers. "Underneath it."

He shook his head and admonished me with the pliers. Apparently, having to remove them from his pocket was very inconvenient. "I turned it down. I hate it when a room's too hot." The tool was returned to his trench coat with a metallic tinkle that indicated it was one of several implements he carried.

"Thanks." I tried to imagine what kind of man regularly toted tools on his person without the benefit of a belt or a box. None of the options were particularly savory.

His eyes drifted around the office, taking in the crates and stacks of files. "You moving?"

I decided to play it casual. Isn't that what you were supposed to do during a bear attack? "I'm putting files into storage to make more space." I returned to the outer office and set the coffee on my desk. He followed me into the reception area and hovered near the dieffenbachia. Without the light behind him, it was easier to see his puss. He had the soft, doughy features of a college athlete. He would've seemed harmless had his face been separated from his imposing body. "I'm sorry, but I didn't catch your name," I said.

"That's 'cause I didn't give it to you." He put his hands in his pockets and surveyed the walls and ceiling. "I figured you'd close up the place with Jim gone."

I leaned against my desk and tore my doughnut in half. "I guess you figured wrong."

He approached Agnes's desk and sat on its top. His hands left his pockets and rested on his knees. "Damn shame what happened to Jim." He met my eyes. His were small and close together like a rodent's. "Seems to me a wise head wouldn't go leaving her office unlocked after something like that."

As menacing as he was trying to be, I found him more irritating than intimidating. Give him a meatloaf and some varicose veins and he could be my ma. "Seems to me a smart man wouldn't go breaking and entering in broad daylight."

He crossed his arms. "It ain't breaking if the door's unlocked." He gave me his profile and recognition flashed through my head.

"I know you!" I snapped my fingers, trying to place where I'd seen his mug. "Jim's viewing—you were there with the other goons . . . er . . . sorry."

If he was insulted, he didn't show it. "I don't know what you're talking about."

My brain kept churning. "There was another time too—the subway the night Jim died. You were hiding behind a newspaper staring at me." He kept his face impassive, resigned to not tip his mitt. "Oh, come on—I know it was you."

He cracked his knuckles. "You don't know from nothing."

"Fine, I don't *know from nothing*." I was officially rankled. "Look, Mister . . . oh, I'm sorry, since you haven't given me your moniker, I'm going to have to make one up for you. How about Frank? Since you're in my office when I'm not, I'm going to assume we're on a first name basis." I took a bite of my doughnut. "Anyways, *Frank,* you can deny everything I say and continue doing that physical intimidation thing you like so much, or you can cut to the chase and tell me what you're doing here. Because I'm awfully busy and I'd prefer you do whatever you came here for so we can both go about our day." I took another bite of doughnut and washed it down with a swig of coffee. Frank kept staring at me. "Would you like some doughnut, Frank?"

His close-set eyes grew even closer. "Yes," he said. "I would."

I reluctantly tossed him the half I hadn't eaten and watched him devour it in a single bite. He searched the desk for a napkin. When one didn't materialize, he wiped his mouth on his coat sleeve, leaving behind a shadow of white powder.

"Word is you're taking on Jim's cases," he said.

"Where did you hear that from?"

His hand grabbed at his chin as though he were feeling for a beard that was no longer there. "I've got my sources."

"And is your source a client?" He didn't say anything. Instead he maintained a stony stare that I suspected he honed through years of practice. "Oh, come on, Frank—you can be square with me." Still nothing, and I knew he was waiting for me to spill. The question was, Why? I was positive Frank was the bruno at the funeral and on the subway, but I didn't understand the reason behind his visit.

I chose my words carefully. "I'm finishing a case or two as a courtesy, but I'm not taking on anything else."

Frank jerked a nod and brushed the crumbs from his coat. The phone shrieked.

"Are we done?" I asked. He shrugged in reply. I rolled my eyes and lifted the receiver. "McCain and Son."

"Rosie?" A little girl's voice breathed my name.

"Just who I was hoping to hear from," I said. "Anybody call?" Jayne had agreed to stay at the house in case I got a callback. My desperation for work had turned to delusion.

"Not yet." There was a frantic quality to her voice that I wasn't used to, a shaky tone that wordlessly implied *your mother's dead* and *the rabbit died*. "Have you seen the A.M. papers?"

I turned away from Frank and lowered my voice. "No. Why?" In the background, Edward R. Murrow brought us up to date on the news from overseas. Was it time for his normal report, or had he chilled the airwaves with the dreaded words *We interrupt this program*?

Had something happened to Jack?

Jayne's voice drifted into a whisper. "Raymond Fielding's dead."

Frank no longer seemed so innocuous. I shifted and spied him from the corner of my eye. "Isn't that something?" I said to the phone. "Don't worry, Jayne—she'll pull through this. My grandmother had the exact same thing and she's still kicking."

"Is somebody there?" Jayne asked.

"Oh, yes," I said, "and Gram's a big woman too. Healthy or not, she could scare the pants off you with a single look."

Frank yawned and cleaned his nails with a pen nib.

"Do you want me to come down?" Jayne asked.

"No, no. You go to the hospital and be with your family. I'll take care of everything."

"If I don't hear back from you in ten minutes, I'm coming over," said Jayne.

"All right. Bye." I put the horn in the cradle and took a deep breath.

Frank stopped his manicure. "What's wrong with your friend's grandma?"

"They're not sure. She's coughing up blood and has stomach pain." There was a bulge in Frank's flogger. When I concentrated on it, I could make out a butt and a barrel.

"She smoke?" asked Frank.

"Only when she's on fire." I picked up a stack of files and aimlessly shuffled them. "Are you staying long? I only ask because I order out for lunch and I'll want to make sure there's enough for two. That half a doughnut left me peckish."

He grunted. "You're an actress, right?"

I stopped shuffling and tried to figure out what gave me away. If he'd been in the office before, it was possible Jim had said something about me. Either that or it was my impeccable posture and well-supported voice. "Let me guess: You're a fan?"

Frank shrugged. "You in movies?"

"Plays."

He shook his head. "Never been to a play." He leaned forward on the desk as if his back were bothering him. "So what do you do then—you pretend to be other people?"

I roosted on a reception chair. "There's a little more to it than that."

"Like what?"

If he didn't have Raymond Fielding's blood on his hands, I would've told him to go climb his thumb. As it was, I fought to explain my craft in twenty words or less. "For starters, there's training. You have to learn how to use your voice, how to move, how to belong to a play."

"I bet memorizing's hard."

I gave him a tight smile. "You get used to it."

His eyes were glued on me. "How so?"

"I don't know—there are tricks to remembering words. Everyone has their own system." Was he worried I'd seen or heard something I wasn't supposed to and committed it to memory?

"And crying," he said. "I'll never figure out how you do that whenever you want to. I bet you poke yourself in the eye when no one's looking, right?"

I decided it wasn't worth teaching him the finer points of emotional recall. "That's right. Lots of eye poking, but only when onions aren't available."

He slapped his hands against his thighs to signal he was getting to his point. "So how does an actress become a gumshoe?"

"I'm not a gumshoe, Frank—I don't have a ticket. I'm just playing one for the moment because nobody else wants the job. That's how I get most of my roles."

He stifled a cough with his hand. "I bet Jim taught you everything he knew."

"Depends on the topic. Jim was pretty close-lipped about a lot of things." Our eyes met and we silently challenged each other. If he wasn't going to tell me his reason for being there, I wasn't going to offer him any more than the basics. Frank looked at his watch, frowned, and began to wind it. "You waiting for someone?" I asked.

"Yeah." He kicked his legs against the side of the metal desk. The office shimmied with the metallic boom. "'S cold outside. That's why I'm here. Waiting."

High-heeled, panicked footsteps sounded in the stairwell. Frank swung his tremendous noodle toward the door and his hand flinched toward the bulge in his trench coat.

"Easy, boy—it's a friend of mine."

His hand returned to his side. "You've got a lot of friends."

"Only two that you know of. Even if we threw you into the mix, we wouldn't have enough people for a party."

Jayne rushed into the office blind to Frank's presence. For someone who'd intended to spend the day sitting by the phone, she was dressed to the nines. "Rosie! Thank goodness you're all right." She saw Frank and slowly spun around to face him. As his enormity became apparent, she shrank until I had to strain my eyes to see her. "Hello there," she said.

Frank rose from the desk as though he were remembering, after years of grandmotherly instruction, that this was what you did when a woman entered the room.

Jayne tilted her head back and stared up at the big lug. "I didn't know you had company." Fear entered her eyes. It was pushed aside by a grin that would've gotten a man slapped and his mother reprimanded.

I played at being hostess. "Jayne—Frank. Frank—Jayne."

Frank returned to his perch. "You the Jane with the sick grandma?"

"That's another Jayne," I said. "This one's an actress like me."

Frank crossed his arms. "You know a lot of Janes."

"It's a popular name. I blame that Tarzan fellow." I raised an eyebrow at my pal, waiting for her to come up with why she was here and how we could leave. She set her open pocketbook on a chair. A newspaper peeked out of the top of it.

"I bet you're wondering why I was worried about Rosie," said Jayne.

"It crossed my mind." Frank's eyes narrowed into twin raisins.

"Well . . ." Jayne paused and shrugged off her coat. Underneath it she had on a navy wool dress that was so snug I could make out the shape of a tissue in her pocket. "Last night Rosie got food poisoning. Bad food poisoning." Her baby voice rose an octave. "I tried to check on her this morning, but she wasn't home. Naturally, I panicked." She turned her calves so Frank could take in her showgirl legs. "So I ran all the way here in these awful heels to make sure she wasn't dead or worse." She patted her platinum hair and widened her eyes. Jayne wore both her hair and her skirts short. It was her way of helping out with the war effort. "I bet I look a mess."

Frank followed the curve of her body. "You don't look so bad to me."

She pursed her lips and wagged a finger at me. Tony B.'s rock winked in the light. "Shame on you, worrying me like that. All this time I'm thinking you're at the hospital and you were here entertaining this big, handsome man."

"You shouldn't have worried your friend like that." Frank unwrapped his arms and pulled at his cuffs. If Jayne was thawing him, it was going to be a long, slow spring.

"To make it up to me, Rosie, you have to go to lunch with me. I'm not going to take no for an answer." She retrieved a compact from her purse and powdered her nose. America's squeakheart was giving the performance of her life. "Get your things and let's scram."

"It's not up to me," I said. "Frank's waiting for somebody."

Jayne put her coat back on. "He can wait in the stairwell."

Frank rose, his girth blocking the light and changing the weather. "Maybe I don't want to wait in the stairwell."

Jayne's coat fell past her shoulders and her breasts led her to Frank. Her voice turned breathy and her skin deepened in hue. "Frank, I know you don't mean to be rude, but your tone isn't going to do. Rosie is going with me, and if you don't let us leave right this minute, we're going to be late. I'm supposed to have lunch with my boyfriend, Tony B., and if I'm not on time I'll never hear the end of it." She put the hand bearing the ring on the lapel of Frank's coat and smoothed the fabric. "You don't want to make trouble for us, do you?"

Frank shook his head and the slightest hint of fear yanked the color from his face.

She winked at him. "Then be a doll, would you, and step into the hall so Rosie can lock up." Reluctantly, Frank did as he was told while Jayne and I applied our lids and grabbed our purses. As we dusted, his eyes burned tiny close-set holes in my back.

"Does that answer your question?" Jayne asked as we hit the street.

I struggled to keep pace with her. "What question?"

"What I see in Tony B., silly."

We walked all the way to Times Square and ducked into Horn and Hardart. The place was plastered with small signs indicating things they were out of and unlikely to be able to create any time soon thanks to shortages: egg salad, roast beef, hamburger. I wrangled my change until I had enough coin for a pair of ham sandwiches, a piece of pie, and two cups of coffee—stretched with chicory—fresh out of the Automat's machine. After Jayne's performance, the least I could do was treat her to lunch.

"So who was he?" she asked as we waited for the counter worker to place a second sandwich behind the glass.

"I'm not sure. He was at Jim's funeral with the rest of the tough guys and I caught him tailing me the night Jim died."

Jayne gasped. "You don't think he killed—"

I cut her off with a wave of my hand. "No. I can't guarantee he didn't bump off Fielding, but I don't think he's responsible for Jim's death. I got the strangest feeling he was there because he wanted me to tell him something, but he couldn't ask me to tell him whatever it was he wanted to know."

Jayne squinted as if the light were hurting her eyes. "That doesn't make any sense."

"I know, but then nothing about today does." We took our trays to the back and hunted for a free table. A group of soldiers on leave clutching maps of the city rose from one of the two tables they occupied and offered Jayne and me a pair of chairs.

"Thanks," she said before helping me slide the table out of their earshot. They could ogle us all they wanted, but we needed our privacy. "Do you want me to ask Tony about him?"

"Why? Does he have a leash on every thug in the city?"

She shrugged. "It couldn't hurt, could it?"

I stared into my coffee, trying to find the best way to express why talking to Tony was a bad idea. If he did know Frank, there was a good chance Tony was involved in whatever was going down and I didn't think either of us needed confirmation of his activities. And it probably wouldn't do me good if word got back to Frank that I was snooping into his business. The last thing I wanted was a follow-up visit.

"Sure, it wouldn't hurt," I said, "but I'd rather forget about the whole thing. I'm fine, and he should have a pretty good inkling that I know nothing about nothing."

Jayne pulled the crinkled newspaper out of her bag and smoothed it with her hand. On page one, above an article blaring NEW YORK OF-FICE OF WAR INFORMATION DECRIES NOW IS THE TIME FOR PATRIOTISM was a death notice for Raymond Fielding, playwright.

"He was a playwright?" I asked.

"I thought you knew," said Jayne.

"Did you?"

"Well, sure . . . after I read the paper."

I pulled the newspaper close to me and scanned the contents. The day before, Fielding's butler had found the recently deceased with a bullet wound to his head in an upstairs bedroom. In the past month, his home had been broken into twice, though it wasn't revealed if the thief took anything.

As far as the victim was concerned, he was a playwright. A prolific playwright. An oft written about and discussed playwright who never achieved popular recognition. He had written at least fifty shows, all produced under the moniker "anonymous," since one of his many theories was that the writer should be invisible to the theatrical ex-perience. There was a partial list of the plays he'd written and not a title among them that I'd ever heard of. He was also deep into theory—he'd written a tome about the modern theater that had be-come standard for college classrooms. He was closely associated with a number of experimental companies. In addition to being a writer, he was an amateur painter and independently wealthy, the son of a long-deceased man who'd made his fortune in rubber right about the time the Ford Motor Company started operating. Fielding had also fought in the Great War, and had received a Purple Heart after losing his leg. He started his own charity for vets after returning home. In fact, he was such a stand-up guy they couldn't fit his entire obituary on the front page. It was continued on page twelve.

"Well, I'll be . . ." I shook my head. "I knew I should've gone to college." I scanned the first part of the article a second time. "If you were a playwright and you lost something important that happened to be on paper, what do you think that might be?"

"A play?" said Jayne.

"Yes, a play. Why didn't he say so? Why all the mystery?"

Jayne stared hard at the upside-down article. "If he was known for writing controversial shows, maybe this play had something in it somebody didn't want to get out."

"It's a play," I said. "How dangerous could it be?" My mind drifted back to the file of programs I'd found in Jim's office. Despite their lack of authorship, they had to be Fielding's shows. If Jim had received the same vague information we had, there was a good chance he was just figuring out what he was looking for right before he died. That certainly explained the Shakespeare quote. But then why, as Fielding claimed, did Jim call him with news that he'd discovered something important?

I plucked off the sugar bowl's lid, ignoring the hastily scrawled note that begged me not to use any more than was necessary. I took four cubes for now and stuck a handful in my purse for later. "And even if the play was controversial, why wouldn't he tell me it was a script that's missing? I didn't need to know what it was about." I flipped through the newspaper, hunting for the conclusion of Fielding's post-mortem accolades. Page twelve was filled with other obituaries, each accompanied by a picture. I searched out Fielding's puss but couldn't locate it. I gave that up and combed the text, looking for his name. "Isn't that funny?"

"What?"

I stabbed the paper with my finger. "They've got a picture labeled Raymond Fielding—only it's not him." Beside the conclusion of the article was a photo of a man with a head full of white hair, half-moon spectacles, and a dour mustache. I turned the paper so Jayne could get a slant.

"It's probably a mistake," she said. "Papers make them all the time. In fact, it always seems like there are more mistakes in the A.M. than the P.M. I wonder why that is?"

I ignored her and bit into my sandwich. "What if it's not a mistake?"

Jayne picked up her fork and stabbed a slice of rhubarb. "Then either there's two Raymond Fieldings or . . ."

"Or the guy I met was lying from the get-go. That would explain why he didn't say what he was looking for—he didn't know."

Jayne lectured me with her fork, spraying the table with speckles of fruit filling. "You should call the cops. Whoever this guy is, he probably had something to do with Fielding's death. They'll want to follow up on that." She dropped her fork and fished a coin out of her pocketbook. "Here." She slid it across the table. "Call them. Now."

I sighed and abandoned my food for the pay phone in the corner. A sign reminded me not to squander my time on the line since "Joe needs long-distance tonight." I fed the phone a dime and asked the operator to connect me with the nearest precinct. Two switchboard operators later and I was connected with the homicide division that was looking into Fielding's murder.

"Can I help you?" asked a secretary whose tone suggested assisting me was the last thing she wanted to do.

"I need to talk to whoever's heading up the Raymond Fielding murder."

"You want Schmidt," she said. "Hold please."

"Wait!" I stopped her before I was plunged into the electronic journey from one phone line to the next. "This Schmidt you're talking about—would this be a Lieutenant Schmidt with a big gut and a bad attitude?"

Her contempt evaporated and was replaced by an acknowledgment of kinship. Apparently, Schmidt had many friends. "That's the one."

I closed my eyes and put my forehead against the rotary. Schmidt's overgrown baby face filled my brain with his mocking grin. If I squealed to him about Fielding, he'd either ignore me or find some way to pin the death on Jim. "Is there anyone else I could talk to?"

She laughed and a metallic buzz signaled she had other calls to answer. "Sister, if it was that simple, don't you think we would've gotten rid of him by now?" She didn't wait for my response. "You want me to transfer you or not?"

"Not," I said, and I hung up.

When I returned to the table, Jayne had finished the pie and was working her way through her sandwich. "Well?" she asked.

I slid into my chair and returned my napkin to my lap. "They're looking into it."

"Good. Now you can wash your hands of this whole thing."

"I wouldn't go that far, Jayne. The police are very busy. This is hardly the only murder they have to concern themselves with."

Jayne's large red lips turned into a tiny rosebud. "We're not going back to Jim's office."

I finished off half of my sandwich. "Of course not. We're going to be far too busy paying a visit to the home of the late Raymond Fielding."

8 The Misanthrope

WE WOLFED DOWN WHAT REMAINED of lunch, then hoofed it to Park Avenue and Forty-second Street. There we fought the crowds at Grand Central and boarded a rattler bound for Croton-on-Hudson in Westchester County. From the depot, we hired a hack to take us to the address the paper had listed. Fielding had lived near Mary Pickford and Douglas Fairbanks's East Coast estate, where the scent of old money wafted through the air like cherry blossoms and where war seemed as if it could exist only at a movie house. Each home had a river view and was set a half acre from the road, buried behind a sea of trees and carefully manicured shrubs. The few buildings we glimpsed were massive brick and stone structures outfitted with porticos and porte cocheres and chimneys that rose from every side like miniature skyscrapers tacked onto the roofs. Despite the solitude, I couldn't shake the feeling that somebody was following us.

I asked the driver to drop us off at the top of the block and tossed him a few clams from the roll the faux Fielding had given me. The chilly morning had given way to a downright cold afternoon. A white blanket of snow coated the rolling lawns from storms that had bypassed the city. The gray sky muttered a warning that more of the same was on the horizon.

Neither Jayne nor I was dressed for a long walk or a cold day, but I forced us to move at a leisurely stroll in case anyone should be watching. While one of my strides may have equaled two of hers, Jayne's legs worked like hummingbird wings so that she could outwalk, outrun, out-everything me if I let her.

"This is a bad idea," she muttered as she passed me on the right.

I grabbed her sleeve and held her in place until I caught up. "Slow down. There's no fire. We're two girls out for a breath of fresh air, remember?"

"I've got snow in my pumps. Snow!" Jayne stopped and emptied her shoes. My own feet gravitated from pain to numbness. The only way I could keep moving was if I squeezed my toes together to conserve heat, but when I did I ended up hobbling like a duck.

I concentrated on the house numbers. "We're almost there."

Jayne rubbed her gloveless hands together. "And what's our plan when we get there?"

I suspected she wasn't asking for the truth. "We'll invite ourselves in, have a drink, and sit before a roaring fire."

Fielding's home was at the top of the hill, set farther back than the ones surrounding it. It looked as if all of New York had used their gas ration coupons to get there. Two rows of cars lined the winding driveway; another lined the street in front of the house.

"What are people doing here?" Jayne asked.

"Maybe it's a wake."

Pine trees bordered the property and broke up a monotonous snow-covered yard. Once we reached a clearing, the house loomed before us. It was Tudor and so large I couldn't take it all in from where we stood.

"Get a load of this place," I said.

It was the perfect retreat for a writer who valued his privacy. A wrought-iron gate topped with decorative spears demarked the space where lawn met road. A flagstone walkway led from the street to the front door, though it was uneven enough to imply that it was intended to hinder not invite. Lead-glass windows were darkened by heavy drapes. Twin griffins guarded the entrance.

The good thing about our physical discomfort was that it distracted us from the stupidity of what we were about to do.

"Follow my lead," I told Jayne as we reached the front door. I rang the bell and we both rapidly tended to our harried appearances:

lipstick emerged from pocketbooks, fingers served as combs, top buttons were relieved of their duties so cleavage (or whatever passed for it) could join us at our task. Within thirty seconds we both looked inviting enough to greet sailors at the dock.

A butler in full livery answered the door and silently gestured us inside.

We entered a dimly lit marble foyer empty but for a large gilt mirror and a pedestal containing a bust. Directly in front of us was a study filled with people who were toting cocktails while engaging in animated conversations before a roaring fire.

"What did I tell you?" I whispered to Jayne. "Booze and a fire."

Hunting trophies dotted the walls, skins lined the floor, and the furniture was a stalwart mixture of deep earth tones and dark woods. The enormous stone fireplace was flanked by bookcases overflowing with volumes in rich leather bindings. To the right of us were French doors leading out to a patio. To the left was a massive carved desk. Additional guests spilled into a doorway that presumably led to the rest of the house.

Jayne elbowed me and I followed her line of sight to the fireplace, above which hung an oil portrait. It was a slightly younger version of the man from the paper. He stood in a fanciful pastoral scene replete with cherubs and a waterfall that could give Niagara a run for its money. A signature decorated the lower left-hand corner. It was a self-portrait.

"That answers that," I said. "The man I met wasn't Raymond Fielding. Do you notice anything strange about the painting?"

Jayne stepped back and squinted upward as people at the Met do when they want to look as if they're serious about art. "It's not very good?"

"No bum leg."

Jayne shrugged. "Maybe he was a vain guy. You think Napoleon didn't ask to be painted a little taller?"

"He started a vet's charity. I find it hard to believe somebody who lost a leg and made it a mission to help out others would have the ego to paint himself with two good getaway sticks."

A servant bearing a tray of half-filled wineglasses breezed by and offered us beverages. We each took one and tried to look as if we belonged. "Who are these people?" asked Jayne.

The crowd was an eclectic mix of shoddily attired men and women who seemed better suited for the Bowery Mission than an elite river-front community. Jayne and I inched closer to a bookcase so we could eavesdrop on a small group huddled in debate.

"Nonsense," said a man in a tattered sport coat. "*The Long Trip* was clearly a retelling of Homer's *Odyssey* and nothing more."

"You have to be kidding me," said a woman wearing large ear-rings. "It was a clever dissection of Hitler's rise to power that used the *Odyssey* as an allegory. Ask anyone."

Tattered Sport Coat rolled his peepers and elbowed a companion to make sure he was getting the joke of Big Earrings's ignorance. "You're putting far too much meaning on the text. I have yet to see a single production that communicated that. Do you want to tell me why?"

Big Earrings tossed her hair over her shoulder. "Because I haven't done it yet."

I pulled out my compact and spied the rest of the crowd through my mirror while I pretended to primp. Fat and Smiley, the director from my miserable audition, was standing by the French doors. His partner in crime, Dull and Dramatic, hovered near the desk examin-ing a letter opener. And Ruby's beau, Lawrence Bentley, sat on the couch surrounded by his court.

I grabbed Jayne's elbow and pulled her into a corner. "Directors and playwrights here to mourn the loss of one of their own and cel-ebrate what his death will mean for their careers."

"No actors?" she asked.

I examined the crowd again but nobody, aside from us, had the lean, desperate look of a performer. "Nope. We're alone. And without our photos."

"Now what?"

I hated feeling like a lamb surrounded by wolves; I wanted to leave. But I also knew we shouldn't waste this opportunity. If anyone

could tell us about Fielding, it was the directors who worshipped
him and the writers who despised him. "Now," I told Jayne, "we
mingle."

Jayne made a lap around the room and looked for anyone who
might be willing to bump gums. I took a more direct approach and
fought my way to the sofa.

"Lawrence? I thought that was you." I plopped beside him and
crossed my legs. His face blared confusion. "I'm Rosie Winter, a
friend of Ruby's."

"Oh." His voice was Connecticut country club, his suit handmade.
"I've never met one of Ruby's friends before."

"Well, you know how she is." I faked a laugh. I could see what
Ruby saw in him. Up close he was very handsome, if a bit of a daisy.
Every time he gestured, it reminded me of tatting lace—he was that
precise. "How is she, by the way?" I asked.

"Honestly? I don't know." He sipped the remnants of his drink as
though he were tasting it for royalty. I found myself seeking out whatever it was that kept him out of the war. Did he have flat feet, poor
hearing, or a daddy with connections? "You know," he said, "now that
I look at you, you seem familiar. Are you an actress?"

I noticed the looks of disapproval on the faces around us and
shook my head. Was it better to be a director or a writer? He might
find the former more endearing. "No, I'm a director. Just starting out.
Off-off-Broadway stuff."

"We all have to start somewhere," he said.

"You're right about that." I needed something to keep Bentley
talking. "I loved *Night Falls* by the way. Brilliant play."

"Thank you." His eyes wandered to his entourage.

"It reminded me of Raymond Fielding's work."

That did it; I roped him. "Really?" I nodded too enthusiastically.
"Which work?"

Stanislavsky, the Russian granddaddy of method acting, boiled
each moment in a script (what he called a "beat") down to three
parts: objective, obstacle, and tactic. The objective was what your

character wanted, the obstacle was what kept her from getting it, and the tactic, which you could change as needed, was the method you used to overcome the obstacle. To put it in simpler terms, my objective was to learn whatever I could about Raymond Fielding. My obstacle was being none too swift about the writer and his work. My tactic was to lie through my teeth.

"Uh . . . *The Long Road* for one," I said to Lawrence. "And some of his earlier plays. While you may not be as political as Fielding, your work shares many of the same sensibilities, although, to be frank"—I leaned toward him so this comment was his alone—"your work is much more entertaining."

He matched my lean, recognizing that a man's wake was no place to be overheard being critical. "I've always felt that too. I admired him, of course, but so many of his works were bogged down by his theory. I often thought if he removed his politics and focused on telling the story, he would have been much more successful."

"True, true." It took everything in me not to roll my eyes. What Bentley wanted was for every writer to create the same garbage he had. "Did you know him?"

"Nobody did. The man was a hermit. I did correspond with him briefly, but I found him to be surprisingly"—he sought the word with his fingers—"difficult."

"How so?"

His tongue danced across his upper teeth as though he wanted to make sure they were free of food. "Despite the fact that he was worshipped by so many, he was a very unpleasant man. Rather than responding to my request for assistance with my work, he wrote me a four-page letter full of poison about how the playwright's ego was destroying the modern theater and we were moving further and further away from what the Greeks intended drama to be. Frankly, I took it as a sign he was mad."

"So if you didn't like him, why are you here?"

"To pay my respects, of course. Just because I didn't like him doesn't mean I don't bow down to the incredible contribution he made to the modern theater." He raised an eyebrow. "If he hated the modern playwright, he despised directors more. Why are you here?"

"The same reason as you, I guess." I lowered my voice. "And curiosity."

He gave me a smug smile. "No need to be coy with me. I dare say every director in this room was hoping they'd find a pile of unproduced manuscripts."

My brain played catch up. "You're on to me. I take it nothing's emerged?"

"Hardly—why do you think people are still here?" He waved over a waiter and replaced his empty glass with a full one.

I cleared my throat and plunged ahead. "I get the feeling, from other people I've talked to, that there's one play in particular they're hoping to find. Have you sensed that?"

He swirled the liquid in his glass until it kissed the rim. "Ah, yes—the great American play. Rumor is that it was stolen out of Fielding's house months ago." His eyes danced around the room, looking for someone more interesting to talk to.

"You seem to doubt that."

"That's because I think it's a fiction created by a mediocre writer who wanted to leave behind a legacy. And all of these people who are so interested in it are going to waste their time looking for it and miss out on the great plays that actually do exist."

Gee, and I wonder who wrote those? "Let me ask you this: Did somebody invite you here today or did you just decide to show up?" Jayne was huddled in the corner chinning with Fat and Smiley. I caught her eye and let her know the pleasure of her company was requested.

Bentley's face grew narrow with thinly veiled disgust. "I was invited of course. Weren't you?"

I plucked a loose thread from the couch. "Of course I was. I just wanted to know *who* invited you."

His hand inched toward mine. "I'm not sure. I received a simple card announcing the event without a host's name listed. You?"

"A phone call," I said. "Though I'm sure your card was very nice."

Jayne sashayed over to us with her coat thrown over her arm.

"This is my friend Jayne," I said. "Jayne, this is Lawrence Bentley."

He rose and delicately shook her hand. "It's a pleasure."

"We've met," she said. "I just auditioned for you." In case Bentley hadn't been sold on her performance, Jayne removed her lipstick from her pocketbook. As she applied it, he followed her every move, his face broadcasting that he found it one of life's great tragedies that he hadn't been born a cosmetic applicator.

I made a show of looking at my watch. "It was lovely talking to you, Lawrence, but I'm afraid we have to be on our way."

"So soon?" he said, as though he hadn't been trying to ditch me for the last fifteen minutes.

"Yes, so soon." I rose and pulled on my coat. "Say, can you tell me which play of Fielding's you consider to be the best example of his work?"

He frowned and strained to answer the question. "Probably *Journey's End*."

"Thanks," I said. "You've been a peach."

9 The Time of Your Life

WHILE JAYNE HUNTED FOR A powder room, I cornered the butler who'd greeted us at the door and asked him for two things: a cab to the depot and the name of his employer. He and the rest of the household staff had been hired for the night by a service. The only information they'd been given was the location of the event, the time it would end, and what food and drink to serve.

Ten minutes later Jayne and I were in a taxi on the way to the station. Our driver was a chatty fellow who smelled like a still, so rather than briefing each other on what we'd learned, we concentrated on keeping the cabbie alert and attentive. The train was no more conducive to conversation; apparently every sailor on the East Coast had been visiting his family and was due to return to the Brooklyn Navy Yard that night. By the time we returned to the Shaw House, it was nine o'clock. As we approached the building, a lumbering shadow left the steps and darted up the street.

Dinner was long over, so we scammed a couple of rolls, two pieces of pie, and a pot of coffee from the kitchen and smuggled them up to our room. Churchill greeted us at the door with a disenchanted mutter that quieted as soon as I offered him half of my Boston cream.

"Cat food," I told Jayne. "Remind me tomorrow that no matter what else I do, I must buy cat food." I shut the window Jayne had left open for Churchill and surveyed the feline's damage. He'd littered the newspaper-covered radiator with his pellets and sprayed the curtains with enough liquid to turn the white fabric yellow. As if that wasn't bad enough, the room was so cold his urine had frozen.

"I hate you," I told him.

"At least he went on the newspaper," said Jayne.

"Shhh," I said. "Don't say a word about it. The minute he figures out you liked something he did, he goes out of his way to do the exact opposite."

Fortunately, gin doesn't freeze, so within ten minutes Jayne had made us cocktails, I'd cleaned up the excrement de cat, and the three of us were sitting on my bed huddling for warmth. Once the hooch had diminished my desire to kill and the weak coffee had restarted my heart, I pulled out Fielding's obit and spread it on the bed before us.

"So what did we learn?" I asked.

Jayne fished out her olive. "Rich people serve cheap booze."

"Do tell me you gleaned more than that." I leaned forward and put my elbows on the bed so I could better examine the newspaper.

"I got an audition."

"Isn't that a pip?"

"What do you want me to say, Rosie? Everyone there was talking theory, and when they weren't doing that they were trying to pump up their own productions. The only thing I learned about Fielding is that nobody knows anything about him and I believe that's the rap we started with." She emptied her glass and replaced it with a coffee cup. "What about you?"

Churchill spied the dinner rolls and batted one of them down the bed. "For starters, I got confirmation that it's a script that's missing. According to Lawrence Bentley, Fielding was a recluse and word is he had a pile of unproduced plays."

"Great, finding *one* of them is hard enough."

I tore the remaining roll in half. I would've killed for some butter. All of us would've. "It gets better. Bentley received a mailed invitation to today's shindig, and I'm willing to bet most of the other theatrical muckety-mucks did too."

Jayne rubbed her eyes. "He just died. I mean, the mails are good, but how on earth could you print an invitation, post it, and get it to someone in two days?"

"Crystal ball maybe?" I dipped the roll in the coffee. It hung limply before disintegrating in my hand. "Needless to say there was no host's name on the invitation."

"What about the household staff? Maybe they know something."

"I'm a step ahead: they were hired for the day and they don't know by who."

Jayne lay back on the pillows. "Wow. Anything else?"

"I think Lawrence and Ruby are finished."

Jayne smiled in spite of herself. "Does she know?"

"I hope not." I smoothed the newspaper. "So here's what we know: someone, who was not Raymond Fielding, hired me to find a missing play of Raymond Fielding's, then bumped off the man he was impersonating but, before he did that, invited every director and writer in New York to a party to honor the victim. The question is why?"

Jayne poured herself some coffee and refilled my cup. "Let's start at the beginning: the murderer wants the play. According to the paper, Fielding's house was broken into twice, but we don't know if anything was taken. If something was, that may be why Fielding hired Jim." Jayne gestured with her cup. A dollop of coffee breached the rim and landed on my quilt. "The ringer gets wind the play is missing and panics because he wants it for some reason. He knows Fielding doesn't have it and he knows Fielding hired a detective, so he visits you to see if you've learned anything."

I shook my head. "You're forgetting all kinds of important things. Sometime between when the play went missing and the ringer came to see me, two men croaked. If Fake Fielding wants to find this thing, it doesn't make sense that he'd kill the only two people who might know where it is."

"Oh." Jayne stretched her legs. "Maybe Fake Fielding isn't our murderer, but he could still be the host of the party. Maybe he thought a writer or director might know something about the play, so he brings them all together hoping one of them might spill."

It was an interesting idea if not entirely plausible. And if he was our host, couldn't he have been in disguise? "Do you think he was there tonight?"

Jayne shrugged. "Sure. Why not?"

I tried to remember if there was someone there who didn't fit, but each face I recalled had the same arrogant artiness of every writer and director I knew. "What could be so important about a play that he'd go to these lengths to try to find it?"

Jayne examined her ring and scraped something off its surface. "Maybe it's worth a lot of money."

"Plays are only worth something if they're a manuscript and the writer's dead."

"Well . . ."

I cut her off with a shake of my head. "Long dead. Shakespeare dead. No, this can't be about dough unless the play was scrawled on the back of twenty large."

A knock sounded at the door. With the speed of a cheetah, Jayne slid the martini glasses under my bed and I tossed a pillow onto Churchill.

"Come in," I said. Ruby peeked her head around the door. Her presence was as welcome as a Burma Shave billboard at the Grand Canyon. "Oh, it's you."

She bared her fangs. "Great to see you, too. Tony's on the phone for you, Jayne."

My eyes rose to the ceiling as Jayne exited with a squeal. "What I meant was I'm glad it's you because if it was Belle we'd have to worry about the cat." On cue, Churchill climbed out from under the pillow. He stretched his limbs—one by one—with a flicker that ended with his left foot, then jumped off the bed and retreated under the dresser. "Close the door, would you?" She did as I requested, only instead of stepping out into the hall first, she lingered in the room like a bad stink. "Do you need something, Rube?"

Her hand disappeared into her pocket and removed a small piece of paper. "You had a phone message." She tossed the scrap onto the bed. "Congratulations."

"It's only a phone message, Ruby. It's not like I got mail." According to her perfect penmanship the end of the world was upon us.

"The drought is over: I'm being offered a lead." An unfamiliar feeling bubbled in my belly until I couldn't help but smile.

Ruby leaned against the door. "Good for you. You'll want to make sure to tell Belle."

"Tell her? I'm going to sing the news while accompanying myself on the harmonica." I read the note a second time and felt my enthusiasm wane. I might've been offered a part, but it was for Dull and Dramatic's war drama. Worse, the company producing it was People's Theatre, a group that had been around since the WPA Federal Theatre Project. They were known for producing experimental shows and politically charged pieces, which meant I'd been drafted for eight weeks of misery.

I forced a smile. I had a job. I didn't have to leave the house. This was good news. Sort of.

Ruby sighed heavily to remind me she was still in the room. I wasn't sure what it would take to get her to leave, but I suspected it involved gunfire and air-raid sirens.

"What's on your mind, Rube?"

Her eyes drifted to the floor. "We lost our backers."

"That's a kick—I'm sorry." Backers were the funding sources big shows depended on to mount. If they lost faith in you and pulled out, you lost the show, an increasingly common occurrence since the war. "I'm sure something will come through."

She lifted her head and pushed the hair out of her eyes. "Oh, I'm sure it will. It's certainly not the show's fault. You know how backers can be." I didn't, but I nodded my understanding all the same. "I can't help but be disappointed though. I was depending on this show."

If Ruby was looking for empathy, we were all out. "Surely Lawrence has other pots on the stove."

A glaze fell over Ruby's eyes, flimsy like crinoline. It had never occurred to me that she felt normal human emotions. I'd assumed her home planet forbade it. "Lawrence and I have decided to discontinue our relationship." It didn't take a grammarian to crab that Lawrence was the noun acting out the verb in that sentence.

I wasn't a mean person by nature, even when pushed to my limits, but being in a better place than Ruby made me forget myself. I wanted her to envy me. I wanted her to feel as I'd felt every day since we met. "Now that you mention it," I said, "Lawrence was acting peculiar."

The tips of her eyebrows bent downward until it looked as if someone had drawn twin black slashes on either side of her nose. "You saw Lawrence?"

"Didn't I mention it? I ran into him this afternoon at Raymond Fielding's wake."

"Raymond Fielding died?" Ruby's face widened in shock.

I fluttered my eyelashes to confirm I'd been crowned one of the elite. "Did you know him?"

"Of course."

I fought a sneer. "Anyway, Lawrence was quite charming, though you're probably better off without him. I wouldn't want to be in a relationship with a man who was so . . . comfortable pitching woo with other women."

Instead of rising to my bait, the long-suffering Camille forced a bright smile across her face and changed the topic as if it was summer drapes on the first day of fall. "I hope Lawrence will be very happy. But enough about him; I was wondering how your job's going. It must be fascinating working for a detective."

The little bit of guilt I felt for teasing Ruby stripped me of self-editing. "Things aren't so good. My boss died and I was, until this moment, on the dole." I looked at the paper again and wondered if this wasn't a cruel joke. I didn't get parts when I needed them. The only time I was ever cast in anything was when I was already cast in something else.

"I'm sorry to hear that. His name was Jim . . . something, right?" asked Ruby.

"McCain."

She nodded as though she'd known the name all along. "How did he die?"

"Heart attack," I said. "Why do you ask?" Her lips quivered as she sought a response. The fog left my brain. "Are you looking for a job?"

Ruby's mouth popped into a no-shaped *o*, but instead of sounding her denial, she nodded.

"Gee, I wish I could help, but like I said, I'm on the shelf." If anyone else at the Shaw House came to me looking for work, I would've combed the ladies help-wanted ads until I found something for them. My lack of desire to help Ruby wasn't so much a personality issue as disbelief that she needed my assistance. If I'd had half as much work as her, I wouldn't have had to take another job until 1954. "There's always the Navy Yard. I hear they're dying for women." The papers were filled every day with pictures of women doing their part for the war effort. While I admired the gumption these Rosie the Riveters showed, there was no way I was giving myself over to some mind-numbing nine-hour day whose only reward, aside from the paycheck, was an *e* for effort.

Ruby gasped. "I couldn't possibly do that."

I figured as much, but the offer was an easy way to measure her desperation. "You might want to ask the other girls. There's always somebody who's leaving a job or knows about one that's opening up."

Ruby's face turned sour. "This isn't the sort of thing I want to spread about. I'd appreciate it if you kept this between us." I nodded my consent and Ruby stomped out of the room. Before I had time to contemplate why the universe was rewarding me and punishing her, Jayne breezed back in and took me by the hands.

"What're you doing on Friday?" She pulled me to my feet and swung me around in an awkward waltz.

"I don't know." The question had a suspect feel to it. "Why?"

"We thought you might want to go out with us. Dancing." She changed directions and tempos. We tangoed toward the windows.

"By *we,* do you mean you, me, and Tony? Or you, me, Tony, and some fix-up you aren't going to tell me about until I get there and I've no choice but to stay?"

She tried to spin me, but her arms couldn't reach over my head. "Tony says he's a nice guy."

I broke free of her grip and sat on the radiator. "Oh sure, a nice guy with a rap sheet."

"When's the last time you had a date?"

"Today as a matter of fact. It's January sixth and it's mine all day."

She tried to pull me to my feet again, but I turned my keister to lead and remained glued to the radiator. "Come on, Rosie. It'll be fun. You need a night on the town."

"Things are looking up for me and I'm not about to spoil them by getting blotto with some Johnson brother."

Jayne fished the martini glasses out from under the bed and deposited them on the night table. "Your boss was murdered, some thug trapped you in his office, and the guy who gave you an impressive wad of cash to find a play turned out to be an imposter and possibly a murderer. If that's your idea of things looking up, I'd hate to see your bad day."

I pulled the scrap out of my pocket and waved it at her. "I got a job."

She put her hands on her face like a silent film star expressing shock. "That's great!"

"Don't get too excited. It's a lousy play with a rotten company."

"A role is a role—this is fantastic news." Jayne succeeded in pulling me to my feet and forced me to hop up and down with her. "See? It's going to be a good year after all."

"As you pointed out, it's only one good thing in a long line of bad."

She grabbed the meat of my upper arms and gently shook me. "You stop that. No bad thoughts. Oh, my goodness—now you have to go out with us on Friday."

I stopped bouncing. "Didn't you hear a word I said?"

"We have to celebrate. I'm not taking no for an answer." She fished out the gin bottle and examined how much remained. "Should we have a toast?"

"We've put down for lesser occasions."

My change in moods coaxed Churchill out from under the dresser and back onto the bed. He stalked about our plates and the newspaper. When he was certain he had my attention, he stepped into the middle of page one and sprayed it with his foul liquid.

"What the hell are you doing?" I screamed. He responded with a second wave of urine.

"Shoo, shoo." Jayne accompanied her weak discouragement with a series of limp arm movements that were supposed to say *Stop that, now!* but in simple-minded feline meant *This joyful arm dance is meant to encourage you to keep peeing.* Churchill rotated like a lawn sprinkler until dehydration set in, then he stepped into his puddle and off the paper.

I stared at the mess pooling on part one of *Raymond Fielding, Playwright*'s obituary. The liquid made a lazy path down the page until it kissed the top of NEW YORK OFFICE OF WAR INFORMATION DECRIES NOW IS THE TIME FOR PATRIOTISM.

"I'm going to kill him," I told Jayne.

"We can get another paper."

"Yes, and we can burn our sheets and put clothespins on our noses, but that isn't going to save his life." I took hold of the paper's upper-right and lower-left corners and lifted them inward. The urine dribbled toward the Office of War Information article and drew a yellow line through the words "New York director Henry Nussbaum."

10 The Watch on the Rhine

"WHAT'S THE OFFICE OF WAR Information?" asked Jayne. I shrugged and scanned the article as best I could without soiling myself. Henry Nussbaum, the man the Fake Fielding had fingered as the lead for the missing play, was apparently the high pillow of the New York Office of War Information. It looked like it was a government agency, but given that such things were a dime a dozen during the war, calling it that was as generic as calling a cat an animal.

I dumped the paper into the wastebasket, marched into the hallway, and rapped on a door across the hall from our own. Restless activity emanated from the room. Paper rustled. A drawer opened and closed. A pen rolled across a hard surface. "Who is it?" asked a distant voice.

"It's Rosie and Jayne," I said. "Can we come in for a minute?"

Harriet Rosenfeld peeked her head into the hall and silently ushered us into the room. She closed the door behind us so rapidly that had Jayne lingered a second longer half of her would've remained in the hallway.

Harriet's upper lip was covered with wax. A strip of paper was drying to the substance so she might, in one painful motion, remove the fine hair that grew too dark beneath her nose. Her hair was in rollers, her eyes magnified by Coke-bottle spectacles. By day she was a very pretty girl; by night she was that pretty girl's homely cousin.

Harriet had no roommate, a choice that upped her rent and her space. Half of it was taken up by the normal trappings of an actress: too many clothes, Max Factor's complete line, piles of plays, back issues of *Variety* and *Cue*. The other half had become a memorial to the war. A wall was covered in clippings, the floor was stacked with newspapers, a shortwave radio hummed with the latest news straight from Berlin. Harriet was a Jew and while for us the war was an inconvenience, to her it was a daily exercise in reminding herself what was important.

"What can I do for you, girls?" she asked us now.

"We thought we'd stop in and say hiya," said Jayne. She looked at me and silently asked how we'd get what we needed without becoming trapped in the room for the remainder of the evening. It's not that we were uncomfortable with Harriet's interest in the war, or that we cared one whit about her religious beliefs, but the girl could jaw about both topics until the cows came home and neither of us was game for that.

"You in anything?" I asked.

She moved toward the actress's side of the room. "I just landed something at the Yiddish Art Theatre." Harriet was one of the few actresses I knew who reveled in political theater. Despite her willingness to prettify herself for public consumption, her concept of what theater should be had moved progressively left. Many nights she sat in the lobby with the other girls, lecturing them about how what roles they took shouldn't be about the advancement of their careers but about the advancement of ideas.

It was a nice thought, but it didn't feed you.

"That's swell," I told her. A light went off in my head. "You ever read any of Raymond Fielding's stuff?"

"Fielding. Fielding." Harriet eyeballed two teetering towers of plays that served as a temporary bedside table. "What did he write?"

What *did* he write? "Lots of stuff. Including a book called *On Theatre* and a play called *Journey's End*. I think most of his work was published anonymously."

Recognition flashed across the Coke-bottle lenses. "I know the guy. Why do you ask?"

"I'm curious about him. He just died and when I read his obituary they listed all these plays he was known for and I realized I'd never read any of them. I figured if he was important enough for the front page of the *Times,* I should probably make his acquaintance."

Harriet nodded, too enthusiastically. "That's great, Rosie. I wish more of the girls around here cared about theater that mattered. If I have anything of his, you're welcome to it."

"Thanks. That would be swell." I lighted on a framed photo of a man in military dress. "Who's the GI?"

"Harold Leventhal." Harriet lifted her left hand and wiggled a chip of ice at us.

Jayne leaped to her side and examined the rock. "You're engaged?! Congratulations. When did this happen?"

"New Year's Eve. He shipped out two days later."

"That's swell, Harriet, just swell," I said. So this was what the war was like for some women; instead of getting the brush-off, they got a ring and a promise. "Where's he been sent to?"

"I don't know and he can't tell me." Her tone suggested she did and he had. "He writes for *Stars & Stripes.*" Harriet moved to the side of the room taken over by the conflict and we moved with her. I had a feeling it wouldn't be much longer until the two halves merged into one, the magazines on the floor growing into a hybrid of audition notices and war propaganda—wanted: women, aged 20–30, average build, with dance training and munitions experience.

Jayne tossed me a look that encouraged me to get to my point.

"Actually, I do have another question for you," I said. "Do you know what the Office of War Information is?"

"You mean the OWI." She sat at a desk piled high with letters vandalized by the war censor's heavy black pen. Beside them was a pad of paper on which she'd scribbled guesses as to what had been deleted from the correspondence.

"That's the one. What's the wire on them?"

Harriet pushed her glasses up her nose. "They used to be part of the COI."

"The CO what?" asked Jayne.

"The Coordinator of Information. It's a government division set up to handle propaganda. Both ours and theirs." She nodded at a bleak poster of a sinking ship captioned, "Somebody talked!" "They're the people responsible for the posters."

"And they're here in New York?" I asked.

She nodded. "New York and Washington. They might have other offices, but those are the two I've heard about. Why?" There was a sense of desperation to the question, as if Harriet wanted to learn there was someone at the Shaw House as concerned about the war as she was. I understood her desire for commonality, but neither Jayne nor I wanted to get roped into a discussion we didn't understand. It wasn't our war the way it was hers, and while it felt cold and small to think that, at the time we believed if we kept our noses out of Europe it would be kind enough to do the same for us.

"No reason," I told Harriet. "Just another mention in the *Times* that made me curious. Jayne and I figured if anyone knew what it was, you would. Any idea where their offices are?"

She dove into a stack of books and newspapers. *The Red Cross First-Aid Manual* collapsed into a pile with *Mission to Moscow* and Walter Lippmann's *U.S. Foreign Policy*. She triumphantly pulled out a copy of the *Times* from earlier in the week and eyeballed an article on U.S. war agencies in New York City. "It looks like they're in Murray Hill. One twenty-two East Forty-second Street. I think that's the Chanin Building. If you want I could . . ."

"No," said Jayne. "That's all we needed, but thanks just the same."

That night I dreamed of Jack. I guess I missed him. It was opening night of the People's Theatre show and he'd gotten leave to come see me perform. As the curtain went down, I spotted him third row center. While the rest of the crowd politely applauded from their seats, he gave me a one-man standing ovation replete with wolf whistle. I tried to get out to the audience, but the velvets and scrim thwarted my efforts. When I finally broke free and made my way into the house, the lights were off, the seats were empty, and Jack was nowhere to be found.

The next morning I awoke with a terrible headache and lay in bed until the light shining through the window no longer made me wish for death. Jayne was up and out, though she'd left a note behind to let me know she'd gone to Fat and Smiley's audition and would like to meet up for lunch.

My dream stayed with me. I'm not one for signs, but I couldn't help but wonder if this meant I was supposed to write Jack. I started a letter in my head but couldn't get past, "Sorry I haven't written," because the apology felt so wooden and inappropriate. We'd never had occasion to write each other before. Oh, there were little cards in opening-night flowers, but the messages were pithy and traditional, not like the woo-pitching tomes I'd seen Jayne unfurl from past boy-friends. I was proud we didn't need to fake sentiment in order to declare our feelings. Like all great actors we expressed our emotions through our actions.

Churchill stalked around my bed, waiting to see if I was going to respond to his lead from the night before and contact Henry Nuss-baum. I decided confronting a total stranger was easier than attempt-ing to mend things with someone I knew, so I dressed and hit the subway. By ten o'clock I was at the ornate Chanin Building on East Forty-second Street, staring at a bronze bas relief of the New York skyline while waiting for the elevator. Ten minutes later I was on the twenty-sixth floor, where I'd found my meat and was crabbing what to do next.

From what I could glean from their lobby, the OWI was a clearing-house for nutcases who believed their neighbors, or their neighbors' neighbors, were secretly assisting the Nazis through wiretapping, illegal use of the mail, or radio waves. A group of very serious people with shifty, nervous eyes waited in a meandering line before a receptionist's desk. I couldn't eyeball the gal in question, but I heard her bark her refrain, telling each Joe to fill out a form, put it in the pile, and if their claim was worth following up on, they'd be contacted. Every third person disputed her order, which only prompted the doll to increase her volume and repeat her message.

I passed the time reading posted government warnings about what would happen if I said the wrong thing to the wrong person. Once the line had dispersed, I checked my appearance in the elevator's doors, cocked my hat jauntily to the side, approached the receptionist, and asked if I could see the man of the hour.

"You don't ask to see Mr. Nussbaum. He asks to see you." She was a heavily made-up gal with an Andrews sister kind of style. She would've been fetching if it weren't for a large mole beside her nose.

"I think he'll want to see me," I said.

She squeezed a pencil between her first and second fingers and tapped out Morse code on a stack of pamphlets lauding the contributions of black soldiers. "And why is that?"

I leaned toward her and lowered my voice. "Because I have some information for him. About the Germans."

She pushed a clipboard toward me. "Fill that out, give it back, and if it's important, you'll be called."

"Didn't you hear me?" I asked. "This war could turn on what I have to say."

The mole shifted, creating the illusion that it wasn't skin but some terrible parasite she didn't know was there. "Look, sweetheart, I see fifty people a day, all of whom are dead certain whatever they know is the key to victory. Nine times out of ten, they're crackpots. So I'm telling you, unless you're Hitler, you're not getting into that office."

I searched the contents of Miss Pleasant of 1943's desk until I found an interoffice memo directed to two women: Violet and Edith. I flipped a mental coin and whipped a pen and notebook out of my purse. "I'm impressed, Edith."

"How do you know my . . . ?"

I opened the pad and scribbled some nonsense on the first blank page before giving her the up and down. "I apologize for the ruse, but you must understand there's no better way to check security than to pretend to be part of the problem. I'm with the Department of Efficiency. I'm afraid we've been fielding a number of complaints about this office."

"Complaints?" She set her chin in her hand.

"The higher-ups have been questioning the numbers coming out of this department. The output isn't matching the input and when that happens you better believe heads are going to roll." Confusion moved the mole north and her kisser south. "There have been some suggestions that instead of routing claims through normal paperwork procedures, OWCs have been sent for a face-to-face, slowing things down especially in instances of dubious claims."

The mole began its retreat, signaling that while Edith may not know what I was saying, she was starting to believe I was who I claimed to be. "What's an OWC?"

A random acronym designed to make me sound officious. "Objective Witness Claim. We call them that because it sounds less accusatory. Anyway, you're providing a great first line of defense. If this is how you handle everyone who comes through this door, I'll assure Mr. Nussbaum that his complaints are without merit."

A wad of gum she must have been storing in her cheek since I'd entered regained its buoyancy. "Mr. Nussbaum's been complaining about me? But he seems so nice. He gave me a holly bush for Christmas."

"May I sit?" I asked.

"Sure."

I grabbed a metal chair and planted myself at the side of her desk. "I like you, Edith. You're clearly a hard worker and, let's face it, we gals in government have got to stick together. What I'm going to tell you is in absolute confidence. I trust you'll keep it between us?"

"Of course," she said.

"Mr. Nussbaum lodged a number of complaints that indicate your professionalism left much to be desired. I came here today to do an inspection at his request, but given what I've witnessed, I'm starting to suspect Mr. Nussbaum is, as we say, passing the buck." I scooted forward in my seat and lowered my voice. "It's been my experience that when someone higher up blames a subordinate for his department's shortcomings, it's because he knows he's failed and wants to make sure we won't trace his mistakes back to him. In his mind, you're clearly dispensable, but if we were to fire you as he wanted . . ."

Her mouth dropped open and the gum plummeted to her desk. "He wants to fire me?!"

I shushed her with my hand. "*If* we were to do that, the same thing would happen to the next person and the one after that. So instead of letting him bunco you, I'm going to pay him a surprise visit and find out what's going on behind his door. Will you help me, Edith?"

She retrieved her gum and straightened her shoulders. "What do I do?"

"Tell him an important claim has been routed back to him that's too time-sensitive to move beyond his office. And tell him my name is Ruby Priest."

Five minutes later Edith deposited me with a knowing wink and cup of lukewarm coffee in a claustrophobic office at the end of a long hallway. I nursed the java while I waited for Nussbaum to appear.

The room was government drab. Gray metal file cabinets lined one wall, a matching desk another. From the heavily blinded windows you could see the magnificent Chrysler Building, but the sparse interior decoration made the view seem like something that had been parceled out in a quantity selected because it would neither harm nor inspire. The walls were dotted with a number of framed newspaper articles lauding Nussbaum's military career prior to his appointment with the OWI. The oldest article, from 1918, relayed how the troops were surviving the harsh French winter. Nussbaum and a man named Alan Detmire were quoted, describing ways to keep the troops' morale up. Nussbaum was fond of sing-a-longs. Detmire liked skits.

So he was a vet with a penchant for campfire songs. That was good to know.

His desk was covered with stacks of paper. One was nothing but the forms Edith had showed me earlier, filled in with a variety of ridiculous claims. The other stacks were a hodgepodge of unrelated materials: novels, radio schedules, newspapers, museum catalogs, theater programs, letters from Hollywood executives announcing impending projects. Either Nussbaum was getting paid to plan his evenings or something else was afoot.

I rifled through what I could and settled on the newspaper at the top of the stack. The front page was predicting what the president would say during his address before Congress that day. I flipped past it and skimmed an article on Errol Flynn's upcoming trial, read a notice that *My Sister Eileen* was finally ending its run after 866 performances, then turned to a brief blurb about Bentley's play securing new financing and planning to open, on schedule, in the middle of February.

I had half a mind to tear it out and tape it to Ruby's door.

"Miss Priest?" A man in a gray pin-striped suit coordinated to match the filing cabinets entered the room. "I'm Henry Nussbaum. I'm terribly sorry to keep you waiting." Nussbaum crossed the room and offered me his hand.

I dropped the paper and returned the handshake. His skin was warm, his nails buffed and manicured. "No need to apologize. I've been catching up on the news."

He removed his jacket with a military precision that suggested he'd been trained to conserve his energy. Charcoal-colored hair emerged from his temples. Fine lines creased his brow and drew fans at the corners of his eyes. He appeared to be in his late forties, but judging from the care he took with the rest of his appearance, he was probably closer to sixty.

"I don't know what you said to my secretary, but she's positively beside herself." He took his place behind the desk and made a tepee of his hands. "What can I do for you?"

I'd been so focused on getting into the office and seeing Nussbaum that I'd forgotten I'd have to say something to him. Outside, the Third Avenue El rumbled past, vibrating the building.

"Miss Priest?"

I sank into my chair. "I lied. I'm not here to report information. I'm here to get some from you." Rather than responding, he tapped his foot in the way people did to let you know the greater value their time possessed. "I was given your name by someone who claimed you took something of his. This person has lied about other things, but I still felt like I had to follow up on it. Just in case."

Nothing in his face revealed that he knew what I was talking about, and yet there was something slightly altered about his puss that made me regret saying anything. What if Fake Fielding had been right and Nussbaum was behind the missing play? Worse, what if I was walking into a trap designed to get rid of me so Fake Fielding wouldn't have to?

"Who are you?" asked Nussbaum.

My brain scrambled for an answer that would satisfy him without making me sing. "I'm an actress . . . and a detective."

"A woman detective?" He said it in a way that made it clear he believed the two terms were mutually exclusive. Strike one against Henry Nussbaum. "Who accused me of this theft?"

I considered my options. Leaving without saying anything more would make this nothing but a trip for biscuits. If I told him part of the truth, I might be able to get a better read on him without fingering myself. "I'm not sure. He claimed he was a man named Raymond Fielding, although it turns out he couldn't be, since Raymond Fielding is dead."

His face remained cool and impassive.

"Does that name ring a bell with you?" I asked.

He frowned. "I'm afraid not. So what did this man claim I took?"

Sitting close to him made it difficult to lie. In the pulps the heroine would moderate her breathing and look the suspect, unblinking,
in the eye. I could do none of those things, so I stood and made a
slow promenade around the room, which served only to emphasize
how big and clumsy my feet were. "He wasn't very clear on that. All
I know is they're papers of some kind."

I crossed to the window and pulled the blinds far enough apart
to look out onto the street. The lower corners of the building jutted
out and I was able to see into some of the other offices. In each was
a man like Nussbaum, pushing around paperwork while drinking
endless cups of coffee.

I turned back to him. "I think it's safe to say if you don't know who
Fielding is, you probably didn't take anything from him."

He leaned back in his chair. "That seems accurate."

"I do feel foolish coming here and bothering you about this, especially when I had so little information to go on, but you were my
only lead." I returned to my seat and crossed my legs. "May I ask what
it is you do here?"

"We are a division of the U.S. Military that carefully monitors any
information being communicated about the war."

I borrowed Jayne's wide eyes and high-pitched voice. "How so?"

I must've seemed harmless because instead of telling me to scram,
he decided to educate me. "The Germans have become very skilled
at using what we term propaganda. Our job is to prevent the spread
of misinformation at home and abroad."

"Judging from the posters in the lobby I take it that in addition
to telling the Germans to mind their tongues, you also encourage
discretion from the rest of us?"

"Everyone needs to do their part during wartime. Unfounded
rumors can be extremely dangerous to morale. At the same time, if
a democratic government shares its plans with its people, they must
encourage their citizenry to keep that information confidential."

I nodded to show him I was plenty swift. "So you probably don't
care much for people who disagree with you?"

Nussbaum met my eyes. "Everyone has the freedom to express their points of view. But yes, we do promote patriotism."

"As in *rah, rah, siss boom bah—go Allies*?"

His smile was as thin as a paper cut. "Something like that. It's important that we promote positive depictions of ourselves and our allies. Conversely, we frown upon stereotyping Axis nations. When a country's at war, its people go through periods when they question their government's actions. Some of these people express this dis- comfort very publicly and, in doing so, encourage more vulnerable individuals to share opinions they may not understand. This can be dangerous, as we saw with the rise of Nazism. If we find something being circulated that may put people or relationships at risk, we take actions to cease the spread of misinformation."

A tickle moved through my gray matter. What if that's what Field- ing was doing? If some of his past plays had been political in nature, he could've written something that not only challenged the govern- ment but put the country at risk. Maybe he even wrote it with no in- tention of it ever being produced, but someone nicked it and planned to perform it, unleashing potentially dangerous ideas and getting Fielding into a jam in the bargain.

If that were the case, though, who was Fake Fielding and why did he care?

"What actions would you take to stop something you thought was dangerous?" I asked.

Nussbaum laughed in a way that he intended to be disarming but which I took as condescending. "People are entitled to their opinions. We certainly don't stop them from expressing them. If, however, there are plans to widely circulate something, we contact those involved and let them know the risks they are creating."

I wondered how those conversations went.

"Do you have any other questions, Miss Priest?"

I licked my lips. There was a problem with my theory. If Field- ing was communicating government secrets, that information was time-sensitive. The play was probably written months before Fielding died, and whatever he'd known had come and gone, or at least lost most of its bite. There had to be more to it.

"What would shock you?" I asked.

Nussbaum held my gaze and I wondered if our government was so advanced that it could read intentions off a glimmer of light reflected from a pupil. "I'm paid to never be surprised."

"I'll remember not to throw you a party without your knowledge, but I wasn't asking about surprise. I was asking about shock." Still his eyes held mine and I had the same odd sensation I got when staring at a mosquito on my arm. As fascinating as the creature might be to witness up close, the boob was still sucking my blood.

He broke the stare and clasped his hands together. "Hardly a quantifiable difference in my opinion. In my line of work, there is no such thing as shocking."

"Thank you." I retrieved my pocketbook and walked to the door. "I appreciate your taking the time to see me this morning."

He rose and offered me his hand. "It was my pleasure, Miss Priest. Can I do anything else for you?"

"Sure," I told him. "Give your secretary my regards. And let her know her job's here for as long as she needs it."

11 'Tis a Pity She's a Whore

AFTER I LEFT NUSSBAUM'S OFFICE, I stopped at the A&P for Cat Chow, then took the subway to Fifty-third Street and Seventh Avenue. It had warmed considerably since the day before, turning what should have been an impressive snowstorm into a relentless rain. Despite the foul weather, the sidewalks were littered with people. Men on bicycles wove in and out of the crowds, trying to get home for lunch. A line trailed out of a butcher shop as women, with coupons in hand, waited for their allotment of meat. A crowd gathered around a newsie examining the A.M. papers while Joseph Stalin, *Time* magazine's man of the year, stared into the rain from the slick's cover. A group of girls patiently stood before a mailbox, each waiting for her turn to drop a handful of V–mail through the slot. A sign mounted on the front of the box asked, "Can you pass a mailbox with a clear conscience?" I couldn't, so I crossed the street.

I hadn't bothered to bring an umbrella so I sprinted the distance between awnings until I at last arrived at the Ziegfeld, where Jayne's audition was taking place. I considered waiting outside for her, but the familiar, gnawing feeling of being watched turned my cold disposition to frigid and falling. I took in every heap, window, and wet passerby trying to put a finger on what rankled me, but that failed to do anything but reinforce the limitless number of people who could be a danger. When I couldn't take the growing anxiety any longer, I escaped into the theater and flattened my nose against the small diamond-shaped windows set in the auditorium doors.

The audition had just ended. The hoofers were gathering their things while a pock-marked stage manager with a voice like Mickey Rooney's reminded them that casting decisions would be posted in two days. Fat and Smiley gestured Jayne over to his table and the two huddled in conversation. As soon as it ended, Jayne's eyes lighted on me and she rushed out of the theater and into the lobby.

"I take it the private powwow was an offer?" I asked.

"Yes, I have just been given my fiftieth chorus part."

"When you make it to one hundred, do you get a watch?" I took her bag from her so she could button her coat.

"I'd better. How awful is this show?"

"I wouldn't call it awful. It's certainly not Lawrence Bentley material, but then not every theater can strive to such heights of mediocrity." We hustled out the door and onto the street. "On the bright side, you're in the Ziegfeld. That's hardly small potatoes."

"Just once I'd like to get a real part." She sighed and pulled on a pair of worn woolen mittens. "How'd it go with Nussbaum?"

"Interesting. In addition to listening to claims about who's spreading pro-German propaganda, the OWI tightly monitors any negative opinions about America's role in the war. And not just newspapers and radio shows—they scrutinize every single movie, book, song, and play that somebody wants to put out there, and if they don't like what it has to say, they bury it."

"Wow," said Jayne. "So what has this got to do with Fielding?"

"I'm not sure." A crowd was gathering outside B&K Furniture, where a radio had been positioned near the open doorway. We joined the group huddled beneath the awning as FDR's 12:30 state-of-the-nation speech began. For forty-seven minutes we listened to the president as he praised our efforts, pleaded for our continued faith, and predicted victory in the coming months. Through the driving downpour he rallied those of us who'd had enough of death and deprivation by reminding us that it wasn't all for naught. "In this war of survival we must keep before our minds not only the evil things we fight against, but the good things we are fighting for. We fight to retain a great past—and fight to regain a greater future."

As the speech came to an end, my brain started focusing on victory on a very different front.

"Rosie?" Jayne waved her hand before my face. "You still there?"

The rest of the crowd dispersed around us, their faces plastered with smiles, their voices light with glee.

"Rosie?"

"What if I hadn't been sent to Nussbaum's to get information? What if I'd been sent there to deliver it? Maybe Fake Fielding told me Nussbaum was a suspect so I'd go to his office and get the government on the trail of the play." That explained why Nussbaum acted like he didn't know what I was talking about when I mentioned Fielding's name—he didn't. I was sent there to put him on the case in the same way Fake Fielding had put me on it.

"Why?" asked Jayne.

"Maybe he thought the more people looking for it, the better."

Jayne took my arm and we moved back into the rain. "This could be good," she said. "If these propaganda people get paid to weed things out, they'll probably find the play much faster than we could, and then we won't have to worry about it anymore." She was right, but something wasn't adding up. I spun on my heel and headed back toward the subway station. "Where are we going anyhow?" I didn't answer. "We're going to your old office, aren't we?"

"Maybe."

"Rosie, you said you wouldn't go back there."

"No, *you* said I shouldn't go back there. I just didn't disagree."

Jayne sighed and tied on her snood. "You're lucky I'm in a good mood," she said. "You've got five minutes. Any sign of trouble and you're on your own."

By the time the train delivered us to Forty-second Street, the rain picked up its rhythm, forcing us to jog the remaining distance to McCain and Son. In the building's foyer, we wrung out our clothes, slipped off our shoes, and wordlessly advised each other to tiptoe up the stairs in case anyone was waiting for us. The building was bliss-

fully quiet, as though all the other tenants had felt so cheered by
FDR's speech that they'd left to celebrate. Despite the silence, there
was a sense of occupation to the place that made us extra mindful of
every dark corner we passed. I had a feeling someone lurked behind
each closed door with his ear to the wood listening to our every move.

My plan was to pinch the file of programs from Jim's office. Now
that I had more information about what I was looking for, I thought
there was a chance I'd missed something in the file the first time
around.

When we arrived on the top floor, my feet were cramping from
the effort to remain quiet. Jayne and I paused in the stairwell and
listened for a sign that someone was inside the office. Once we were
certain there was no noise aside from our own breathing, I turned
the knob and found the door unlocked.

I prepared myself for an unwelcome visitor who stood with his
back flush against the wall, his rod raised and ready to strike. Instead
of being told to grab air, we entered an empty office. Someone had
made a clean sneak; all of the furniture and, more to the point, all of
the files were gone. Only the phone remained.

"Who would do this?" I asked.

"Maybe Agnes put them away somewhere." Jayne prowled the
outer office and searched the cupboards.

"Does that sound like Agnes to you?" I went into Jim's office and
found it equally bare. Even the trash bin I'd dropped his gun into was
gone. I paced the length of the room, snapping my fingers to try to
force my brain to work at a faster rate. Why would somebody sneak
the files now, when there was plenty of time to take them before? If
the killer had wanted them, he could've taken them the night Jim
died, unless he was afraid someone would notice their absence and
didn't want to raise any questions as to whether Jim had really committed suicide.

"What about the thugs?" asked Jayne. "Didn't you say you overheard them at the funeral talking about their plan to clean the office?"

"Of course, it had to be them." Although I sounded confident, I didn't feel it. The goon I'd dubbed Frank was a professional and I found it hard to believe he or his crew would take everything, including the furniture, to erase the few clues linking them with Jim.

"Can we go?" asked Jayne. "This place is giving me the heebies."

We put on our shoes and gathered our things. As we headed out the door, the phone began to jangle.

"What do I do?" I asked.

"Don't answer it," said Jayne. "It could be a trap. Maybe whoever took the files is watching us."

We hadn't turned the lights on in the office—there was enough daylight to see by—and it would've been impossible to spy us from the street. Of course that didn't mean someone didn't see us go into the building. "But what if it's somebody who knows something?" I asked. "What if it's Fake Fielding?"

Jayne bit her lip and the two of us watched as the phone shook with effort.

"I'm answering it," I said. Jayne's fingers plucked the air, but I lifted the receiver before she could stop me. "McCain and Son."

"It's about time," said Eloise McCain. "I've been trying to reach you all morning."

I mouthed her name to Jayne and sat on the floor beside the phone. "I'm terribly sorry, Eloise, but I do have a life aside from this office. What can I do for you?"

"Are the files packed?"

"Yes," I said, because they were. Somewhere.

"And did you find anything unusual in them?"

"No," I said. "But I was working quickly."

"Thank you for trying." Her voice held as much gratitude as bears had table manners. "If it's all right with you, I'll send you a check."

I gave her the Shaw House address and listened as she ordered someone to fetch her a pen and piece of paper. The items were swiftly delivered and a voice murmured a question to which Eloise responded that that was all she needed for the time being and the silver polish could be found with the other cleaning supplies.

"New maid?" I asked.

"How on earth could you tell?"

"Different accent, faster reflexes. I bet she also answers to a different name."

Eloise sighed. "If you are done castigating me for the ways in which I discern my help, I need to be going. Do you have anything else to tell me?"

I swallowed the truth until my voice was shiny and happy. "No. I think that's everything."

"I do thank you for your assistance, Rosie."

This was the point where we were supposed to offer each other help in the future. Instead, there was an awkward pause in the conversation that I ended by saying, "You're welcome. Good-bye."

Jayne tapped her foot as I hung up the horn. "You didn't tell her the files were missing."

"She didn't ask. And odds are she won't. She'll send people over to retrieve the crates, and they'll get hell when they tell her the files aren't here. Let someone else take the rap. I'm washing my hands of the whole thing." I rose to my feet and brushed off my skirt.

"So that's it, right? You're not going to look for the play anymore?" asked Jayne.

"I don't think we have to. If it's out there and whoever has it intends for it to be seen, I'm sure we'll know about it soon enough."

"And in the meantime?" she asked.

"We wait."

12 The Beaux Stratagem

FRIDAY JAYNE AND I SPENT the better part of the day milling about the Garment District looking for a dress that met two requirements: it made me look like a knock-out and I could afford it. When neither qualification co-existed in one spectacular gown, we went back to the Shaw House where I sulked about, proclaiming this was a sign I was supposed to stay home that night.

"But you can't!" Having no clothing dilemma of her own, Jayne found it hard to empathize with mine. She planned on wearing one of several frocks Tony B. had bought her that were cut so low and slit so high that the only part of her guaranteed no exposure was her stomach.

I retreated to my bed and shifted a stack of magazines to my lap. "Trust me: it's better for everyone if I stay home." The plan was to go to a gin joint the civilian shortage had turned into a gangster hangout. I'd never been there before, but I knew the kind of place it was. A girl had to be dressed to the nines if she wanted to survive the night.

Jayne pursed her lips and threw her arms across her chest. "I'm not taking no for an answer." She stomped out of the room and slammed the door behind her. Churchill and I ignored the melodrama and instead examined a woman poured into a red dress and sprawled across the cover of *Detective Fiction Weekly*. Now there was a dame who was dressed for a night out with Tony B. She even carried a gun.

I flipped through the magazine, looking for a story to grab my attention. Instead, a circular shoved inside fluttered to the bed, announcing that the publication may be reducing its frequency thanks to the war-induced paper shortage. In addition to irking me, the note reminded me of Jack, who was not, at that moment, trying to find something he could wear on a blind date.

"But he would," I told Churchill. "If he could."

"Rosie?" Jayne opened the door and stuck her head into the room. Her body followed and was joined by a second form. "It's our lucky day—Ruby has offered to lend you a dress." Filling Ruby's arms were ten evening gowns in a variety of styles and colors. She eyed my choice in literature and looked heavenward.

"Thanks but no thanks." I gave a queenly wave to dismiss them. "I don't feel comfortable wearing Ruby's rags."

"If you're worried about stretching them," cooed Ruby, "I can lend you a girdle."

That did it. I tossed aside the magazine, rose from the bed, and sucked in my stomach. "That wasn't my worry, though I appreciate your concern." I grabbed a dress and held it in front of me. The bureau mirror reported that the color was nice but the cut all wrong.

Ruby sat on the bed and smoothed the remaining dresses across her lap. "Jayne says you're going on a fix-up tonight."

"Oh, she did, did she?" I tried to meet Jayne's eyes and found her gaze focused out the window.

Ruby fluttered her lashes. "If you're looking to meet someone, I might know a few fellows about your age."

"Gee, that's swell of you, Rube, but I'd think you'd want to concentrate on your own love life." I relieved her of the other dresses and went behind an Oriental screen we'd stashed in the corner. "How's the job hunt going?"

"You're looking for a job?" asked Jayne.

"No," snapped Ruby. "As a matter of fact, several things have come through for me."

I pulled a red sequin-encrusted number over my head. "Good for you. I'm assuming one of them isn't Bentley's play? I understand he got new funding." I zipped the dress and peered around the screen until I could see my reflection in the bureau mirror. The gown bagged at the bosom and made my hips look like a boy's.

"I don't know what Lawrence is or is not doing," said Ruby. "WEAF hired me for a weekly show and I was cast in a play at People's Theatre."

Jayne's head volleyed from Ruby to my reflection. I receded into my corner. "I thought it was cast?" I asked.

"Oh, it was, but the director decided to go in a new direction."

I yanked off the sequined dress and replaced it with something black and itchy. "What does that mean?"

Ruby touched her fur-trimmed collar the way rich old women fawn over little dogs. "I'm not sure. All I know is they called and offered me a sizable part. I didn't even have to audition."

Jayne cleared her throat and I rose onto my tiptoes and caught her eye in the mirror. She misread my attempt to shut her head and raised her squeaky voice. "Aren't you in that show, Rosie?"

"Nix on that," I said between clenched teeth.

"Is that so?" Ruby threw me a look that was so condescending it wore a crown. "This will be our first show together. Won't that be fun?"

"Loads."

She glanced at her wristwatch. "If you'll excuse me, girls, I have other things I need to be doing." She opened the door. "Take your time picking out a dress, but be careful. Some of those gowns are very expensive." As she exited, I emerged from my cave.

Jayne slouched onto the bed and dragged Churchill into her lap. "That's a pretty dress."

"Yeah, all I need are a couple of balloons in my bra and it will fit perfectly." I struggled with the zipper and dropped the gown to the floor. "Why did you have to ask her for help?"

Churchill's tail wrapped around Jayne's wrist. "I wanted you to come out tonight."

"Now not only do I not want to go, I want to kill her."

Jayne sank her fingers into Churchill's back. "You know you don't mean that."

I stepped on the dress, crushing wrinkles into the delicate fabric. "All right, I don't want to kill her, but I'd be interested in seeing her get a very bad bruise. She's stealing my part."

"You're off your nut."

I kicked the dress out of spite. "There are two women's parts in that show: a moll and a Mother Hubbard."

"She said they were going in a new direction. Maybe he decided to add more women to balance things." Jayne's hand caught Churchill beneath his chin and ruffled his fur.

I retrieved another dress and pulled it over my head. "Or maybe Ruby called in a favor and got me booted." My arms made it into the sleeves, but my head couldn't find its hole. I staggered blindly until Jayne came to my aid and directed my noggin upward.

"She didn't even know you were cast in the show."

The shoulder seam let out a satisfying rip. "Oh, she knew. She's the one who gave me the message. This is her revenge."

"For what?"

I rapped my noodle, hoping to shake a logical explanation loose. One fluttered free and I acknowledged it with a snap. "Right after Bentley broke up with her I told her, we'd met him and he'd been on the make."

"And you think she'd use that as a reason for getting even with you?" Jayne was losing patience with me. "It's Friday, Rosie. If they decided not to cast you, they would've called. They wouldn't let you show up on Monday and tell you you're fired."

I examined myself in yet another overpriced, ill-fitting dress. "They would, if Ruby asked them to."

By eight o'clock I was decked out in Ruby's most expensive gown (brown taffeta enhanced by my thickest socks) and an updo that showed my neck to good advantage. While Jayne finished drawing seams on the backs of her bare legs, I took refuge from the cat hair and went down to the lobby with an issue of *The Shadow*.

"Aren't you gussied up," said Belle as I came down the stairs. In her hand was a feather duster that matched the plumage-lined purple dress she'd donned to clean the house.

"Just the woman I wanted to see." I'd been waiting for the perfect moment to tell her about the People's Theatre gig. I gracefully left the stairs, twirled her way, and tripped over a pile of luggage.

"Going somewhere?" I asked.

Belle shook her head. "It's not mine. It's Veda Dale's."

Veda Dale was a dancer who'd moved into the Shaw House a few months before. She was a talented girl with the grace of Ginger Rogers and the face of Fred Astaire. "No work?" I asked.

"No brother," said Belle. "Her folks called this morning. He was gunned down in North Africa. If you know of anyone who needs a room, we've got an opening."

My desire to rub in my new job instantly disappeared. It was funny how other people's grief hit me. I was devastated for them, but I also felt like I'd dodged a bullet. I still believed there could be only so much death in the world and each time someone else died they were taking up a slot that might have been Jack's.

Belle continued along her path to the kitchen. "I understand congratulations are in order."

I followed after her. "What are you talking about?"

"The job you just got, you sap. Ruby told me about it. She was so happy for you she couldn't keep it to herself." I let out a noise like a low growl. Belle flicked her feathers in the direction of the lobby and lowered her voice. "By the way: your visitor's here."

"My what?"

She tipped her head toward a man sitting with his back to me. "Your visitor." She winked, then disappeared behind the kitchen's swinging door. I stepped toward the lobby and paused at an angle where I could better see my companion's back. Close-cropped dark hair ended above a wool navy peacoat. The shoulders were square and strong. He held his head at an angle that suggested he was a man who knew from posture, probably because a director had told

him that slouching was appropriate only if your character's name was
Quasimodo.

My dream *had* been a sign—Jack was home! I gave my breath a
quick check and verified there were no sweat stains in my armpits.
I put my arm on the banister and fixed a gentle smile on my face.
"Couldn't stay away, could you?"

Edgar McCain turned around and sliced his face with a grin.
"From the look of the place, I never would've guessed there were
dress requirements."

I ignored the hand he offered me and hid my disappointment
beneath layers of carefully applied disgust. "I've got a blind date." He
made a move to respond, but I continued rattling. "And before you
come up with some witty retort, let me say I'm amazed a member of
your species can walk upright, which is proof that miracles do happen, my own plans notwithstanding."

His eyes drifted chest level. "I was going to say you look nice."

"They're socks and you're a pig." I covered myself as best I could
and stepped away from him. "To what do I owe this unexpected and
wholly inappropriate pleasure?"

He reached into his coat and pulled out an envelope. Through the
thin paper I made out the outline of a check. "My mother asked that
I deliver this to you."

I took it from him and shoved it into my evening bag. "And you
have—good-bye."

"Don't I get a thank-you?"

I curtsied as anyone in an evening gown should. "Thank you. In
the future, might I recommend you use the post office? They've made
a business of this delivery stuff and do a bang-up job from what I
understand."

He tilted his head as one did when talking to a very small child.
"But then I wouldn't have gotten to see you."

"I'd be flattered if I didn't know you better."

The half smirk disappeared. "What do you say we grab a cup of
coffee?"

"If by *we* you mean you and me, I say no. Look, Mr. McCain, I have things to do. There's the floor, and there's the door. I guarantee if you follow one it will lead to the other." I clutched the pulp to my chest and turned toward the stairwell.

"Don't call me Mr. McCain."

I kept my back to him and rolled my eyes. "Fine: *captain, lieutenant, whatever.*"

"I mean my name's not McCain."

Curiosity got the better of me and spun me around.

"Jim McCain wasn't my father. He was my stepfather." He removed his hat and rested it in the crook of his arm. "My last name's Fielding. Is that incentive enough for you to join me?"

13 Arms and the Man

I LEFT WORD WITH BELLE that I'd gone up to Charles Street to grab some java at Louie's, a hash house known for its cheap food and dim lighting. Within ten minutes Edgar and I were in a corner booth stirring condensed milk into twin cups of joe and bumping gums about the war. When it became apparent that I had less to contribute than Sally Rand had clothes, he lit a cigarette, extinguished his match, and jumped to his point.

"Who were you expecting?" he asked. He removed his coat, revealing the same stark blue uniform I'd seen him in at Jim's funeral. A gold eagle nested on his lapel, watching me in judgment.

I tapped my spoon on the lip of my mug. "What do you mean?"

"Was your date supposed to pick you up?"

Since he offered the lie, I grabbed it. "Yes."

He mulled this over a drag on the gasper. "Funny, I thought you said it was a blind date."

"Don't worry: that steel trap you call a brain is accurate."

He nodded, his butt bobbing along with his head. "Yet the first thing out of your mouth was 'you couldn't keep away, could you?'"

I narrowed my gaze. I wasn't about to share any fantasies about Jack returning to me. "What's your point?"

He leaned into the table and turned discomfort into a threat. "I know when you're lying."

I chased his malice with a slug of coffee and willed myself to show no fear. He couldn't do anything to me. It was a public place. "It's been quite a week for you, Ed. Both your dad and stepdad killed in one day."

"Don't call me Ed."

"Then drop the military mind games." Nerves yanked my voice to a pitch that left dogs begging for earmuffs. "While I enjoyed hearing about your family tree, what do you want?"

"I need to know where the files went."

I fluttered my eyelashes in my best impersonation of innocence. "Last I saw they went into crates which presumably went into a moving truck."

"The office was empty when the movers arrived."

I cocked my head and toasted him with my coffee cup. "Gee, I'm sorry to hear that. Next time you might want to consider hiring a guard in addition to a file clerk." Before my cup reached my lips, Edgar's paw knocked it from my hand, sending steaming liquid all over the table and the front of Ruby's gown. "What the hell are you doing?!"

"This isn't a game," said Edgar.

"And this isn't my dress." Anger pulverized whatever fear I felt until all I could think about was shoving my spoon in his eye. "Who the hell do you think you are?" I rose and pushed at the table as hard as I could. Its metal-lined edge bounced off Edgar's abdomen while the legs slammed into the floor. The impact grabbed everyone's attention. The cook and busboys filled the kitchen doorway and watched us warily from a distance.

Edgar grabbed my wrist and attempted to pull me back into my seat. "Lower your voice."

I wrenched myself free and reprimanded him with the stained napkin. "Lower my voice? Look, pal, you're the one who turned things nasty." My volume increased until it lingered near Medea's. "If I feel like screaming my lungs out while I buzz the coppers, I think I'm entitled."

"You all right, miss?" asked a tentative black man in white chef's garb.

"She's fine," said Edgar. Again he made for my arm, but I moved before he could touch me. His teeth clenched, turning his voice from a snarl to a hiss. "Let's start over, Rosie."

"You must have me confused with some other chippy. I'm leaving." I reached for my evening bag on the booth seat and couldn't find it. I located the purse with my foot and bent down to retrieve it. As my hand made contact with the strap, Edgar joined me in the dark cavern beneath the table.

"I don't think your leaving is such a good idea." He took hold of the bag and we engaged in a momentary game of tug-of-war.

"Give me one good reason why I should stay."

"I have your purse."

It was a nice purse. More to the point, it had my lipstick, compact, and Eloise's check in it. "I have other purses."

His voice slipped just above silence. "I also have a gun."

I struggled to get out from under the booth, but in my panic my head hit one of the table's metal supports. Dull pain reverberated from the center of my skull to my lower back. Edgar released my purse and took hold of my wrist.

I think I said, "Let go of me," but the ringing in my noggin was so loud it was impossible to tell the difference between what I was thinking and what I was saying.

Edgar kept his voice low and calm. To anyone listening, his tone would've been gentle and reassuring but his words indistinct. "Ponder this: You think anyone here's going to help you? The dark meat in the kitchen's not going to protect you. I'm an officer in uniform." He was right. I may have been a regular, but that didn't mean the staff would take a slug for me. Given how little I tipped, the waitress would probably help Edgar aim the gun.

I stared at the top of the table and counted six wads of petrified chewing gum and a mysterious blob I feared once resided in a human orifice. I didn't want to die here.

"Here's how this is going to play," said Edgar. "We're going to get up and sit back in the booth. You're going to act like a remorseful girlfriend and go along with whatever I say. Then you and I are going to have a little chat." I evaluated my options. I could scream, assuming my mouth still worked, but gun or no gun Edgar was goofy and my angering him further wasn't going to get me home. He had the bulge. "What do you say, Rosie?" I nodded my consent, closing my eyes against the pain of my noodle sloshing about my skull. "If we get up and you run, I'll fire. Be certain of that." He released my wrist and I scooted backward until I made contact with the booth. Slowly I pulled myself into the seat and made a pact with God that if the room stopped spinning, I'd be a very good girl.

All eyes were on us. The kitchen staff waited in the doorway, uncertain whether to flee or charge.

Edgar's voice returned to normal and his eyes crinkled under the strain of his false smile. "You overreacted. There's no other girl for me. You've got to know that."

So that was the role I was supposed to play—the brave sailor's jealous girlfriend. If there was a bright side to the situation, at least I got to sink my teeth into a part I'd normally be passed over for. "Golly, I'm sorry." I tried to widen my eyes, but the pounding in my head wouldn't allow it. "I do know how you feel for me. I don't know why I'm always gunning for trouble." Motion returned to the room. The kitchen staff disappeared and the noise of the swinging door joined a chorus of conversations that eclipsed our own. A very pregnant waitress silently mopped up the remaining coffee and produced a tumbler of club soda to use on the dress's stain. As I cleaned myself, Edgar retrieved a menu and feigned interest in that evening's specials.

The waitress waddled over to a new table full of women dolled up for a night on the town. Edgar slid his hand, palm up, across the table and gestured for me to do the same. I did as he instructed and like two lovers we played with each other's fingers and bent into our conversation.

"I'd like to start by apologizing," he said. I snorted, then covered up the contempt with a fake cough. "As you said, it's been a very bad week for me."

"You're not the only one."

He closed his hand over mine. "I won't hurt you," he said.

"That's a funny pledge from a guy packing heat."

His eyes drifted down to the table. "I lied. I don't have a gun."

"Then I don't have a reason to stay." My keister rose into the air as my hand slid free of his. Like a snake, his arm followed mine, again making contact.

"Don't you want to know about Fielding's missing play?"

I froze, rump north, while common sense did battle with curiosity. The latter won out and I lowered myself back into the booth. "I'm listening."

Edgar took a sip of coffee, then directed his cup back to his saucer with the kind of care one took landing planes. "Are you surprised I know about it?"

"Should I be? You were his son."

He spun his cup until the handle rested at twelve o'clock. "My father loved the theater. As a writer he believed art should challenge the audience and force them to think."

I squeaked forward in my seat. "Sounds like a right guy."

"I'll leave that assessment to you. Have you read much of his writing?"

I could fake my way through many things, but this wasn't one of them. "No."

He nodded, pleased with either my honesty or my ignorance. "As I'm sure you know, he wrote much of his work anonymously. His reasoning for this was explained in *On Theatre*, a book most universities continue to inflict on their students." As Edgar spoke, his manner changed as though his recent installation into military life didn't often allow for these detours down a past that had been filled with college and other hoity-toity pursuits. And he missed it because while being in the service allowed for many things, it didn't give him the chance to freely express his intellectual superiority. "He wrote that his ideal play was one that appeared to have been produced organically, without any sign of the writer in it. He thought the playwright should be as our best actors are: so completely submerged in their parts that, were the play removed from the stage, it would be impossible to tell where the character began and the actor ended. To this end he touted the merits of complete realism. He also believed the easiest way to remove someone from the distancing of theater was to make sure whatever story he was telling was so astounding the audience would lose themselves in what they were hearing rather than the method by which they were hearing it."

I thought of Jim's note scribbled on the outside of the file folder: What would shock you? "So he liked to surprise people?" I asked Edgar.

He nodded. Our hands sat in grim prayer, his naked and wind-chapped, mine painted and ready for a night on the town. "I came to see you tonight because I believe Jim was very close to locating my father's missing play and I believe this information was documented in his files. When I found the office had been burgled, you can imagine my dismay."

"Actually, I can't," I said. His arm stretched like a waking cat, revealing a wristwatch with a plain black leather band. It was going on 9:30. Jayne would be throwing an ing-bing if I didn't show up soon. "While you've told me many interesting things, and shown me parts of Louie's I never would've visited on my own, I still don't understand why you want this play."

He rubbed his chin. Hair was starting to peek through his skin as though spending an hour with me required him to be at his most masculine. "It was my father's last work and it was important enough for someone to kill him over. Is that enough of a reason for you?"

"Is it worth something?" I asked.

"Not monetarily. Given the passionate response its existence has caused, I think it's safe to say that it's worth a great deal to someone and not much at all to most everyone else."

"So why not let that someone have it then?" I asked. "I mean, if the play was worth killing over, why would you want to put yourself at risk?"

Edgar sighed and released his hold on me. "It's far too complicated to make you understand."

It wasn't, but I knew better than to go over the edge with the rams.

"What I need to know," said Edgar, "is what was in Jim's files?" His eyes locked on mine. He tapped his foot expectantly.

I concentrated on my pulse and heart rate, begging my body to relax as spies did right before submitting to lie detectors. "Like I told your ma, there was nothing in them. I went through everything, every last scrap, and never even found a folder with Fielding's name on it."

His head sank into his hands. "I told her we should've taken them out of the office from the start."

"Gosh, I'm sorry." I rose, unencumbered, and tucked my bag under my arm. "Can I ask you something, Edgar?"

He lifted his head. "Sure."

"What exactly was your ma's relationship with Fielding?"

He paused before answering, his lips as thin as the gold lines drawn on his cuffs. "They never married if that's what you're asking."

"Far be it for me to be judgmental, but Eloise doesn't strike me as the kind of gal who would be comfortable having a kid out of wedlock."

"My father didn't give her much choice in the matter."

It was hard to picture Eloise taking that lying down. "Did Jim know who your real father was?"

"Most likely, yes." It was an odd answer and he knew it, and yet somehow I could tell that it was the most honest answer he could've given me.

"Did he ever talk to you or your ma about Fielding's script?"

"By the time the play went missing their relationship was sufficiently strained that I doubt Jim would've considered talking to her."

I could believe that. If the circumstances of his murder were any indication, Jim wasn't in the habit of coming home regularly. And I doubted, when he did appear, that either he or Eloise was up for conversation. "What about you?"

"Jim was my stepfather in name only. We had no relationship."

A chill passed through me. Why had Jim resigned himself to a loveless marriage, uniting himself with a son who wouldn't know affection if it bit him on the leg? It couldn't always been that way, could it? Nobody would choose to become trapped in a relationship like that. "When was the last time you saw Fielding?"

Edgar's eyes lingered on mine, their fierceness overtaken by something much more pathetic. "It's been years. He hated to be thought of as a weak man. After he lost his leg in the war, he became a recluse."

"Were you close to him?"

Emotion softened the lines of his face until he looked like a much younger version of himself. "Extremely. I may not have seen him, but he communicated almost daily through letters and telephone calls."

I might have believed him if he'd been mentioned once in the obituary.

Edgar paid for the coffee and insisted on ankling back with me. The temperature had dropped during our hour inside. Light snow drifted lazily to the ground, turning our path white while making a mess of my shoes. I kept my eyes on the ground, seeking out patches of ice so I wouldn't have to rely on his touch to regain my balance. Neither of us spoke during the walk and this quiet monotony lengthened the road and shortened my stride.

A lifetime later we arrived at the Shaw House. We paused at the stoop of the building and I pondered which farewell would make it clear I hoped to never see him again.

"I am sorry about before," he said.

"Don't think of it. You've been through a lot and I can try the patience of a nun." I'd left the Shaw House in such a hurry that I hadn't grabbed my wrap. I hugged myself to keep the wind from my wet dress.

"You said it, not me." While I shivered, my knight in naval dress pulled his coat tighter about his body. "Since the files are gone, I guess we won't be needing your services anymore. In fact, you probably don't need to be concerning yourself any further with this play."

I translated what he was saying. "You're right about that. I work for money."

"Good," he said. "So where's your blind date taking you?"

I wondered if I possessed the same power as Jayne, if the mere mention of a name could send a warning that I wasn't to be touched again. "I'm not sure. We're doubling with my girlfriend Jayne and her fellow. He's one of Mangano's men. Maybe you've heard of him— Tony B.?" Edgar shrugged. I made a note to encourage Jayne to date more recognizable thugs. "The *B* stands for bones, which he's fond of breaking. Anyway, my date's some friend of his, which means the guy probably has a short temper and a long record." The wind picked up, but Edgar showed no sign of leaving. I rose onto the first step and teetered. "I hate to be rude, but if I stay out here another minute, you'll have to chisel me off the walk."

"Of course." He removed his hat and replaced it. "Enjoy your date."

Jayne was in the lobby, ruining her otherwise perfect appearance with a scowl. "Where have you been?"

I headed over to the mirror above the fireplace. "Java at Louie's. I told Belle to tell you."

She approached me from behind and lectured my reflection. "That was over an hour ago." Her eyes landed on the dress's bodice and widened in horror. "You do know the cup goes to your mouth, right?"

"Is it that noticeable?"

"Only when I look at it."

The continent of Africa began at my bosom and ended at the first of the skirt's pleats. While, mercifully, the dress was brown, the coffee had the nerve to appear a darker shade.

I turned away from the mirror and headed toward the stairs. "I'll change my diapers."

Jayne grabbed my arm and steered me in the direction of my waiting coat. "Oh, no you don't. It took you all day to decide on this and we're already late."

I checked my watch. "We're fine. Tony's not even here yet."

Jayne whipped out a tube of lipstick and blotted it on without pausing her lecture. "He's been here and left. I told him I'd wait for you and the minute you showed we'd be over." She pinched her cheeks until color rose into her pale skin.

"Go without me—I'm not fit for man or beast."

Jayne picked up my coat and forced my arms into it. "You're going and that's final." Her dainty, well-manicured fingers pushed buttons through buttonholes with such force that I expected to hear wool rip. "The car's waiting for us."

I sighed and pinched my own cheeks until they matched the ruddiness of my nose. "Far be it for me to keep a car waiting."

14 Cure for Matrimony

We hopped into Tony's boiler and a mute driver lost beneath a large fedora drove us too fast down side streets still slick with snow. With each turn the heap made, a stack of forged c-ration gas coupons slid the length of the dash until the driver stilled them. I waited for Jayne to ask me who I'd had coffee with and why I'd ended up wearing most of it, but she kept her eyes locked on the window, working her hands into the nervous knots she always made when she was concerned she was displeasing Tony.

Tony, Tony, Tony. I shook my head in rhythm to his name and found myself growing sick at the thought of spending an evening with the great Tony B., a man so powerful he could make my otherwise secure friend turn into a quivering spaniel. I pushed him out of my mind and tried to replay my conversation with Edgar. Something wasn't adding up beyond his familial ties. There had been plenty of time for him to retrieve the files on his own, even if the papers had been in disarray. No, Edgar's visit couldn't have been just about determining the files' current location. His mother must've wanted to verify what—if anything—I knew about their contents. And I couldn't shake the feeling that if I'd been square with them and told them about the file of programs I'd found, I'd still be lying under that table staring at the remnants of someone's chewing gum while the life leaked out of me.

We careened down Fifty-second Street and pulled in front of Ali Baba's. The driver opened the door and helped both of us to our feet, before he went to some secluded garage where he wouldn't get

fined for being at a nonessential location. We walked under a bright
red awning and were ushered through glass and brass doors by a
man in a monkey cap. A sister with so much bosom she could have
rented herself out as a porch took our coats and directed us down
the hall to the powder room. There, in a sea of elaborately dressed
platinum blondes, we jostled for mirror space and took the shine off
our noses.

Ali Baba's was part clip joint, part dance hall. In the twenties it
had been a heavily populated speakeasy, but when it was no longer
necessary to hide its activities from prying eyes, those who'd made
money off bad booze pumped the dough back into the club until it
became one of the places to see and be seen. Tables ringed a gigan-
tic, dimly lit room decked out to look like Hollywood's concept of a
sheikh's palace. Spaced a stumble apart were bars attended by men
in white sheets and women in belly-dancer gear. If that was too far
for you to wobble, in the space between booze venders were crystal
fountains flowing with cheap champagne, which you could collect
in a shoe or a hat or, for the more conservative, one of a hundred
spit-cleaned glasses stacked in a pyramid. At the edge of the tables
was a brass banister designed to keep the eaters from the hoofers. In
the center of the room was an immense marble dance floor and in its
center was a stage outfitted by a big band playing a somber rendition
of "I Left My Heart at the Stage Door Canteen."

It was striking to see such ornate entertainment at a time when
we were being cautioned to conserve and think of our boys in blue.
Unlike Hollywood's Lucky Jordan, Alan Ladd's gangster who became
a war hero, the clientele of Ali Baba's had bought their way out of the
war with cabbage so dirty it left a mark on your hand. Their pockets
bulged with rolls of ill-gotten bills and their profiles tattled on arm
holsters packed with rods still warm from last night's raid. Since the
war, Tony B. and the like had made this their joint, discreetly letting
the public know it was invitation only and anything that went on
there was to be forgotten by dawn. Most of the women who decorated the tables with bright hair and shiny fabrics were cardboard

stand-ins, the wives being too preoccupied with raising children and mourning their lost youth to participate in these entertainments. These common bims had chosen this life instead of the war plants or the Women's Army Corps because it was easier to be quiet and pretty than to stand on their own. Even though laughter filled the room and flowed from the amber fountains, there was an air of sadness about the skirts as though they knew they were playing Cinderella only for the weekend. Come Sunday they would go back to their dingy brownstone apartments filled with black-market gifts, waiting for the horn to blow with an invitation for another Friday night.

"There he is," squealed Jayne as we entered the restaurant. She took me by the hand and pulled me across the room to where Tony B. was holding court at a table near the dance floor.

"Dollface." Tony rose from his throne and the crowd that had been around him dispersed in silent acknowledgment that whatever business they'd been conducting was adjourned for the evening. "Don't you look beeyouteeful." Tony liked to drag out long words as though to remind the listener that one of the many powers he wielded was the ability to stop time. He was also loose with his verb choice, which had convinced me long ago that despite his business smarts, he thought grammar was his mother's mother.

Tony landed a kiss on Jayne's cheek and patted her well-girdled keister.

She stepped back and put her arm around my waist. "You remember Rosie."

"Do I remember her? Of course I remember Rose!"

"It's Rosie, not Rose," I said. I was pretty sure Tony knew I didn't like him, but I still liked to remind him of it whenever the opportunity arose. He moved toward me like he was going to engulf me in a hug but stopped when I offered him my hand. Instead of shaking it, he planted a kiss on it, then gestured Jayne and me into two chairs separated by an empty one.

"What are you ladies drinking?" Tony plopped into his chair and signaled for one of Ali Baba's women to come our way.

"Champagne," said Jayne. "We've got celebrating to do." The band announced it was going on a ten-minute break and a Glenn Miller platter was piped through the speakers. Tony gave the girl our order, instructing her to pull a bottle from his private stock. She disappeared into the crowd and Tony returned his attention to us.

"I understand congrajoolations are in order," he said. "Jayne says you got yourself a swell part in some play."

I ignored evidence to the contrary and decided that for tonight's purposes I did indeed have the lead in a good play. "I'm not the only one," I said. "Jayne got a chorus part in a great musical."

Tony took Jayne's hand and played with her fingers as though they were an expensive piece of jewelry he'd asked to see up close but which he knew he couldn't afford. "Can you believe this one? Another lousy chorus part."

"Tony." Jayne's eyes shifted to the table as a blush colored her cheeks a deep maroon. One of the many things I admired about my pal was she never used Tony to get ahead. She insisted any work she got was on her own terms, despite the strings he could've pulled.

"I'm proud of you, babe. I'm just saying a girl as beeyouteeful as mine needs to be up front where everyone can see her." This was one of Tony's refrains, always dragged out when Jayne was cast in something new, and always interpreted by Jayne to mean she'd failed. The thing was, he *was* proud of her. He was just befuddled that he was the only one who recognized Jayne's value and that made him mad because she was the only investment of his that hadn't paid off.

"I like being in the chorus," Jayne told her lap.

"It's a revival of a great musical," I said, even if repeating the lie didn't make it true.

Jayne lifted her head and pushed her hair out of her face in a way that said she was a star no matter what she was cast in. A smile washed across her features as she prepared herself for the next scene in that evening's play. "Well?" she asked Tony. The secret language of people who spend far too much time together passed between them, encoding that single word with an entire conversation.

"Bathroom," said Tony (the word missing its *h*). "Nervous bladder."

"Oh," said Jayne. "That's sweet."

"Does my intended have a moniker or just a medical condition?" I asked.

"His name's Al and he's a great guy," said Tony. "First thing he said to me when he got out is he wanted to make things right for his ma."

I wasn't sure which part of that sentence to tackle first. "So he's been in the stir?" I nudged Jayne's thigh and shot her a sidelong glance that said, *See what you've gotten me into?*

Tony pulled at his shirt cuffs until a pair of bright gold cuff links appeared. "You didn't tell her about him, doll?"

"You knew he'd been in jail?" I asked her.

Jayne sank farther into her chair. "Maybe Tony mentioned it."

I reached for my evening bag and struggled to rise from my seat. Tony showed me his palms. "Whoa, Rose. Calm down. I wouldn't set you up with some lowlife. Al's one of the biggest gentlemen I know." I had a feeling that claim was to be taken literally and the fellow in question would not only have a rap sheet but a girth and height that made him tower above the rest of the room. "Ain't a guy in here who ain't been in the joint. Don't make them bad people."

I pointed at him with my bag. "You and I have different standards, Tony."

He surrendered with his hands. "It's not like he murdered some-body."

"Is that the measure you use?"

He ignored me and downed the finger of scotch he'd been nurs-ing since before our arrival. "He got the bum's rush. Al passed some orphan paper is all."

"Some what?" I asked.

"Forged checks."

I dropped my purse into my chair. "Gee, I can't even believe that's a crime."

Tony leaned into the table and I was reminded that this was a man with blood on his hands, a man who, with a snap of his fingers, could have parts of my body distributed in trash cans throughout the city. With a gesture so sparse I would've missed it if I hadn't been watching for it, he urged me back into my chair. I obeyed. "He was dizzy for this one dame. Real cheap sort, but he didn't see it. She writes him a Dear John, says she found someone who can keep her in the style she likes. He can't eat, he can't sleep. He's sick about it. At some point he decides the way to win her back is to buy her anything she wants. He gets her a car, furs, jewels, a nice apartment—you name it, that cupcake got it. Everything's going great until the bank tracks down the checks he's paying for all this with. Every one of them's forged. Al does a three spot and this girl of his forgets his name in under a week."

Jayne put her hand on mine. "It was for love, Rosie. Isn't that sweet?"

I couldn't have been more touched if my arms were fingers.

"A man," said Tony. "A man'll do anything for love." His broad, angular face softened and for a moment I lost myself in the fairy tale that said irresponsible, criminal behavior was something a woman should long for.

Fortunately, it passed.

Tony tapped the table with his index finger. "You will, of course, keep this between us?"

"Of course," I said.

The waitress deposited four flutes and a bottle of bubbly nestled in a silver-plated cooler. She popped the cork and dribbled some liquid into each of the glasses.

"I got to tell you," said Tony, "Al was reluctant to come here tonight. He even tried to tell me he was coming down with something. I think he's intimidated by you being this big-time actress. I told him ain't nobody can show a fellow a good time like Rose Winter."

I ignored him and tipped a long swallow of champagne. As a warm ebb started in my neck and slowly moved upward, Tony leaped to his feet and ceremoniously deposited his flute on the table. "And here he is: the man of the hour." I kept my eyes locked on my drink, determined to postpone the inevitable. Jayne turned to see Al, then spun back toward me, her face as pale as our tablecloth. "We've been waiting for you," said Tony. To strengthen my resolve, I downed the rest of my champagne, then rose as gracefully as a wooden boy.

Behind me the man who'd visited me at the office—"Frank" the enforcer—cracked his knuckles and shifted his weight from one foot to the other. I searched the air behind him, hoping to find my date.

Tony wrapped an arm about my waist. "Al—Rose. Rose—Al."

"Frank?" I asked.

He continued his nervous dance. "It's Al," he said.

Tony elbowed me in the ribs. "Youse know each other?"

Al shot me a look that begged me to go along with whatever he said.

"I must've been mistaken," I said.

"I got one of those faces," said the man formerly known as Frank. "Happens all the time." Behind us, the band returned from its break and struck up "Moonlight Serenade." A sea of people rushed onto the dance floor, where two by two they became one.

Tony offered Jayne his hand and pulled her to her feet. "What do you say, doll? Let's cut a rug and give these two a chance to get to know each other." Jayne mouthed *scream if you need help* and followed Tony out to the dance floor. While I plotted my revenge against her, the crowd swallowed them whole until they became just another gangster and his blonde.

Al attempted to collapse into himself until he was no longer visible.

"Sit," I told him.

He did as I ordered. "I didn't want to come here tonight."

"So I heard."

His eyes sank to my chest and lingered there.

"My eyes are up here, Al."

"What happened to your dress? You spill something on it?"

I crossed my arms. "It's not a stain—it's a design. You'd know that if you were a dame."

"Fair enough." He gestured toward the fourth, untouched flute. "That for me?"

"No," I said. "For me." I threw back the champagne and slid the empty glass across the table. I figured it was fair turnabout for the doughnut. "There're two ways to work this, *Al.* Either you spill what last week was about or Jayne and I let Tony B. know you threatened us. I know you don't like that idea, so I'm going to encourage you to be forthright."

He waved over a server and asked for a whiskey, neat. As the waitress disappeared, Al set his forearms on the table and, like a flat tire encountering a pump, regained his bulk. "I didn't threaten you."

"Say what you will, I have a feeling Tony will disagree."

A smile peaked out from the corners of his mouth as he shook his head at me. "Name one thing I said that meant I was going to hurt you."

I tried to recall why I'd felt threatened and came up empty. "Maybe you didn't say anything, but the threat was implied."

"How so?"

I counted off the reasons with my fingers. "You entered my office without an invitation."

"The door was unlocked."

I ticked off my next point. "You wouldn't let me leave."

"No, *I* wouldn't leave. You were free to come and go as you pleased."

I trudged forward without a finger to stand on. "You ate half of my doughnut."

"You offered it to me."

I ended my illustration and played with the stem of my empty champagne flute. "Let's say, for the sake of argument, that you weren't threatening me. If that's the case, why were you there?"

His eyes drifted to the table. "I can't tell you."

"Did you come to take the files?"

Bewilderment washed across his features. Either Al was made for the stage or he had no idea what I was talking about. "What files?"

"For crying out loud, I heard your friends at the funeral talking about cleaning Jim's office. All of his files, even his furniture's gone."

The confusion disappeared and was replaced by prideful astonishment. "Hey, when we clean an office, no one knows about it. We only take what's ours. We don't got nothing to do with Jim being robbed."

"Then why were you there?"

He sighed. "Like I said before: I can't tell you."

I crossed my arms. "Then maybe you can tell Tony."

The fear he'd donned earlier returned. His eyes were bloodshot, the bags beneath them big enough to pack for a trip on the *Queen Mary.* "I didn't do nothing wrong."

"Then tell that to Tony. If your nose is clean, why would he care?" Scheherazade deposited his drink and dribbled bubbly into my empty glass. She walked away with a rustle of fabric we could hear above the band.

Al gulped his drink, then rested the half-empty glass in his open palm. "What I was doing I wasn't doing for Tony."

I wasn't following him and told him so.

"That day, the reason I was there, wasn't for Tony."

I wrapped my hand around the flute. "Oh, so you were freelancing? And apparently that's a problem because . . . what? It's harder to figure out your income tax?"

Al finished off his drink and raised the empty tumbler into the air. "Tony says when you work for him, you work for him. That's all."

I pushed the champagne bottle toward him and he gratefully splashed some into his glass. The band switched to "String of Pearls" and Tony and Jayne appeared in the center of the dance floor. They were so caught up in dancing that the crowd had to back away to give them room. Tony was a passable dancer for a guy who spent his days sitting on his can dipping the bill, but Jayne was dazzling. She flashed her best Broadway smile and followed up each of Tony's perfunctory swings with the kind of flourish one could pick up only after working in a dozen chorus lines. The crowd cheered them on, offering catcalls at the sight of Jayne's skirt lifting in the air, at the way she played with the men around her, giving them winks and knowing nods. Tony ate it all up, his own steps growing looser as he gave in to the music and rhythm that was Jayne.

"She's a good dancer," said Al. I nodded and emptied the rest of the champagne into my glass. I had a buzz on that was half a flute from knocking me on my back. "I was doing a favor for a friend," said Al.

"What?" I screamed above the music.

"That day. I was there for a friend. There wasn't no money involved, nothing like that, but my time is Tony's, see?"

I guzzled the drink with the enthusiasm of a parched bulldog and set the empty glass on the table. "What did your friend want you to do?"

Al grunted and put a napkin to his sweaty brow. "Just check in with you. Make sure you're okay. That kind of thing."

The bubbles from my glass transferred to my brain, making it very difficult to complete a thought. A dozen shadows ducking behind pillars, up alleys, and through doors flashed through my mind. "You've been tailing me, haven't you?"

Al loosened his tie. "It's not tailing—it's checking."

"Son of a gun. For days you've been following me. How long is this supposed to go on?" Al didn't say anything. In his hand the tumbler was reduced to a pill vial. "Who are you working for?"

The song quieted and so did his voice. "I can't tell you."

"Maybe not with words, but you're going to spill all the same." I tried to poke his arm to show him I meant business, but whatever cement he was made of was unyielding. "I'll ask you a question and you clap once for no, twice for yes. Are you working for Edgar Fielding?" He gave me a long, indignant look before clapping once. "Henry Nussbaum?" The irritation stayed and was paired with lack of recognition. Again he clapped once. "Eloise McCain?" He paused long enough to tell me I'd landed on it. "What does she want with me?"

"It ain't her."

I got in his face until his beady eyes were the size of a normal mortal's. "You hesitated."

He bridged the distance remaining between us until he was so close I could taste what he had for lunch. "And I told you: it ain't her." I stared into his eyes until I knew every red vein threaded through the white. He was on the square. Worse, up close Al was a hard guy to hate. His bulk became softness, his hard lines curves, and his little peepers possessed a warmth and pain I'd begun to believe men didn't have access to.

I put my hand atop his and gently squeezed. "Please tell me. I need to know."

He held my gaze and cocked his head to the right, his way of relenting. "It was Jim."

15 The Butter and Egg Man

IN ADDITION TO WORKING AS a gumshoe and providing private security, Jim made money serving as a personal liaison for the imprisoned. Sometimes he paid their bills and helped get rid of anything incriminating that hadn't yet been brought to the law's notice. Other times he was the gun you called on to send your ma flowers for her birthday and let your enemies know your debts wouldn't be met for another year or two. He didn't make a lot of money doing this, but he worked with the expectation that as soon as you were out of the pen you owed him a favor. Most thugs became Jim's bill collectors. When Al was released for writing bad checks, he got me.

"That explains all the letters from Attica I found in his office," I said over the roar of the band. "So if he put you on me, did he know something was going to happen to him?"

Al shrugged. "Every guy in here thinks something bad's going to happen to him. Maybe Jim was a little more worried when this Fielding stuff started or maybe he wanted to cover his bases, just in case."

"Just in case?" You wore clean drawers just in case. You paid your insurance bill just in case. You didn't hire a thug to follow your file clerk around *just in case*. "What did Jim say?"

Al's flippers flailed through the air, illustrating everything he said in a manner that was totally unrelated to the point he was trying to make. "He told me if something happened to him I was to make sure you stayed out of it."

That got my hackles up. Jim hadn't been worried about harm

coming to me; he was trying to keep me from snooping. "Fine job you did. What about Agnes?"

"He didn't think she'd be a problem."

I laughed at that. Agnes meddled more than a hairdresser on a windy day. "Why not?"

"She don't gum things up. You though—you're worse than the SS."

"He said that?"

"Maybe not in so many words, but that was the gist."

I put my elbows on the table and rested my head in my hands. "If he was so concerned about me, maybe he should've taken better care to see to it that I wasn't dragged into this mess. I didn't go looking for trouble, Al. It found me."

"You can stay out of it now."

Even if I wanted to, there seemed to be some force that kept dragging me back in. If I didn't see this through to the end, who would? "I don't think I have a choice."

Al glanced at his wristwatch and, noting the time, sank further into himself. Was he back with the tomato whose greed had sent him to prison, or was there another duty that demanded he be home soon and up early? "There's always a choice, Rosie. That's why Jim asked me to tail you. I'm your choice. I'm your ticket out of trouble."

"And if I turn in my ticket and board your rattler, who's going to see to it that whoever killed Jim is punished?"

What I expected was a list of underworld enforcers who were already on the job. What I got was another shrug. "These things have a way of working out."

I laughed and shredded my cocktail napkin. "Then I guess we'll have to wait and see what happens, won't we?"

Before Al could reply, Jayne and Tony joined us at the table. Another bottle of champagne appeared and I quickly passed the threshold between buzzed and blitzed. Rather than surrendering to a pleasant drunk, I let the memory of Jim tip me a few more drinks until the tackiness of Ali Baba's and the sadness of his women became something resplendent and joyful, so much so that I had to sing about it.

"Easy, Rosie," said Al. "Get off the table like a good girl and sit back in your chair."

I gently kicked him in the stomach and toasted the room with my eighth glass of bubbly. "I'm singing, Al. I've got great pipes and I fully intend to use them."

"Let her go," said Tony. "There's no harm."

He was right, so right that I stepped off the table and into his lap. He took my free hand and helped me to the floor. I settled rump first on his thigh and became fascinated with his bow tie. "I don't like you, Tony, but you're a good egg." My voice didn't sound right. It was fast and crisp in my mind, but out loud it was loose in the middle and soft around the edges. I followed his tie upward and traced the skin beneath his nose. "You should consider growing a mustache. It'd soften that schnozzle of yours."

Two of him grinned at me, which emphasized his need for facial hair. "I'll take that under consideration. Why don't you like me, Rose?"

I finished glass number eight and tried to put it on the table, but the darn thing moved, sending the flute crashing to the floor. "In the first place," I told the one of him on the left, "my name's Rosie. I hate being called Rose. And in the second place, I don't like the way you treat Jayne." Saying her name reminded me she was somewhere in the room, so I stood up and located a pair of her standing next to Al. "Come here, Jayne," I said. Both of her did as I instructed. I put my arm around her waists and the three us looked down on the twin Tonys. "This is my best friend, Tony, and when I hear you're putting her down or you're not calling her or something, it breaks my heart. You know why?"

The merriment was gone from his face. "Why?"

I tried to put a hand on Jayne's shoulder and missed. "Because she's a good girl. A devoted girl. And she deserves a fellow who'll give her the moon."

"I'd give her that and more. All she's got to do is ask." He took Jayne's hand in his and my favorite blonde swayed from side to side until her skirt rose into the air. She looked like a flower then and the sweetness of Tony B. holding my roommate who became a flower made me start to cry.

"What's the matter, Rosie?" asked Jayne.

"Nobody." I struggled for breath. "Just nobody has ever made me a flower."

When I'd stopped crying long enough to identify my coat and blow farewell kisses to the band, Al offered to see me home. Tony's driver followed a meandering path that coaxed the champagne out of my stomach and onto my skirt. On the upside, it camouflaged the stain.

"Where's Jack?" I asked as I stewed in my own filth.

"Who?" asked Al.

The stench cleared my head. "Jayne. Where's Jayne?"

"With Tony," said the man of few words. "She'll be home in the morning."

I leaned my head against the car window and let the icy glass bring me back to myself. "You got a sweetheart, Al?"

"Naw. Not anymore. " He spread his arms wide and rested them on top of the back seat. "I've got a ma."

"I've got a ma," I said, as though having a mother were as unique as having a twin. "What's yours like?"

Al pondered the question. "Feeble. And easily disappointed. Yours?"

"About the same, though she could probably take yours in a foot-race. Mine hates that I'm an actress."

Al rubbed his eyes. "Yeah? Next time she says something about it, tell her at least she's not visiting you in the joint."

I smiled at that. Clearly he didn't know my ma. "So what did Jim say when he told you to watch out for me?"

"Nothing really. Just to keep an eye on you because you were his girl."

I sat so straight my head hit the car roof. "That son of a bitch. We weren't . . . you know . . . like *that*, Al. I barely knew the guy. He was my boss and I was his employee. That's the crop."

Al winced, probably from the unnatural pitch my voice was reaching. "Whatever you say. Ain't no skin off my back."

"Well, it's skin off *my* back. The guy was more than twice my age. There was no funny business going on between us. I was his file clerk."

"You were obviously more than that," said Al.

"What's that supposed to mean?"

"Just that you meant more to him than that. Don't take it wrong." I caught sight of myself in the window. My hair was astray and my eyes were so shot they should by all rights be dead. "How am I supposed to take it?"

Al sighed. "You got a father?"

I leaned against the door. "I've got a grave in Brooklyn."

"How 'bout a brother?"

I hadn't heard from my brother since the war started. He only contacted me if he wanted to brag about something or needed help out of a fix. "Only when the weather's good."

"Then there's your problem. I don't know if Jim wanted to"—he raised his eyebrows up and down—"or not. You're an attractive broad and ten to one the idea went through his head. But when a guy calls you his girl and takes pains to make sure trouble stays away when he's not there to protect you, it could be because he cares about you like a brother or a father, see?"

I burned with embarrassment. Score one for my overinflated ego. "I'm one dumb bunny." Al didn't disagree. "Couldn't he have left me money in his will?"

"Trust me, this is better. You can't put a price on protection."

By the time we arrived at the Shaw House I'd scraped the sick off my dress and was feeling more like myself. The last hour had become one of those hazy dreams you're sincerely glad didn't happen because the humiliation would be worse than anything you could imagine.

"You want me to walk you in?" asked Al.

I shook my head and fumbled with the door until I figured out how to open it. I stepped out of the car and onto the curb. A patch of black ice masquerading as cement yanked my dogs out from under me. Whatever buzz still lingered took the run out to make room for searing pain.

Al used two fingers to wrench me to my feet. "I'm walking you to the door."

"Change walking to carrying and you've got a deal."

The Shaw House had no formal curfew, although there was enough of an implied one to make you carefully plan your evenings. After 11:00 on weekends, Belle went to bed and we had to use keys to get into the lobby. If you lost your key, you were out of luck until morning since no amount of knocking, honking, or screaming could wrestle Belle from slumber. Keys were issued once, on the day you moved in. If you lost yours—tough luck. Belle believed anyone who lost something once, would lose it again, excepting, of course, her virginity.

I asked Al to drag me close to the streetlight so I could dump out my purse and search for my brass friend.

"You got a key?" asked Al.

The situation didn't look too optimistic. "Jayne's got a key." I sifted through the few things I'd bothered to cram into my evening bag. "I have a hairpin and a stick of gum."

Al blew on his gloveless hands and examined the door. Before I could tell him about the futility of knocking, he returned to my side and claimed the hairpin for himself. As quick as a cat, he wrestled with the lock until it opened with a triumphant click.

"If you can do the same thing for stains, I might have to keep you around."

He offered me his hand and pulled me to my feet. "That leg of yours is going to feel like hell in the morning."

"It's not feeling all that fabulous right now. You want to come in for a cup of tea?"

His eyes danced up the street; I was keeping him from something. "I better not. I'll see you around."

"I'll be looking for you." As he climbed back into the car, I hobbled up the stairs and into the lobby. I decided if I continued at my current pace, I wouldn't make it to bed until sunrise, so I swallowed the pain and rushed up the stairs as fast as I could. Churchill greeted me from the depths of the dark, empty room. As I eased my way to the bureau, hard nuggets of Cat Chow crackled like burning wood. I clicked on the lamp and surveyed the dress in the mirror. It was, in a word, destroyed. In addition to the stains, when I'd fallen I'd ripped both the knee and a side seam.

Churchill came to my side and sniffed my skirt. He identified the source of the odor and with a scowl leaped onto Jayne's bed.

"If you think that's bad, try wearing it." Balanced on one foot, I removed the dress, balled it up, and tossed it into the waste bin. I'd figure out what to tell Ruby in the morning.

I didn't wake until early afternoon. My head pounded, my vision was blurred, and my ankle had swelled to the size of Boris Karloff's neck in *Frankenstein*. I wasn't in a state to deal with the ruined dress, so I decided the best thing to do was leave the house and lie low. As I left my room, I tripped over a stack of books placed outside the door. True to her word, Harriet had located her copies of *On Theatre* and *Journey's End*. I stuck them both in the crook of my arm and limped two blocks to Cora Deane's, one of the few places where a gal could get breakfast at any time of day without the waitress tsk-tsking her for keeping a pro skirt's hours.

While I downed a quart of java and some plain toast, a booth full of women behind me took turns reading one another V-mail from their newly acquired military pen pals. I couldn't stand lis-

tening to their excitement over men they'd never met so I turned
to my reading material. I decided to start with *On Theatre* since I
had a feeling understanding Fielding's theory was going to increase
my understanding of his play. The book was surprisingly slim—only
a hundred pages. Despite its brevity, it was as clear as the news
from the Russian front. If Raymond Fielding had an audience (and
I doubted he considered such things), it was lofty, erudite thinkers
who held the common man in great disdain even as they helped to
pay his bills.

That's not to say I didn't understand *any* of it. From what I could
gather, the gist of his thesis was that theater was nothing more than
an attempt to imitate life, and until we recognized this goal and
focused our efforts on better achieving it, theater as a form would
fail. He hated plays that flaunted *artistry,* a term he decried as "the
unfortunate result when a participant places their ego above their art;
when we speak of someone's artistry we are automatically negating
the possibility for a theatrical piece to succeed."

Fielding's favorite word was *invisible,* the state in which he believed all facets of a production should be. The set, actors, direction,
and writing should be so true to life as to be unrecognizable as
anything but reality. Fielding believed the worst thing to happen to
theater was putting it on a stage, a remove which immediately suggested it was apart from, rather than a reflection of, life. The second
worst thing was the director.

Of course, you couldn't place real people on a real set and call
it theater. One key element separated drama from real life: conflict. Sure, life had plenty of it, but much of our everyday activity
was void of any dramatic push and pull. Fielding wrote, "While
we strive to mimic daily goings-on, there's no reason to be boring
about it. Some events in our lives are made for observation; others
are undeserving of an audience. We must carefully discern between
the two."

Journey's End matched *On Theatre* for length and density. The basic plot was that a man, in the midst of an unnamed war, struggles to

get home to his exiled family. Along the way he encounters a variety of characters he needs to spill about his family's whereabouts. It was clearly intended to be a political allegory, but I wasn't swift to what he was trying to say. All I knew was that if this was the best example of Fielding's writing, the only reason it should be prompting anyone's death was from boredom.

16 There Shall Be No Night

JAYNE DIDN'T COME HOME on Saturday, and by Sunday I'd convinced myself that Tony had whisked her away for a romantic weekend. I went to bed early that night to avoid Ruby. I'd managed to duck her the entire weekend, but it was going to be impossible to continue dodging her if we were in the same rehearsal hall. From nine o'clock on I tossed and turned, thinking about Jack in the arms of some nameless French nurse with a face like Rita Hayworth's, thinking about Jim hanging from a rope that creaked with every swing. The images merged until it was Jack I kept finding in Jim's closet. Despite the noose around his neck, he was still alive and every time I opened the door he presented me with a marked deck of cards while Churchill whispered, "Aces are high."

At ten o'clock I turned on the lights and let sleep know I was giving it a rest for the night. Churchill was sprawled belly up against Jayne's pillows. He opened one eye at the return of lamplight, then rotated his head until the pillowcase better blocked his vision.

I rifled through back issues of *Dime Detective* but couldn't find a single tale that held my attention. I returned the pulps to their teetering pile and retrieved a stash of blank V-mail from under my bed.

Dear Jack . . .

I passed the next half hour staring at his name, trying to decide on the best opening. We'd left things bad. Very bad. While no one had officially declared the relationship over, it was obvious he believed it to be the case when he packed up his troubles in his old kit bag and left without saying good-bye.

Our problems stemmed from the age-old rule that actors and actresses should never date one another. When and why these two creatures became incompatible I couldn't guess, though I suspected the Elizabethans employed cross-dressing to get around the problem. The life of an actor could be an agonizingly lonely one. It was tempting to look for camaraderie among like-minded individuals if for no one other reason than because you believed similarities beget understanding. Plus there was something to be said for the attraction one felt when she witnessed someone succeeding at his craft. A talented man was a powerful aphrodisiac.

The problem with both people in a relationship pursuing the same thing was that inevitably they achieved different levels of acclaim. Before he enlisted, Jack was heavily in demand, so much so that he no longer auditioned for work. I wasn't bothered by his accomplishments, but I'd grown to dread the way it altered his attitude toward me. Suddenly, he believed he knew the secret to succeeding as an actor and rather than sitting back and supporting my admittedly minor victories, he doled out advice in a way that used my achievements as an example of what I shouldn't have done.

It's not that Jack didn't support me, but he had a different notion about being an actor than I did. I believed acting was a job like any other and if that meant I sometimes did stupid things to guarantee my financial survival, so be it. I took whatever parts I could, working for companies that would be gone tomorrow or reduced to theatrical punch lines. To me it made good sense; to Jack I was compromising myself. In the heat of an argument he once told me that my taking parts that were beneath me was the reason that people thought the word *actress* was synonymous with *whore*. Right before I clocked him, I reminded him that his first name was half of the word synonymous with *donkey*.

Jack had to believe everything he did was Art (capital A), from the production of *A Doll's House* set in the human digestive system (Nora's exit wasn't so much a choice as an expulsion) to the version of *Twelfth Night* that played out over as many evenings so the audience could no longer connect what had just happened in the play with what had occurred two weeks prior. In Jack's mind what counted wasn't your paycheck but how each role would serve to make people remember your name as a performer. This was a decision he could afford to make because he hailed from a wealthy family. I, on the other hand, had rent to pay and a nasty desire to eat three squares a day.

Even if I didn't have all those responsibilities hanging over me, there was no guarantee I would've achieved greater success by being more particular about what roles I accepted. We didn't live in a perfect world where every actor with talent was guaranteed meaningful work. Putting aside the nepotism and politicking that took most casting decisions out of the realm of logic, I wasn't a contender for every good part. I was tall and imperious onstage, no matter how I tried to hide it, which limited the kinds of roles I could play. Jack didn't see that though. If I failed it was because of something I hadn't done rather than something I couldn't.

Jack enlisted because of me. We'd been having one of the many fights that characterized the end of our relationship. He'd taken me to task for working for Jim, an arrangement he believed was my way of declaring I was abandoning my acting career once and for all. I explained that that wasn't the case, that when one job didn't pan out, you took another to get through the lean times, but he would hear none of it. Before I knew it, I was challenging him to descend his throne and try living like everyone else for once. I had no idea he'd use that as rationale for the Actor to become a soldier.

That's not to say that I was the *only* reason he signed up. You couldn't get through the year since Pearl Harbor without feeling that you should be doing something to help. Friend after friend of ours joined up and shipped out, until Jack was one of the few actors in his twenties still working. It must've bothered him, though he never admitted it, just like it had to drive him crazy when soldiers passed him on the street and laughingly referred to him as the Home Guard. I wished I knew that side of him. It might've helped me handle his going off to basic training better. And maybe, when he finally returned,

I wouldn't have greeted the news that he'd received his orders with a torrent of tears and accusations about how he was doing this to punish me—that he'd never really loved me. That had to make it easy for him to leave without saying good-bye.

I picked up my pen and scribbled beneath the salutation, "Please don't die," then I crumbled the paper into a ball and threw it at the wastebasket. Shortly thereafter I must have fallen asleep because the next thing I knew, Jayne had turned off the lights and was creeping about the room with a stiffness that suggested she was aiming for invisibility.

I rose up on my elbow and clicked on my bedside lamp. "Hiya, stranger."

She kept her back to me and struggled to take off her clothes. "Hiya, yourself. You can turn off the light. I don't need it. I'm almost changed." There was an air of insistence to her voice that told me to either obey or face her wrath. Jayne was happy-go-lucky to a fault so hearing her tone set on edge signified something was seriously wrong.

I clicked off the lamp and watched her form struggle to dress by the light of the pulsing neon motel sign across the street from us. "You all right?"

"Fine. Just tired." With her back still to me, she slid into bed and pulled the covers past her neck. "You have a good weekend?"

I laughed at the night and pulled the sheet to my chin. "Allow me to boil its bleakness down to one activity: I spent a large part of the evening trying to write Jack."

"That is bleak."

The room grew strangled with a silence so oppressive only Churchill's snores could be heard. My instincts told me to leave Jayne alone, but I had a feeling doing so was the last thing she needed. I climbed out of bed and took a seat on the edge of hers. As gentle as a butterfly, I set my hand on her shoulder and squeezed. Her arm vibrated in response and I realized Jayne hadn't stopped speaking because she wanted to but because it was the only way she could quiet the sobs wracking her body.

"What's wrong?"

She turned to me, her hand on top of mine, and showed me through the throbbing light what had kept her from the Shaw House for two days. Her left eye was lost in a shadow that started above her penciled eyebrow and ended below the top of her rouged cheek. Her lips rippled as though she'd hastily eaten a piece of cake without wiping her mouth. I turned the lamp back on and the shadow became a bruise, the cake a poorly healed scab. A crevice ran vertically from her upper lip to her lower, making her mouth appear like lava that leaked from a wound in the earth.

"That son of a bitch! I'll kill him." I rose from the bed but made it no farther than the iron footboard before Jayne pulled me back down beside her.

"Don't, Rosie. Please."

"Why? Because he's a good guy? Because you deserved it? Give me one good reason why I shouldn't clean his clock."

Jayne again turned off the light as though she believed the wounds disappeared when I could no longer see them. "Just don't. Okay? I need to think. Then maybe . . ." Her voice trailed off. She fumbled with her nightstand drawer until she located a cigarette and lighter. The flame momentarily illuminated Tony B.'s damage before again masking it in darkness.

"When did this happen?"

She tilted her head back and exhaled. The smoke drew a lazy line in the air. "Friday. After." She rested the hand holding the cigarette by her cheek to ease her pain with its warmth. "I don't know what happened. We were dancing, having a good time. Everything was great." Tears choked her words. Jayne's eyes lit on a spot on the wall opposite her and I had the same feeling I had the one time she was miscast in a tragedy. Her hands moved too much; her facial expressions were too extreme. Jayne played drama like a clubfoot tap-danced. "Then some guy starts making eyes at me, only Tony's not game for it. I told him off, but it wasn't good enough for Tony. He made out like I was asking for the attention." I thought back to Friday night. It didn't make sense that someone could go from loving the spotlight to bashing the bulb in. "I tried to tell him he's the only man for me, but everything came out wrong and before I knew it . . ."

"He was hitting you."

Her face changed and her eyes left their spot and returned to me. "I just stood there. I kept thinking he'd stop. He'd see the blood and he'd stop." She pulled down the front of her gown and showed me what I couldn't see from a distance: her chest, her shoulders, her back—all of it was black and blue.

I was overcome with a mix of pity and anger. I was mad at Jayne for not telling me the truth and bewildered by the clear evidence that someone had hurt her. How could I make things right when I didn't know what had happened to begin with?

A better person might have been able to get the real story out of her, but I tripped and stumbled over my fat tongue and asked, "Why didn't you stop him?"

Her eyes went blank, as if I'd asked her a complicated math question. She ran her index finger over her split lip and winced. "I couldn't stop him."

"Of course you could. You could've hit him back. You could've screamed for help. You could've done something."

"I couldn't." Her voice grew more forceful. "He's stronger than me, see? He was too far off the track. And I knew if I tried to do anything to stop him it would make it worse." She wielded the cigarette with such ferocity that I had to duck out of the way to keep from getting burned. "If I yelled, no one would've come. If I'd hit him, he would've hit me harder. I'm not smart. I'm not good at defending myself. All I could do was stand there and take it. I'm sorry if that wasn't good enough for you." She curled her legs toward her body and hugged her knees. Never had I seen Jayne so defeated.

"Have you been with him this whole time?" I asked.

Her fingers searched her lips and plucked a stray hair from the scab. "No. I went home." Jayne's family ran a dairy farm two hours north of the city. Since I'd known her, they hadn't come to see one of her shows; nor had she ever bothered to go home for a visit. "I couldn't stay there, but I needed to get away, you know? I was scared he'd find me."

I nodded. "What are you going to do?"

She rolled over until her back was to me. Churchill delicately picked his way across her bed and settled in the hollow beneath her stomach. "I'm going to sleep."

17 The Rivals

I GOT UP EARLY THE next morning and tiptoed about the room while Jayne continued to sleep. Churchill remained in the curve of her belly, one grave eye set upon me as I went about my business. By eight o'clock I was downstairs and eating breakfast alone in the dining room, a treat I usually missed out on. In exchange for our sugar ration coupons, the Shaw House provided us with two hot meals of varying quality. If you were up before ten, you got a stack of wheats and a cup of joe. As delectable as this might sound, the house cook, Ellen Deering, was a cousin of Belle's. What Belle was to hospitality, Ellen was to food, meaning the pancakes were the consistency of paving brick.

Still, I wolfed down the food, hoping speed would bump off taste, and entertained myself with an abandoned newspaper. Babe Ruth was making personal appearances at movie theaters to get kids involved in the war effort. Jane Russell was the number-one pinup choice of the armed forces. Twelve percent of the motion picture industry had enlisted, including Jimmy Stewart and Clark Gable. It was a good heartwarming look at how fame could be a positive thing, but it couldn't trump the news that five brothers were missing after fighting the same battle in the Pacific. All five from one family gone in an instant. Now *that* was reality.

I was about to put my cup down and declare breakfast conquered when Ruby promenaded into the dining room and blocked the exit with her body. She was wearing a stunning royal blue silk shantung suit (bought, I assumed, before the ration kicked in) and matching mules. Her hair and makeup made it clear she'd been up since six to make sure nobody at rehearsal looked better than she did.

"Eating all alone?" she cooed.

"Finishing actually." My cup met its saucer and rattled a warning.

"You're lucky you're so tall. I can't imagine a smaller woman eating what you do and getting away with it." Ruby left the doorway and sat at the table. "How was your date?"

"Swell."

She sat with her back straight, her hands palms down on the tabletop. Despite this front, there was something hinky about her, as though she was as disturbed by me as I was by her.

"What about you, Rube—what were you up to this weekend?"

"Me?" She fluttered her eyelashes to communicate how strange it was for her to jaw about herself. As if I'd believe that. "Why, I didn't really do anything."

I raised a questioning eyebrow and pushed forward. "So you were here all weekend?"

"Here and there." Her napkin lighted into the air and settled gracefully on her lap. "By the way, when should I expect my dress back?"

"Soon. I took it to a dry cleaner." I'd never had anything drycleaned in my life, but I hoped the process took a while and ended with the garment looking worse for wear.

Ruby's forehead crinkled with concern. "You didn't get anything on it, did you?"

I rose from the table. "I was on a date, Ruby. I was nervous."

She pursed her lips into a tiny red oval. "That dress cost a hundred dollars."

Overcooked pancakes leaped from my stomach and lodged in my throat. My entire wardrobe didn't cost $100. I'd hoped no one's did. "Let me finish, would you?" Faster, brain, faster! "I was nervous and thought I'd better get the dress cleaned in case it . . . um . . ." I checked the door and lowered my voice. "In case it smelled."

"Oh." Her acrylic smile returned and she shifted her body to further increase the distance between us. "I appreciate the thought. So why are you up so early? Did you get another job?"

"No, I'm going to rehearsal. With you. Remember?"

Ruby nodded deeply as people will do when they're pretending to learn something for the first time. "That's right, you're in *my* show." Her show. *Her* show. Jayne had been beaten and was lying about why. Jack had shipped out. My boss was dead. And the one potential bright spot in my life had been snatched by Little Miss Did It First and Did It Better. No longer was I worried I'd destroyed her dress; I only wished I'd set it on fire.

Ruby retrieved a wheat from the platter and carefully scraped away its burned outer layer. "Maybe we can share a cab to rehearsal. What time were you planning on leaving?"

I plastered a fourteen-karat smile on my face. "That's awfully swell of you, but I have a few things I have to do this morning. Maybe we can share a cab home?"

Her own smile grew, silently spilling that the original offer had been a sham. "Unfortunately, I have to go uptown. I have a lunch date, and then I have to work on my radio show."

I snapped my fingers. "Oh, that's right—you got that little radio gig."

A deep, throaty laugh sounded in her chest. "I'd hardly call it *little*. I'm the lead."

"Well, that's swell, Rube. Really, truly swell." I should've dusted then, but I couldn't help myself. If Ruby was going to ruin my day, I could ruin her meal. "You know, it's wonderful that you're so secure about taking radio work. I've heard some directors assume anyone on the radio is using their voice to compensate for other . . . shortcomings."

Ruby's fingers, still bearing the pancake's carbon, danced along her hairline and pushed her glossy curls into place. "Obviously that's not a problem for me."

"Obviously." I started to leave but paused long enough to admire the crumbs glistening like black pearls against white silk. "But give it time."

•   •   •

Since I had nowhere to go and an hour and a half to kill, I decided
to walk to rehearsal. People's Theatre was north of the Shaw House
on West Fourteenth Street, an address that had served many other
theaters with small budgets and big mouths since the beginning of
the century. The morning was warm enough that street vendors assumed their stations and grocers spilled their wares onto the sidewalks to compensate for their cramped, overstocked spaces. A mix of
accents—some Irish, some Italian—hawked produce I didn't need and
couldn't afford. A pair of sailors wandered among them, their eyes
lighting on each sight as if they were attempting to commit every
detail to memory in case they should never see it again. Across the
street a courier checked an address from the list in his hands while
women peeked around the drapes in their living rooms, their faces
tensed in preparation for the starred telegram they might be getting.
"The War Department regrets to inform you," it would say, the rest
of its text unreadable once their tears began.

By the time I arrived at the theater a light mist had saturated my
coat and hat, turning my formerly neat appearance to wrinkled, wet,
and odorous. I was still a half hour early and the building appeared
empty, so I ducked into the ladies' room and did my best to pat myself
dry. Once I was less waterlogged, I took a stroll around the lobby and
examined framed photos and reviews from the last several shows.

People's Theatre specialized in realistic, contemporary productions, many of which had a political bent. During the Depression,
they'd become world-renowned for a musical about the Triangle
Shirtwaist factory fire, starring real-life survivors of the accident instead of actors. Many of their productions had been endorsed by
labor unions while being defamed as subversive and reckless by local politicians. The photos from the shows told of gritty, realistic sets
and actors made human by uncombed hair, smudges of dirt, torn
costumes, and stark lighting. Had they not been identified as pictures

from plays, I would've thought all the images were *Life* magazine portraits of people pushed to their limits so those of us safe in our living rooms could humanize the tales we read in our papers.

In addition to the photos, there was a large brass plaque lining one wall, engraved with the names of those who'd helped People's Theatre establish, grow, and continue to exist. The usual suspects were listed—well-to-do families and captains of industry who supported the arts not because they cared about theater but because they had a quota of plaques to appear on. There were also well-known performers, directors, and writers who may have pursued their careers elsewhere but believed enough in People's Theatre to continue to contribute to its efforts. There was even a name that had been removed, its shadow a tale of someone who'd withdrawn his support after something he didn't approve of was done.

That didn't bode well. I didn't want a company with an agenda. I wanted a job.

To warm up for the read-through, I began to read the names on the plaque aloud, exaggerating each syllable until the monikers lost their meaning: Sarah Plotkins. Amos Carraway. Alan Detmire. Georgia T. Boyles. Raymond Fielding.

I stopped and went back to the last name. Fielding's work had been performed here. Here! And that other name—Alan Detmire. Hadn't I seen his name in one of the newspaper articles in Nussbaum's office?

"Like what you see?" A male voice sounded behind me. I whirled around and found the director from my audition—the one I'd dubbed Dull and Dramatic—standing at attention.

"Uh, hiya," I said. "It's certainly . . . interesting stuff. You guys aren't afraid to take a stand." I sidestepped back to the photos and he joined me, looking upon them like a proud father displaying the artwork of his children.

"The only way theaters in this town get noticed is by being controversial." He offered me his hand. It was a nice hand. "I'm Peter Sherwood."

This was Peter Sherwood, the mysterious guy who had invited me to the audition in the first place? "I'm Rosie Winter, and unless I'm mistaken you just cast me."

He peered through small wire-rimmed glasses that were fashionable ten years before but had since fallen out of favor. "You're the 'Tea for Two' girl."

Prickles of embarrassment burned across my hairline. "That's me."

"My apologies for not recognizing you sooner."

"Perhaps I would've been more familiar if you'd encountered me feet first?" What I took from a distance as boring and serious, was, up close, much more exciting. He was in his early thirties and possessed a bookish charm that doomed him to a life behind the scenes. His hair had a shaggy irregularity that suggested he'd either cut it himself or paid someone too little for the privilege. Stripped down or dressed up, he would've been a handsome man but left as he was, he was much more interesting.

"Don't take it personally, Rosie. I rarely remember the actors I cast, which is half the reason I cast them." Peter shifted a book he had wedged beneath his arm. A long German title stood stark against a woven red and tan cover. A sticker on the spine identified it as having come from the New York Public Library.

"Good book?" I asked.

He appeared startled to find the tome, as though the discomfort from having six hundred pages shoved into his armpit was something he'd grown to accept as normal. "Interesting book. I wouldn't say anything the Germans are churning out these days is good." He winked. "You never know who might be listening."

"That seems dangerous."

"That I'm reading their literature or that anyone has access to it?" He leaned in close to me and I inhaled a scent of oatmeal and Ivory soap. I bet he had a mother who didn't understand what he did but still came to every show he directed.

"Both, I guess," I said.

"If we're ever going to understand the enemy, shouldn't we know what they're being told?"

I had a feeling Henry Nussbaum wouldn't agree with him.

I wanted to ask him why he'd invited me to the audition and if he'd ever met Raymond Fielding or Alan Detmire, but before I could, two women I didn't recognize entered the lobby. Peter greeted them and instructed them that the read-through would be upstairs.

"Are you rehearsing two shows today?" I asked.

"No, just the one."

I waited for further explanation. When none came, I plowed forward. "Then are you sure I'm supposed to be here? The show I auditioned for needed two older men, an older woman, and me, and now you have several much younger female faces traipsing through your lobby."

"You're very observant."

"I don't know if I'm observant or paranoid. I've had a hell of a two weeks and I'm running low on sleep, so if I'm getting canned, please do it before I climb two flights of stairs."

"Don't worry: I'm not letting you go." He crossed his arms and shifted his weight. His left shoulder was curiously higher than his right. I followed the line of his body, seeking out the reason for the inequity. One of his legs was shorter than the other.

"Polio," he said.

My eyes snapped to his face. "I thought I was being more subtle than that. I'm sorry."

"Don't be. It's kept me out of the war. My mother swore I'd eventually be grateful for it."

I couldn't decide what was safe to set my eyes on, so I held his gaze and changed the subject. "So about the show—why the new cast?"

"We've switched shows. I'll be telling everyone about it today."

Ruby was right—that alone was vexing.

Before Peter could tell me any more, the lobby door yawned and the devil herself glided into the room, affecting an accent not heard since Philip Barry's last play.

"Peter, darling!"

At the sight of the ethereal beauty with the evil disposition, Peter forgot about me and limped into Ruby's arms. "Ruby! It's so good to see you. I was worried you wouldn't show."

She pulled out of the embrace and castigated him with a wagging finger. "I'd never disappoint you, darling. I overslept. I rushed over here so fast I must look a mess." She looked exactly as she had at breakfast, excepting the crumbs she'd wiped from her hairline.

Peter stepped back so he could better take all of her in. "If this is your idea of a mess, I'd hate to see what you do when you have time on your hands." Although the distance between them increased, there was intimacy in the way they stood that hinted that if they weren't lovers yet, they would be soon.

Ruby turned from him and focused on me. "Rosie, it's so good to see you."

I raised an eyebrow. Surely she didn't expect me to play like we were long-lost pals? What had she told Peter about me? If it were negative, would he have been so chummy with me? Or perhaps he'd forgotten whatever had been said and just now realized I was foe not friend.

Whatever it was, it didn't look as if I was going to find out. Peter glanced at his watch and clapped his hands. "Shall we go upstairs, ladies? It's time for rehearsal to begin."

Seven actresses other than us were seated elbow to elbow in a rehearsal room on the second floor. At the head of the table was the stage manager, a woman identifiable as such because of the timepiece she had set before her, the stack of paper she was collating, and a look on her face that made it clear some predetermined schedule had already been violated. Peter took his place beside her, and Ruby and I squeezed our way into the two remaining chairs. The other actresses tossed us quick glances intended to assess who we were in relation to

them. Two of the women were in their forties, one in her sixties. The
rest were our age or younger and all, while attractive, didn't possess
the kind of beauty that made you look at them twice.

Peter sighed and planted a smile on his face as a way of signaling
to us that we could be at ease. "Welcome, ladies. Let me begin by
introducing our stage manager, Hilda Cuthbert." Hilda nodded and
continued assembling her mimeographed pages. Her job was to keep
us in line and on schedule, not be our friend. "I appreciate your coming out today, especially since for many of you this was on such short
notice." He gave Hilda a knowing nod and thick packets of paper
began making their way around the table, each ominously stamped
SAVE PAPER, SAVE YOUR JOB. "As you know, we have opted to change
plays at the last minute. We have been given the opportunity to do an
exciting new work, one that is more prescient. I have appended the
cast list to the copies of the play, which are going around now. Before
we begin the read-through, I should point out that in many ways this
play is different from the works previously produced by People's Theatre." My heart leaped. "While we are certainly no stranger to contro-
versy"—he paused here and his audience tittered appreciatively—"this
play is the first for us that not only examines the war in Europe but
looks at it from the point of view of each nation's women. I think
you'll agree that this is a most unusual way for a play to proceed."

Again, the other women mumbled their consent. I slumped into
my seat until my head barely cleared the table. A stack of scripts
made its way toward me and I reluctantly accepted my meat. While
everyone else whispered with excitement, I stared at the cast list,
searching for what awful role I'd been assigned. Something wasn't
right; the character's names were listed with the actresses' names
beside them, but mine wasn't among them.

I flipped to the next page and found a list of who was assigned
which part. Here, at last, was my name, though beside it was the most
unsavory term imaginable: understudy.

I sucked in air so quickly the page drifted toward my mouth.
Understudy! Understudy? Maybe I was misunderstanding something.

Could it be this play was about plays and the characters were given names that were the generic terms one used in the theater? I scanned the rest of the page and found relatively normal monikers that gave no hint of theatrical terminology.

I gasped at confirmation of my demotion. How could I have gone from being cast in a lead role in a lousy show to this insulting position? Beside me, Ruby silently plowed through her script to verify she had more lines than anyone else. Of course—this was her doing. Never had I been assigned such indignity. I'd been in choruses and cast as nameless characters who were servants and ladies in waiting, but I always had a part I could call my own. An understudy wasn't a part. It was an insurance policy for someone who thought she was more important than me.

I couldn't decide what to do. My pride wanted me to stomp out of the room while uttering a melodramatic "I won't be so insulted," but my ego couldn't bear such a scene before a room full of people who would see to it the story circulated faster than C-rations at lunchtime. I decided to stay for the read-through in hopes the situation might be clarified. If that didn't happen, I could at least use the time to plot my revenge against Ruby.

I closed my eyes and silently counted to ten. When I opened them, Peter suggested we go around the table and introduce ourselves, indicating which character we'd be playing.

I clenched my teeth as the introductions began, each woman not being satisfied with merely listing her name but also her recent accomplishments and any accolades she'd received. When my turn arrived, I'd worn the enamel off my molars.

"I'm Rosie," I said, deciding that listing both my full name and recent roles would do nothing but highlight my descent. "And apparently"— I added a chill to my voice suitable for *Hamlet*'s Gertrude—"I'm the understudy." Peter raised an eyebrow, waiting for me to say more. I clasped my hands together and smiled sweetly to signal I was done.

Ruby began her monotonous recitation of recent print ads, radio work, and stage performances, pausing every now and again so her adoring fans could comment that they knew they'd seen her some-where and my but wasn't she good in *what's it called*? Another stack of papers began to make its way around the table, and I silenced the angry voice in my head in case this was a corrected casting list held back until now as part of some kind of stupid exercise.

"This," said Peter, "is a final formality. I must caution you about one thing: we've been asked to keep the fact that we've been given access to this play confidential. In fact it's so confidential, I can't tell you the writer's name. I know this is unorthodox, but no one in this room is permitted to discuss the script. Everything that occurs in this building must remain a secret. If you can't agree to this, we'll have to excuse you from the production."

My fury momentarily took the run out. Was this it? Could I have walked right into the missing play? As Peter instructed Hilda to be-gin reading the stage directions aloud, I stared at the script, hoping the play would alleviate my anger. It did just that, for as the reading began, my rage blew and was replaced by relief that I'd narrowly escaped being cast in a dog of a show.

The working title of the play was *In the Dark*. The unfortunately unlit were eight women of different nations and backgrounds whose lives were connected to the war and whose exposure to propaganda left them, as the title implied, "in the dark" about what was really going on. There was a Nazi sympathizer, a German hausfrau with no party affiliations, a Polish Jew, a Russian, a British aid worker, a fas-cist, a Japanese woman living in an American relocation camp, and a U.S. Women's Army Corps lieutenant. This cast of characters should have made for explosive drama, but the writer never examined the women's experiences in their own cultures. Instead, he showed mo-ments from before and during the war that served to express one common idea: they needed the war and they needed the Allies. The play couldn't have been more red, white, and blue if it were printed with colored ink.

Ruby played the saintly WAC, which was the best of the eight parts, though given the overall shortcomings of the play, that was a bit like being the whore with the nicest teeth. As the reading progressed, I overcame my amusement at the play's defects and found myself combing through the text—pen in hand—looking for something remotely inflammatory. There was nothing. If someone wanted to keep this play from being performed, it could only be because they respected audiences too much to inflict this poorly written garbage on them.

So this play wasn't *the* play. I had two strikes for the day.

The reading came to an end and Peter asked if anyone had any questions. One woman requested clarification about pronunciations, then Hilda passed out the rehearsal schedule and announced that we were all to be present at each rehearsal, regardless of whether or not our scenes were being blocked. The actresses slowly shuffled out of the room with Ruby as their caboose. I mulled following them, but my body was unwilling to move until I had an explanation for what had occurred.

Peter lingered at the head of the table with Hilda, quietly communicating instructions for the next rehearsal. Once Hilda was done noting her tasks on a stenographer's pad, she collected her mountain of remaining paperwork and left. Peter attempted to do the same, but before he could dust, I cleared my throat.

"I didn't realize you were still here," he said.

"Apparently I'm easy to overlook." I stood and we faced each other with the table between us. "I think you owe me an explanation. I'm the understudy, am I? That's a hell of a thing to tell a girl and a hell of a way to tell her."

"Ruby thought you'd be pleased."

"Pleased?" I put my hands on the table in an effort to look more massive. "I believe the words you're looking for are insulted and mortified. Why, pray tell, would I be pleased?"

"She mentioned a difficulty with your boardinghouse. She said this would help to secure your living arrangements." He continued to look bewildered and I wondered if what I'd originally taken as thoughtfulness was simplemindedness.

"Next time you decide to make a decision like this, why not let me in on it?"

"I apologize. And you're right: I should've contacted you before today, but there simply wasn't time. Besides, I was concerned if I told you beforehand, you wouldn't have shown up."

I laughed, no longer caring how horrid it made me look. "Wow, you're a prognosticator. It's good to know you have something to fall back on if this show flops. If you wanted to give me work so badly, why didn't you cast me in a part? I could've played any one of those roles."

He sighed and set his stack of paper on the table. "Most of these women have worked here previously. This is a very important production and it was vital to our board that we use performers who were . . . known quantities."

I didn't know how to take that. On the one hand, it was a perfectly rational reason, especially in light of the awful script. If you had to do a bad play, you needed good actors. On the other hand, I was no slouch. I'd worked enough that anyone should've been comfortable hiring me. "Why Ruby Priest? She hasn't worked here before. Was it her looks? Her talent? Because I can act circles around her."

Peter sat on the edge of the table. "I don't expect you to understand this, but it was an economic decision. I needed a name."

"And my parents didn't bother to give me one?" I huffed and I puffed and I blew my credibility down.

His focus shifted to his hands. "I understand why you're angry."

"You can't begin to understand." My voice shook the building like a bass drum. "I gave up other parts—real parts—to do this show because I wanted to work with this company." So I lied, what of it? "And now, instead of furthering my career, you expect me to be a second banana whose name's listed between the assistant lighting designer and the prop master."

He removed his cheaters and rubbed his eyes. "All I can say is I'm sorry, Rosie. I was under the impression this was something Ruby had discussed with you. It was a last-minute change. Had I done the other play, I would've kept you in the lead, but this piece came up and the opportunity was such that I couldn't turn it down."

"And a fine opportunity it is. I don't know what's worse—getting booted or getting booted out of a lousy play."

He ignored my stab at literary criticism. "I need you. I need a reliable understudy. Ruby has other commitments that will prevent her from being at many of the rehearsals. And all sorts of things can go wrong between now and opening night. You'll still get paid full scale and I'll make certain you get to play at least one performance."

"Yeah, a Sunday matinee in the smallest part available. I know the drill." I picked up my script and hugged it to my chest until the paperclip left its impression on my skin. "Why did you ask me to audition in the first place?"

"I don't know what you're talking about."

"Is that how you're going to play it?" I wanted to tell him where he could put his need for an understudy, but Belle's face projected itself on the wall opposite me. I may not have wanted this job, but I needed it. "You're lucky I'm desperate, because if I wasn't I'd . . . I'd . . ." I couldn't think of a good threat so I waved my hand at him and stomped out of the room.

I let my rage propel me down the stairs while I tried to convince myself not to cry. I failed, and by the time I arrived in the lobby hot tears poured down my face and dirtied my blouse. I plopped onto one of the lobby benches and mopped at my eyes. The gesture primed the pump until I wondered if it were possible to drown in my own salty water.

Calm down, I urged myself. *If this is rock bottom, things can only get better.*

"Rosie?" Ruby emerged from the ladies' room and approached me. Had I been a cat, I would've hissed. "Is everything all right?"

I tried to roll my eyes, but they bobbed above the waterline. "What do you think?"

Rather than taking the hint that I lingered on the knife edge between vile and violence, Ruby sat beside me. "You must be awfully disappointed." She passed me a handkerchief she had ready for just this purpose and I defiled it in a variety of ways before mashing it into my hand. "My heart broke for you when I saw the cast list. I guess the good news is, since you're still being paid, Belle can't throw you out. And I'll bet rehearsals will be loads of fun. I hear Peter loves to experiment."

I couldn't handle her forced merriment any longer. "How'd you pull it off, Rube? Did someone make a phone call? Or was a conversation with Peter enough for you to get your way?"

Ruby put a hand to her chest and gasped. "I can assure you I had nothing to do with this. Honestly, I can't believe you would accuse me of such a thing when it's obvious how bad I feel."

I laughed and my nose leaked. "Bad enough to give me your part?"

"I couldn't do that!" She shifted and replaced outrage with pity. "But if there's anything else I can do for you, anything at all, I'd do it in a second."

I had a laundry list of things, most of which would get me arrested. I discarded the worst of them and settled on the most practical. "Well, if you really mean it . . ."

"I do, I truly do." Her sincerity was so thin you could be arrested for wearing it in public.

I smiled. "I get a favor from you in the future—any favor I want."

"Within reason," she said. "Anything else?"

"Yeah, forget about your brown dress."

18 In Search of Justice

Ruby departed for her show at WEAF with a muttered assurance that my price (her dress and a future favor) would be met. I spent another ten minutes on the lobby bench before I was ready to face the world.

I was exhausted and opted to nix lunch and head back to the Shaw House for a nice long nap. I boarded a standing-room-only subway at West Fourteenth Street and Seventh Avenue and spent the entire ride glaring at a man who was too busy reading *The Song of Bernadette* to offer me his seat.

When I arrived home, Tony B. was sitting on the Shaw House steps smoking down the remains of a cigar. "Hey, Rosie! Can I have a word with you?" He toed a pile of ashes dotted with his telltale Cuban butts. He'd been waiting for me for a while.

I attempted to pass him on the stairs. "I don't want to talk to you."

"Jayne around?"

"She doesn't want to talk to you either." I shoved past him with my pocketbook clenched in my hand. If he so much as looked at me wrong, I'd slam it into his groin.

"Can you at least give her these?" He offered me a bouquet of red roses, which had been lying on the ground beside him.

I took his gift, smiled sweetly, and chucked it into the street. "I'll have her open the window and give them a looksy. Good-bye, Tony." I showed him my back and attempted to climb the remaining stairs. Before I could reach the door, he grabbed my elbow. "You've got five seconds to take your mitt off my arm or I start screaming."

He released his grip. "I've got to know if she's all right. That's all."

I whirled around and was pleased to find him two steps beneath me. At this level his eyes barely made it to my chin. "You want to know if she's all right? Isn't that sweet of you. As a matter of fact, she's not. She's got a goose egg above her eye, a split in her lip, and enough dark marks on her body that she could pass for a Dalmatian in the right light. Proud of yourself?"

He stumbled backward and took hold of the railing to steady himself. "What the hell happened to her?"

"Is that your game? She's supposed to forgive you because you don't remember what you did?"

Tony licked his lips and his tone softened into that of a remorseful boozehound the morning after another ruined family outing. "What did I do?"

I lowered my gaze until a perfect forty-five-degree angle could be drawn from my eyes to his. I wished I were one of the villains from *Astounding Stories* who could level her enemies with an infrared light that flashed red and burned like fire. "You beat her up."

All hint of machismo dripped out of his body and onto the pavement. "I swear to God, I didn't lay a hand on her."

"She might fall for your act, but I don't have time for it. Goodbye, Tony." Again I turned to go, and again his hand grasped my arm. "The same threat applies as before. Only this time, it's four seconds before I sing."

"Look at me, Rosie. Please." His voice was wet and desperate. Despite my better judgment, I turned toward him. His stature was more diminished than the step alone could account for. "Look at my hands." He released me and held up his manicured paws as though he were a cosmetic girl at Gimbel's who wanted to demonstrate how effective a new hand cream was. "You see anything? Anything at all?" I moved closer and examined his flesh. There wasn't a mark to be found. "Does it look like I beat someone up?"

"Maybe you were wearing gloves, or maybe one of your palookas did it for you. You've hit her before." Tony blanched. His mouth rippled with a fib I wasn't about to let find sound. "I'm wise to you. I see the way she is when you're around."

His head descended toward the sidewalk. "Once." His finger rose in the air to better connect me with the number of lapses. "It happened once."

"Once is enough."

His head lifted, his hands met in prayer. "I swear to you and God and anyone who'll listen that I ain't laid a hand on her since. She made it clear to me—that one night—she made it clear what I'd done could never be done again. I promised her and I meant it."

"And then you bought her a ring to cement the pledge."

Amazement flickered past his eyes. He didn't bank on my being able to put two and two together.

"A few weeks is hardly a marathon, Tony. You can understand why I consider you a suspect when my girl comes home black and blue."

He nodded again, so deeply his chin hit his chest.

"What happened on Friday?"

"She was mad at me and blew out of Ali Baba's not long after you did. I tried calling her the next day, but I was told she wasn't there." It was possible he was on the square. As scarce as I was in my efforts to avoid Ruby, there was no way I would've known if he'd called. "I decided to give her time, let her cool down, so I called here this morning to apologize and now I'm being told she won't talk to me. I came all the way over here and your den mother wouldn't let me past the front door."

God bless Belle; she may have forced me into taking a rotten job, but she knew when to say no and mean it. "Why was she mad at you?"

Tony scratched his ear and kicked an expensive wingtip into the step above his. It left an ugly ding in the leather. "There was this old girlfriend of mine, see? Jayne saw us talking and jumped to conclusions."

"You were just talking, Tony?"

He removed his fedora and studied its rim. "Maybe she gave me a little sugar when we were saying good-bye. It was nothing."

"Not to Jayne."

He kicked the step again. "In her shoes, I would've thought something was going on, too. I wouldn't have gotten mad at her for it, though. Would that make sense?"

Of course it wouldn't, but then logic and Tony B. weren't fast friends. Still, even if he wasn't a man familiar with sincerity, his concern for Jayne felt real.

"If she left you at Ali Baba's, how did she get home?"

"She waited until my driver got back from dropping you and Al, then he took her home."

"When the car dropped her off, did the driver wait for her to go inside?"

"Knowing Joe? Probably not. He's not up on the finer social graces." Tony returned his hat to his head and stuck his hands deep in his pockets. "You believe me—right, Rosie?"

"The jury's still out." Damn if there weren't tears in his eyes. They may have smelled like booze and burned at the touch, but they were tears all the same. I gently punched his arm. "I believe you, Tony."

"That one time, I was off my nut. I never would've done that in my right mind. I know you don't like me, but I love Jayne." I wasn't listening to him anymore. Instead, I was crabbing who the culprit could be. If Jayne had left not long after we did, she would've made it home less than an hour after me, so there was no way I could've missed her return. Whoever the hood was, he must have been waiting for her in front of the building.

But that still didn't explain why she didn't return right after it happened and why she was claiming Tony was the one who did it.

"How bad was she hurt?" asked Tony.

My fingers were growing numb from the cold. I squeezed my hands into fists until blood rushed back into my extremities. "She'll live, but somebody was trying to tell her something."

He turned and landed a roundhouse on the stone banister. Instantly his puss reflected regret at his bravado. "You find out who did this, Rosie." He shook his bloodied fist and a dribble of red splattered on the ground. "I swear to God I'll take down whoever touched her."

"I'll do what I can."

His uninjured hand parted his jacket lapels and ducked into a hidden breast pocket. He pulled out a pen and paper and hurriedly scribbled an exchange. "You need anything, call me." He handed me the page and backed down the remaining stairs, his eyes combing the street for the man who'd tangled with his girl. "And tell her I was here and I'm sorry."

Jayne was sitting on her bed, propped up by pillows, and flipping through *Life* magazine too quickly to be reading it. Churchill lounged in her lap and batted at the glossy pages more, it seemed, for the pleasure of the noise than to irritate Jayne. Two kids in military uniforms grinned from the slick's cover, both of their legs raised as they half-skipped, half-marched toward a war they couldn't possibly understand.

"You been in here all day?" I asked. Churchill shot me a look that urged me to leave his mistress alone.

"I didn't want to have to explain what happened to anyone. It's been nice. I took a long nap." In the daylight her bruises were shocking motor-oil drips on white taffeta. While the deeper blacks had faded to grays and yellows, there wasn't a spot on her face that hadn't suffered damage.

"You hungry?" I asked. "I could get you something."

She shook her head and turned yet another unread page. "Maybe later."

I dumped my script and pocketbook on my bed. Jayne registered where I'd come from and opened her mouth to utter the unasked question. I stopped her with my hand. "Before you speak, let me forewarn you that you'll receive an earful. Proceed with caution if you choose to proceed at all."

She plowed forward as only one still groggy with sleep could do. "How was rehearsal?"

I sat on my bed and piled my hands in my lap like a schoolchild preparing for a recitation. "Not only did they change the play, Ruby Priest got the lead and I'm an understudy."

Jayne shook off the remnants of her nap. "You're a what?"

"You know: an understudy—all the work, none of the billing."

She slammed the magazine on the bed. Churchill yowled and shot to the floor. "They can't do that!"

"They can and they have."

"But you were invited to the audition."

"Not to hear Peter Sherwood tell it." With Jayne outraged on my behalf, I no longer found it necessary to be angry. Instead, I plastered an amused smile on my face and pretended I was recounting someone else's misfortune. "I haven't told you the best part. The lousy Polish play has become red, white, and blue. You'll never guess who I think the author is."

Her brow wrinkled as she thought hard on the question. "Lawrence Bentley?"

I shook my head. "Oh no—even better. Raymond Fielding."

Jayne's mouth opened and closed, but no sound came out.

I fell backward onto my pillows. "Don't worry: if it is by him, it's not the play we're looking for, just a rotten coincidence. It's all hush hush, so don't breathe a word about it." I moaned and my moan threatened to become a scream. "My life is being ruined by Ruby Priest and Raymond Fielding."

Jayne winced. "What are you going to do?"

"What can I do? It's still a credit and a paycheck. If I drop out, there's no guarantee I'll find either of those before the week's out. I'm stuck."

Jayne twisted her fingers. Tony's ring caught the light and echoed his promise across the walls. "I think you should quit."

I started at the decidedly un-Jayne-like advice. "What?"

"You were dreading working with them anyway. You'll get another job."

"Didn't you hear me? I can't depend on getting another gig fast enough to please Belle."

"So you move out for a while. Would that be the worst thing?"

"In case you haven't heard, there's a war on. I'm as likely to find an apartment as Hitler is to surrender." I closed my eyes, hoping when I reopened them Jayne would be back from her mental vacation. Instead, *Life* magazine's mini-cadets continued their motionless struts, hinting that war was so much child's play. "Are you trying to get rid of me or something?"

"No . . . it just seems if things are so bad, maybe somebody's trying to tell you something."

I couldn't argue with her logic; nor was it fair to nitpick when we had more important things to deal with. "I don't have to decide right now. You should've seen the big act Ruby put on when I confronted her about it. She had the nerve to imply I was being paranoid when I suggested she was behind this. I'm telling you, she's got it in for me."

Jayne shrugged and slumped onto her pillows. As she landed against the cotton cases, she winced. Churchill climbed back onto the bed and offered her a hesitant paw to see if it was safe for him to return.

I rose and went behind the screen to change. "By the way—you had a visitor."

Her voice became piano wire. "Who?"

"Who do you think?" I shimmied out of my blouse and skirt.

"Oh." She paused a moment too long. I peeked between the screen's seams and watched her exchange longing for irritation. "What did *he* want?"

I pulled on a sweater and a pair of trousers and went back into the room. "To see if you were all right, for starters."

Jayne batted Churchill's paw away. "I hope you gave him a piece of your mind."

"Two pieces, and I hurled the roses he brought you into the street."

She froze. "He brought me roses?"

"Yeah. Expensive ones. If you look out the window, you can probably still see them."

She eased out of her nest and grimaced as bruises on her chest and ribs resisted movement. She kneeled on the radiator and peered at the street below, where afternoon travelers had turned Tony's roses into vivid red splotches.

"You didn't have to throw them away," said Jayne.

"And you didn't have to lie to me."

Her spine grew taut. "I didn't lie."

I joined her on the radiator and set my hand atop hers. "Tony didn't do this to you. He may be a no good rat bastard with a history of putting his hands where they don't belong, but he didn't do this."

She turned to me as her eyes overflowed with tears. "But he did. He hit me."

"Over Christmas? Sure, I know that. But he didn't touch you Friday night."

She squeezed my hand until I started from the pain. "He's lying to you, Rosie. Who're you going to believe, me or him?"

I pulled my mitt free and tested the fingers to make sure they weren't broken. "If you want to sit here and blame him, be my guest, but I have to tell you something for your own good: when you're not onstage, you're a terrible actress. I can tell you're lying and, more important, I can tell he's not." I again touched my skin to hers as though this would allow for the transfer of truth. "Who did this to you?"

Her lips looked ready to again form Tony's name, but before she could, she closed her mouth and swallowed. "I don't know." Her head drifted downward and studied the steel coil. "After the party, Tony's driver dropped me off. I went over to the streetlight—you know, to look for my key—and this sailor buzzes me. At first he starts talking real nice, acting like he's seen me in a show. He wants to know if he can buy me a cup of coffee. I thought it was safe—he was in uniform and everything. I was mad at Tony, so I said sure and we started walking toward Louie's." I froze at the coincidence. "Before we get there, his whole tone changes. He says I should tell you, you make a better actress than snoop, and if you know what's good for you, you'll stay out of this Raymond Fielding business. I thought that was it, he was going to let me go, but then he says he's worried I won't deliver the message as intended. He hits me across the face, and before I can register what's happened, he's beating me all over. I've never seen a man who was so strong. He finally stops, only he's holding me in place and telling me if you don't keep your nose out of other people's business, he's going to see to it Tony suffers an unfortunate accident." Tears rolled down Jayne's cheeks. Her hands grasped the windowsill and squeezed until her knuckles turned white. "I was so scared. I thought if I said Tony did it you wouldn't ask me why I wasn't seeing him anymore. If I stayed away from him, maybe this guy would leave him alone, you know, thinking we'd broken up."

"Oh, Jayne." I put a hand to the small of her back and rubbed it as my ma used to do for me. "Where did you go all weekend?"

"I got a room at the Martha Washington." The Martha Washington was a flophouse with two kinds of clientele: pro skirts and those who were too scared to go home. I ached at the thought that Jayne had been mistaken for either. "I was thinking, with a good night's sleep my face would be better, but . . ." Her tears came faster, turning her breath staccato. "You've got to stay out of it. Please. For me."

"I am, Jayne. I will. Have I said one word about it since last week?"

She grabbed my wrists and pulled me down to her level. "But this play . . . I know you. When this guy finds out . . ."

"I'm not positive it's a Fielding play, and even if it is, he's not going to find out. I told you it was on the Q.T. They even made us sign something."

She shook her head, silently confirming that wasn't good enough. "I don't want to be afraid to walk out of the building. And I certainly don't want to spend the next week praying that when the bruises go away I'll still be pretty."

"Of course you'll be pretty." I fetched a hanky from my bedside table and offered it to her. This wasn't the way things were supposed to happen. She was my sidekick in this adventure, the scintillating siren who distracted the bad guys long enough for me to get to the root of what was going on. She wasn't supposed to be beaten black and blue.

She dabbed hard at the corners of her eyes as though all she needed to stop the tears was to force them to flow in the other direction. "If you got another part in something, would you drop out of this show?" Jayne folded the hanky and blew her nose again.

"It's not likely to happen, but sure." I tried to hide my irritation at her fear. Shouldn't what happened drive us to action, not force us to retreat?

And shouldn't I care enough about Jayne to do whatever she wanted to keep her safe?

I pulled my coat back on and slung my pocketbook over my shoulder.

"Where are you going?" she asked.

"I . . . uh . . . you just reminded me. I forgot about this thing I said I'd do. I'll be back later."

19 She Stoops to Conquer

I HAD NO IDEA WHERE I was going, but I wanted to get out of that room. I stood outside the Shaw House and toed the ashes Tony had left behind. I wasn't mad at Jayne; I was mad at myself. Since Jim was cut down, I'd been living my life like some story in the pulps, never thinking there could be consequences to what I was doing. Jayne could've been killed because of me, and if I could fix that by quitting a lousy part in a lousy play, it was the least I owed her.

That and giving her peace of mind.

The morning's rain had turned to snow flurries, disguising the dirt and refuse of the Village in a coating of powdered sugar. I headed south on Hudson, pausing now and again to examine hats, dresses, jewels—whatever caught my eye in shop windows.

On my fifth stop, a human form ducked two shops above where I stood. I made like I was going to walk into the store whose display of the new, war-plant-friendly corsets so captivated me, then spun around in time to catch Al as he struggled to catch up.

"Aha!" I said.

A cigarette dangled from his mouth, and he wore neither hat nor gloves. Since I'd last seen him his appearance had degenerated from disheveled to death warmed over.

"What the hell are you doing?" he asked, though even this was stated on the sly to keep attention from us.

"I'm trying to talk to you," I said. "You got time for a late lunch?"

Al remained frozen in his path, his eyes jostling down the street, looking for danger. "I got things to do."

I turned down Christopher Street with Al on my tail. To the right of us the door to Schrafft's was ringing with the last of the late lunch crowd. "Things to do, eh? Let me put it this way: I'm going in there to have a cup of joe and some chow. It will be easier and more comfortable for you to observe me doing so if you also go inside." I bobbed my head toward the door to confirm the sincerity of the invitation and entered the restaurant. A pink-clad waitress with pencils stabbed into her pompadour directed me to a seat at the counter. As I opened my menu, Al slid onto the stool beside to me.

"Doesn't take much to convince you," I said.

He wrenched a second menu loose from the condiment caddy and flipped it open. "I like lunch."

As we read about the various plates that could be had for a little bit of silver, a group of girls still young enough for saddle shoes lingered by the candy display, giggling over their blackout sundaes. The waitress deposited two cups of coffee and a pitcher of condensed milk before us and then bustled away, distracting Al with the sway of her hips.

"So how are you?" I asked.

"I got no kick."

"You look like hell."

He wrapped his hands around the coffee cup, then lifted them to his face so he might absorb their warmth. "You don't look so good yourself. Were you crying this morning when you were leaving that theater?"

My morning with Peter and Ruby flashed before me. I no longer had private moments—every humiliation of mine was observed by Al. "I had a rough rehearsal. It's an emotional play."

He shrugged; experiencing pain for the sake of entertainment was a foreign concept to him.

I closed my menu and entwined my hands atop it. "Look, you can't keep following me and working for Tony. It's going to kill you."

"It's my decision."

"Be that as it may, I think I might have a way for you to continue doing both without jeopardizing your job. You interested?"

He shifted until his bulk was as close to me as the fixed stool would allow. "You've got my ear."

"Here's the thing: Jayne was worked over Friday night. Badly. She's too scared to leave our room, much less go outside. I'm with her most of the time, so I figure if you suggest to Tony that you tail her, you can watch both of us on his time, without having to kill yourself."

The practicality of my plan slid past Al. He'd heard only one thing. "She going to be okay?"

"She'll heal. On the outside." I sighed and shook my head. If I laid it on any thicker, I'd topple over from the weight. "But as long as she thinks this could happen again, I'm afraid she'll never be all right."

The waitress reappeared and tapped her pencil on her order pad until she had our attention. We both ordered the Spanish spaghetti and sat in silence until she left.

"Who did it?" Al freed his napkin from his silverware, causing the latter to clang as it bounced across the counter.

"I'm not sure." I chased the lie with some java. If I told Al that I thought Edgar Fielding was behind it, he'd have no choice but to point out that Jayne never would've been hurt if I hadn't started to look for the play to begin with. I couldn't bear that. "And another thing: not only did this guy threaten Jayne, he also said he'd put the hurt on Tony."

Al clenched his napkin until it could fit into a soda straw. "Nobody puts the hurt on Tony B."

"You don't have to tell me, which is why it's important you stick to Jayne like hair on a dog." His lips wavered but found no sound to accompany them. "I'll talk to Tony for you. It'll be my idea."

He pondered this. "And what about you? Where are you going to be?"

I didn't care about me anymore. "I'm not sure, but wherever I am, you can rest assured I'll be staying out of trouble."

•   •   •

After lunch, I bought Jayne some Schrafft's fudge and ordered Al to go home, get some sleep, and report for duty Tuesday morning outside the Shaw House. I refused his offer to escort me home and instead ducked into a phone booth in plain view to assure him I wasn't doing anything I wasn't supposed to. I deposited a dime and recited Tony's exchange. A gruff, male voice gave me the third before agreeing to put Tony on the horn.

"Charming secretary," I said by way of greeting.

"You can't be too careful. How's our girl?"

"Increasingly honest. And scared. I have a favor to ask, Tony. I want you to put someone on Jayne day and night 'til this thing blows over."

"I'll do it myself."

"Nix on that. I think you need to keep your distance for a while. Whoever did this to her threatened you, and I don't want her worrying about your safety on top of everything else."

"Oh." Tony didn't believe me, but he also knew if he wanted to see Jayne again, he'd do as I asked. "I'll put No-neck on her. He used to be a prizefighter. Anyone looks at her wrong will end up with two googs and a busted schnozzle."

"Um . . . not No-neck," I said, as though I were acquainted with the appendage-lacking gentleman in question. "I'd rather you use Al."

"Al?" Tony's tone made it clear that in a class full of goons Al was the dunce.

"Sure—Al. Jayne knows him, so if she crabs she's being tailed, she won't panic. I don't want her to think someone else is coming after her. Trust me: we need a friendly face."

Tony sighed and a pencil scratched against paper. I wondered if he had an enormous scheduling roster where he kept track of which tough guy was on which job. Maybe he even made them clock their hours. "Okay, Al it is. Tell her I'm asking about her, would you?"

"Sure thing, Tony." And with that I hung up.

•   •   •

I left the booth and tried to dope where to go next. I was glad I'd done something for Jayne, but it wasn't enough. Whoever did this to her was still out there, roaming the streets with his medal-adorned chest puffed up like Helen Hayes at the Drama League Awards. . . .

"Rosie?"

Peter Sherwood stood behind me, wrapped in a worn camel-hair coat and a tartan scarf that swallowed half his face. I didn't know if I should run or brace myself for a hit.

"Oh, hiya." My smile was so false we could've recycled it for scrap. I pulled my coat closed, not because of the cold but because I hoped it would help me disappear.

To his credit, Peter looked less than thrilled to see me, but did a better job of hiding it. "You live around here?"

"Visiting a friend," I lied. "You?"

"About a block up."

We both nodded at this information as if it were the most fascinating thing we'd ever heard. Behind us, a member of the Junior Red Cross rang a bell asking for donations. Across the street, a pair of young girls jumped rope in unison, singing, "Whistle while you work. Hitler is a jerk. Eany, Meany, Mussolini, Put Tojo out of work . . ." The wind picked up and sent a newspaper into our path. I caught it before it made it into the street and read and reread a *Blondie* comic. Not only was our heroine mad at Dagwood, but she was irritated more people weren't saving kitchen fats.

"Well . . . see you," said Peter.

I looked up from my reading material. "See you." He turned to go, and like a simpleton, I watched after him. He hadn't traveled ten yards when he stopped and looked back at me.

"I *am* sorry, Rosie."

I shrugged and shoved the newspaper and my hands deep into my pockets. I hoped he would take that to mean I was giving him the gate, but instead he limped the distance between us and hunted for words that would bring him forgiveness.

"I'm new at People's Theatre," he said. "I'm not sure you knew that. This is my first show." I hadn't been aware of that, not that his newness excused anything. "There's an enormous amount of pressure on me to ensure this production is a success and that forced me into some decisions I wouldn't otherwise have made. Please believe me when I say that under any other circumstances, I would've gladly cast you in a real part, but my hands were tied."

"That's good to hear." I didn't want to believe him, but like Tony, his sincerity polluted the air to such an extent that if I didn't acknowledge it, I'd gag on the stuff. I chewed my lip and willed myself to remember Jayne's face. "Unfortunately, I'm going to have to drop out of the show. I feel like I need to be doing something more substantial with my career."

Peter pursed his lips and nodded. "I can understand why you might feel that way. So you've worked things out with your boarding-house?"

My stomach churned. "Absolutely. They were very understanding."

He glanced at his watch, then took stock of where we stood. "I was thinking about grabbing a drink. Would you care to join me?"

I couldn't tell what his intentions were. Either he was determined to appease me so I wouldn't go wagging my tongue about town, or he wanted to convince me to stay in the show. And while I may not have relished the idea of rehashing why he was wrong and I was right, I was curious to hear his reasoning.

Plus, I'm a sucker for a free drink.

"I could be persuaded," I said.

We headed toward People's Theatre and landed at John Kelly's, a small corner Irish pub where a giant mutt of a bartender served one kind of beer and one kind of whiskey from casks that looked as if they'd come over on the boat with him. We sat at a table near the door, where we were blasted by frigid air every few minutes as patrons filed in and out.

The gin mill was dark to afford privacy to everyone in its confines. Unlike most such establishments, this one didn't try to dress up what it was by displaying ethnic memorabilia and pithy sayings. Instead, its decor disappeared into dark wood and dim lighting as a reminder to us that someday we too would vanish. Its sole concessions to the war were a vase of miniature American flags set in the storefront window and a photograph of FDR hanging above the bar. The air was heavy with smoke and body odor and the putrid combination of oil and gasoline that usually lined the nails of military mechanics. A phonograph whose speed needed to be adjusted played "In the Mood" much too slowly, stripping it of its merriment and turning it into a funeral dirge.

"Charming place," I said.

"What it lacks in charm, it makes up for in potency." Peter waved over the bartender and requested two mugs of beer. The man disappeared with a grunt, then installed himself behind the bar to portion out our drinks. He returned to us with both mugs in one hand and deposited them with a splash in the center of the table. Wasting no time on hospitality, he again disappeared.

"What if I wanted the whiskey?" I asked.

"Trust me," said Peter. "You don't." He lifted his mug and we clinked cheap glass against cheap glass. I tossed back the giggle juice until my tongue loosened and my nerve thickened.

"So . . . ," I said. "How long have you known Ruby?"

"A few years. I stage-managed a show she was in." Peter's eyes glistened in the murky light and his mouth drew itself into a lazy line that seemed better acquainted with pitching woo than conversation.

"One of Lawrence Bentley's?"

Headlights from a hack swinging past the bar window momentarily illuminated Peter's face. "No, this was before Lawrence. In fact, this was before Ruby. She was working under her real name back then." I was dying to know what ethnic monstrosity Ruby had been saddled with but knew now wasn't the time to ask.

"So I take it if she changed her name, the show wasn't a success?"

"Again, I commend you on your perception." He toasted me and emptied his glass to the halfway mark. "The play was very good but not in demand. A little too experimental, I'm afraid. You probably haven't even heard of the writer."

My stomach clenched. "Try me."

"Raymond Fielding."

"Ah." There he was again. "I'm familiar with him. In fact, I saw you. At his wake."

He raised an eyebrow. "I wasn't aware you knew Raymond Fielding."

I dropped my hands into my lap and twisted them into pretzels. "I didn't. A friend of mine was a big fan of his work, so I tagged along. Did you know him?"

Peter shook his head no and tilted his glass so he could better see the remnants of his beer. "Not personally, though I did correspond with him for a time."

"Is that why you decided to change to one of his plays?"

Surprise wiped the color from his face. "You're the first cast member to figure that out."

"Does that mean I win my part back?"

He ignored my joke and mopped the table with his coat sleeve. "I'm a tremendous fan of Fielding's work. I did my dissertation on him and committed *On Theatre* to memory by the time I was eighteen."

"So you were obsessed?"

He smiled. The wooden boy did have human feelings after all. "I prefer 'preoccupied.' Anyway, one day I got the nerve to write him and for several months we corresponded about his theories—or, rather, he expounded and I flattered. Eventually, the dialogue ended with the rejoinder that if I wanted to learn about theater, I'd be better off spending my time doing it than talking to some old theorist about his ideas. So I started stage-managing—his play was my first job—and once my feet were wet, I tried my hand at directing." He finished his beer and stared into the mug as though mystified that it didn't immediately refill itself.

"Did you ever hear from him again?"

He held up the empty glass and the bartender tipped him another. "He wrote me a few brief notes when plays I directed received good notice, and one much-deserved scathing commentary on a piece of rubbish I was involved in that was loved by the public and reviled by anyone with a brain. As my experience grew, I planted the idea in his head that I would love to direct one of his pieces. Months passed and then one day I received a letter from him indicating he was working on something he thought I'd be the perfect person to bring to life. He promised more was forthcoming. . . ."

I finished the sentence for him. "And then he croaked." Two new beers were dropped to the table and our old glasses were swept away. "So is *In the Dark* that play?"

He wrapped both hands around his mug until his fingers met. "No. There's been a rumor circulating for some time about this incredible play that would change theater forever. Everyone with a subscription to *Variety* had heard about it, but nobody had seen it or knew what it was about. Fielding so much as confirmed for me the play existed and had poured from his pen. This was the play he had promised me." I was feeling jingle-brained and not just because the room was filled with smoke. "I'm very happy to be directing anything of Raymond's, especially a premiere. I'd be lying, though, if I didn't admit I was disappointed in *In the Dark*. I have a feeling this is something he abandoned and never intended to have produced."

The second beer put me on the roof. "The feeling is mutual."

"You really didn't like it?"

A dozen callous responses danced through my head, but I still had the wherewithal to choose something diplomatic. "It has . . . uh . . . weaknesses, don't you think?"

Someone corrected the speed on the phonograph and changed the platter to Spike Jones and His City Slickers. As Spike told us what he wanted to do "right in Der Fuhrer's face," Peter removed his glasses and rubbed his eyes. "I suspect the work was intended to have more bite than it does. I know it comes off as terribly facile, but with some smart choices I think there might be a strong story to tell."

Right. And I've got this bridge in Brooklyn . . . "So how did you end up with *In the Dark*?"

"A very good question." He paused and emptied his second beer. "The play was sent to me anonymously, though I suspect it was someone close enough to Raymond to know we had a working relationship. I knew immediately it wasn't the right play, but I thought . . ."

I leaned into the table until my chest made contact with it. "You thought what?"

He rolled his eyes as if he were going to dismiss away the whole matter without ever telling me, but something stopped him and he plodded forward. "I thought maybe it was a test of some kind, which is why I committed to doing it. If I succeeded with *In the Dark*, then whoever it was Fielding left as custodian of his remaining work would send this more important play my way." He emitted a short burst of air to label his theory unworthy and ridiculous. "I know that sounds incredibly naive. . . ."

"I wouldn't say that."

He sighed and rotated his glass as though a change in perspective could alter the taste of the drink. "I think it's my way of avoiding the painful reality that he never intended for me to have the monumental play and this other script was to be my consolation prize: a poor play for a poor director."

Oh, boo hoo, I thought. *At least you have a job.*

"What are you thinking?" asked Peter.

Since I couldn't share my real thoughts, I blurted, "What if he *couldn't* give you the other play?"

"What do you mean?"

I traced a line down the layer of frost on my mug. "What if something happened to it before he could give it to you? You said a lot of people heard rumors about the script. What if someone filched it?"

He licked his lips and moved as close to me as the table would permit, so close I could see the faint white line of a scar on his nose, long since faded by sun and age. "Are you merely positing a scenario to make me feel better, or do you know something?"

A chill from someplace other than the door crawled up my body. This was the last thing in the world I should've been talking about, and yet I felt I owed it to him to tell him. I knew what it was like to wait for something that might never come. "I've heard a rumor from a credible source that the play was nicked."

Peter receded into the darkness until I could no longer read his expression. "In his obituary they noted his house had been broken into twice." I nodded, more frantically than I should have. "With all due respect, Rosie, I don't think that proves anything."

"I used to work for a private dick Fielding hired to find the play."

"Has this detective had any luck?"

I lowered my gaze to the table, where the dim overhead light reflected back on me. "No. He was killed at about the same time as Fielding and his files disappeared."

"Are you kidding?"

"I wish I were. Anyway, that should be all the proof you need that the great American play is missing and not being kept from you until you prove yourself. The question is, Who would've taken it?"

Peter splayed his hand across the table and tapped his fingers as he listed the possibilities. "A rival playwright. A bitter lover. A shunned actor."

"See, I think the play isn't just this theater-altering masterpiece. I think it reveals something about someone or something. Something shocking." Damn the beer—it was making it impossible for me to self-censor. "I think whoever took it wanted to keep whatever information it revealed from getting out."

"Interesting theory. So you intend to find it?"

I bit my tongue. "No. If my boss and Fielding died because of this thing, I don't want to be the next victim."

Peter frowned. "I had you pegged differently. After your display this afternoon, I assumed you were someone who was willing to go after whatever she wanted."

"What can I say? I'm all bark."

"I don't think that's true. In fact, I'll make you a deal: if you find this play and let me see it before anyone else, I'll see to it that you star in it."

I laughed; I couldn't help it. The last thing I wanted was to star in one of Fielding's disasters. "Let's revise that: if I change my mind and find the play, I'll let you see it before anyone else, but I get to choose if I want to be a part of it. *In the Dark*'s got me thinking that the only good Fielding play is a lost Fielding play."

Peter smiled. "Touché, though I do promise you he produced some remarkable work." In one smooth gesture, Peter glanced at his watch and signaled to the bartender that he was ready to pay up. "Forgive me, but I didn't realize we'd been sitting here so long. Is there somewhere I can walk you?"

"No thanks. I can hoof it on my own."

The bill paid and the remnants of my glass emptied, Peter helped me into my coat and we walked, side by side, into the night.

"Is there anything I can say to change your mind about leaving *In the Dark*?"

I chewed my lip and longed for a clear mind. Think of Jayne, think of Jayne, think of Jayne. "I don't think so, Peter."

"What if you stay with the production for the time being but continue auditioning for other roles? If you get a better offer, you're free to leave, no hurt feelings."

All he was doing was offering me the same arrangement Jayne had proposed. There was nothing wrong with accepting, especially if I promised myself I would absolutely, positively leave the production the minute another gig came along. And if, in the process, I learned more about Raymond Fielding, it would only be a coincidental benefit. "I could do that."

20 The Measure's Taken

As I approached the Shaw House that night, a man in an orange public works helmet turned off the last of the streetlamps, sending the block into a darkness so complete it was a wonder daylight could ever emerge. The interior of the building was no better. The lobby was empty and a lone lamp threw its meager radiance in a sphere extending only a foot from its base. I stumbled in this near blackness to the staircase and crept upward, half-expecting to find all of the other residents frozen like Sleeping Beauties removed from the activity of normal life.

The door to my room was closed, though from inside came voices engaged in a heated discussion. The male of the two was unrecognizable and much too refined to be one of Jayne's normal companions. The female's voice was low and soothing, even when made ragged with rage. I couldn't figure out what they were talking about, but the fact that they'd invaded our space to chin meant something was very, very wrong.

I armed myself with a gun made of my hand. As I eased the door open, mindful of its squeak, our unwanted guests revealed themselves to be nothing more than Jayne, Churchill, and a new radio resting on the radiator.

"Hiya, Rosie!" Jayne chirped from her bed. Her welcoming grin became a pout as she observed the lump I'd shoved into my coat. "Is that a gun?"

I removed my hand to assure her I was unarmed and disentangled myself from my winter things. "You scared me half to death. Where did the radio come from?"

Her smile returned; only now it rippled with the warm suggestion of a secret. "Tony sent it over as a gift during my recovery."

It was a newer Magnavox, smaller and more modern than the one in the lobby, with a glossy mahogany box that looked as if it would've made a very nice piece of furniture. Fibber McGee and Molly ended their argument for a brief word from Johnson's Wax.

"I've got news." Jayne sat Indian-style, which only accentuated how childlike she was. Her bruises had faded in the few hours I had been gone and that, plus her changed attitude, stripped her face of its ghastliness.

"Well?" I asked.

Her lips disappeared into her mouth, than reemerged with less lipstick than they'd had the moment before. She shuddered with excitement.

"Out with it," I said.

She took a deep breath and put her hands in her lap. "I've been cast in Lawrence Bentley's new show."

I hesitated, waiting for the punch line. "Really?"

"Really!"

I went to her side and gave her a clumsy hug. Her hair was freshly washed and smelled like gardenia. "When did you find out?"

She bounced as she returned to the bed. "Lawrence called me this afternoon. Personally. It's a speaking part and everything."

I tried to push aside the coincidence of Jayne's getting the radio and a plum role all in the same day. Tony knew how Jayne felt about his making arrangements for her. Surely he wouldn't risk her wrath when things were so shaky between them.

"What's the script like?" I asked. "Is it awful?"

She put her palms on the bed and stretched catlike. "I don't remember; the audition was ages ago. I'm sure it's bad, but who cares!"

"So you're not going to do the musical?"

"Of course not. I already called them and gave them my regrets. Bentley's rehearsals start in a few days." Her hands traced her cheekbones and lips. "I figure with a little powder and lipstick I'll be ready for my public."

"Absolutely. You'll look great."

"So where have you been?" asked Jayne.

I turned down the radio's volume and tried to remember what I'd told her earlier. Rather than selecting a lie that might contradict an earlier one, I offered the truth, or part of it anyway. "I had lunch with a friend. I brought you a little something." I removed the sack of fudge from my pocketbook and passed it to her.

She opened the bag and seemed ready to devour both my gift and my explanation until she remembered that all of my friends were her friends and if I was dining without her, it meant she'd been deliberately excluded. "Who?"

"Al."

Her eyes widened and she rose onto her knees. "If he's bothering you, say the word and I'll tell Tony . . ."

I waved her down. "Easy—no reason to call out the cavalry. We're friends."

Her eyebrow rose and whispered possible lewd interpretations of that word.

"Just friends," I said. "Nothing more. It turns out he was pretty close to Jim and has been keeping an eye on me as a favor. We had a nice chat and on my way home I ran into Peter Sherwood."

"Did you talk to him about leaving the show?"

The beer reexerted its force and I struggled to strip our conversation down to its relevant points. "Yes. He was surprisingly nice about the whole thing. He said I can stay with the production until I find something else, so either way I have a job."

"Oh. That's good." Her tone suggested otherwise.

"Just so you know: this isn't a Raymond Fielding thing; this is a money thing." I could've repeated that claim all night long and she wouldn't have believed me. There was only one rationale Jayne might be willing to accept. "Plus, I find Peter Sherwood . . . intriguing."

Jayne pressed her right hand against her left until her fingers contorted into an *L*. "What about Jack?"

"What about him?"

Her voice became irritatingly precious. I half-expected her to use baby talk. "It's strange hearing you interested in someone else is all. Especially with Jack having just shipped out."

"He didn't just ship out; he's been gone over a month. And you're the one who sent me on a fix-up the other night, remember? I didn't realize my ex-boyfriend's being at war meant I couldn't look at another man."

"It doesn't, but"—she switched hands and mauled the fingers on her left—"I didn't realize you'd officially broken up."

"If we haven't, he has a very peculiar notion of what a relationship is. Why?"

Jayne shrugged. "No reason. I thought, since you talked about writing him, maybe, you know . . ." She swallowed the end of her sentence, which was just as well; I'm sure I wouldn't have liked what came next.

"You've been listening to too much radio," I said. "Just because Jack went off to war doesn't mean either of us has grown up."

"People change."

"People? Maybe. The only way an actor changes is if there's a dresser, another costume, and a long enough scene to warrant it." I left her side and sat on my bed. "He's the one who left without saying good-bye. The last thing he deserves is my loyalty."

"All right already." Jayne lowered her eyes to her lap.

"I'm sorry." A pounding started at my temples and threatened to take over my whole head. I squeezed my nails into my palms and changed the subject. "Where is everyone tonight? It's a graveyard downstairs."

Jayne shifted onto her backside and stretched her legs. "Rehearsals, I guess. Belle decided to take advantage of the quiet and go see Sonja Henie in the ice show at the Garden."

"What about Ruby?" I kicked off my shoes.

Jayne smiled and rubbed her hands together. "She's out too, and I have some interesting information about her. Remember how she's supposedly in a new show at WEAF that was starting today? I've been listening since you left and I've yet to hear a peep out of her. Not only that, but when Lawrence called, he asked that I have her call him."

I lay back and closed my eyes. "Maybe they've etched the show in wax instead of broadcasting it live. So what? I'm her understudy, Jayne, not her mother."

A childlike lisp strangled Jayne's words. "No, she was definitely lying. Aren't you a little curious why she would've made something like that up?"

Because she's evil and wanted to make me feel bad about my own accomplishments just when something good was starting to happen for me. "Who knows?"

Jayne shifted and lowered her voice to the pitch used by German spies. "Here's my theory: when Lawrence called, I asked him who else was going to be in his show. He listed some names but said he still hadn't cast the leads and was planning on seeing a few more people before rehearsals start. I'd bet my left arm he's trying to get Ruby to rejoin the cast."

If Jayne was right, that would explain why Ruby needed an understudy. She took the People's Theatre part to guarantee she had work, knowing if something better came along she'd have somebody ready to take her place to alleviate any guilt—or professional damage—dropping out of the show might cause.

"Anyway," said Jayne. "I told Lawrence I knew somebody he should have read."

"You want me to audition? Why would I do that? The part's as good as Ruby's."

Jayne smacked me on the thigh. "You've got more talent in your pinkie than she's got in her whole body. If I forget to give her Lawrence's message, but tell him I did, he'll think Ruby wants nothing to do with him. Not only might you get a good part in a high-profile play, you could fix her good for what she did."

Plus, I'd get out of the People's Theatre show. I knew her grift. So that's why Jack was suddenly boyfriend of the year. If I was still thinking about Jack, I wouldn't be thinking about Peter. And if I wasn't interested in Peter, I wouldn't have any excuse for not leaving the People's Theatre show for Lawrence Bentley's gig. She was pulling out all the stops to make sure I had nothing to do with Raymond Fielding and his missing script. "He wouldn't cast me, Jayne. I'm a nobody."

"You know that's not true. He cast me, didn't he?" *Yeah,* I thought, *but only at the urging of the butter and egg man.* "Rosie, you're too talented to be an understudy. We both know that. I've got a good feeling about this. I know if you show up tomorrow he's going to give you that part."

Even if I was part of whatever deal Tony had cut, I had what it took to be in one of Lawrence Bentley's shows. And there was no telling what an enormous effect being in such a show would have on my career. But . . .

I rose and moved toward the window. "I don't want to audition for Bentley. I'm sorry about what happened to you, Jayne, but just because some thug decided to strong-arm us doesn't mean we should ignore what happened to Jim and Fielding. Two men have been murdered. We can't pretend like that didn't happen."

"I'm not suggesting that. I'm just saying things have gotten dangerous and it's time for us to step back and let the cops take care of it."

"They won't."

"Of course they will . . ." Her voice faded as she noted the look on my face. "You didn't call them that day, did you?"

"I tried to, but it was the same lousy copper they put on Jim's case. The guy's crooked."

"Then you talk to someone else," said Jayne.

"There wasn't someone else. There was just him."

"You lied to me." Her face crumbled. I'd never disappointed her before. It was an awful feeling.

"I'm sorry. I won't do it again."

Her expression told me she didn't believe me. If I wasn't careful, from this moment on I'd always be a liar to her.

"Look, I know I should've been straight from the beginning. But I also know part of you understands why I did it. Why else wouldn't you have buzzed the cops the night you were worked over?" I'd gotten her there. She couldn't have spent all these months with Tony without realizing there were moments when the law was an insufficient remedy. "I didn't intend to become wrapped up in this, but everywhere I turn it's like someone keeps trying to drag me back in. I could walk away from it and play it safe, or I could get to the bottom of what's going on. It's like the president said the other day: we know the fight's going to be hard, but that's no reason to back down, not when we're doing it for the right reasons."

"He'll kill you, Rosie. Whoever he is, he'll kill you."

"I know now," I said. "I know that this person means business and I have to keep my yap shut. From this moment on, I won't tell a soul that I'm looking for the play. And I'll make sure nobody else comes after you."

"How can you promise that?"

"You have protection." I told her about Al. "I'll do this if you want me to, Jayne. I'll audition for Bentley and hide in his show and never say Fielding's name again. But I'm asking you to reconsider."

Jayne's hand followed the line of her jaw before landing in her lap. I was wrong that her bruises had faded; they were still there, as crisp as stained glass.

"All right," she said at last. "Do what you need to do."

21 The Theatrical Illusion

I OVERSLEPT THE NEXT MORNING and took a cab I couldn't afford to People's Theatre, arriving fifteen minutes late for our first rehearsal. I sneaked into the theater and took in the auditorium for the first time. It was surprisingly large and ornate for an experimental space. It looked as if it could seat close to five hundred, though I doubted they ever got that many people to come to their shows without papering the house. The cast was spread out among the first row, some flipping through their scripts, others carrying on quiet conversations. They greeted me with the enthusiasm Park Avenue wives reserve for their maids, so I retreated to a seat in the rear.

Ruby was absent, which meant I got to pretend I was both the star and the lead. To start us off, Peter had us pair off with the person we believed our character would have the greatest disdain for. I teamed up with the "German woman," an actress named Heidi Lambert who matched me height for height. We introduced ourselves and bumped gums while the other women assembled themselves into their pairs. Once Peter was satisfied everyone had found their appropriate antagonist, he asked one person from each pair to join him in the lobby. When enough time had passed for those of us who didn't accompany him to go from uncomfortable to bored, Peter and the four women returned.

As our first exercise, Peter had us stand face-to-face with our partners and mirror each other's movements. Those of us who'd remained in the room led the exercise, while the others mimicked our motions, taking pains to do things at the exact same rate we did them. Once Peter was satisfied we'd achieved whatever nameless objective he'd set for us, he had the four of us he hadn't talked to don blindfolds while our partners led us by the hand about the theater, alerting us when obstacles were in our paths. After this exercise was complete, we did a few other trust-oriented activities most of us had done a thousand times before. Once we had built up simpatico with our partners, Peter had us switch roles so I was the one mirroring Heidi, leading her around, and catching her when she fell.

Strangely, Heidi never developed a rhythm with me. Rather than letting our mirrored motions become predictable—as they should— she attempted to trick me so I wasn't able to anticipate her move- ments. When I led her blindfolded about the theater, each step she took was hesitant, as though she expected at any moment to fall off a platform. There was something about me Heidi didn't like and didn't trust. Since we'd barely spoken two words to each other, this was incredibly disconcerting.

By two o'clock I was ready to jump ship and beg Lawrence Bentley for a part. Exercises like this were as experimental as putting butter on bread—every milquetoast theater company did something similar to build up trust and compatibility in its cast. Aside from developing insecurity about how someone I didn't know had grown to despise me, I was getting nothing out of the experience.

After a brief break, Peter explained that for our final activity he would assign each pair a relationship and have us improvise a scene in which a specific conflict had to be addressed. Because he wanted us to feel unself-conscious during this exercise, he asked the other groups to retire to the lobby so we could work independently with him.

When it was time for our scene, Peter asked for a moment alone with me. He ushered me over to the edge of the stage and we huddled as if we were about to make a football play. "You're getting married after a whirlwind courtship," he said. "What I want you to do is tell your mother the news and convince her it's a good thing."

I struggled to keep from rolling my eyes. Did Peter think all of this was innovative and exciting? What was next—having us don cos- tumes and speak words written by someone else?

We started the scene and all was proceeding quite normally until I announced that I was getting married. I expected Heidi to belittle the groom-to-be or to express concern that the marriage was too soon. Instead, she slapped me across the face, called me a whore, and exited the theater.

Needless to say, I wasn't prepared for *that*. Once I was done gasping in pain, I sank to my knees and curled into a ball.

"You're supposed to leave."

I started at the sound of Peter's voice, afraid that it was Heidi returning for another go at me. When I was sure I was safe, I plopped onto my keister and sought him in the dark audience. "I'm afraid that's not possible at the moment. Since I'm only an understudy, why don't you tell me what the deuce that was all about?"

Peter left his seat and came around to the apron. "Can we keep it between us?"

"Absolutely."

He smiled and his face turned pale pink. "I like to call it a trust diminishment exercise."

"And what's the purpose of such a thing?"

He awkwardly pulled himself onto the stage and took a seat on the floor beside me. "If I want this show to be more than patriotic blathering, I need to have each character attempt to convince the audience of the supremacy of her point of view. Each of the eight women believes her position is the only position and everyone else is the enemy."

I rubbed my cheek to make sure I still had feeling in it. "So everyone went through this?"

He crossed his arms about his knees. "In different ways. I told your partners vile, hideous things about each of you to put them on their guard throughout the day."

"Such as?"

He cleared his throat. I wondered if he was torn about revealing his magician's tricks or worried that I'd squeal to Actors' Equity. "Well, you, for example: I said I was forced into using you by a board member and you had made it very clear you had no intention of remaining an understudy and would do whatever necessary to get the part you believed should have been yours—the German woman. There were a few other things—total fictions, of course—that I selected based on what I knew about Heidi. Then I gave her a detailed character history for the upcoming scene, something she's been able to stew over for most of the day. I put Heidi in the position of being an old-world immigrant who was working day and night to create a better life for you. Back in the homeland you were a little darling, but since you immigrated you've ruined yourself by pursuing what you perceived as the American way: dabbling in booze and dope, and selling yourself to anyone who possessed either of those."

I had to hand it to Peter—his exercise was effective. Even though acting was acting, I wouldn't go near Heidi again if he paid me.

"Forgive me?" he asked.

I wasn't sure what I was forgiving him for: putting me through this exercise or ruining the experience by telling me his plan. "There's nothing to forgive."

"That's a relief." He pulled himself to his feet and offered me his hand. I rose with such force that we almost toppled over. For a moment we stood—still touching—in the middle of the stage, our eyes lighting on each other like two kids in a high school production of *Our Town*.

Then the moment ended.

"Ahem." Hilda cleared her throat to make her presence known. She stood at the rear of the auditorium, her arms crossed against her clipboard. "I'm sorry to interrupt, but I was wondering if I could have a word with you, Peter."

Peter dropped my hand like . . . well, like it was *my hand* and squinted into the distance. "Absolutely, Hilda. Absolutely." He turned back to me and wiped the hand that had held mine on his pants. "I'll see you tomorrow, Rosie."

•   •   •

It poured the whole way home. By the time I reached the Shaw House I was so wet I sloshed when I walked. Half the house was assembled around the radio in the lobby listening to a program I couldn't identify. No doubt something had happened with the war.

Let Jack be all right. *Please.*

"You ever hear of an umbrella?" asked Belle. With a wave of her hand she directed me off the wooden floor and onto the rug.

"I was dry when I left," I said.

Belle returned her attention to the radio. "Keep it moving; we don't need a puddle."

"What's everyone listening to?"

Ella Bart, a Rockette who was determined to parlay her gams into a career in the movies, pulled a lollipop out of her mouth and directed it at the Magnavox. "*Cavalcade of America.* Paulette Monroe's on."

I nodded, relieved it was nothing important and irritated that they could be focused on something so trivial. Paulette was one of the Shaw House's success stories. Two years before, she'd left us for Hollywood, where she played second banana to a number of much better known stars in the pictures. Whenever she appeared on film or radio, the Shaw House took notice as though we believed we could catch success as easily as a cold.

I left them to their listening and climbed the stairs to my room. Inside, Jayne was sitting on her bed, Indian-style, with her back to me. Churchill sat at her side, his gaze switching between her and the wall as he tried to figure out if she'd gone goofy. To this featureless bit of plaster she whispered, "I missed you, Jonathan. Not a day went by when I didn't wonder what you were doing and who you were with. Did you miss me? I like to think so. I like to believe that even as you fought I was there in your mind, watching over you."

I snorted at Bentley's sappy writing. Jayne whirled around, revealing the script nestled in her lap. "Hard at work already?" I asked.

She turned the script upside down to protect it from further ridicule. "I thought I should use my time wisely." An odd glow had come over her complexion. For a woman who'd been beaten black and blue, she looked radiant. "Plus...he's changed my part. I'm now playing the lead."

"In Bentley's show?" She nodded her confirmation. "Wow . . . that's swell. Really swell." She deserved bigger and better congratu-lations, but I was so surprised I wasn't sure what to say. "I guess he's given up on Ruby then."

"Yep. I asked him about her and he claims she's sticking with the People's Theatre gig." She paused and tried to read my reaction. "I'm sorry, Rosie."

"I made my bed."

"I know, but if he'd cast Ruby you might've gotten a better part out of the deal."

"And then you wouldn't have. Believe me—things are fine." I came to her side and offered her my hands. "Things are better than fine. You're the star!"

She returned my squeeze, then pulled her arms away to keep the water still dripping from me from making contact with her. "You're soaking!"

"Not anymore. Now I'm just dripping." I put on my bathrobe and wrapped my hair turban-style in a discarded towel.

"How was your rehearsal?"

"Both tedious and fascinating." I kicked off my mules and my feet came in contact with small, hard knobs. I lifted my leg and discov-ered black beads clinging to the bottom of my stocking. I followed the trail into the cavern made by my dresser. There, my one good evening bag lay in shambles.

I lunged at the bed. "I'm going to kill him."

Jayne rose and filled the distance between Churchill and me. "Take it easy. He's a cat. He doesn't know any better."

"The hell he doesn't!"

"It's only a bag." Jayne bent down to survey the damage. "Maybe it can be fixed."

I couldn't bear to look at the extent of Churchill's deed, so I stared down the feline until he leaped from the bed and retreated into the closet. "You touch anything in there," I told him, "And I'll be repair-ing it with catgut."

"It's not so bad." Jayne brought over what remained of my purse and gingerly laid it on her bed. "If you sewed the beads back on, I bet nobody would even notice." She fingered the loose handle and opened the purse's clutch to tuck it inside. As she did so, the contents of the purse peeked out, including Eloise McCain's check. "What's this?"

"I got paid for organizing the files," I said.

Jayne pulled the check all the way out and stared at it. Friday's date was emblazoned in Eloise's impeccable hand. "That's why you went to Louie's—to get paid?" I nodded. "How did you end up with coffee all over you?"

"A friendly visit turned nasty. Eloise's son came by not only to deliver the check but to find out where the files were. He was none too pleased when I told him I didn't know."

Jayne's head snapped up. "He's in the navy, isn't he?" I nodded. "Do you think he's the one who worked me over?"

"Edgar? I'd put money on it. And get this: he claims he's Raymond Fielding's son."

She traced the engraved address at the top of the draft. "Why didn't you say something?"

"Because you wanted me to stay out of it."

She jerked a nod and her gaze fell to Tony's ring. For a long time she stared at it as though the stone had hypnotized her. The room grew so quiet I could hear Churchill breathing.

"We could tell Tony," I said. "He could take care of Edgar for you."

She shook her head. "If Edgar's going around threatening you and me, he must be pretty worried that we'll find something." She paused and tucked her hair behind her ears. "We should go over there."

"Where?" I asked.

"Eloise's house." She picked up the check and carefully smoothed out its creases. "We need to figure out why she and her son are so interested in the play."

"Are you sure you want to do that?"

Jayne lifted her head and met my eyes. "Definitely."

22 Every Maid Her Own Mistress

WE TOOK THE SUBWAY UPTOWN and lost ourselves in the growing foot traffic. It was just before 5:00, but already the walks were crammed full of suits making a mad dash for the next train out of the city. The locals moved at a more leisurely stride, pausing to pick up the P.M. papers, which screamed with the headlines from overseas. It was good news as far as the war went. Nazi land forces were weakening around the African front. British bombers were continuing their attack on Germany's Ruhr region. The American government was halting rising corn prices so our farmers could produce more dairy and meat. People grinned at the front page, relieved that casualty numbers weren't clogging up the headlines with all their zeros. They were still there, though. Even when the dead didn't achieve the quantity that earned them two-inch letters, you could count them between the lines.

We paused at a traffic light and entertained ourselves by reading the signs plastered on telephone poles. WACs urged us not to marry unless we were marrying a GI. A tearful mother announced in bold type, I GAVE A MAN! WILL YOU GIVE AT LEAST 10% OF YOUR PAY IN WAR BONDS?

I'd have to get back to her on that one.

"What's the plan?" I asked Jayne.

She steered me right. "We need to get into her apartment and look around. Maybe one of us can provide a distraction while the other person searches the scene."

I stopped midstep. "You've been reading my pulps, haven't you? You do realize they're fiction, right? They're not how-to manuals."

"That doesn't mean you can't use them as a guide."

I couldn't argue with that.

I'd never had any reason to go to Jim's house before. In fact, I'd had no idea where he lived. The address on Eloise's check took us to Park Avenue and Fiftieth Street. We marched up and down the block twice before realizing the number we sought had been before us all along: the Waldorf-Astoria.

"She lives here?" breathed Jayne.

The limestone and brick building towered forty-seven stories above the street, a monolith to money and the things it could buy. Outside, doormen adorned with gold-colored epaulets opened car doors and assisted guests in and out of the building. Flags from a foreign land flew above the entrance while shoeshine boys and newsies kept a respectable distance, hawking their wares with knowing nods rather than the irritating chatter they used in our part of the city. We walked into the building as if we belonged and tried our best not to gawk at the marble floors and ornate bronze and wood decor. Scattered throughout the lobby were delicate antique chairs easily flummoxed by human weight and brightly colored Oriental rugs that bore no evidence of the foot traffic they endured on a daily basis.

A crowd was gathered at the lobby desk, drawing the attention of the hotel staff and house dicks who should've been monitoring our arrival. Foreign words flew through the air so rapidly that I doubted even those who spoke the language were able to follow them. The employees interjected apologies they addressed to "Madame" and "your Excellency," but despite their efforts, the haranguing continued, escalating like an aria until I was certain one or the other of the complainants would use up their air and collapse to the floor.

"If we go up, we go now," I told Jayne. "Follow my lead." I took her by the elbow and led her to the elevator bank. Between the doors was a marquee listing the permanent residents' names and suite numbers. Mrs. James McCain lived in the East Tower on the forty-fourth floor. We identified which car would take us there and pushed the signal button. An elevator operator so old he predated the inventor of the device greeted us with a smile that revealed an ill-fitting set of dentures. "She's going to kill us," I told Jayne. "We're a half hour late and Eloise was fit to be tied the last time that happened."

"You're her favorite niece," said Jayne. "She won't stay angry. She's grieving."

The operator followed our gab as if he were watching a tennis match and when we paused for breath interjected the question we were hoping he'd ask. "Going to Mrs. McCain's?"

"Yes, please," said Jayne with a smile and a wink.

"Forty-fourth floor, here we come." He pushed a brass button, then wiped his glove's imprint from the surface. As though it were afflicted by the same age-induced inertia as its operator, the elevator chugged upward at a pace designed to remind its passengers that while we might be too lazy to use the stairs, that didn't mean we were going to get there any faster.

After a lifetime the elevator came to a heavy stop and its shining doors slid open to reveal a modest lobby decorated with two potted plants that had managed to survive without any available light source. Eloise's scent lingered in the air, then coiled back on itself like a snake she'd charmed into threatening whoever should pass her threshold.

"Forty-fourth floor," said the operator. We exited the car and it closed with a *whoosh* that shouldn't have been assigned to so sluggish a device. There were two doors on the floor, one that bore only a number and another adorned with a tasteful plaque announcing MRS. JAMES McCAIN. I fingered the plate beneath the embossed metal letters, trying to read if Jim's name had ever appeared with his wife's and, if so, how recently it had been removed. There was nothing there to tell me.

We put our heads to the door and listened as Eloise's terse voice barked an order that her companion "use more care when mopping the floors." After she delivered her what-for, her footsteps grew in volume until it was a matter of seconds before she appeared.

We backed away from her entrance and hunted for a place to hide. As we were planting ourselves behind the plants, Eloise emerged from the apartment.

"Oh," she said. "I didn't realize someone was here." She was dressed to the nines in a black pantsuit with a matching veiled hat. Slung over her arm was a fur, too warm for the journey to the lobby, and an alligator clutch that matched her reptilian shoes.

I stepped around a scrawny palm and thumped myself on the head. "Ah, so *this* is your apartment. We were having the darnedest time figuring out which number went with which door."

Her ringless left hand caressed the fur; it purred in response. "What can I do for you?"

I urged my mind to think of something clever. When that failed, I begged it to think of anything at all. "Money." I pawed my (cheap, tattered) purse until I came up with her check. "Edgar delivered this, which I was terribly appreciative of, but I'm afraid the sum doesn't cover the other money I was owed. He told me I would have to take up the matter with you."

Her penciled eyebrows tipped toward her nose. "I thought my generosity more than covered both debts."

Even if I hadn't been desperate for an explanation for why I was there, Eloise's sum *was* short. I was owed six weeks' back pay, and while she may have guessed at what my rate was, the figure didn't begin to approach Jim's scale.

I matched my hoity to her toity. "I'm afraid it doesn't."

"How much will it take to resolve this matter?"

I named a figure that was only slightly more than what I was owed, since it seemed my inconvenience deserved a little juice. The alligator bag devoured her hand, then, recognizing the number was greater than what she carried on her, she sighed for the third time and announced she would need to retrieve her checkbook. She started back into the apartment and made as though she were going to close the door.

Jayne lunged after her and stopped the door with her hand. "May I come inside?"

Eloise took in the unmanicured mitt and stepped backward. "Whatever for?"

To snoop, of course.

"I need to use your powder room," said Jayne.

Eloise stared her down, searching for a sign Jayne was lying. Jayne shifted her weight in a subtle demonstration of her bladder's fullness.

Eloise pushed the door open its full width and gestured her inside in such a way that said since we'd already inconvenienced her, one more misuse of her time wouldn't tip the scales. "It's down the hall, first door on the right." She moved to again close the door, but I shadowed Jayne and wedged myself into the hallway.

"Do you need to use the powder room too?" she asked.

"No, but I assumed you wouldn't be so rude as to leave me out here by myself."

Eloise waved me into a sitting room, then disappeared into the same hall Jayne had turned down. The joint had as much in common with Jim as bunnies had with blitzkrieg. The apartment was sparse and modern. Bright white walls served as the backdrop for brilliantly colored abstract murals and sculptures. Stark wooden furniture void of cushions sat before a fireplace made of an amalgam of metal and stone. I admired the artwork or, at least, pretended to, since on closer inspection it was clear they were amateur attempts.

I moved closer to the canvases to identify the source of mediocrity. They were hung so high and the signatures were so small that the only way I could make out the artist was to stand atop a spindly wooden bench that wobbled the minute I put my big toe on it. I balanced as best as I could, then stretched as high as my legs would allow until I could read "E. Fitzgerald."

Eloise cleared her throat. I bobbled atop the bench and gracelessly climbed to the floor. "Did you do these?" I asked.

She sat at a small secretary, flipped open her checkbook, and licked the pen nib. "Yes."

"They're very good. Have you ever had a showing?"

Eloise signed the bottom of the draft with great flourish. "Many, many times."

"Do you still paint?"

For a second, something softened in her face. Though it was completely out of character, it looked as if she was about to let her guard down and speak to me not as a woman who was beneath her but as an artist who might understand her turmoil.

Then it passed.

"I don't see how that's any of your business." She handed me the check, taking care not to smudge the ink. "Where's your friend?"

"Still in the can, I presume."

Eloise cocked her head toward the hallway. "I don't hear water."

"Maybe she's not ready for it yet."

She met my eyes. Her eyebrow ascended in a silent question that she didn't bother to let me answer. She turned and headed into the hall.

On cue, Jayne appeared. "Sorry that took so long."

Eloise pointed us toward the door. "I assume you'll be leaving now?"

"Of course," I said.

She didn't see us out. We rushed out the door and into the lobby. Jayne signaled for the elevator while I waved the check until it dried.

"Anything?" I asked.

"She likes nice soap and thick towels," said Jayne. "Aside from that, nothing. You?"

"She's an artist. Not a very good artist, but at least that's something new. We need to get back in there."

Jayne nodded. "What if we wait until she leaves and see if the maid will let us in? We know she's on her way out, so it shouldn't take long."

Old and Speedy appeared and signaled for our descent. An eternity later, we exited the lobby and picked up a copy of the *Times* from the stand outside the Waldorf. We lingered near the newsie, taking turns spying the entrance to the building, shielding our faces with the news that the French had won a pass in Tunisia. Eloise emerged five minutes after us and climbed into a hired car. As soon as the bucket was out of sight, we returned to the lobby and asked Old and Speedy to take us back up to her floor.

We knocked on Eloise's door for a good twenty seconds before the maid answered. She cracked it open a sliver of a sliver. "Yes?" She had a husky voice flavored with an ethnicity I couldn't identify.

"Hiya," said Jayne. "My friend and I were just here and my friend believes she may have left something in the living room. May we come in and get it?"

"Mrs. McCain's not here." With more words to go by, her accent sounded Eastern European, but there was something forced about it, as if she were from somewhere else but had picked up English while visiting Warsaw.

"I understand she's not here," I said. Where was this belligerent attitude coming from? Given Eloise's past behavior toward me, I found it hard to believe she treated her staff well enough to earn this kind of loyalty. "I ran into her in the lobby, and when I told her I forgot what I forgot, she told us to come upstairs and get it. I know if we have to come back, she's going to be very disappointed."

There was a long pause on the other side of the door. Babies were born. Soldiers fell. "You are lying. Mrs. McCain would not tell you that. She does not like you."

"That's why she told us to come up here," I said, fists clenched, body ready for action. "She doesn't want to see either of us again. And she's going to be none too happy with anyone who's responsible for our return visit." I thought I'd convinced her, but rather than accepting defeat and letting us enter, she started to close the door. I no longer cared about snooping through Eloise's belongings, but I was determined to get into that apartment and give the maid my what-for. I pushed against the door, throwing her off balance and sending her onto her backside.

"Hey!" she shouted in unaccented English. Or at least someone did. Someone in a maid uniform who looked an awful lot like Ruby Priest.

23 The Lady Has a Heart

"Ruby?" Ruby Priest—stripped of makeup, hair in an untidy bun—lay sprawled, dogs in the air, drawers on display. I shook the confusion out of my noodle and leaned against the wall for support. This wasn't happening. I was seeing things.

Ruby walked her hands up the wall and rose to her feet. Irritation creased her face. "You need to leave. Now."

"What are you doing here?" asked Jayne.

Ruby grabbed us by the upper arms and attempted to escort us out the door. "I'm serious."

We stood our ground and leaned away from her hold. "I know you're serious," I said, "but we're not going to move one toe until we know what's going on."

Ruby's mouth opened and closed as she hunted for a threat to wield at us. When nothing emerged greater than the damage we could do, she released her hold and started toward the living room. "Then at least close the door and keep your voices down."

We clammed up until we were back in Eloise's museum of bad art and uncomfortable furniture. "What's the story, Rube?" I asked.

She sat on the bench with a huff and examined a hole that had sprouted in her stocking. "I'm doing research for a part."

"Let me guess: *The Servant with Two Masters*?"

She narrowed her eyes and I could tell she was doing battle with whether to continue protesting our presence or to tell us the truth and hope it would encourage us to sneak.

"Whatever it is you're researching," I said, "it's not for WEAF. See, Jayne's been listening and she has yet to hear your voice on air."

Jayne nodded her confirmation.

"So now you're both detectives? I told you I needed a job."

I sat in a chair that resembled a medieval torture device and offered the same level of relief. "You've got a job. You've got *In the Dark*, not to mention everything you've raked in from Bentley's swill. You must be rolling in dough." I was angry and I wasn't sure why. It just seemed Ruby wasn't supposed to be cleaning up after people. She was supposed to be wearing a Dior gown and having drinks under the clock at the Biltmore while plotting the next part she intended to steal. "Are you in trouble?" I asked.

She tilted her face heavenward. "I just need money. Is that so hard to understand?"

"Frankly, yes. I've seen your collection of glad rags. You don't need money—you need a day in my shoes."

She clasped her hands together and pleaded with some unnamed force to give her strength. "I didn't buy those things, Rosie; I was given them. If I could've gotten cash instead, I would've gladly taken it."

Numbers filled my mind and began to waltz. How could she be on the nut? We lived in the same rooming house, chewed the same food (and when she ate better it was on someone else's dime), encountered identical costs. Where was this great drain on her pocketbook that forced her to lower herself to polishing Eloise's silver? "Why?"

Ruby's eyes filled with tears. "It's none of your business."

"I thought we'd established that it is now. Put us wise or we'll start making things up."

She bowed her head. "My parents are in Europe. I promised them I'd get them out before things got any worse."

My stomach fell to the floor; I couldn't have been more surprised if she'd told me FDR had joined the Bund.

"Where in Europe?" I asked.

Ruby paused a breath too long. If I were directing the scene, I would've told her to pick up the pace so it didn't look like she'd forgotten her line. "Um . . . Poland."

I raised an eyebrow at her.

"Do you have a problem with that?" she snapped.

Jayne put her hand on mine and dropped into the seat beside me. "Of course she doesn't. So you're not American?"

"Technically, no, though I've been here for years. My aunt raised me."

Jayne scrunched her forehead. "But you don't have an—"

"Accent?" finished Ruby. She laughed to establish that even in this she had superiority. "I learned English at a young age and realized that if I wanted to be an actress, I would have to be an American." She paused and flashed me an accusatory look. "So now you know."

"I'm sorry." I bowed my head. Maybe she was telling the truth. It was possible she was not only human but loved people enough to make an enormous sacrifice for them. Who was I to question her? I couldn't even write a letter to Jack.

"Why not go to Hollywood?" asked Jayne. "There's money in pictures. You're good enough for them."

A flicker of pride passed through Ruby's eyes. "I know I'm talented, but the Shaw House is the only address they have." She picked at her skirt, removing something only she could see. "I haven't heard from them in over a year. The Nazis . . ." Her voice broke. "All of my letters have come back unopened."

I didn't have a witty comeback for that. Nobody did. "I'm so sorry, Ruby."

She cut the air with her hand. "What do you care? This war wasn't worth your attention until they bombed Pearl Harbor."

I fought the urge to retaliate. "You're right. It must be very . . ." My voice trailed off. "My . . . Jack shipped out last month. I know it's not the same, but I have a sense, maybe, of what you're . . ." No, I didn't. Even with my loose connection to the war, I didn't have a clue what she was going through. "I wished you'd said something before."

"Why?" Her eyes were dark and striking, no longer brilliant in their china-doll blue. "So you could have more of a reason to hate me?"

"We don't hate you."

She rolled her peepers at the lack of conviction in my voice.

"You can be difficult," I said. "Trying even. But we never hated you. Right, Jayne?" My pal nodded. "And knowing you're Polish wouldn't have changed our feelings one way or another."

Jayne twisted her fingers into a church, then a steeple. "Does Lawrence know?"

"God, no. Lawrence can't even stand foreign food."

"What about this job?" asked Jayne. "Doesn't Eloise know who you are?"

Ruby smiled and stared down at broken fingernails lined in kitchen dirt. "For somebody as wealthy as she is, she isn't a very cultured person. Besides, I don't play myself here. I figured if I was going to demean myself, I wasn't going to demean *myself*. I created a character who bares no resemblance to Ruby Priest."

Judging from her appearance, that meant she bathed biweekly at best. "How long are you planning on doing this?" I asked.

"Until I have enough money." Her eyes again grew moist. She took a deep breath intended to bury her emotion.

Jayne pulled a hankie out of her pocketbook. "You can cry, Ruby. It's all right."

"I don't want to cry." Her eyes lit upward as she fought to keep her impulses in check. It was beautiful and sad, and yet I was finding it harder and harder to buy what she was selling. An immigrant actress overcoming her past to succeed in the New World? Beloved parents missing in a faraway land? The brave and beautiful heroine forced to sacrifice her burgeoning career for her family? It was starting to sound too much like a Twentieth Century Fox flick.

"You can't tell anybody," said Ruby.

"We won't," said Jayne.

"I'm serious. Not a word about the job or my family. I know how you two are."

The lady was protesting too much. We were hardly the worst of the leaking buckets at the Shaw House. "Now that you mention it . . ." If she was telling the truth, I was about to make myself look colder than Charles Lindbergh denouncing the Allies at an America First rally. "It's not like Jayne and I owe you any favors. As a matter of fact, I believe you owe me one."

"What are you saying?"

I stood and walked the length of the room. "Just that you're asking an awful lot. Keeping quiet about your family isn't that big a deal, but in order to forget about this job of yours, Jayne and I will have to queer things to a lot of people who've been asking questions about what you're up to. If we're going to keep this secret, it's going to require quite a bit of effort on our parts."

Ruby rubbed her hands together. "What do you want?"

Jayne could barely contain her fury at my behavior. "Rosie—"

I dismissed her with a wave. "We need a spy," I told Ruby. "You have something we need: access to this apartment. We want you to find whatever dirt you can on Eloise."

Ruby crossed her arms. "I'm not about to get involved in something illegal. If you think you can blackmail me into doing your dirty work, I'd rather have the whole world know the truth about me."

"Oh, give us break," I said. "We're not asking you to do anything below the board." She held her stance, arms rigid, face haughty. If she'd had a sword, she would've been Joan of Arc. "We're looking for a play," I said.

"You said you'd keep your mouth shut." Jayne stomped her foot like a petulant child.

I ignored her. "Look, supposedly Raymond Fielding's great masterwork went missing right before he died. It turns out your new boss was his lover and her son is the fruit of that relationship. Fielding hired Jim McCain to help him find the missing play, and both he and Fielding ended up dead shortly thereafter. I think the play revealed something about someone that they didn't want to get out. A number of people are awfully interested in where it's gone off to, including Eloise and Edgar. We want to know why, and I'll bet dollars to doughnuts the reason exists in this apartment."

Ruby eased into a recline. She was now Cleopatra. "So you don't believe Eloise has this play?"

"Not yet," I said. "But she and her son seem to be working hard to find it. Do we have a deal?"

Ruby nodded and smoothed her skirt across her knees. "I think so."

24 A Lady Detained

"YOU PROMISED ME YOU'D KEEP your mouth shut," said Jayne. She and I were on the street, heading away from the Waldorf. Ruby had advised us to scram before Eloise returned.

"The opportunity was too good to pass up. You know as well as I do that if there's something in that apartment, Ruby will find it."

Jayne couldn't meet my eyes. "I just can't believe you were so . . . cold. You were practically blackmailing her right after she told us—"

"A bunch of hooey." I buttoned up my coat and bent into the wind. "I don't believe a word she said."

"War doesn't discriminate, Rosie. All victims aren't likable people."

"Oh, I believe that; I just don't believe *her*. She thinks we're a couple of saps."

"Because she's Ruby or because the story doesn't wash?"

"Both," I said. "Think about it, Jayne: the Ruby Priest we know wouldn't think twice about selling her grandma if she thought it would put her in a better position. Plus, there's a servant shortage on. You can't tell me that out of every mucky-muck in New York who needs a maid, she just *happens* to end up working for Eloise."

Jayne scrunched her nose while she pondered the evidence. "How could anyone lie about a family torn apart by war?"

"When it comes to Ruby, I think it's better not to ask any questions," I said. "For now we've got some help, even if it does come attached to a sour puss." We were heading down Park Avenue as evening turned to night. I hadn't been in this area past sundown since the dim-out started. It was unnerving to see that even the opulent hotels and homes had to obey the law and lower their lights. In the near dark there was no telling rich from poor; with our cheap coats and handbags we could pretend we belonged.

Jayne paused to pick a pebble out of her shoe. As she refastened her pump, a flivver pulled up beside us and popped open its rear door.

"Get in," said a familiar voice.

"Run!" I told Jayne.

Everything that followed came in a blur. The voice repeated its command, stressing its sincerity with a disembodied hand bearing a gun. I turned to make sure Jayne had heeded my advice and found her still planted beside me. A second hand emerged from the car and grabbed hold of my wrist. The gun pressed against my temple and my body went limp. As I was maneuvered like a rag doll, I was overtaken with a horrendous case of nausea. This, it turned out, was my body's way of responding to fear.

"You too, blondie," said the voice. "Climb on in here nice and quiet and Rosie won't even get a bruise."

My temple throbbed that it was already too late for that.

I made it into the backseat of the car, closely followed by Jayne. I swallowed hard against the rising acidic mix of lunch and terror. The doors closed and I blinked at my dark surroundings, trying to make sense of where we were and who was with us. At last Edgar Fielding came into view. Seconds after I made him, Jayne gasped in recognition.

The good news was I was familiar with our adversary. The bad news was I was familiar with our adversary.

I clucked my tongue and put a reassuring hand on Jayne's. The nausea left me and in its place my lower body began to shake as though the temperature had plummeted. "I see you found a gun, Edgar; good for you, though I'm starting to take this very personally. If I'm to believe we're friends, I must insist you be unarmed in my presence."

He angled his revolver until I was staring straight into the barrel. "Still being smart?"

"Still being dumb as a box of hammers?" I squeezed Jayne's hand to will the chill out of her flesh and put an end to my ridiculous shaking. If we were going to get out of this, we both needed our full wits. The car continued to idle at the curb. The front seat was separated from the back by a closed panel that prevented us from seeing the driver but not him from hearing us. I had half a mind to tell him to think of our boys in blue and kill the engine.

"Forgive my rudeness," I said. "I believe you've met Jayne?"

"She was looking better the last time I saw her, but, yeah, I've met her."

Jayne bristled beside me and her hand clenched mine so hard I was certain my fingers would never be straight again.

"Now that the small talk is over, what do you want, Edgar?"

He lowered the rod. "I understand you paid my mother a visit today."

My eyes flickered around the vehicle, trying to determine if there was anything that might assist our escape. Aside from ourselves and the gun, the backseat was bare. "I don't know if I'd call it a visit. She didn't even offer us a beverage."

Edgar smiled—or at least sneered. It was hard to tell in the dark. "I was surprised when Mother told me you stopped by, especially when she said you claimed I insisted you do it."

"All this over a little fib? If you're going to get upset every time I lie, this relationship isn't going to go anywhere." I sighed and shook my head. "Pipe this: I didn't bother to look at the check you gave me until today and I realized I was still owed some dough. I needed to be paid and I figured the only way that was going to happen was through a personal visit. Forgive me, but a girl's got to eat."

He responded to my monologue with slow clapping that didn't resonate very well with the rod in his hand. "Bravo. That was Mother's explanation as well, but I give you more credit than that. I think you went to see her for another reason."

"You do have the nicest bathroom in Manhattan."

"And if all of this was over payment, why is it you're just now leaving the Waldorf?"

"Dinner," Jayne croaked.

"You expect me to believe you two dined at the Waldorf?"

I followed Jayne's lead. "What can I say? Your ma's check burned a hole in my pocket and the concierge was more than happy to cash it on her behalf. Perhaps next time you can join us? Have your girl call our service." I reached across Jayne for the door handle.

Edgar cocked his gun. "I'm getting tired of your flippancy."

I receded back into my seat. "Imagine how we feel."

"I told you to stay out of our business, but since you two seem incapable of doing that, I guess I'll have to take further measures to ensure your silence."

I held my position and my tongue. If he was going to pump me full of lead, it was going to be because of his itchy finger not my big mouth.

Jayne shifted until her skirt kissed the tops of her thighs and left the rest of her on display. "Isn't this getting silly, Edgar?" she asked. "All this excitement over a little play. Surely it's not worth killing someone over?"

Edgar smiled wide, showing an impossible number of teeth for the size of his mouth. "What's two more bodies?" He knocked against the panel separating us from the driver. "Drive."

The car slipped into gear and Jayne's hand shattered my fingers. Before we could pull forward, a light tapping sounded outside Jayne's window.

Edgar ignored the noise and again signaled to the driver. "I said drive on."

"I can't," said a muffled voice. The speaker had a lisp, which made me hope we were being chauffeured by a small child who could easily be overcome with a stern reprimand and a promise of sweets. "Somebody's out there. Blocking me."

Edgar gestured for Jayne to roll down her window. As she worked, he took my arm and planted the butt of his gun firmly in my back. I held my uncomfortable position as the glass descended and Al came into view.

"What can I do for you, pal?" asked Edgar.

"I thought that was you," said Al. "Here I was walking down the street and I see these two dames and think to myself: there goes Jayne and Rosie. How're you two doing?"

"We've been better," squeaked Jayne.

"I heard about what happened to your face, Jayne. Rest assured, Tony's given me full rein to do whatever I like to whoever was behind it." He cracked his knuckles. "I'd just love to get a hold of that guy. Who's your friend?"

"This is Edgar Fielding," I said. "Jim's stepson."

"Good guy, Jim. He was practically family to me." Al glanced at his watch. "Say, I'm going to meet Tony B. right now and I know he's dying to catch up with you two. Why don't you let us buy you a drink?"

Edgar rammed the gun between my ribs. "Busy," I gasped. "Real busy."

Al put his elbows on the door and stuck his head through the window. "Ah, come on now—no one's too busy for Tony B. You know Tony B., Edgar?"

Edgar shook his head.

"He's a good guy, but he's got these two flaws: he hates it when people mess with his girl and he don't take too well to being insulted."

The gun found my kidney and rested on it like a tumor. "All the same, we're booked up for the night," I said. "Give Tony our regards."

Al nodded slowly. "Will do." He pulled himself out of the window and spun away from the car. Before he could complete the pivot, he turned back to us and put a large red hand on the door. "Say, you wouldn't happen to have a rod in your back, would you, Rosie?" The butt went deeper than should've been possible without surgical intervention. "'Cause your friend here might want to know there's a piece trained on the back of his head on the other side of the car. Now, he could choose to shoot you, which would be unfortunate, or he can let both of you out of the car and we'll walk away like nothing ever happened."

The gun left my insides and disappeared into the upholstery. "You're overreacting, pal," said Edgar. "The ladies and I were just having a friendly chat."

Al rattled the door to let us know he could rip it off its hinges if he had to. "Be that as it may, the ladies are leaving with me." He pulled open our door and yanked Jayne out of her seat. I scrambled after her and ducked behind Al. From this vantage there wasn't another soul on the street. Every movement we made echoed.

"I'm going to count on you to stay away from these ladies from now on," said Al. "Even one of your tires rolls near them, I'm going to see to it that iron of yours ain't the only thing shoved between your seats." Al slammed the back door shut and pounded on the driver's window. The flivver pulled away with a squeal of tires.

Jayne and I huddled as close as twins in the womb. I had an overwhelming desire to hug Al, but before I could act on it, he took a deep breath and made like he was going to say something. His index finger rose into the air, ready to tick off whatever point he wanted to make. The impulse escaped him, and he took another breath and again sliced the air with his hand. "Don't ever get in a car with an armed man," he said.

"We didn't have a choice," I said.

"There's always a choice. A guy with a gun in the back of a bucket ain't got no intention of you leaving that backseat any way but in a meat wagon. Get it?" He shook his head in what I imagined was a perfect impression of his mother catching him in some childhood crime. "Is that the guy who worked you over, Jayne?"

She talked to her feet. "Maybe."

"What would you have done if I hadn't been following you?"

"We had a plan," she said.

I disentangled myself from her. "We did?"

She elbowed me in the ribs. "Of course we did. We didn't walk into this blind."

We were in front of a storefront filled with photos of veterans from this war and the one before. Even in the darkness I could make out the stark black-and-white images. Some lay in hospital beds, their abdomens swathed in bandages. Others sat in wheelchairs or posed on crutches, their fifty-watt grins not bright enough to hide their missing limbs. A large sign sitting in the center of the images reminded us, ONE PINT CAN SAVE A MAN. It certainly didn't take much to sustain a life, and even less to end one.

Al turned his attention back to me. "I thought you were going to stay out of this now. What are you doing going to see Eloise McCain? That's asking for grief."

Jayne rose onto her tiptoes and addressed Al's chest. "It wasn't her idea—it was mine."

He glanced at his watch, then looked at the rising moon as though it were a more dependable portent of time. "I got to go. I'm getting you a yellow back to your house. You guys get inside and don't leave your room until morning. And you'd better hope I don't tell Tony about this." He turned to leave.

Jayne darted after him and blocked his path. "We're not children."

"I don't remember saying you were."

She stabbed him with her index finger. "You might as well have with all that talk of telling Tony."

"I'm here to protect you, see? That's my job. You want to get worked over again? 'Cause those are the options."

Jayne puffed out her chest. "I happen to think Rosie and I were doing just fine on our own. Do you see a bruise on us?" Her tone was clipped and irritated. Almost being killed had put her in a foul mood.

"Fine. You two don't need my help, then I won't be around no more." He stepped backward, the light from a passing car illuminating his face for the first time since he'd appeared. His eyes were red-rimmed, his schnozzle stained the same bright crimson.

"You got a cold?" I asked.

"Never mind about me." He pulled a hankie from his pocket and blew his nose. "I'm going. You two take care."

I crossed my arms and leaned against a lamppost. "Don't be that way, Al. We need you." He shrugged and showed me his back. "We're on the verge of putting this whole thing together and the fact of is, neither of us wants to back down until it's done. Before you showed up, Edgar so much as told us that he and his ma had killed some-one."

"So?"

I widened my eyes. "So maybe that someone was Jim." Al looked unconvinced. "Look, I'm starting to think Jim and Fielding aren't the only stiffs this play's going to leave in its wake. We've got to get to the bottom of this for them and whoever might be next."

Al turned back to me. "What do you two expect me to do?"

"We've got some questions for you," I said.

A wet cough wracked his body. "Maybe I've got some answers." He pulled out a deck of Luckies that looked as if it had spent most of its life beneath a couch cushion.

"You shouldn't be smoking if you've got a cold."

He patted himself down, looking for his lighter. "If I wanted a lecture, I'd call my ma." He tapped out a cigarette and within seconds wielded its glowing red ember.

"We need to know what you know," I said.

He exhaled a thin line of smoke that hovered above his head like a question mark. "You're tooting the wrong ringer."

"I'll be the judge of that." My foot traced a circle on the sidewalk. "Why did Jim marry Eloise?"

"I can't tell you that."

Jayne put her hand on his arm. "Can't because you don't know or because you're not allowed to say?"

Al's eyes landed on her hand and lingered there. "Can't 'cause I don't know." He backed away from her touch. "Look, me and Jim were business associates—that's all. Agnes knew loads more about him than I did. I didn't even know he was hitched till he died."

Agnes—of course! If there was one person in this world who knew Jim, it was his secretary and mistress.

The dimmed streetlights simultaneously shut off. A mechanical wail pierced the night. It was an air raid siren. In tandem, we all looked at the sky for enemy planes that might be flying in the vicinity. Spotter station lights danced across the blank canvas, their beams capturing nothing.

Al crumpled the cigarette package and shoved it into his pocket. "You two want to end up dead, that's your business. From here on, I'm out of this."

"Al . . . ," I said.

"I mean it. Don't come running to me."

"All right, break it up," said a high-pitched voice. We were held hostage by a flashlight's globe. "There's a drill on," said a boy who couldn't have been more than fifteen, though his demeanor made it clear he wanted to be taken as older. He was the neighborhood's warden, assigned the precious duty of making sure blackout blinds were pulled, lights extinguished, and streets cleared of anyone who didn't have a reason to be there. "You're not supposed to be here."

"I'm hailing the ladies a cab," said Al. On cue a hack with dimmed headlights pulled up. "We done here?"

"Absolutely," I said, then I followed Jayne into the backseat.

25 A Woman of No Importance

I GOT UP EARLY THE next day and left in ample time to see Agnes and still make my twelve o'clock rehearsal. I'd thought about calling her first, but something told me a personal visit would be more effective. Separated by miles of phone lines, Agnes would find it easy to change the topic or wallow in her grief (not that she wasn't entitled). I needed her to focus on Jim in life not death.

I took a cross-town bus and stopped and bought Agnes a houseplant on Orchard Street, at a shop overflowing with carnation crosses dyed red, white, and blue. Although it was early to me, the city was alive with people trying to use the war to inspire others to act. Next door to the florist, a group of coeds adorned with the unit patches of their boyfriends begged me to consider donating any extra clothing I might have to Bundles for Britain. At the storefront next to them a furrier had replaced his goods with a sign requesting donations of old coats so that he might make warm vests for the merchant marines. And across the street, in a more dubious attempt at patriotism, mannequins were modeling military-style jackets and urging me to buy them, because, "even if he's 4F, he can dress like a hero."

My plant and I arrived at Agnes's Lower East Side apartment just before ten. The windows surrounding hers had service flags with blue stars on them, signifying husbands and sons gone to war. Only Agnes's window was bare. As I rang her bell, her drapes fluttered. I stepped back onto the stoop to assist her in making me and plastered a smile on my face. She cracked open the door and in her weakest voice asked, "Yes?"

"It's me." No recognition showed in her eyes. "Rosie. Rosie Winter?"

"Rosie?" her weak, tinny voice echoed. Slowly, she opened the door its full width, and I was greeted by the sight of Agnes in a bathrobe with no makeup and an unruly head of hair that hadn't seen shampoo for several days.

"You all right?" I asked.

"Oh, you know . . ." Tears welled in the long red-stained corners of her eyes. She plugged her ducts with a tissue before rivulets could stream down her cheeks. "Please, come in. This is a lovely surprise." She looked down at herself and seemed to notice for the first time that she was in a robe. "I should change." Her eyes flew about the room, trying to identify where one did such things. "I'll be right back."

As she disappeared up the stairs, I entered a dark, unkempt living room and busied myself by making a pile of newspapers on the sofa. Still evident vacuum tracks and a lingering scent of pine hinted that there was a time when the joint was much more orderly. I circled the room, eyeballing her collection of knickknacks. There was something very odd about the place. While a mess, the furniture was higher end than one would've expected on a secretary's salary. And the colors were the dark, brooding sort one would expect in a man's den rather than the home of someone like Agnes. By a window sat a reproduction Chippendale chair and a small table loaded with slicks. I lifted their edges and uncovered a year's worth of *The Saturday Evening Post, Dime Detective,* and a songbook put out by the International Workers of the World.

No wonder Jim didn't seem to belong in Eloise's apartment. This was his home.

I peeked around a corner and found a kitchen in disarray. Dirty dishes towered above the sink. Unfinished meals rotted on the counter. A coffeepot sat cooking on the stove, though the burning smell made it clear its liquid had long since evaporated. I clicked off the burner and moved toward what should've been the dining room. Instead of housing a table and chairs, our office furniture formed a barricade that made it impossible for anyone to enter.

Agnes's footsteps banged overhead. She was on her way back down.

I rushed back into the living room and assumed my place on the couch. Upon her return I remembered the plant and thrust it toward her. She gave it a dazed look, as though she worried the world had changed so much in the past few weeks that people now donned flora instead of hats and purses. "It's for you," I said. "A gift."

She accepted the plant and tears again bubbled from the corners of her eyes. "That's just lovely of you, Rosie. So lovely." She sighed back her sobs and ceremoniously deposited the plant on the front windowsill. "It's funny; I feel like a widow and yet I haven't gotten one flower or note acknowledging the role I played in his life. This is the first . . ." Again the tissue was thrust into the corners of her eyes. "It means a great deal to me that you see me as more than just another mourner." She stared at the plant and came to some silent conclusion about it. She lifted the philodendron and wiped away the dust beneath it before carefully centering the plant on its chosen spot.

I sank into the sofa and the room filled with its aging melody. "I'm sorry to see you've been doing so badly, Agnes."

She shrugged and turned the plant until the side with more growth faced us.

"You need to give yourself time, but you can't let Jim's death rule your life. He wouldn't have wanted that."

She sniffled and returned the tissue to its previous purpose. "Someone has to grieve."

"People are—lots of people. Not a day goes by that I don't think about him, and I know a number of his former business acquaintances are lost without him." My comparison felt trite and cruel. I barely knew Jim; who was I to think I could barge into what was left of Agnes's life and demand she assist me? Where had I been when she desperately needed someone around? "You can't stop living because he has. What if you'd died instead of him? Would you expect him to wallow around the house not eating or sleeping or bathing?"

She thought about it a second too long, and I realized that, to Agnes, there was a direct correlation between the display of grief and the depth of love. She would mourn forever if it meant that her relationship with Jim would be validated as more than a mere affair.

I patted the couch and urged her over to me. "You're still young, Agnes. There are plenty of men out there who would appreciate knowing you. Jim's death isn't your end."

"I guess." She sank onto the pile of newspapers beside me, her feet dangling inches off the ground. In her feigned resignation I found a black ugly core of despair I'd been dodging for weeks. Who was I to tell Agnes to go on with her life? I had nothing.

Focus, Rosie.

"Why is Jim's office furniture in your dining room?"

Her head popped toward the entrance to the room in question. "Oh. You saw it."

"It's kind of hard to miss."

She bit her lip and turned her head away from mine. "I didn't want her to have it."

"Her?"

Agnes rubbed the sofa's arm. It was made of a plaid fabric that hid decades of stains and cigarette burns in bold, dark stripes. "His wife."

"How did you get it all here?"

"I paid some movers. Friends of my brother's."

"Did you take the files, too?"

She looked at me like a small child caught in a lie. "Yes." Her face drooped while she hunted for a rationale. "It's all that's left of him." Her fingers walked the distance between fabric lines. "Have you seen her?"

Was I being insensitive if she was the one who brought up the topic I most wished to discuss? I decided no, especially if I pretended that jawing about Eloise McCain was the last thing I wanted to do. "Uh, yeah. I've seen her once or twice."

Agnes inhaled sharply. "And how is she?"

"Fine, I guess. It's hard to tell. She's a very cold woman." Agnes nodded enthusiastically, urging me to go on. I paused to feign reluctance. "I was a little surprised by her lack of grief. It doesn't seem like she's behaving as a wife should."

A smug smile lit across Agnes's face. She leaned back on the sofa and spread her arms until it no longer looked like she was sitting on the furniture so much as conquering it. "I'm not surprised. She didn't love him. She never did."

"Then why did they get married?"

Agnes scooted closer to me. The grieving lover left and was replaced by the office gossip I adored. "Do you know who Cromwell Fitzgerald was?"

I thought back to Jim's funeral, when the man with the wine-stain birthmark had given me an earful. "The steel manufacturer?"

"And Eloise's father. He was a very influential man in this town. At his height, he had the entire police force in his pocket. Fitzgerald hated what the unions were doing to his business. Whenever rumors began that there was a strike on the horizon, he'd call the police commissioner and fifty men would be sent over to break up any organizing and arrest anyone Fitzgerald felt was a troublemaker."

I was so busy hanging on her every word that I forgot to breathe. "On what grounds?"

Agnes shrugged. "What did it matter? Most of it was trumped up, which the officers knew and ignored."

"How does Jim fit into this?"

"How do you think? Jim was a cop, and when he figured out the force was nothing but a puppet for Fitzgerald, he was outraged." I tried to picture Jim as an idealistic young man and couldn't. "Instead of forgetting what he knew and keeping his nose clean, he went straight to the top and wrote a letter to the commissioner, believing the guy didn't know the score. A few days later, Jim was called in for a meeting, and when he showed up, it wasn't just the commissioner waiting for him but Fitzgerald and a couple of goons from the force who Jim knew were turncoats. They railroaded Jim into believing he had only two options: continue down his current path and suffer the same fate as the union or shut his head, leave his job, and disappear with his reputation intact."

"That doesn't sound so bad."

Agnes smiled. "There was one other condition. Fitzgerald had a daughter who needed a husband fast. If Jim took the more pleasant path, he would also have to take a wife."

There it was—the thread that finally tied them together. I plucked it from the air and worked it around my fingers. As I did, I conjured Lieutenant Schmidt's smug, swollen face blathering on, the night I'd found Jim's body, about how Jim had been a corrupt cop. It had to look like that. One didn't blast the boss in one breath and marry his daughter in the next. "I don't understand why Fitzgerald selected Jim to marry Eloise, though. He seems like the last person he'd want to marry his daughter."

Agnes opened a crystal candy dish nesting on the coffee table. She plucked a handful of Starlight Mints from their resting spot and offered me one, which I gladly accepted. The room filled with the sound of sticky cellophane. "That was the point. He wanted to punish them both."

"Why?" I asked.

The candy clicked against Agnes's teeth, then lolled across her tongue like a beach ball tossed in the surf. "Eloise scandalized the family by . . ." She lowered her voice to a whisper, for whose benefit I couldn't guess. "Let's just say her son wasn't conceived with the benefit of marriage. By making her and Jim get hitched not only did she have to suffer the scandal she'd created, but she wouldn't be allowed to marry the kind of man she wanted to end up with."

"Someone with money and a reputation."

"Exactly."

I tried to imagine Eloise being so meek that she obeyed her father's every command. Hadn't she always been the queen bee? "Something isn't adding up here. How could Fitzgerald force his daughter to marry someone?"

Agnes snorted, which propelled the candy into her throat. She pounded on her chest until the projectile was dislodged, then coughed as insurance that the blockage was really gone.

"Are you all right?"

She waved me off. Relief turned her face from red to white and I knew that a single Starlight Mint had just confirmed for Agnes that she really did want to live. "I'm fine. What was I saying?"

I bit my own stale candy in half, then pulverized it into tiny bits. "You were explaining to me how Cromwell Fitzgerald could force . . ." Something was niggling me, something else the man with the wine-stained birthmark had said. "Wait a second—someone at Jim's funeral told me there was a rumor that years ago Eloise was up on murder charges and ended up escaping the rap."

Agnes couldn't have looked happier if I'd just told her Eloise was the one who'd been iced. "Even with all her money, people still talk about it."

"Talk about what?"

Agnes shook her head, and suddenly she was no longer my peer but a much older woman with more experience of the world than I'd ever have. "Edgar's father was an artist, someone Eloise was head over heels for. She became pregnant and expected him to marry her. When things didn't go her way, he turned up dead two days later."

"Wait a second—I thought Raymond Fielding was Edgar's father?"

"Who?"

"The playwright."

"Never heard of him. According to Jim, the guy was a painter. Eloise was the prime suspect in his murder, but apparently her father bought her way out of a trial and a potential prison sentence. In exchange, she had to do whatever he asked, including ending her painting career and marrying whomever he wanted. If she didn't do as he ordered—forever—she'd be cut off from the family fortune."

I followed my train of thought to the window. "So we have the reason for the marriage, but I don't see why Jim would've stayed.

He didn't like Eloise, so why keep up the charade for all these years, especially if he knew what she'd done? I would've left her the minute the old man turned cold."

Agnes cracked open the mint. "Let's just say that she made him an equitable business deal. Cromwell Fitzgerald may not have known it, but some of the money he gave his daughter was being used to help prove the innocence of wrongly accused union members. McCain and Son couldn't have existed without it."

26 You Can't Take It with You

I ASKED AGNES IF I could come back to look through the crates of files and she agreed that I could stop in in the next morning. I ran to rehearsal, where I perfected the art of thinking about one thing while doing another. During our mid-rehearsal break, I ducked into the lobby and called the Shaw House. Jayne answered on the first ring.

"I've been waiting for two hours! Why didn't you call me from Agnes's?"

"No time," I said. "Get this: Agnes took the files."

"Jim's files? No!"

Behind me, the other actresses shuffled to and from the bathroom. I lowered my voice and crouched closer to the horn. "On my honor, the crates are sitting in Agnes's dining room exactly as I packed them. She also took the furniture. She wanted it as a memento. And if that wasn't the find of the day, I know why Eloise married Jim." I quickly recounted Agnes's story.

"But what does all of this have to do with Raymond Fielding?" asked Jayne.

"I'm not there yet, but give me time. I'm going back to look at the files tomorrow."

Peter rapped on the lobby wall and announced that it was time for rehearsal to resume. I bid Jayne farewell and disconnected.

We spent the afternoon shattering the last remaining alliances in the cast, which wasn't too hard since already nobody was speaking to anyone else and the tension in the theater could've held a rhino at bay. When rehearsal came to an end, I grabbed my stuff and attempted to breeze. Peter caught up with me as I was on my way out the door.

"In a hurry?" he asked. It was a stupid question since I was posed with one foot on the street, but I told him no anyway. "I just wanted to let you know that Ruby is returning tomorrow."

I knew it was bound to happen sooner or later, but I'd been banking on later. I pulled my leg back into the lobby. "I'm amazed that you're so comfortable with her coming and going like this."

"I do meet with her privately."

I raised an eyebrow. "You do?" I conjured Ruby in a room at the St. Regis, wearing a flimsy negligee while eating bonbons in bed.

"Of course. We've been meeting in the evenings, though naturally the rehearsals are different in nature."

"Naturally." I forced a grimace. "How well do you know Ruby?"

Peter frowned. "We're not romantically involved, if that's what you're asking."

The room at the St. Regis disappeared. "I'm not."

His expression made it clear he didn't believe me. "Ruby's a bit of an enigma. For someone who loves attention, she's a surprisingly private person. But then I guess she gets that from her parents."

"Her parents?"

"Yes, the old man's a minister and the good wife supports the flock. Very conservative, very quiet. They came to Ruby's first show, the one I told you about."

I couldn't help but feel relieved. Ruby had definitely been lying. I was not an awful person. "They're here in New York?"

"They used to be. Upstate, I think. They were none too fond of Ruby's chosen vocation, and I think they had a falling out over it. It wasn't long after that show that she took her stage name. A rather ironic choice for a minister's daughter to become a 'Priest,' don't you think?"

"Ruby always was a clever one."

He leaned in to me, though instead of feeling put out by the gesture, I was warmed by the intimacy. "I'm very grateful to you, Rosie.

While Ruby may be returning, I want you to know that I still consider
you an integral part of this production."

"Thanks, I guess."

"I've been very impressed with your performance. I've told a number of people about you. You may not get the visibility you want
out of this production, but I guarantee you'll get work." He gently
brushed my hair out my eyes. My scalp tingled.

If Agnes was ready to move on with her life, shouldn't I be too?
Jack was gone, our relationship was kaput, and life was barreling on
without me. I could do a lot worse than Peter Sherwood.

I stopped his hand with my own. "Would you be interested in
getting a drink?"

His smile was delicate and sad, drawing the length of a missed
opportunity. "I'm afraid I have other plans tonight." He grasped my
hand until a touch became a hold. "Can we do it another time?"

I held on to him a moment too long. His palm was smooth and
dry. "Absolutely."

I struck a compromise between my desire for safety and my lack of
dough and took the subway home. Jayne was out, so I scammed some
dinner from the kitchen and had a picnic on my bed with Churchill
and *Burns and Allen*. We were halfway through our second roll and
the first commercial break when a knock sounded at the door.

Before I could ask my visitor to identify herself, Ruby poked her
head around the corner. "Busy?" she asked.

"In a manner of speaking. What do you want?"

Her eyes arced across the room, taking in the details of Jayne's and
my slovenly lifestyle. An ancient cup of tea coagulated on a dresser. A
bra wound its wire-filled tendrils about the radiator. The clothes I'd
worn to rehearsal were splayed about the floor like a bear-skin rug.
She sighed at the sight of our squalor and approached my bed. "How
are rehearsals going?"

I turned the volume down on the Magnavox. "Swell, though not a day goes by that we don't miss you. Fortunately for all of us, I hear you're coming back tomorrow."

"Was Peter talking about my return?"

"That and nothing else." I gave Churchill the remainder of my roll. He lay on top of it, his almond eyes challenging me to try to steal it back. "Hear anything from your family?"

Ruby sighed again and shook her head. "No."

"That's a pity, but I wouldn't give up hope. The mail can be awfully slow between here and upstate. I mean, those letters have to travel a good hundred miles through the war-torn Catskills. Fortunately, there's no summer stock to impede them."

Ruby backed up and pushed the door closed. "What do you want?"

"The truth." I left the bed and met her eye to eye. "And not that bowl of hooey you fed us the other day. I know about the minister and his wife, and neither seems to be overseas."

If Ruby had been any more shocked, we could've powered the chair at Sing Sing for a week. "How did you find out?"

I folded my arms and attempted to mimic her stance. "Never you mind: the point is I did. Why are you working for Eloise?"

Her nostrils flared. It was not a good look for her. "I don't have to tell you that. You don't have leverage anymore. Go and tell everyone you like that I lied. I won't care."

I thumped my finger against her breastbone. "You might not care about the house knowing your background, but you sure wouldn't want Mrs. McCain to know you're a fraud. She and her son aren't known for their hospitality toward snoops."

Ruby blanched. As fast as the fear arrived, it left. She buoyed herself until her head seemed an inch from the ceiling. "I have information for you," she said. "I've learned loads about Eloise's connection with Raymond Fielding. But if you insist on threatening me, perhaps I'll just forget what I found."

"So you've been holding out on me?"

A lazy smile stretched from ear to ear. "I prefer to think of it as waiting to divulge information until a more fortuitous time."

That was a good dodge; I'd have to remember it for later. "How do I know you're not lying again?"

"The evidence will make it clear. Of course, I have no intention of showing you anything unless you promise not to say a word to Eloise about me."

I was taking a chance, but something told me Ruby was on the square. "Go ahead. My lips are sealed."

She settled on Jayne's bed, her skirt billowing around her as though she were about to sing a solo. "Eloise was accused of murdering Edgar's father—his *real* father, not Raymond Fielding." She looked at me expectantly, waiting for applause or huzzahs or at least a gasp of amazement.

"Skip to the picture—I've seen the newsreel and I hope for your benefit that there's more to this information than that. Eloise killed her artist lover. Pop Fitzgerald was able to get the crooked coppers already in his pocket to get her off. In return, she had to obey his every word, including marrying a man she couldn't stand."

Ruby swallowed her disappointment and continued focusing on one-upping me. "Or face disownment. While Eloise put on a happy face for her father, she had no intention of being the dutiful daughter for the rest of her life. She was good friends with Fielding. He was just starting his career, and word was he wasn't quite the man he claimed to be."

"He was a nance? So are half the guys in theater."

Ruby flipped her hair. "This was before the Great War, Rosie. People weren't quite as accepting of those . . . sorts of relationships." I didn't need to ask Ruby where she stood on the issue. "Apparently Fielding was concerned this was doing injury to his career, so he and Eloise decided to circulate a rumor that Edgar was his, further distancing her from her lover's death and giving Fielding the manly reputation he needed. In exchange, Fielding would unofficially declare the child his son, going so far as to provide for him in his will. When

Fielding died, Edgar would get his estate, and Eloise would have the financial freedom to separate from her family and from Jim."

Things were getting weirder and weirder. "Sounds like an awful long time to wait."

"I don't think she intended to wait long. After all, this is a woman who's killed before."

It was a good story with plenty of motive, yet I couldn't help but wonder why Ruby was willing to share it with me. "Where's this evidence you mentioned?"

"Isn't my word enough?" With a look, I let her know it wasn't. She reached into her pocket and pulled out a packet of papers. "These are letters between Eloise and Fielding documenting the entire arrangement and a copy of his will." I grabbed for them, but she lifted the stack out of my reach. "I need to return them tomorrow."

"And you shall." She surrendered the papers and I quickly scanned them. Things were exactly as Ruby had said. Letters between Fielding and Eloise depicted two people desperate to change their circumstances. Fielding needed a reputation. Eloise wanted money so she could break from her father and Jim for good. I shook my head in amazement. "Why on earth would she save these things?"

"Apparently, she wanted to make sure she had legal proof of their deal just in case he should ever contest it."

"Why would he do that?"

If her smile could've wrapped around her head, it would've. "There's a catch: no one could ever reveal Edgar's true parentage, or the arrangement was off."

"That doesn't sound like a problem. Clearly Edgar and Eloise want the money and, clearly, they have no desire to dredge up the dead artist."

Ruby cocked her head to the right. "Of course they didn't, but that didn't mean Fielding didn't. If he found someone more deserving of his inheritance, say a lover, he may have been motivated to expose this information on his own."

Jayne came home an hour later. I tipped us a couple of drinks and filled her in on my afternoon.

"So Eloise and Edgar think the play reveals that Raymond Field-ing isn't Edgar's father?" asked Jayne.

"Yep. And if that's the case, they need to make sure it doesn't see the light or they lose out on all of his dough."

"Interesting." Jayne dipped her finger into her glass to sop up any residual gin. "So if Ruby really was lying to us the other day, why is she working for Eloise?"

"Why does Ruby do anything?" I thought we had our prime sus-pects already identified, but Ruby's behavior was more than a little odd. "Maybe Ruby's looking for the play too. It would've been easy enough for her to overhear us talking about it. You know how she's always poking her nose in our room. She could've put two and two together and figured out who would most likely have the script."

"I suppose anything's possible," said Jayne. "Why would she want it, though?"

That was a question I couldn't answer. "Maybe Ruby doesn't want it for herself. Maybe she's trying to find it for a certain playwright."

"You mean she's doing this for Lawrence Bentley? That sounds a little far-fetched."

"And Eloise and Edgar's motives don't?" I stifled a yawn. This whole thing was wearing me out. "At Fielding's wake, Bentley made it clear to me that he was disgusted by everyone's interest in the missing play. He even tried to convince me it didn't exist. What if he's wor-ried that if it does turn up, his new play will be overshadowed? After all, he had a hard time getting funding for it. It makes sense that he would want to prevent any competition."

"So Ruby and he fake a breakup, she gets cast in the People's Theatre show, eavesdrops on us, and starts working as a maid for the person who's most likely to have the play?"

I nodded. "And we helped her out by verifying that she was on the right track."

•   •   •

I pondered the suspects for the length of my drink. I dozed off in mid-thought and probably would've slept through the night—glass still in hand—if the phone hadn't started shrieking just before midnight.

"Rosie!" shouted Belle from the landing. I dropped my glass to the floor, where an oddly positioned Churchill hissed at me. "Rosie! Phone!" The only news that ever came in the middle of the night was bad news. My heart pitter-pattered as I stumbled into the hallway and took the receiver from Belle. Her tone matched her appearance: disheveled and ripped from much-needed slumber. "Do you know what time it is?"

"Not quite late enough to be tomorrow?"

Her stubby finger jabbed my shoulder. "This better be important. And whoever it is better not call at this hour again."

I nodded my understanding and attempted to shoo her away. She didn't move. "Hello?"

"Rosie? It's Agnes. I'm sorry to call so late."

I was so relieved that it was her that I went weak in the knees. I leaned against the banister and slid to the floor. "It's all right. What's the matter?"

She sucked in air so fast I expected to be dragged through the receiver. "The files are gone."

"What?" My head bounced against the banister. In a rare show of humanity, Belle sensed that now wasn't the time to aggravate me and drifted away.

Agnes moaned again. "A man came over and demanded I turn over the files."

"What man?"

"A big man in a naval uniform. He didn't give a name."

He didn't have to. The only way Edgar could've made his presence more obvious is if he'd left a calling card. "And you just let him take the files?"

Her voice reached a Wagnerian pitch. "They weren't mine to keep." She was right, of course, but that did nothing to squash my frustration.

"Did he hurt you?"

Her voice lowered. "He had a gun. And a mean disposition."

"Don't take it personally. He's like that with everyone."

"He asked me to give you a message."

I pictured amputated fingers floating in a jar filled with murky fluid.

"He said to tell you thanks."

"That son of a bitch." I clicked on the lights so Jayne would have no choice but to sit up and talk to me.

"What's the matter? Who was on the phone?"

"Agnes." I sank onto my bed. "Edgar showed up at her place tonight and took the files."

"How did he know they were there?"

"He must've tailed me." I punched a pillow. Feathers took flight and sank to the bed.

Jayne shielded her eyes from the light. "So now's he got . . . what exactly?"

"I don't know, but whatever it is, it was enough to get Jim killed. The play's as good as his."

Jayne sighed and pulled her blanket up to her chin. "Is that the worst thing? This proves once and for all that Eloise and Edgar are behind all this. If they have enough evidence to find the play, doesn't that mean the killing is done?"

I wrapped myself in my quilt and pondered her words. While Edgar stealing the files was a long way from Jim getting justice, if the files led him to the script, no one else would die. And while I wanted to see the darn thing to satisfy my curiosity, if he found the play and destroyed it, it would be a whole lot better than attending another funeral.

"You're right," I told Jayne. "Assuming Edgar finds what he's looking for, this is good news." And if he didn't . . . well, I didn't want to think about that.

27 Blind Alley

RUBY DESCENDED ON REHEARSAL THE next morning and I went from director's pet to persona non grata. Not only was my role at rehearsal greatly reduced, but Peter began to limit his contact with me, as though I'd been a stand-in for Ruby both onstage and behind the scenes. For the next week and a half I spent much of rehearsal sulking in the audience, alternating between telling myself that Peter had to devote his attention to Ruby in order to get her up to speed with the rest of the cast and convincing myself that Peter's ignoring me was all part of his effort to make me feel as alienated and bitter as everyone else.

To make matters worse, Ruby continued to avoid suffering the same indignations as the rest of us. Peter scheduled a rehearsal for an unheard-of Friday night but told half of the group one call time, and the other half another. Naturally, I was part of the first group and wasted an hour of my time pacing the lobby. When the second group finally showed up—initially apologetic, then self-righteous—the rehearsal was canceled since so much time and energy had been wasted arguing over who was right to begin with. Conveniently, neither Peter nor Ruby showed.

When Hilda declared rehearsal a wash, everyone silently took the gate in search of something to do to redeem their evening. I was the only one who didn't have plans, so rather than dwelling on what I could've done that night, I was overtaken by resentment that I now had an entire evening spread before me with nothing to do. I hoofed it out of the theater and onto the street. It was going on 8:00 and I wasn't tired or hungry or any of the other things one could rely on to fill their time, so I decided to walk home.

January was giving way to February, but what should have been the deepest part of winter had momentarily surrendered to springlike temperatures. I still had to wear a coat, but once I got my pace going, I was able to shed my hat and gloves and enjoy nature's reprieve. I wasn't the only one taking advantage of the good weather. All around me people had their apartment windows open, hoping to air out a winter of fear and sacrifice. The breeze carried their evening radio programs down to the street, weaving *This Is War* with *The Lone Ranger* and the glorious voice of Lily Pons performing *Lucia di Lammermoor* at the Met.

I let my irritation at Peter propel me forward, but after four blocks and careful analysis of how wise to human nature he really was, my anger subsided. I decided I would stop off at the Shaw House, find out where Jayne was, and meet up with her in time for a drink.

As my mood changed, my anxiety at walking home alone grew. One by one the lights around me disappeared as people pulled their blackout blinds into place. A bedraggled woman on a defense poster warned me, THERE'S DANGER WHEN PEOPLE TIRE TOO EASILY, WHEN MINDS ARE SLOW TO THINK, WHEN BODIES CAN'T FIGHT DISEASE. She had that right. But then there was also danger when pausing too long to read signs. There weren't many cars on the road, but I still kept my ear trained to every tire humming against wet pavement in case Edgar, disappointed with the files, should decide to host another impromptu meeting. Each time a vehicle came my way, I receded into the shadows of awnings long since extinguished of their shop light. I was feeling pretty self-congratulatory about my attempts at safety when a hand locked on my shoulder.

"Ruby Priest?" asked a male voice.

I shrugged the hand off and prepared to bash my purse into the head of whoever was behind me. "You're got the wrong dame, pal."

His footsteps ended, along with his pursuit. "I'm terribly sorry. Please don't be afraid. You look like someone I know."

I took a few steps back and turned to meet my companion. Henry Nussbaum, Fake Fielding's first suspect and the head of the New York Office of War Information, stood with his palms extended to assure me he wasn't a threat.

He shook his head. "I must tell you, the likeness is uncanny."

That's right—I'd told him I was Ruby the day I visited him at his office. "It should be because I'm her. I mean me. I'm me." If I could've subtly smacked myself, I would've. "I'm sorry, Mr. Nussbaum, you scared the skin off me and a girl can't be too careful."

"Of course. I understand." He removed a pair of leather gloves the mild weather had declared unnecessary. "I must say this is seren-dipitous. I was just thinking I should give you a call. Of course, then I realized I didn't have a way of contacting you."

"Sorry about that." Was he following me? I hadn't told him where I lived, or, rather, where Ruby Priest lived. Perhaps the name alone had been enough information to track me down. "Why were you thinking about calling me?"

"After you left my office, I became intrigued by our conversation. Did this imposter ever find what he was looking for?"

I took care not to pause, bouldering forward before he'd put the period on his sentence. "I'm not sure. After I saw you I decided it was probably best I stay out of his business."

"That was wise."

I struggled to recall what else I'd told him, but the rush of things I'd queered over the past few weeks became tangled, making it im-possible for me to remember what I'd told whom. If this continued, I'd have to start writing things down.

"It was nice to see you," I said, "but I should probably go."

He tucked his gloves into the crook of his arm. "May I walk with you?"

He seemed safe enough, but as Jayne's experience proved, one couldn't be too careful. I'd make sure we kept to Seventh Avenue, close to the road, and at the first sign of funny business, I'd sing until my lungs popped.

"Sure," I said.

We took the first block in silence while Nussbaum batted about whatever question had led him to me in the first place. Despite the temperate evening, I began to shiver. I buried my hands in my pockets and still my body shook.

We came to a traffic signal and stood waiting until the light changed. As though this were the permission he'd been waiting for, Nussbaum cleared his throat and came to his point. "After you left, I did a little research on Raymond Fielding. I'm embarrassed the name hadn't rung a bell when you first brought it to my attention."

"Did you know him?" I asked.

He continued forward, his stride so long I had to jog to catch up to him. "I knew of him." Nussbaum pursed his lips in imitation of someone mulling something over. "Given Mr. Fielding's background, I'm wondering if the missing item in question might be a play?"

I almost snorted at this belated revelation but decided it would be more appropriate to nod seriously. "Could be. So why do you think this imposter claimed you were the one person who would know where this missing item was?"

He removed his hat and studied the brim. "Perhaps he believed that the play or whatever it contained is something dangerous. If something controversial is being circulated, ours is one of the first organizations contacted."

"But he didn't say the Office of War Information; he said your name."

He returned his hat to his head. "I'm the New York regional director of the OWI. It's only natural that my name has become synonymous with the organization."

We came to another four-way intersection and paused until the pedestrian light beckoned us forward. Nussbaum plowed ahead, in the direction of the Shaw House. I darted in front of him to block his path. "You know what—this is my stop. Thanks for the company and the conversation. I'm sorry I couldn't be of more help." I spun around and headed toward the House.

"How's the acting career going, Miss Priest?"

I froze. Had I told him I was an actress? Even if I hadn't, it wouldn't take a master spy to turn up the career of the real Ruby Priest. "Better than detecting, that's for sure."

"You know, the OWI creates its own projects from time to time for radio and film. If you're interested, I might be able to send some work your way."

Was he trying to bribe me? Why? "Thanks, but I'm doing pretty good on my own."

"Are you in anything right now?"

If he knew what Ruby did for a living, he probably also knew if she was cast in something. I turned back to him and feigned a stumble to buy myself time. What if he had more than a passing interest in Fielding? Could he be connected to Edgar and Eloise, sent in their stead to find out what the files couldn't tell them?

"As a matter of fact, I'm doing a show at People's Theatre. I've just come from a rehearsal there." He didn't respond in any way to the news, which meant he probably already knew this but didn't know the particulars of the show being produced.

"What's the name of the play?"

I fluttered my lashes and played the coquette. "I'm not allowed to say, and truth be told, you probably wouldn't have heard of it. It's never been produced before."

He nodded, then turned in the direction we'd come from. "I might have to come see it. I've always enjoyed obscure theater."

I went inside and skulked up to my room. The encounter with Nussbaum left a bad taste in my mouth that I didn't think a martini could wash away. There was something rotten about him, but he'd managed to pull off our conversation without tipping his hand. In fact, the only thing that didn't add up was how he'd managed to find me.

I abandoned my plan to meet up with Jayne and instead climbed into bed and nursed my irritation with Cab Calloway and back issues of *Variety*. Churchill joined me, risking closeness in exchange for warmth. As he lay long against my side, I found myself resisting the urge to stroke him. I had been much too long without human companionship if I found myself fighting friendly impulses toward a feline.

As I read about auditions that had already happened and productions that had opened and closed, my eyes grew heavy and I began to nod off. Just before my face met the pillow, a knock sounded at the door.

I snapped up and rubbed the sleep from my eyes. Churchill sprang from my body as though I were the ugliest girl at school and he feared his friends were about to catch us together. "Come in," I said to my visitor.

Ruby slinked through the door and closed it behind her. "Are you alone?"

Very, very alone. "Just me and the cat." Churchill shot me a look that made it clear he'd rather not be associated with my company. "What do you want?"

"How was rehearsal?" she asked.

"Canceled. Which you would have known if you'd attended."

"I had a personal matter to attend to. Why was it canceled?"

Since she showed no sign of leaving, I gave her the rundown on Peter's latest game.

"That was a mean trick," she said.

Were we just having a normal conversation? I wasn't sure. "It may have been mean, but it was ingenious."

"I hate having my time wasted. He knows that." I expected her to flounce out of the room, having spent time with me only to find out what she'd missed, but instead of doing so, she curled up on my bed and patted the coverlet to lure Churchill over to her.

"That was the point of the exercise, Rube. And the nice thing is, Peter never does the same thing twice, so we can rest comfortably, knowing this is the last time we'll be wasting a Friday night for this show, public performances aside."

Ruby rolled Churchill onto his back. "Did you miss out on anything tonight?"

I hated to admit I had no social life, so I invented plans. "A picture. A drink. The usual."

Churchill batted at her hair and received a stern reminder that one does not touch Ruby Priest without invitation. "Did your friend catch up with you?"

"What friend?"

"An older gentleman, very handsome. He was lurking outside the building when I got home and asked me if you were around. I told him you were probably still at rehearsal."

All of my muscles simultaneously stopped functioning. "And he asked for me?"

Ruby fluttered her lashes. "He called you *Rosalind.* In his mouth it was pure poetry."

My mind zipped about trying to determine how Henry Nussbaum knew I wasn't Ruby. "Did he ask you anything else about me?"

She kneaded Churchill's belly until his leg shook with satisfaction. "Just which theater you were at. I gave him directions and he left."

The photos! He must have called around and found out Ruby lived at the Shaw House, entered the building, and seen the headshots on the wall. Mine identified me by my full name. All he had to do was realize the moniker didn't match the puss and *poof*—my trick was revealed.

"I have something else I need to tell you," said Ruby. "Edgar Fielding is dead."

I shot up so fast Churchill hit the wall. "What?"

"They found his body in Eloise's apartment this morning. That's why I wasn't at rehearsal tonight. The police say it was a single gunshot to the temple."

For a brief moment I felt glee at Edgar getting his what-for. Almost as quickly as it arrived, it vanished. Edgar may have been a louse, but I didn't think he had this coming to him. More important, what did this mean? Was Edgar's murder a random killing, or did we have to assume that while he may have wanted the play, he wasn't the only one after it?

"Did anything get delivered to their apartment in the last week or so? Say a bunch of crates?"

Ruby shook her head. "Not that I know of, but I wasn't allowed in his room. The whole apartment was ransacked. Eloise brought me in to help her clean up."

Eloise wouldn't have killed her own son for the play; that wouldn't make sense, especially if the files were missing again. But Nussbaum might have, or Lawrence Bentley, or—

"Are you all right?" Ruby asked.

"I think I'm getting a cold," I said.

Her hands flew up to her face to create an impromptu mask. "A cold? Maybe I should go. I would hate to jeopardize the production."

"Understood," I said.

Once Ruby was gone, I coaxed Churchill back to my side and burrowed beneath my covers. So the killer was still loose. And the files and the play were still missing. And Fake Fielding was—

"You two make a nice picture." Jayne entered the room and slung her evening bag onto the dresser. Churchill rose and stretched reverentially. "I thought you had rehearsal tonight?"

"It was an alienation exercise. We were done being set against one another by seven thirty."

Jayne removed her coat and plucked a pair of rhinestone earrings from her lobes. "That's crazy. Your whole night wasted for nothing. Unzip me?" She had on a spectacular bronze gown that plunged to her waist. She showed me her back and I coaxed the zipper past her girdle. "You should've come out with us. Tony took me to dinner at the Copacabana."

"You went out with Tony?"

"I figured it was safe. With the files back where they belong, I didn't think Edgar would be threatening anyone any time soon."

"You can say that again—Edgar's dead."

Jayne held her position for an eternity before slowly turning back to me. "When?"

"They found the body this morning. And it looks like the files are missing again."

She sank to her bed and clasped her hands in prayer. "Oh, God." Her face crumbled and her eyes grew watery. I couldn't begin to understand where the emotion was coming from. Two men had already died; why this grief for a third who'd worked her over then threatened to kill her? "He said he wanted to celebrate, but he wouldn't tell me why. I figured business was good."

"Who are you talking about? Tony?" Jayne nodded. "What are you saying?"

"Al told Tony who slapped me around." Her eyes held mine and communicated everything she feared had come to pass.

"He wouldn't," I said. "That's not the way Tony operates. He'd rough him up, sure. Teach him a lesson. But he wouldn't . . . not where . . ." I stopped myself before I finished the thought. "This has nothing to do with Tony. It's the play, Jayne. It has to be. We weren't the only ones who didn't want Edgar to find it." Was it better to suspect Edgar had been murdered by the same unknown killer who'd zotzed Jim and Raymond or to hope that Tony had intervened and we had nothing to fear but him?

"You're right," said Jayne. "Of course you're right." She stood and wiggled out of the dress. "So if the killer's still loose, who is it?"

"I have a couple of thoughts." I told her about my strange escort home. As I gave her the lay, I attempted to make sense of Nussbaum's renewed interest. What did he and Fielding have in common? They were both men, approximately the same age, but other than that, there were no similarities. The only connection between them could be the play: something Fielding wrote that Nussbaum, as the director of the OWI, wouldn't want to see released. And the only thing Nussbaum was putting the screws on these days was the war.

The war.

"Rosie?"

The words came out in a rush. "Nussbaum was a Great War vet and so was Fielding." I rose from the bed and went to the window. "What if the connection between them wasn't the work they're doing now, but the work they did then?" There would be an official military record that could verify if they'd served in the same unit or had any other opportunity to cross paths. But it's not like I could just pick up a phone and have access to that.

Jayne read my thoughts. "How do you prove it?"

"I can't."

She tapped her nails against her teeth, then heralded the arrival of an idea with a snap. "What about Harriet? I bet she'd know how to find out what we need."

Jayne threw on her kimono and we rushed out of our room and into the hall. Harriet Rosenfeld, our resident war expert who'd helped us understand what the OWI was to begin with, opened her door much more quickly than she had on our last visit. This time the homely girl in spectacles and depilatory cream didn't greet us. This was her good-looking cousin.

"Rosie? Jayne? What a nice surprise. What can I do for you girls?" She ushered us into a room that had undergone a transformation since our last visit. Gone were any signs of her theatrical avocation. The war had taken over.

We would've commented on it if we could've taken our eyes off Harriet. She was wearing a red velvet dress that displayed every curve like a topographical map.

"On your way out?" I asked.

She nodded and fussed with a small beaded bag. "I'm having a late drink with the head of the USO."

"What does your fella think about that?" asked Jayne.

Harriet checked the door and urged us over to the outside wall of the room. "It was his idea." She lowered her voice. "I'm gathering information. Harold and I are working on an article on the USO and what it's doing with its money."

"For *Stars & Stripes*?" I asked.

"For whoever will take it. I'm his field reporter."

I had to admire Harriet. She may have been single-minded, but she knew how to get results.

"What about you two?" asked Harriet.

"We're not up to anything that exciting," I said. "Just thought we'd pop by."

Jayne walked the room and pretended to read the clippings on the wall. "We did have a question, though. How would someone find out about a Great War vet?"

Harriet nodded and paused long enough for me to believe she'd forgotten the question. "If you're talking about getting access to someone's military record, you can't."

"Oh." I hadn't anticipated that what we wanted to do was impossible. "So nix on that?"

A wry smile crept across her face, turning her pretty features into something even more striking. "*You* can't access someone's military record, but there are people who can."

"Like who?" asked Jayne.

Harriet tilted her head toward her fiancé's photo. "Harold's allowed to call up military records as a way of verifying career details for the men he profiles. He's done it for me on a number of occasions." She picked up a pen and pad from her desk and stood at the ready. "So who do we ask him to research for you?"

I looked at Jayne to see if I should proceed. She shrugged, so I barreled forward.

"Raymond Fielding to start with."

Harriet scribbled the name. "Anyone else?"

"Henry Nussbaum."

Harriet's pen hovered above the pad. "The New York director of the OWI?"

My first instinct was to play dumb. "I don't know. Is there someone by that name who works there?"

She bought my act. "Sure is." I waited for her to ask us why we wanted to know about him, but she didn't. Harriet seemed to understand that doing us a favor was one thing, asking us what we were up to was quite another. "Pulling his record might be tough . . . unless Harold can convince the higher-ups that he's writing a piece about the war at home and the efforts the military uses to counter propaganda." She lifted her chin. "In fact, I bet such an exposé would be fascinating." She wrote Nussbaum's name beneath Fielding's. "Anyone else?"

"That's all," said Jayne.

Harriet flipped the notepad shut. "I'm not sure how long it's going to take to get what you need, but I'll do what I can. It's great to see both of you becoming so interested in politics."

28 Miss Information

THE MURDER OF U.S. NAVAL Captain Edgar Fielding was verified in the A.M. papers. His two-column inches also made it clear—by what it didn't say—that Edgar left this world still claiming he was the son of Raymond Fielding, and his mother was in no hurry to dispel that myth. There was a service two days later, but the location was hush-hush. As curious as I might've been to see the state Eloise had found herself in, I didn't think it was right to crash the festivities. Instead, I relied on Ruby to give me the scoop on what was taking place at the apartment.

"All she does is pace, day and night. I'd say the woman is legitimately grief stricken." Ruby and I were walking together to rehearsal two days after the murder. I still didn't trust her, but I found it strangely reassuring that she continued working for Eloise when evidence about the play's whereabouts could no longer be in her hands. If Ruby didn't know about the files, then it was unlikely either she or Lawrence Bentley were behind Edgar's—or anyone else's—death.

Our conversation ended as we entered People's Theatre. Peter had instituted a no-talking rule that was enforced from the moment we entered the building until we left at the end of the day. To further frustrate matters, we were required to arrive one hour before starting rehearsal to give ourselves time to prepare. The only communication we were allowed was whatever was scripted. As much as I hated this artificial attempt to puff the script with meaning it didn't possess, I had to admit it was working. The rage everyone built up during the wasted hour of sitting in silence gave their poor, underwritten characters a fire they couldn't have possessed if the script had been printed with accelerant. The desire to talk also forced everyone to find new ways to say the only words they were allotted for the day, as though they were determined to make an impact no matter how feeble their ammunition.

Of course, Peter couldn't let the environment of antagonism he'd so carefully created disappear along with permission to speak. At the end of each rehearsal he picked apart our performances by describing them as wooden, childish, unprofessional, embarrassing, staged, and frightfully inadequate. As we sat in silent protest, he turned the criticisms more personal by lamenting that we were aging, unattractive, overweight, and possessing personal hygiene that would make the incarcerated blush. Some nights we weren't dismissed after these cruel words but forced to climb onstage and run through the play again while we were still feeling tired, hurt, and furious. That's when things really got interesting. No longer were the few words we had enough to say what we wanted to put onstage. The cast stomped their feet until the boards shook, threw shoddily constructed furniture until it audibly split, and set their rage upon their fellow performers until each actress bore a hand-shaped bruise on her upper arm. In a way the anger he stoked was incredibly liberating. I imagined it was what war felt like.

It also transformed the play. I'd gathered from backstage gossip that I wasn't alone in thinking the script stunk. While an octet of angry actresses hardly redeemed the material, it did guarantee the performances were astounding enough to overlook the writing's shortcomings. It may have been a bad play, but it was going to be an amazing show.

When I was being cool-headed, a part of me was grateful to be the understudy. I didn't know if I could bear to be part of a production that forced us to dig into so many dark places night after night. In order to feel the rage that Peter demanded the few times I'd stepped in for Ruby, I'd had to replay Jack's departure again and again. When that no longer brought me to tears, I invented scenarios. Jack captured. Jack in a work camp. Jack wounded. Jack dead. The beauty of being an actress is that you can imagine anything, convince yourself of any reality. The horror of being an actress is that you feel it all so deeply, five nights a week and twice on Sundays. That's too often for anyone to grieve.

On the bright side, after a week of not speaking to me, Peter once again approached me after rehearsal.

"Do you have a minute, Rosie?" I fought the urge to check behind me to see if there was some other Rosie he was referring to. Had Ruby taken my name as well as my part?

"I guess." I reentered the lobby and slumped over to the bench.

Peter smiled reassuringly, recognizing my low mood but not identifying that he was the source. "What did you think of today's rehearsal?" he asked.

"Cruel," I said. "I think every woman in that theater wants to see you dead." His post-rehearsal comments had been particularly harsh, so much so that I was certain he'd spent the day preparing so he could hit each actress's most vulnerable spot.

"Good, good. I was afraid I was running out of anything useful." He smiled in the intimate way he had that made me think I was the only person in the room (an easy task since I was). I should've been charmed or at least content he was talking to me again, but the whole situation made me glum.

I wrapped my arms about my torso as if I was readying myself for a crash.

"Rehearsal's over, Rosie. Let go of the anger."

"I couldn't bear to. It goes with everything I own." I released my body and attempted to force the tension from my shoulders. "What's the last week of rehearsals going to be like? Air raids? Land mines? Chinese water torture?"

He laughed and gathered the stack of books he'd set down beside him. "No, tomorrow there will be other people to contend with. I don't dare let electricians and stagehands be privy to my methods or, before you know it, every theater in town will be using them." His smile faded. "Care to join me for that drink?"

"I don't think I'd be very good company tonight."

He tapped my leg with his index finger. "It's a process, that's all. It's nothing personal."

Was he talking about rehearsal or us? I couldn't tell. All I knew was I was tired and couldn't bear having my emotions toyed with. "I know it's a process, Peter, and you know that you don't drag an actor through hell without her ass getting singed. If we're good at what we do, it goes home with us."

"Then we won't talk about the play. We'll talk about something else."

I met his eyes and found he was being sincere. If I had to determine which Peter was the real Peter, the one before me was making an argument for his supremacy.

I smiled. "I'm an actress and you're a director. What could we possibly talk about aside from theater?"

"I imagine we could come up with something." We stared at each other, each waiting for the other to confirm that this was all right, that no unwritten rules were being violated. Our faces moved forward, mine right, his left, then in and out as though our heads asked, *Is this permitted*?

We didn't have time to find out. Before our lips could part, meet, touch, and recede, a knock rattled the theater door, sending us leaping to opposite sides of the bench.

"Yes?" Peter called out.

"We're looking for Rosie Winter," said a voice muffled by the door.

I rose and peered through the glass. Two female silhouettes stood by the streetlight. Peter unlocked the door and opened it until the lobby light illuminated Jayne and Harriet. They stood side by side with their hands in their pockets and their hats tilted over their left eyes.

"What are you two doing here?" I asked.

"We thought we'd go do that thing," said Jayne. "And maybe you'd want to join us."

"The USO thing," said Harriet. "That we talked about the other day."

Light penetrated clouds and I nodded that I finally caught on. "Right. I forgot that was tonight." Peter cleared his throat. "This is my roommate, Jayne Hamilton, and our friend Harriet Rosenfeld. This is Peter Sherwood."

Harriet shook his hand. Jayne did the same, at half the speed to give her time to size up the man in question. "Charmed," she cooed.

"I'll see you tomorrow, Peter," I told him, then I grabbed Jayne and Harriet and pulled them into the night.

We hurried away from the theater as though escaping Peter were our primary objective. A man in a worn bowler and houndstooth coat blocked our path and thrust a stack of handbills at us. Jayne and Harriet hurried around him while I absentmindedly took what he was offering. "Of Race and People" the paper read. "Why do you believe the lie of equality?" I crumpled up the handbill and shoved it into my pocket before Harriet caught wind of it. To make sure the man knew how much I appreciated his gift, I stuck out my tongue and gave him a Bronx cheer.

When we were far enough from the building that there was no way Peter could overhear us without employing Gestapo techniques, I slowed down and took in the lay of the land. "Why all the secrecy? Couldn't this have waited until I got home?"

"Peter's cute," said Jayne. "A little worn around the edges, but you could do worse."

A blush started at my belly and catapulted to the top of my head. I poked her shoulder. "Answer the question."

"We were in the neighborhood," she said.

I ushered them over to John Kelly's, the bar Peter and I had gone to weeks before. We staked a claim on a corner table dominated by an overflowing ashtray.

We were the only girls in there. A band of older gents sat hunched around a pitcher of beer telling a story that necessitated lowering their voices upon our entrance. Two solitary men sat at the bar, one lost in a newspaper and the other preoccupied by the scarred wood his drink sat upon. Diagonal to us were three midshipmen who took our arrival as a sign the evening was looking up.

We ordered a round of beer, which was delivered in a soiled pitcher bearing the fingerprints of many who had come before us. From the phonograph Sammy Kaye and his orchestra begged us to "Remember Pearl Harbor." As though we could forget.

"What's the wire?" I pulled my handkerchief out and wiped the outside of my glass.

Harriet checked the room and scooted closer to me. "It seems your men have more in common than past military service."

I leaned toward her and wrapped my hands about my beer. "Go on."

Before she could, one of the midshipmen approached us. His naval hat was nestled beneath his arm and his shoes were so polished they reflected us back on ourselves. He was the only clean thing in the joint.

"Good evening, ladies. My friends and I were thinking about going to a dance hall up the street and we were wondering if you'd care to join us."

The friends waved to us from their post. Jayne fluttered her ring. "Married."

Harriet bowed her head. "Missing."

I clutched the hankie. "Mourning."

His face turned paler than his uniform. "Forgive me, ladies. Have a pleasant evening."

With that formality out of the way, we each took a long sip of beer. The bartender turned off the phonograph and switched on a radio for the Rangers game. The announcer rattled on about how the Chicago Black Hawks were losing their left wing to the army the next day and it was only fair that the Hawks should win to give him the send-off he deserved.

"Fielding and Nussbaum were in the same platoon together," whispered Harriet.

"Were they friends?" I asked

She shook her head. "Doubtful. Nussbaum was the platoon leader and Fielding was one of the grunts. It appears there was some question as to who was responsible the night Fielding lost his leg."

"Meaning?"

"The loss didn't happen in combat. They were in camp and Nussbaum decided to play a prank in retaliation for something Fielding had done to him. Nussbaum put what he claimed he thought was a firecracker in the outhouse. The firecracker was in fact a mortar shell—leading to the loss of Fielding's leg and an inquest. Any misdoing went unproven and Nussbaum's record was expunged."

"Why?" I asked.

"I'm getting to that. Before he lost his leg, Fielding's platoon spent a long, cold winter in France with little action and even less food. The only way they survived the monotonous conditions was to entertain one another. To keep morale up, Fielding and another soldier, who had worked as an actor before the war, would put together skits on camp life, often incorporating information from the other platoon members' lives. As the winter progressed and spirits diminished, they turned their wit on their commander, putting together an evening of burlesque at Nussbaum's expense."

All of this sounded strangely familiar. Hadn't the articles on the walls in Nussbaum's office recounted a similar tale of the troops entertaining one another during the war's harshest months? "And this was why Nussbaum put the mortar in the john? Because of a few jokes?"

Harriet downed her beer until her glass was half empty. "In the official report about the accident, the men who were present described the skits as nothing out of the ordinary. Nussbaum seemed to take the lampooning well and Fielding and his actor friend weren't believed to have done anything out of malice. In the inquest transcript, there's a dispute about whether or not something set Nussbaum off, and then it stops."

The men at the bar groaned as the Black Hawks scored a goal. "Stops?"

"Fielding defended Nussbaum and declared that his actions were an accident, nothing more. All charges were dismissed and Nussbaum's career was allowed to blossom without any taint from the incident." I mulled this over between sips of my drink. Perhaps Fielding decided that by mocking Nussbaum he was partially responsible for what happened to him, so he decided to help get the guy off. Or maybe Nussbaum influenced Fielding's change of tune. Regardless, Nussbaum must've believed that twenty years later Fielding regretted the decision and decided to get his revenge by writing a play that depicted his version of what had happened and punished Nussbaum sufficiently for causing him to lose his leg.

If this were true, it made sense that Nussbaum would want to find the play to prevent his career from being tarnished. Of course, it was equally plausible that the play told the true tale of Edgar Fielding's parentage, a truth that would have caused Edgar and his mother to lose out on Fielding's substantial fortune. How was it that two very different people came to see this play as being about them?

"What about the actor?" I asked. "Who was he?"

"I had a feeling you'd want to know about him." Harriet whipped out a notepad and checked the name. "His name's Alan Detmire."

I almost tipped over my beer glass. Alan Detmire?! That name was in one of the articles in Nussbaum's office. And I'd seen it somewhere else, too . . .

"Have you heard of him?" asked Jayne.

"And then some. Fielding and he are both immortalized on a plaque at People's Theatre."

Jayne shifted beside me. "That's not the only space they shared. If the information in the directory's right, Detmire's been living with Fielding for the last ten years."

29 The Dictator

THE NEXT MORNING I WAS up and out by 9:00 and headed toward People's Theatre for the first of a week's worth of technical rehearsals. When I arrived, the lobby was empty but the auditorium was alive with the sound of hammers and other scene-building implements. Inside, half the cast was spread about the seats watching as a group of middle-aged carpenters—the only ones who hadn't been drafted—struggled to connect a series of painted flats. My brain couldn't take the noise, so I retreated into the lobby and settled on a bench with the latest issue of *Detective Comics.*

No matter how hard I tried, I couldn't focus on the continuing adventures of shamus Slam Bradley and his sidekick Shorty Morgan. I searched my coat pocket for something to mark my page with and found a wad of paper. I unfurled it before I realized what it was: the anti-Jewish flyer from the night before. I was about to tear it up when the subtitle caught my eye, "Why do you believe the lie of equality?"

In the newspapers, we were constantly bombarded with how there was the truth and then there was what the Axis nations told their people. Clearly their governments were smart enough to tell them lies that appealed to them, compelling them to accept horrific conditions and treatment because, ultimately, it would be for the good of their countries. By appealing to whatever their people valued most, these nations kept their soldiers fighting and their homefronts willing to sacrifice.

Believing in something could make you do just about anything. It could even convince you that a script was so dangerous you had

The War Against Miss Winter

to kill someone to make sure it didn't fall into the wrong hands. The question was, how could it do that to more than one person when the information they were responding to was very different? Was someone deliberately misleading people about the play's contents, or was something else afoot?

"Heavy reading?" Peter appeared beside me, wearing paint-splattered dungarees and the kind of shirt I imagined lumberjacks in Ontario donned for a day on the job.

I shoved the flyer into the pages of the comic book. "I like the brightly colored pictures. Don't tell me you're responsible for building the set as well as directing the play?"

He sat beside me and concentrated on rolling the cuffs of his too large shirt. "I'm assisting, though to hear the designer talk, I'm staging a coup."

An electrician entered the lobby hauling a coil of cable. Before him he held an enormous spotlight, as if it were a lantern guiding his way.

"Can I ask you a question?" I said.

"Shoot."

"Wasn't Fielding against all this brouhaha?"

Peter watched as the electrician forced his way into the theater, the light banging against the heavy oak doors. "While Raymond was a brilliant writer, I think it's unreasonable to demand we dispense with everything theatrical. What I'm doing will accentuate the play, not dominate it."

Somehow I doubted Fielding would see it that way.

"Incidentally, Ruby isn't available until this afternoon. I hope you don't mind stepping in until she arrives." I nodded my consent and his expression turned serious. "How did things go with your friends last night?"

I ran my hands over the cover of the comic book. "Fine."

"Did you meet anyone?"

"Excuse me?"

He stood and stepped away from me. "It's none of my business."

That's right—he thought we'd gone to a USO dance. "No—it's all right. I didn't meet anyone."

He smiled at the floor. "I'm glad to hear that."

Well, well, well—this was an interesting development. Could it be that Peter was as insecure as I was? "I'm sorry I ran out on you last night. I didn't want to." I bit my lip and tried to decide if he'd be impressed or disgusted by my shenanigans. "We didn't go to a dance. I didn't want you to know what I was really up to."

"Which was what?"

I winced as if I was readying myself for a hit. "I've been looking for that stupid play."

He frowned and rejoined me on the bench. "Raymond Fielding's play?"

"That's the one."

"That doesn't sound so stupid to me."

"Maybe stupid isn't the right word. Anyway, I had a lead on where it might have ended up and my friends were kind enough to do a little investigating on my behalf. They decided they wanted to tell me in person what they'd found."

"I appreciate your honesty. I was starting to take last night very personally."

At least he knew how it felt.

"You said you thought you had a lead. Didn't it pan out?"

"Yes and no." It couldn't hurt to ask Peter his thoughts on what was going on. At worst he'd think I was crazy. "You probably know more about Raymond Fielding than anyone, right?"

"That's arguable. Why?"

I braced myself for the question I dreaded asking. "Do you think there's a chance there's more than one play?"

Peter chuckled. "I suppose anything's possible, though it's not the way it was presented to me."

He was about to say more when Hilda rapped on the wall behind us. "Everyone is here and ready," she announced. She lifted and lowered her eyebrows to question why we were the only two people in the lobby.

Peter stood and offered me his hand. "Shall we?" He hoisted me
to my feet, which would've been quite chivalrous if I'd paid more attention to my balance and less to his touching me in Hilda's presence.
He released me once I'd gained my equilibrium and with a salute
instructed Hilda to lead the way into the auditorium.

Technical rehearsals are boring affairs for the actors and juggling
acts for the director. Finally, after weeks of preparation, you're at the
stage where your unpolished gem is ready to receive the design elements that will elevate it from script to spectacle. The problem was,
like most theaters, People's introduced all of the pageantry simultaneously so that we had to contend with lights, set, sound, costumes,
and props for the first time in a single rehearsal. All those weeks
of perfecting character and motivation went out the door while we
struggled with props that weren't what we'd imagined, set pieces that
were more cumbersome than planned, and clothes that restricted
movements we'd come to believe were integral to our roles. Blinded
by lights, deafened by music, disoriented by the presence of people
in the auditorium after weeks of being used to our small clique, it felt
very much as if all of our practice had been for naught.

Despite the inconvenience, from my perspective in the audience
the introduction of lights, sound, and set were completely worthwhile.
The cast may have appeared more bumbling than believable, but the
technical elements legitimized what we were doing and why we had the
nerve to charge people to attend it. This may have all seemed artifice to
Raymond Fielding, but I could see where Peter was coming from. We
needed this stuff to distinguish the everyday from the extraordinary.

While I was cheered by the process, Peter's mood swiftly declined
from frustrated to foul. A war was raging between him and the technical staff, and rather than appearing the kind, easygoing man I'd just
spoken to, Peter was looking more and more tyrannical by the minute.
The lights were wrong, the costumes hideous, and the set he'd helped
construct was nothing like what they'd talked about. Clearly someone had undone all of his hard work the minute his back was turned.
He strong-armed carpenters to get out of his way, stomped across the

stage, and shifted platforms with such ease that I expected his shirt to burst open to reveal a physique Mr. Universe would've killed for. The only way I could stomach watching the display was by assuring myself that this was another one of Peter's experiments designed to pit the cast against him. I was fine with this read until he set his guns on me.

"Rosie, find your light. Move left—stage left." I moved two steps to the left and looked downward for the pool of light I was supposed to find, but which was too dim for me to see. "Are you deaf? I said stage right." I wasn't and he hadn't, but I obeyed anyway, well aware that no matter what I did it wouldn't resemble what he believed he'd asked me to do. Indeed, it didn't. Peter climbed onstage and moved me back to the position I'd been in to begin with. Above us an electrician altered the direction of a light, causing the clamp to grind into the pipe with a frightful moan. I prayed the klieg light would break free of its mount and land on Peter's head.

I wasn't the only one he behaved this way toward, but after the fifth reprimand I was no longer able *not* to take it personally. I alternated between wanting to cry and wanting to push the flats until they collapsed in a pile like dominoes. After four hours of this abuse, Peter announced we would break for lunch in the lobby; we had e*xactly* a half hour until we resumed rehearsal. As we collected our things and silently filed out of the theater, Ruby popped her head in and waved.

"Are you back for good?" I asked. A table of sandwich makings had been set up at one end of the lobby. She and I took our places at the end of the food line and kept our voices low so they couldn't be heard above the buzz of other conversations.

"Why? Miss me?"

"You have no idea," I muttered. "How was work?"

"Dull." Ruby flipped her hair and a whiff of pine-scented cleaner filled the lobby. "I'm thinking about quitting. Eloise becomes more abusive by the minute. Plus, the job may no longer be necessary."

"And why is that?"

"I have other opportunities on the horizon. I certainly had no intention of being a maid for the rest of my life." I squirmed. Where would she turn up next: Henry Nussbaum's house or in the employ of the mysterious Alan Detmire?

We ate cold cuts on rye and washed down what remained of our humility with Coca-Colas and small stale gingersnaps. The rest of the afternoon was a virtual repeat of the morning's tortures, with Ruby in the lead instead of me. At 5:00 rehearsal was complete and Peter momentarily assumed his human form to thank us for our patience and remind us that we'd run the entire show from top to bottom starting the following evening. I scooped up my belongings and followed the cast through the lobby and out onto the street.

"Calling it a night?" Peter stood framed in the theater entrance. He wore neither coat nor hat, which meant he'd followed me outside hoping to stop me.

"It's been a long day," I said. The wind picked up and my scarf flopped toward my chin.

"I was hoping we could continue our conversation."

If he had been nicer to me that day, I would've leaped at the chance to spend some time with him. As it was . . . "Maybe another night. I'm bushed."

He put his hand on my arm and moved closer. "Come on, Rosie, it's early." His doe eyes widened to full capacity; he was assuming whatever stance he usually took in order to make people yield to him. And it was working: no longer did I want to punish him for being both a difficult director and an incomprehensible man. I just wanted to sit with him in some quiet out-of-the-way place and talk until the sun came up.

Unfortunately, there were more important things for me to deal with than nursing my hurt feelings.

"Let's do it another night," I said. "I've reached the point where if I don't head home now, I'm going to curl up and sleep on the lobby floor." His face fell and I hated myself for continuing this bizarre dance of ours. I swallowed my sense of propriety and gave him a peck on the cheek. His frown reversed and he loosened his hold on me.

"Another night," he repeated. And with that, I hailed a cab and headed toward Penn Station.

30 The Noble Experiment

JAYNE MET ME AT THE station and we took the train back up to Fielding's manse in Croton-on-Hudson. I had no idea if Alan Detmire still lived there, but I figured it was as good a place as any to start looking.

"How's Lawrence?" I asked her on the trip out of town. Jayne had also come straight from rehearsal and neither of us was going to win any prizes for our moods.

"The same," said Jayne. "Why?"

I told her about Ruby's claim that she'd be leaving Eloise sooner rather than later.

"Well, if Ruby did find the play," said Jayne, "Bentley's doing a fabulous job of hiding it. He couldn't have been less pleasant today if we skinned him alive."

It was a long shot that Bentley was our man. He didn't have a motive, beyond his fear of competition, and I found it hard to believe that a man with his ego would be concerned about another play's success. But Bentley was a known quantity and accusing him was easier than imagining that Nussbaum or someone we hadn't even met yet was behind everything.

"I've been thinking about Detmire," I told Jayne. "The obit said Fielding had a servant. Remember? That's who supposedly found him."

"So you think Detmire was his butler?" Behind Jayne, cigarette ads geared up for battle: CAMELS ARE FIRST WITH MEN IN THE SERVICE but LUCKY STRIKE GREEN HAS GONE TO WAR.

"Or at least posing as one. Ruby said Fielding was a nance, so maybe Detmire was his lover. That would explain why we haven't heard much about him."

We arrived at the station and hired a hack. Once we arrived at Fielding's, we followed the winding path to the front door. There was no car in the drive, but enough lights glowed behind the windows to let us know someone lingered inside. Halfway up the walk we heard a tinny radio crooning, "I'll Be Seeing You."

Jayne rang the bell and we both repeatedly cleared our throats as if we were orchestras tuning our instruments. A form distorted by the door's glass panels loomed toward us. A voice assured us he was coming as fast as he could.

The door creaked open and a stooped man gazed at the two of us. "May I help you?" His was an accent that had faded, a remnant from a land he hadn't lived in or visited for many years.

"We're looking for Alan Detmire," I said in my best Humphrey Bogart.

The man eyed us for a moment too long, then came to a silent decision. "I'm Alan Detmire. Won't you come in?" He ushered us in with a hand that shook like a wind-up doll, then proceeded ahead of us. He had a funny way of walking, all stiff-legged, as though he were one of Hitler's goose-stepping storm troopers. We passed through the familiar foyer and joined him in the library, where the portrait of Raymond Fielding by Raymond Fielding watched us from above a fire. Alan directed us to the sofa and we both sat with our knees pressed together and our feet flat on the rug. "Are you with the police?"

"No," I said. Who was he fooling? Since when did the coppers hire a pair of dolls in uncomfortable shoes?

He nodded at this news and took slow, deliberate steps to the desk. "Care for a drink?"

"Sure," I said. "We'll both take some of that scotch."

Alan made the drinks with the practiced hand of someone who'd held a cocktail shaker longer than a rattle. He delivered our drinks at the same maddeningly slow pace as he did everything else. I couldn't decide if his speed was always this sluggish or if he'd downshifted as a way of irritating us. I decided to give him the benefit of the doubt.

"Mr. Detmire," I said at last. "My name's Rosie Winter and this is my friend Jayne Hamilton." He didn't say anything in response, so I plodded on. "You ever heard of Jim McCain?"

His brow creased and he shook his head. "Can't say that I have."

"How about Henry Nussbaum?"

He stroked his bare chin. "Forgive me, but I don't recall why you said you're here."

"We didn't." I dipped a sip of courage. "We want to know about the play."

"The play?" A satisfied smile spread across Detmire's face. In a blink, it disappeared and his brows and mouth dipped downward. "Which play are you referring to?"

"Fielding's magnum opus, the one full of so much dirt that everyone's tripping over themselves trying to make sure it doesn't get produced."

"I don't know what you're talking about." Alan paused and carefully selected his next words. "Raymond Fielding has no unproduced plays."

"What about *In the Dark*?" I asked.

"That play is *about* to be produced, Miss Winter, so I don't think it qualifies. Let us say that today Raymond Fielding has one unproduced play, but this weekend he shall have none."

Was it possible he really didn't know anything about the play? I couldn't get over how deliberate he was, as though everything he said and did was for our edification. Part of it, no doubt, was retained from his days as an actor, constantly telegraphing to an audience too unsavvy to comprehend emotions at a distance. There was something hinky about him, though. I had the feeling we were engaged in some sort of game.

I turned my attention to the painting of Fielding by Fielding, then again set my sights on Detmire. Could I have met him before, possibly at the wake? I didn't think so, but I couldn't shake the feeling I'd encountered him previously. It was like running into a big-name star at the Stage Door Canteen. You were so used to seeing them with wigs, makeup, and distance that when you examined them unadorned they were practically unrecognizable.

I rose from the couch and approached him. "You're Fake Fielding."

"Pardon me?"

All he needed was a neat Vandyke beard and a smooth bald head. "That day, at Jim's office, you're the one who came in claiming to be Raymond Fielding. You're the one who hired me."

His smile grew larger, but he said nothing to dispute my claim.

"So there *is* a play. And you know about it."

He crossed his arms and reclined against the desk. "Do I?"

"Of course you do. You have to unless . . ." My brain fell into the next thought faster than a barrel careening down Niagara Falls.

Jayne boarded my train and came to my side. "Unless this whole thing has been some sort of scam from the beginning."

Alan's smile died and he seemed to grow more massive, as though we'd been looking at an earlier, unfinished version of him until this time. "I can assure you there is a play. There always has been."

Jayne stepped toward him. "Then where is it?"

He clucked his tongue and refilled his glass. "That is what we paid Mr. McCain and Miss Winter to find out." He took a sip of the amber liquid, then held the glass up to the light. "Are people talking about it?"

I decided to throw the guy a bone. "Some people, sure."

"Good, good." Detmire lowered the glass and dipped his pinkie into the drink. "I suppose you two should be going now."

I put my hands on my hips. "Every road led us here, so we're not leaving until we know what's going on. Where's the play?"

Alan glanced at his watch and sighed. "At this moment, it's hard to say. Uptown, perhaps. In a government office. Beneath an actress's bed. In a rival playwright's drawer. Or, maybe, right here in this room."

"What's your game?"

Detmire examined the nails of his free hand. "Game, Miss Winter? I'm not playing any game."

"I don't care what you call it. The fact is, you're not being straight with us. Use all the double-talk you want. Jim, Raymond, and Edgar have all been murdered over this play, and instead of speaking in riddles, you should jump to the point and put us wise to where the damn thing is."

He met my eyes and smiled. "I just did. You're the one who's looking for Chinese angles."

That did it for me. I leaped toward him, determined to ring his neck until the color drained from his face. Before I could reach him, Jayne grabbed me from behind and pulled me away. "Let go of me, Jayne. He's got this coming to him." My arms flailed like windmills, trying to make contact with anyone or anything. I expected Jayne to go sailing over my head, but she held her ground and kept me planted.

"Easy, Rosie."

"Don't 'easy' me. This guy is conning us. And if he won't tell me where the play is, we're going to stage an impromptu production of *Salome* and put his head on a platter."

Jayne looped her arms through mine and restrained me. "You do that and we'll never find out what's going on. Is that what you want?"

I turned toward her, but it was impossible to meet her face-to-face. "Who says he's going to tell us what we want to hear?"

"I do," said Detmire.

Jayne released me.

"Why don't you both sit down?"

I didn't oblige.

"Really, Miss Winter, it will be much more comfortable for you to do so. When I'm done saying what I have to say, you're welcome to resume threatening me." Detmire produced a silver cigarette case and offered us smokes. Jayne accepted for both of us, then steered me onto the sofa. "You found your way to me, which is impressive, but I must say I'm disappointed you've come to me looking for information rather than bearing it. I warned Raymond that he couldn't expect everyone to have the intellectual prowess to get what he was trying to do. I suppose this was to be expected with two women on the trail."

It would serve him right if I clocked him even if he told us what we'd come to hear.

"Get what?" asked Jayne.

"The play of course." Detmire opened his arms wide enough to engulf the entire room. "I've told you where it is and yet you continue to fail to see it."

"Can you blame us?" asked Jayne. "You haven't given us a lot to go on. The play's here, it's there, it's everywhere. What is this, old MacDonald's farm?"

I put my hand out and signaled for her to close her head. There it was: one idea meeting another until I finally understood what was going on. "All the world's a stage and all men and women merely players," I whispered.

Jayne nudged me with her elbow. "Now's not the time to quote Shakespeare."

I spun until I was facing Detmire head-on. "That's what you said the day you visited me and I'm just now starting to understand why. We're the play. That's the crop, isn't it? There is no play; there never was. But we—what we're doing here, what everyone is doing as they search this thing out—that's the theater Fielding was hoping to create: the ultimate play, without intrusion from author or director. He provided the conflict, we provided the characters, and now you're sitting back to see how the whole thing plays out."

Detmire smiled again, wider than the Cheshire cat. He began to applaud in that slow way people use to simultaneously praise an effort and belittle it. "Very good, Miss Winter. I'd be more impressed if you'd come to this conclusion without my hints, but I'll give credit where credit is due." What a guy. "Raymond was obsessed with defining theater. Everything he wrote came back to that central question:

What is theater? If you addressed the audience, did it change? If you removed the set, did it change? What if it was no longer on a stage? What if the actors were real people? Everything he wrote took away more and more of the conventions we'd come to associate with the form until all that was left was drama and spectacle, and still people came to see it and called it art."

Pity he didn't explore this side of himself until after he wrote *In the Dark*.

"Eventually, he came to define theater as the artificial incitement of conflict. But he needed one more test to ensure this assessment was accurate. That's what this is."

"We're the play?" asked Jayne. "How can that be?"

Detmire took a cleansing sip of liquor and cleared his throat. "He knew early on who his cast of characters would be, most of them anyway. You two were unnamed minor players. He created the idea of a play that revealed something about each of his main characters, something they hoped would never be made public. At first, the threat of confidential information getting out was a sufficient catalyst for the action, but Raymond grew worried the conflict wasn't developing swiftly enough. He loved the form of the mystery since human curiosity is an extremely powerful moti- vation. So he introduced a new element: the play, which may have remained unproduced in Raymond's hands, had been stolen by somebody with dangerous intentions. Raymond hired Jim to lend credibility to the idea that there was something to find and to further drive the cast by having someone poke into their histories. And when both Jim and Raymond were killed, I encouraged the show to go on, so to speak, by approaching Rosie and by hosting a wake that would keep the theater community talking about the missing script."

I sat down; I had to. I couldn't continue to stand in a world where a man mentioned two stiffs with the same regard given to recipe in- gredients. "Why would you do that? Men were murdered. Why would you keep this ridiculous experiment going?"

The grin left Detmire and with it the sense of immorality I'd attributed to him. "Because I was asked to. My job was to record what happened, no matter what, and to keep it moving until it's natural end. I promised Raymond. It's impossible for you to understand the degree of dedication he had to this project. He believed it was the culmination of his life's work, and if that meant he had to lose his life in the process, so be it."

"That's great," I said. "That's his life. What about Jim's? What about Edgar Fielding's? What about the next person some kook bumps off to keep a play that doesn't exist from being produced?"

"Things have taken a course Raymond couldn't have anticipated. It's unfortunate, but it's not his fault."

I couldn't keep it in anymore. Jim had been reduced to a wrong turn on a country road. A sob left me and a big, fat, betraying tear slid down my cheek. Jayne put her hand on my shoulder and squeezed.

"Naturally you're angry," said Detmire. "I was too. But I realized that great art elicits emotions. Instead of resenting that we're experiencing them, we should be grateful for the pain."

I shook free of Jayne's touch. "This isn't a play. This is life. Real men died."

Jayne again put her arm on mine, more for restraint than comfort. Detmire put his hands in the air. "Be angry if you must, but don't be angry at me. I am merely fulfilling a dear friend's wish. As my honesty proves, I was never trying to deceive anyone. I've never lied throughout this project." I started to protest and he pierced the air with his finger. "Not once. All anyone had to do was tell me what they believed was happening and I would've verified it for them."

"Is that supposed to be reassuring?" I wiped my face and imagined it disordering itself into a Cubist painting. If my eyes were where my nose should be, would this start to make sense? "All we had to do was find a man who deliberately kept himself hidden and ask him the magic question and he'd let us into Oz? Now why didn't I think of that to begin with?" I clocked myself on the head. "I'll tell you right now: The show's over. Your curtain just went down."

Detmire ran his tongue over his teeth. "It can't be over yet, Miss Winter. There's still a murderer loose and a mystery to solve."

"I'll leave that to the police, thank you. Once they get wind of what's really going on, I'm sure they'll be happy to take over."

Detmire crossed to the fireplace and rubbed his hands before the dying flames. "Will they? If you repeat any of what I've told you, I'll tell the police you're lying. You know as well as I do what they thought of Jim. Any assistant of his would be viewed as similarly suspect." He paused and buttoned his jacket. "No, the show isn't over yet. You must let it play out to its natural end, just as Raymond wanted."

Jayne released me and stepped forward. "We'll tell everyone. This can't continue if everyone knows what's going on."

Detmire removed a brass poker from a stand on the hearth and encouraged the logs to burn. "Who would believe you, Miss Hamilton? What sort of evidence could you have to prove something never existed? It's a dilemma, isn't it? I know because I've pondered it many, many nights." He replaced the poker in its stand and stared into the rising flames. "Even if there were clear, irrefutable evidence, how would you propose making people aware of it? A letter-writing campaign? Radio time? Newspaper ads? It would take something of that magnitude. You have no idea how large this production is. You two have met a handful of people who are involved, but that doesn't mean they're the only ones—just the ones your characters would have access to. What if you were to tell everyone you think should know only to find out months later that the one person you didn't inform continues to live this fiction? If someone else dies—maybe a total stranger this time—you would have failed." Never had I been so cold. I wrapped my arms about myself and struggled to keep my teeth from, chattering. "You can't walk off the stage now. There's a second act to finish, and if you two aren't present, I have a feeling a third act will develop, then a fourth, and a fifth, until Raymond and Jim and Edgar are joined by a chorus of corpses. Do you want to be responsible for that?"

Jayne shook, as I did, and rubbed her hands on her upper arms. "We wouldn't be responsible. It wouldn't be our fault."

Detmire looked at her and cocked his head. "Wouldn't it, Miss Hamilton? You're in the know now, and that means you're complicit. A moment ago you indicted me for failing to stop things after Raymond died. I tried to find a way to do so, believe me, just as you'll try the minute you walk out of this room. But what I learned, as you will learn, is that art takes on a life of its own."

Defeated, we left Detmire. As we waited for the train home, Jayne and I stared at each other, stumbling to start sentences that didn't seem to want to come. How could we make sense of the insensible? Jim and Edgar were dead because they had been looking for a play that never existed to begin with. Raymond Fielding was dead because he was so obsessed with his art that he would do anything keep a fictional drama in motion. If all of that wasn't bad enough, whoever had killed the three of them still believed that a play was missing and that it revealed something so devastating about the killer that they would be willing to kill again just to make sure it didn't emerge.

We gave up trying to talk. In silence we rode back to the city and in silence we returned to the Shaw House. Once in our room we simultaneously sank onto our beds and wrapped our arms about our legs. For a long time we stayed that way, until the gnawing cold forced us to shift positions in tandem.

Bad things keep happening and we just have to accept them.

I cleared my throat. "On the bright side, the play's no longer missing."

"And here I thought there was no silver lining." Jayne wiped at her face and turned her head away from me. "By the way—thanks for bringing me along."

"Don't blame me; act two, scene four said you were supposed to accompany me."

She turned back to me and smiled for the first time since we'd left Detmire. "Tell me that one again tomorrow. Maybe by then it will be funny." She sighed and looked at her feet. "You know what I miss? I miss genuinely believing there's nothing I can't survive. Edgar Fielding stole that from me and I think Alan Detmire guaranteed I'll never get it back." She sighed and propped her head on her hands. Churchill leaped to the end of her bed and stared at her as though the conversation were directed at him. "What are we going to do?"

I shrugged. "We'll keep going to rehearsal and in a few days, I'll open as an understudy in a crappy play. Maybe somebody tries to kill somebody, or maybe this is like war and it goes on much too long and makes very little sense in the end."

I left the bed and went to the window. The dimout had brought the stars back to the city, filling the night sky with the hazy lights of other atmospheres. "It seems unfair that whoever killed Fielding, Jim, and Edgar was manipulated into doing it. If Fielding never had this lousy idea, the murderer never would've felt threatened enough to commit a crime. It's like the strawberry hankie."

"The what?" asked Jayne.

"In *Othello*. Othello kills Desdemona because he's led to believe she's been unfaithful, his one piece of evidence being her strawberry hankie. His jealousy is his tragic flaw and so when Iago deceives him, his downfall begins."

"I think it begins before then."

"Fine, this isn't dramatic lit class. My point is, it doesn't seem fair that whoever our murderer is became a murderer in the first place. Who knows what might've become of them if Fielding never began this stupid experiment."

Jayne shifted and her bed groaned. "But isn't a tragedy a tragedy because it's destined to happen? I thought tragic heroes did what they did because of fate not flaws."

"Fate?" I turned away from the window and leaned on the radiator.

"Sure. Whoever our murderer is wasn't made that way because of what Fielding did. He or she was destined to kill."

31 The Very Idea

I ARRIVED LATE TO REHEARSAL the next day. They'd already begun act one, and while I should've been relieved that my delay went unnoticed, I wallowed in how insignificant I'd become to the production. The return of Ruby meant I had little to do other than sit at the rear of the auditorium and dwell on the events of the day before, and, frankly, that's the last thing I needed.

If we really couldn't stop what had already started, was there any way to speed things up? The end of the "play" had to be the revelation of the murderer and there were only two ways that was going to happen: a confession or somebody else got zotzed with one of us standing by. Since I could no longer be certain how many suspects there were, it would be almost impossible to get a confession. The pattern of homicide had been to kill anyone who may have knowledge of the play's whereabouts. So if I wanted to prompt another attack, all I had to do was convince the "cast" that the play . . .

"Rosie, why don't you take over for act two?"

I snapped to attention at the sound of my name and found Peter staring at me from the stage apron. "What?"

"I'd like you to do act two."

I disentangled myself from my seat and tripped over my pocketbook. Ruby scowled from upstage, but her scorn wasn't directed at me; she was staring daggers at Peter. Had I missed something? Last time I'd looked everything had been proceeding normally.

Ruby climbed offstage, muttering something indecipherable under her breath while rolling her peepers. I took her place and for the next delicious hour, pretended I was a real actress. By 7:00 I was back to being a civilian.

"Are you walking?" asked Ruby as I gathered my things from the back of the house.

"Home? Yes, I think so."

"Mind if I walk with you?" Ruby asked.

I wanted time to clear my thoughts, but I was curious about why I'd been given the chance to take over the show when Ruby was there and available. I decided I could think all I wanted at the house; I deserved a little harmless gossip.

We left through the main doors and took the path she preferred home. The meandering series of illogical turns she followed were clearly designed to avoid running into other cast members.

"Why'd he make you take a powder tonight?" I was feeling brave. What was Ruby's scorn in the face of murder?

Ruby sighed and picked a cat hair from her coat. "Peter's mad at me."

"What did you do?"

She looked aghast and put her hand over her heart. "I didn't do anything. I merely responded to what he did. *I'm* the victim."

"So what did *he* do?"

She raised an eyebrow and waited for further kowtowing to establish victim and offender. When none came, she rolled her eyes and sighed a second time. "It's this ridiculous advertising policy of his. Did you see the posters?" I shook my head. "They're all black with no title, no author, no mention of *me*. All they have is some ridiculous teaser that suggests if you want to know anything about the play, you need to come see it."

"People are curious animals. I'm willing to bet it will be a very successful campaign."

The wind picked up, sending her hat askew. "Sure, for the *fringe*." She said the word like it burned her tongue. "But there are plenty of people in this city who are unwilling to leave their homes unless there's a guarantee of reputability."

"I wasn't aware you could guarantee such a thing."

She removed her hatpin and wielded it before her. "This is nothing to joke about, Rosie. Known playwrights and performers legitimize a production. Otherwise, why would they come see us instead of a production of *Hedda Gabler* at a garage in Hoboken?"

"People's Theatre does have a reputation. They've been around for a while."

She looked heavenward. "God—you sound like *him*."

I fought a smile at the thought that my words matched Peter's. "So did you talk to him about his advertising policy?"

She refastened her hat and flipped her scarf about her neck with the sort of flare one reserved for a feather boa. "Somebody had to. It's going to be the ruin of this production."

My temples throbbed. Why couldn't Ruby just tell me what happened without editorializing? "And what did you say to him?"

"Well . . ." She steeled herself as though she were about to perform a monologue about her terrifying escape from the Nazis. "I didn't have time to talk to him before rehearsal, so I decided to do it during Beverly Dwyer's scene. I mean, let's face it, everything she's in is a yawner." I nodded. Beverly was nice enough, but she took the concept of naturalism in acting too far. Everything she did conveyed a slothlike world-weariness that made you wish she were on film so you could make the reel go faster. "I told him that if he expected to sell this show, he had better take drastic actions in the next few days. I also told him I was extremely disappointed my name was not being sold in conjunction with the production and that the fact that I didn't appear on the posters may be a contractual violation."

If I could figure out how to harness Ruby's hot air, gas rationing could be a thing of the past. "And what did he say?"

"He told me that ticket sales were brisk and there was no need to worry about something that wasn't my concern to begin with." She gulped air and her hands fluttered through the air as though she were a conductor directing this opera to its crescendo. "And if I didn't like the way he was promoting his show, I was welcome to leave.

Naturally, I told him that while he may not be using me to get people into the theater, I was going to be the only reason they stayed, and if he thought for a moment an understudy could achieve the same effect, he was even more deluded than I thought." Ruby paused and noted the look on my face. "No offense."

"None taken."

"Obviously he didn't take things well, since he asked you to perform the second act." I waited for her to explain how ludicrous a decision that had been, but for once Ruby showed restraint. "Frankly, I don't know if I want to be part of a show that won't even make an effort to promote itself."

It took everything in me to keep from yelling, *Then quit!* "He's not not promoting it," I said. "He's using Raymond Fielding's methods as a way of marketing the show. It's a pretty clever plan."

"That's all well and good, Rosie, but it doesn't put people in seats. A few posters won't entice the *important* people. I'm not against the creativity of leaving the title and author unknown, but the man hasn't even sent out a press release. What are we, heathens?" She stopped walking and tapped the air with her index finger. "If I had half a mind . . ." *Don't tempt me*, I begged. "I'd promote the thing myself."

"What?"

"Don't look so aghast. I'm not talking about ruining his stupid surprise. I just mean contacting the people who should be in the know that an important play is about to be performed"—she tapped her chest with her hands and smiled at the sky—"by me."

I was about to tell her why this was the stupidest idea I'd ever heard of when something stopped me. Nussbaum was intrigued by the play the minute I said I wasn't allowed to talk about it. What if Ruby got word out that a new play, never before produced, and terribly shocking and important was about to open? Wouldn't that bring everyone out of the woodwork?

"You should do it," I said.

"Really?"

"Absolutely. But make sure no one knows the information came from you, you know, so Peter doesn't get upset. And don't tell them too much. Just that it's important and shocking and rumored to be an unproduced play by an important writer. Oh, and mention yourself being in it."

"Hmmm." Ruby tapped her teeth with her nail. "I could do that."

"You'll have to do it fast, though. We open in two days."

Ruby tossed her head back and laughed. "Honey, I can make a rumor circle this town twice with ten minutes' notice."

By the time we returned to the Shaw House, I was feeling fifty pounds lighter. I climbed the steps two at a time and decided I would spend the rest of the evening reading the pulps and thinking about nothing that could possibly happen in real life.

"Hiya." Jayne sat on her bed. Her eyes were red-rimmed and a series of well-worn hankies were sprawled around her. Churchill was entertaining himself by batting the wads of cotton between his front paws.

I sank onto the bed beside her and flicked a sodden handkerchief out of Churchill's reach. I scanned the room for the source of her grief. Had there been a bad radio report? A starred telegram? A visit from an officer who thought we should hear the news firsthand? "What's the matter?"

"He wants to recast my part."

"Bentley?"

Jayne wove her fingers together. The hankie rested in the middle of them like an egg in a basket. "Apparently Ruby has expressed interest in joining the cast as well as becoming his girlfriend again."

"Wait a second—she's leaving *In the Dark*?" It didn't make any sense, unless she was using the lack of publicity as her excuse.

"No. He's decided to push back his opening for her. His funders would prefer someone more known in the lead." She made no attempt to stop the flood of tears this time. "Things were going so well. Lawrence was always telling me how talented I was. I mean, I know I never would've gotten the part without Tony . . ."

"Jayne—"

"No, it's okay. I know. I'm not dumb, Rosie. A girl like me doesn't get a chance like this on her own. It just . . . it just really stinks to have this taken away. I've been working so hard." She mopped at her face and blew her nose, but the tears just kept coming. I hadn't seen her this inconsolable since Carole Lombard had died the previous January. "Look who I'm talking to. She did the same thing to you."

"You should talk to Tony," I said.

Her face crumbled again. "He's done enough. He doesn't need to know I messed this up."

I gently slapped her leg. "You didn't mess up. And Tony's going to find out one way or another. Better it be now when he can fix the situation than after the show opens and he feels the need for retaliation."

"I don't want to tell him." Her jaw was set, her hands clenched.

"Is this about Edgar Fielding?"

She shrugged.

"Tony didn't have anything to do with that, Jayne. You know that. If nothing else good came out of meeting Alan Detmire, at least we know whoever killed Edgar was the same nut who took down Jim."

"We don't know that for sure." She wrapped a finger in the satin edge of her blanket. "I'm thinking maybe I shouldn't see Tony anymore. Maybe someone's trying to tell me something with everything that's going on." She twisted the blanket so tightly her finger turned red. "Besides, it's not fair to make him step in every time I want my way."

"Do you think Ruby's playing fair? Yeah, we'd all like to get great parts based on our talent, but you know that doesn't happen. There's always going to be a Ruby Priest who relies on her looks or her connections to get what we deserve. And if you want to come out ahead, you have to be willing to do the same."

Jayne stared at her feet and wiggled her toes. "I'll think about it."

"I mean it, Jayne; you can't take this lying down. If you don't call him, I will."

She met my eyes and nodded. "I said I'd think about it."

I rose from the bed and went to my dresser. "I had a brainstorm today: What if we leak to the press that People's Theatre is about to do a show that bears a striking resemblance to the missing Fielding play?"

Jayne's outrage melted away; with it went her posture. "Isn't that dangerous?"

Was it? While luring a potential murderer anywhere may have seemed like a bad idea, I was under the impression that luring him or her to a play rather than a person would be safe. The worst thing that ever happened to me in a theater was being demoted to understudy. "Of course not. All we have to do is sit back and watch to see who shows and how they react. The first move someone makes to block the production and—*pow!* We know we've got our man."

"And then what do we do?"

I was trying very hard not to be irritated at Jayne for making me nail down details. I knew I needed to figure this stuff out before opening night, but there was no reason I had to decide it now. I trusted that I'd know what to do when it really counted.

I locked my eyes on hers. "The walls have ears. Let's just say I have it worked out."

"I'm glad to hear that," she said, though I knew she believed me as much as I believed she'd pick up the phone and call Tony. Which is why I called him the next morning on her behalf.

32 Dark Victory

THE NEXT TWO DAYS PASSED in a blur. Rehearsals started early and ran late. Peter was so consumed by the production that my only chance to talk to him was during those rare moments I was onstage, and then our interaction was limited to comments about my performance. Teasers crept into the papers about the show. Critics and gossip columnists alike printed items such as, "Rumor has it that the play no one will talk about is the play everyone's been talking about and if you don't know what I'm talking about, come anyway and join in the fun. I understand it will be a shocking good time." Never one to stay in the shadows, Ruby made sure her name was uttered again and again in banal comments such as, "Wondering whatever became of up-and-comer Ruby Priest? Her whereabouts are as mysterious as the play she's rumored to be starring in. She won't take our calls, but we understand that on Thursday night at People's Theatre she'll be saying a mouthful about things plenty of people wish she'd keep quiet about." I expected Ruby to be full of herself over the success of her "campaign," but rather than rubbing my nose in it, she kept quiet about the effort. Apparently, she had other things on her mind.

"What's the matter, Rube?" I asked her the evening of our final rehearsal. She'd been stomping about the theater since her arrival, causing everyone to back away from her lest they encounter her wrath.

"Nothing. Everything's fine." She continued to slam, smack, and push items that entered her path. At last I realized the source of her rage: I was witnessing the dance of a woman scorned. Tony must have stepped in and secured Jayne's part.

I maintained a safe distance and whispered. "You sure?"

She looked at me, torn between whether to confide the enormous disservice she'd been done or to swallow her agony until she'd set her stomach afire. She decided on the latter. "I said I was fine."

It was a standard belief in the theater world that a bad last rehearsal meant a good opening night. You didn't actively seek out a poor performance, since we believed that theatrical voodoo wouldn't reward a conscious effort at failure. But when you managed to put on a rehearsal that made hand puppets appealing, you reassured yourself that the show wouldn't be a complete disaster by remembering that suffering through this guaranteed success the next night. And the fact was that every show I'd been in had had at least one outright disaster at the final dress rehearsal that left us all sleepless with anxiety only to redeem ourselves with an audience the next day. Fear could do a lot to improve a show. So could adrenaline.

So it was with a mix of glee and peculiar hope that all would go well on opening night that I watched Ruby give the worst performance of her career. Whatever had set her off took the heart out of every line until it seemed I'd stumbled upon some grade school Christmas pageant. Each scene she was in resulted in a gaggle of off-stage tittering as the other actresses rushed to confirm they'd seen what they'd just seen. Peter remained stony throughout the display, hoping, I think, that it was retaliation for his method exercises. When no one yelled "surprise" as the final curtain went down, he put his head in his hands and made a noise that was a cross between a whimper and a moan.

Before the run-through had begun, he'd announced that it wasn't his practice to give notes at the last rehearsal, and that we were all to gather our things and leave as soon as we were out of costume. As though they feared he would change his mind based on what he'd just seen, the cast rushed to the dressing rooms to disrobe and left the theater on mute tiptoes. I decided to stick around for a minute or two, since I suspected if I didn't lend Peter my ear, the local gin mill would be given that honor.

"How bad was it?" Peter limped across the house and settled in the chair beside me.

"The technical stuff was great and I found the ending very moving." I picked at my nails, then realized this gesture might be perceived as evidence of my fibbing.

"You can be honest, Rosie. The critics will be."

I sat on my hands to prevent their further destruction. "Ruby was a little off."

Peter laughed with such enthusiasm that his head bounced off the back of his seat. "A little? I tell you, between this and the leaks to the press . . . I don't know what I'm going to do."

"What leaks?"

Peter rolled his eyes and scowled. "Come on, Rosie—I'm not dumb. Haven't you seen the items in the papers? Ruby made it clear to me she was upset the show wasn't being publicized. This is her revenge."

Guilt nibbled at my stomach. "At least she's keeping up the air of mystery. I haven't seen anything that revealed the title or author." Did I wear my complicity like too much rouge? "Have people been calling?"

"Nonstop. The whole weekend's sold."

I punched him lightly on the shoulder. "See? That's a good thing."

His arm turned rigid at my touch. "It was already selling. And I find her tactics more than a little dishonest. In the first place, I forbade her to do any promotion. And in the second, the promotion she has done makes this sound like another play entirely. Surely you've caught that?"

"Is that really so bad? If it gets them here . . ."

He swatted at an imaginary fly. "If it gets them here, they'll be disappointed that our play isn't the one they were hoping for. After the first night, word will get out that this isn't Raymond Fielding's long-lost masterwork but something much less exciting. That will kill the production."

I hadn't thought about that. In fact, I hadn't thought about anything beyond opening night. I hated to think my scheme would be responsible for *In the Dark*'s demise, especially since I wasn't likely to step foot onstage until several weeks into the run. "You've created a great show, Peter, one that will stand on its merits. Maybe people will come expecting Fielding's long-lost play, but I have a feeling that after they see what you've done with *this* show, they're not going to care about the other one."

"Don't be so naive," Peter snapped. His face changed and he set his hand on my arm. "I'm sorry. That came out wrong. I just feel like Ruby's ruined something by doing this. I suppose you and I are in the same boat. We've both been working very hard for something we'll benefit very little from."

"At least the checks cash." I pulled my belongings onto the seat on the other side of me and made sure I had everything I'd brought with me. "And if I'm being naive, I think you're being melodramatic. It really is a good show. I'm not trying to soothe your wounded ego. I thought nothing of this play a month ago, and now I'd kill to be in it on opening night. Doesn't that tell you something?"

"Just that I made a casting mistake." He reached out and gently touched my cheek. "I am sorry. You're a good actress."

My hand met his. "Thanks, but I wanted to be great."

"You're a great actress." Then, just like that, he kissed me. It was the kind of kiss that made you take back things you didn't steal. Twice I opened my eyes and twice I realized how odd it was to watch someone while their eyes were closed. At last we separated, and I was so dumbstruck that I could do nothing but touch my lips.

"I like you," he said.

"You'd better. Some girls would take that as a proposal."

He gave the room a furtive glance. "How about we get out of here?"

I was tired and knew I should head home, but the kiss had temporarily removed the word *no* from my vocabulary. "What did you have in mind?"

"A drink. Maybe two."

He made a cursory sweep of the room, shutting off lights and bidding farewell to a few lingering crew members chatting in the lobby. I went to the windows and watched as a light snow began to fall. Outside, a young couple paused before the *In the Dark* poster. I could see the woman clearly—young and pretty, her long dark hair dusted white—but the only thing I could make out about the man was his navy uniform. As they read the sign, he wrapped his arms around her, put his chin atop her head, and pretended to snooze. She laughed at him and turned to meet him face-to-face. The dimmed streetlight illuminated them and for one awful moment I thought it was Jack who held her, Jack who made her laugh, Jack who kept her warm.

Was it like this for him, too? Did he see me in places I couldn't possibly be?

"Ready?" Peter asked.

My head ached, my stomach swirled. "I think I need to call it a night."

Peter approached me and lightly set his hand atop my shoulder. "Why?"

A sob gripped my throat. *Keep it together, Rosie. You can cry all you want on the way home.* "I'm not feeling so good."

His hand brushed my cheek. "Can I walk you home?"

I backed away from him as the first tears blurred my vision. "No, no. I think I'll hail a hack and spend some of that money I've been working so hard for. Thank you, though."

It took me forever to fall asleep. While Jayne lightly snored beside me, I put the radio on low and listened to the late-night news on WNEW. The Japanese had stepped up attacks near the Solomon Islands in an effort to get control of that area. Days before there had been rumors that they had sunk two Allied battleships and three cruisers, though now our navy was insisting that this was a gross exaggeration; we hadn't lost nearly the number of men the Axis were claiming. Still, men were lost and I couldn't help but wonder if Jack was among them.

If I loved him enough, could that save him? Or did the men who were loved die as easily as those nobody missed?

Eventually, my body gave up and let me doze. I slept as if I were in a Pullman upper during an overnight trip in the driving rain. My dreams played out the various scenarios that might happen on opening night, but I never got to see how each possibility ended. Instead, the scenes blurred one into the other until it seemed that there would never be resolution, just moments that spurred on an infinite number of other events.

"Rosie? Rosie? Wake up."

I blinked until a series of disconnected images formed an outline of my roommate. I rubbed my eyes until the shape filled in and Jayne's face loomed large before me. "What?"

"Do you know where Ruby is?"

As it was not the question I would expect to hear first thing in the morning, I struggled to make the meaningless words form a coherent thought. "What?"

Jayne sighed and repeated the question at a rate reserved for the ancient and deaf. I sat up and struggled to make out the hands on my bedside clock. "Ruby? No. Why?"

Jayne slumped onto the edge of my bed and I realized she was fully dressed. That meant it had to be going on 11:00. "Peter Sherwood has been calling for her for the past hour. She was supposed to be at the theater and didn't show."

I sank back onto my pillows. "She's probably on her way. Ruby wouldn't just not show up." I yawned and stretched my arms. "Is Peter still on the horn?" With distance between me and the night before, I felt sheepish about my quick exit. I'd been tired; that was all. He would understand.

"No, but he told me to have her call him the second I see her." Jayne smacked my leg. "How can you be so calm?"

"To start with, I'm half asleep, though the pain now coursing down my leg is doing wonders toward waking me. Why are you so worried?"

Jayne put her hands on her hips. "Don't you consider it a little strange that after getting out the word that Fielding's missing play is going to be performed tonight, the one named cast member is missing?"

I shook the final remnants of sleep from my head and searched the floor for my shoes. "I forgot about that."

"You forgot?!"

"Are you going to be repeating everything I say today?" I wasn't irritated by her; I was mad at my own stupidity. "I'm sorry. Look, you're right. This could mean something has happened to Ruby, but it could also mean she's throwing an ing-bing at Peter and decided she's not showing up until she's good and ready." I crammed my dogs into my shoes, then realized they didn't match. Off came one in exchange for the other's mate.

"So you think she's all right?"

"Stubborn and bitter, yes, but in danger? Absolutely not." I changed the rest of my clothes and convinced Jayne to join me at Cora Dean's for a late breakfast. I needed to chew and I was willing to bet that by the time we made it home the situation with Ruby would be resolved. I was a mess at breakfast, so clumsy with nerves that I managed to knock over my coffee. I wanted to take my mind off whatever was coming to pass that night, so I dragged Jayne to the Roxy and we took in an afternoon short.

By the time the final reel reminded us that we could buy war bonds and stamps in the lobby, it was 3:00. The minute we returned to the house, Belle assaulted us.

"You need to call Peter Sherwood. Immediately."

Jayne and I exchanged panicked looks before I took the stairs two at a time and announced to Diane Lemus that if she didn't hang up the blower, she'd be wearing it. The phone rang and rang at People's

Theatre. I decided to give it twenty jangles before heading over on foot. Peter picked up on number nineteen.

"Ruby?" he gasped.

"Rosie," I said. "Are you dying or just out of breath?"

"Both, unless you have good news. Ruby was supposed to be here at nine this morning and has yet to show. Please tell me you know where she is."

Jayne came to my side and tipped the receiver so she could eavesdrop. "Nope," I told Peter. "She's not here. Why were you meeting her so early?"

"After I left you last night, I ran into her. We had words and a rather ghastly falling out. After I apologized profusely, she conceded that maybe she hadn't done her best job and that it might be useful to have one final rehearsal."

"So you left on good terms?"

"Absolutely," said Peter. "I'm frantic, Rosie. I've called the police, the hospitals, everywhere I can think of. She's just disappeared."

"Did you try Lawrence Bentley?"

"Of course."

I was sick to my stomach. Jayne didn't help matters by gasping at each new revelation as to why we needed to be worried about Ruby's disappearance. I sent her away from the phone with a sharp tilt of my head and put my back to her. "I don't know what to tell you, Peter. If Ruby was mad at you, I could see her doing this, but if you left on good terms . . . well she still could've gotten distracted by something. You shouldn't give up hope."

"I'm not giving up hope," said Peter. "But we open in five hours. We need a contingency plan and I'm afraid you're it."

I looked over my shoulder at Jayne to make sure she hadn't heard what Peter had said.

"Did you hear me, Rosie?" he asked.

"Loud and clear."

"It's a full house tonight and there are a number of reviewers in attendance. I can't cancel things, and while the situation isn't ideal, I know you'll do a great job."

I was torn between feeling jubilant that I would get to play the part and terrified that Ruby was lying in an alley somewhere because of me and my big mouth. If Ruby was dead, then just as Detmire predicted, my attempts to smoke out the killer had succeeded only in causing more loss of life. "Will you do it, Rosie?"

I slid to the floor and knocked my head against the banister. "Do I have any choice?"

33 Stage Door

"YOU'RE DOING THE SHOW, AREN'T you?" Jayne was on me before the phone hit the cradle.

"He needs me."

"What he needs is to cancel the show. Don't you see that?" She followed me back into the room and guarded the door while I threw what I needed into a bag.

"It'll be fine, Jayne."

"I'll remind you of that at your funeral."

"I know the situation isn't ideal, but I don't have a choice in the matter. This is our last chance—after tonight everyone's going to know the play doesn't exist. The safest place I could be is onstage." Jayne pondered this logic while I hid my lack of conviction beneath a hastily applied layer of lipstick. Too many stories in the pulps pointed out the flaw in my theory. If I wasn't shot during my big monologue, any number of accidental catastrophes could befall me—falling rigging, poisoned water, knife-wielding henchmen waiting in the wings. Suspect though they may be, careful planning on the part of the culprit could make it possible for whatever happened to me to be ruled an accident. And given my experience with the bias of the local flatfoots, I doubted anyone was going to dicker with a misdiagnosis.

I just wouldn't stand beneath any lights, beside any flats, or drink any liquids I didn't prepare myself. Oh, and I'd wear an iron girdle beneath my costume.

"I'm going to need more reinforcements for tonight," said Jayne. "If you're going to be onstage, me scoping out the crowd won't be enough."

I applied my hat and coat and did a final search of my bag. A horrible thought crept through my head as I performed what had become my mundane routine: What if this is the last time I ever did this? Would I wish I'd spent more time doing ordinary things?

Should I have written Jack?

I gave Jayne a wide, false smile. "Bring whoever you've got to bring—Tony, Al, whoever—but don't worry. I'm going to be fine."

Churchill yowled and rubbed against my legs. There it was: verification of my impending demise. When even the devil's nice to you, you know you're in trouble.

"Knock it off, Churchill."

"He's wishing you luck," said Jayne.

"He's bidding me farewell." I gently kicked him out of my way, and with a hiss he approached the dresser. As I pinned on my hat and pulled on my coat, he began to use a mahogany leg as his scratching post. Since it wasn't my dresser or, technically, my cat, I ignored him. He wasn't happy about this; he increased his damage and his volume.

"You'll miss me," I told him.

Jayne hugged me with the intensity of a war bride, then pulled away and studied me as if she was trying to cement the image for posterity. "You're right—everything will be great. And all things considered, this may turn out to be quite a night for you." Her face lingered somewhere between a grin and a scowl, confirming that while she intended her words to be upbeat, they really were nothing more than one of my ma's attempts to placate me when I was sick. Ma would reassure me that I wasn't dying and that whatever symptoms I had were ones she herself had weathered, but the minute I turned my back, she was on the phone crowing to the doctor about her baby's descent to death's door.

I'd survived measles, mumps, and smallpox; I'd survive this, too.

·   ·   ·

When I arrived at the theater at 4:00, Peter wasn't there, which was fine by me. The last thing I needed were his opening night hysterics further complicating what was bound to be a difficult evening. Hilda let me inside, then resumed her work preparing the lobby with flowers, photos, and a more conducive arrangement of the benches.

"Where's Peter?" I asked her.

"Running errands, which means he's probably holed up at John Kelly's doing shots." And here I thought he didn't drink the whiskey.

I picked up a program and was disappointed to find the printer lacked psychic abilities. Ruby was prominently listed while my name was nowhere to be found.

"There'll be an insert," said Hilda.

I nodded, trying hard to look like I couldn't care less if my performance was acknowledged. "Big crowd tonight?"

Hilda nodded toward the end of the bench, silently asking for my assistance in moving it. "Huge. The biggest I've seen at this joint yet. And we've not only got bodies, we've got names. Rumor has it LaGuardia's coming."

"The mayor?" I wondered what kind of dirt he thought Fielding had on him.

"Yep. And his wife."

I tried to keep up my air of not caring, but it was impossible to do that while hauling heavy furniture. "Any chance I could see who else is on the list?"

We lowered the bench into its new position and she stepped back to assess that all was as she wanted it. "Look, Rosie, opening a show you didn't intend to open is bad enough. I'm not going to let you dwell on who's going to be here when chances are you won't be able to see beyond the first row. Concentrate on you and leave the rest to me."

You had to admire a woman who knew how to deal with paranoid actresses. On another night, I might've even appreciated it. "Thanks, Hilda, but I just want to make sure my friends got reservations."

"Assume they're in. Anyone tells the box office your name will get a seat, even if I have to kick out my own mother. Do you need anything else?"

I pondered the variety of intoxicants that could get me through the night and shook my head. "An hour alone in the theater would be good."

"Done. The costumer is due here in forty-five minutes, but she's never on time. The other girls are coming at five thirty to run through your scenes. Until one or the other shows up, I'll protect those wooden doors with my life."

I disappeared into the auditorium and found they had yet to adjust the heating in the building to levels compatible with human life. Overnight they'd painted the stage floor black to hide the weeks of scuff marks we'd left on the wood. Small pieces of tape replaced the heavily drawn lines we'd relied on to find our marks.

To summon the emotions I needed for my character, I tried to recall every moment I'd felt slighted and insignificant, from Jack's silence and Peter's mixed signals to Ruby's and Eloise's more direct attacks. I walked the stage whispering my lines, no longer thinking of the words but of the meaning. As I progressed from the beginning of the play to the end, tears welled up in my eyes and I implored invisible characters to find it in their hearts to forgive me.

Applause sounded from the rear of the auditorium. I stopped what I was doing and located Peter standing with his back to the wall. "You've restored my confidence," he said.

"I wasn't aware you'd lost it."

"Call it temporarily misplaced." He met me at the edge of the stage and offered me a hand to help me to the floor. I landed with a wobble that increased as I caught a whiff of booze on his breath.

"You've been celebrating early."

"Can you blame me? If your life were about to end, wouldn't you allow yourself a little pleasure?" He wore a blue serge suit that had started clean and pressed and deteriorated into a wino's Sunday best.

"Your life isn't going to end, Peter. It's one production."

He looked toward the ceiling. His eyes were red-rimmed, his face splotchy. He'd been crying. "It's so much more than that."

I pulled out a hankie and gently cleaned his face. "Why? Why does this production matter so much to you?"

He stopped my hand with his and studied my fingers as though it were the first time he'd really seen those odd digits that separated man from beast. "I wanted to prove myself. I wanted to make it clear that I was ready for bigger and better things."

"That is clear. Ruby isn't taking that away from you."

He released me and leaned against the stage. "It's not just Ruby. It's *In the Dark*. We've done good things, but when all is said and done, this production is going to be forgotten."

"That's a bleak outlook."

He turned to me and cocked his head. "It's an awful play, Rosie. We both know that. To do the first production of a really important play allows something of what you've created to be preserved. My direction, my revisions to the script, my cast—they all become indelibly connected to the play. I had to do this production, and maybe someone will see it and think good things about me as a director. But even if the run's a success, it will not be the play that will make my career."

"And what would that play be like?"

He smiled faintly and swept my hair off my shoulder. "For starters, my performers would be very different from this production. Not only would they be talented, but they'd influence every decision I made. I'd pick actresses not because of who they are and what they'd been in but because of what they meant to me."

His face was inches from my own. We breathed the same air and his afternoon cocktail no longer seemed so terrible. "And the play?"

"It would be important, well written, controversial—everything this play isn't."

"What if such a play doesn't exist?"

He stepped away from me and took my hands in his. "It does. I just have to find it."

I should've told him the play he wanted was no more, but I couldn't stand the idea of shattering his illusion, especially since I was to blame for the position he was in. "You will find it," I said. I searched out my next words. They felt cruel, but if it helped Peter get through the evening, I didn't see the harm. "In fact, I think I already have."

"You found the play?"

I stuttered, immediately regretting saying anything. "I have a very strong lead."

Peter smiled and nodded. "I've waited this long. What's a few more days?" He landed a feather-light kiss on my cheek. "The other girls are here and you have work to do."

He opened the auditorium door, and the rest of the cast came pouring through, greeting me with "Congratulations," and "Isn't this exciting," and "I'm so glad you're playing the role instead of Ruby." I stood dazed as they gathered around me, acknowledging their words with a mumbled thank-you while wondering if it was too late to scram.

I didn't have a chance. For the next hour we went through my scenes to make certain I knew all of the blocking. Peter sat quietly in the audience, nursing his drunk with a strong cup of joe while contributing nothing to the effort beyond a growing sense of doom. As soon as we'd done the final scene, I was banished to the dressing rooms where Joan—the costumer—awaited with assorted implements of her trade and a WAC uniform that was much too ample in the bust.

"Nervous?" she asked. She was a large woman with a mass of curly hair she'd pulled back from her face with a scrap of gingham. All about her enormous bosom were pins she'd stuck through her dress lapel. You could see the pins' heads and tips, but the centers disappeared beneath the fabric so that it looked as if she'd pierced her skin.

I shrugged at her statement of the obvious and decided to be contrary for the heck of it. "I don't get nervous."

She smiled at me and I knew she felt my lie in the way my pump raced beneath her touch.

"Things seem pretty normal to you tonight?" I asked.

"What do you mean?" She had a space between her front teeth you could drive a flivver through.

"You know—does this seem like an ordinary opening night to you?"

"You're the first understudy we've had step in if that's what you mean." It wasn't, but I had a feeling I wasn't going to get the answer I needed without outright telling her why I was asking. "Peter must be feeling pretty good about hiring you."

Peter was feeling a lot of things tonight, but good wasn't one of them. "What do you mean?" I asked.

"You're the first understudy People's Theatre ever hired. They're not in the budget." She laughed and fished a needle out of her dress. "Heck, I'm not in the budget. Peter fought tooth and nail to get you for this show, though. Of course, once word gets out, I imagine every director is going to insist on the same. Board's going to love that." She threaded the needle and bit the thread free from its spool. "I'm going to have to sew you in for tonight. If this ends up being a regular deal, we'll look into making some more permanent changes."

I nodded and braced myself as she pushed the needle into the fabric beneath my left armpit. "I thought Ruby insisted she needed an understudy?"

Joan shrugged, which changed the needle's path until it pricked my skin. "I just know what I hear. Rumor was Peter claimed it was the way professional theaters did things, and if we ever hoped to be considered one, we'd do the same. 'Course, he may have been worried that Ruby would pull something like this. I tell you, that one could make a bear eat its own cubs."

She was wise, this woman. "But why me?"

"Why not?"

Hilda entered our enclave and rapped her clipboard against the wall. "Twenty minutes to places."

Joan bit free the thread that joined her to me and tucked a neat knot inside the new seam. "I know you're not nervous and you don't need it, but break a leg, kid. You're going to be fantastic, knock on wood." She gave me a solid pat on the back and picked up a basket containing an assortment of thread, needles, and fasteners. As she left, she rapped her fist on my vanity to solidify the good fortune I so desperately needed.

The other girls bustled into the dressing room and pulled on the simple shifts designed to represent their various nationalities. The air grew heavy with powder and nervous chitchat that predicted all the horrible things that might happen that night. They all talked over one another, until their overlapping voices became a symphony of everything that might go wrong.

"I know I'm going to trip. Right in the middle of my monologue I'll go facedown, and with Brooks Atkinson in the house."

"Just make sure you wear a slip. I walked onstage opening night of *Taming of the Shrew* and no one bothered to tell me that you could see my drawers when I found my light."

"I'd kill for something like that to happen to me. I'm so forgettable in this lousy part that they printed my name in the program with invisible ink."

The girls cooed remonstrations at one another, assuring themselves that they were talented, lovely, and destined for greatness. I smiled to myself as they fluttered about, wondering how it was that after weeks of enforced tension, the group had managed to gain the camaraderie of any other cast. Peter would've been mortified.

I walked out of the dressing room and crept into the wings. I peered through a hole in the grand drape and spied the audience as they found their seats. Eloise McCain was seated in the third row, center, her veiled black hat obscuring her face. Henry Nussbaum sat house right, talking to a stylish older woman who might've been his wife. Lawrence Bentley in a well-tailored suit and a lingering scowl sat on the aisle. Hail, hail the gang was all here.

"Dabrowski's Mazurka," Poland's national anthem, blared through the house speakers, only to be cut off and replaced by "The Star-Spangled Banner." The audience cheered as the familiar piece started, only to gasp when it was replaced by Germany's "Deutsch-landlied." If that shocked them, they were in for a long, uncomfortable night.

I backed away from the curtain and put my hands over my ears to temporarily block out the crowd. Behind me was the prop table, heavily laden with the various implements we'd be using throughout the night. I released my ears and rapped my hand against the wood. Everything would be fine, knock on wood. Nobody would die, knock on wood. I wouldn't humiliate myself, knock on wood.

I started to walk away, but the leg of the table snagged my skirt. The wood had been so damaged that it looked like a banana with its peel half off. Clearly this piece of furniture had been salvaged from someone's home, where evil reigned with its almond-shaped eyes. The calm left me and Churchill weighed heavily on my mind. Stupid cat with his random acts of destruction. We'd be lucky if any of the furniture remained when we got home. And since when had he developed a taste for wood? The only time I'd ever seen him touch it was the day I'd found Jim and that was clearly to alert me . . .

Wood?! When Fake Fielding visited me at Jim's office, Churchill had scratched his leg. He hadn't bled; he hadn't even reacted until he saw the cat dangling from his limb. And that portrait, that damn portrait in Fielding's library, depicted a man with two good getaway sticks. Fielding would never have painted a self-portrait—it didn't fit in with his idea of the artist being invisible to his art. Plus, Fielding was the one who'd lost a leg in the war, not Detmire, so why would Detmire sport a bum leg? Could they both have sustained the exact same injury, or was the man who claimed to be Alan Detmire as bogus as the painting that was supposed to be a self-portrait?

The music in the theater began to fade and with it went the house-lights. Someone took my arm and led me back to the wings, then gave me a gentle push onto the stage.

34 The Devil Takes a Bride

IN TOTAL DARKNESS I SOUGHT my marker on the stage floor and took my position for the opening montage. As the lights came up, I forgot about Raymond Fielding and gave in to the peculiar energy of a rapt audience. My anxiety and nervousness mixed until everything but the moment before me was blocked out. I was terrifying, proud, and strong. If for a fleeting moment I pondered the stability of the klieg lights above me or the reactions of the darkened crowd before me, the sense of responsibility I had toward my character quickly quieted those distractions. By the time we whirled toward the end of the first act, I'd forgotten there was anyone there other than the seven women who shared my stage.

At intermission, we traveled en masse back to the dressing room and on Hilda's command were not allowed to talk to anyone lest we lose the sense of tension we'd ended the act with. For fifteen minutes we clammed up while the building buzzed with audience members traveling to restrooms, having a smoke, and buying hooch from a temporary bar in the lobby. All the while we knew they were talking about the play. With the show halfway over, was anyone still worried that the information they feared would emerge in the second act?

A bell sounded that the audience was to return to their seats. Hilda barked the amount of time remaining until places, and we each gave our attention to the row of lighted mirrors where our faces appeared large and unfamiliar. Makeup fixed, hair pinned, costumes donned, we returned to the backstage area, took a collective deep breath, and plunged into act two.

The show passed more quickly than before, and though we each dreaded the deep emotion that might or might not come when it was supposed to, I was jubilant when tears began to fall and the sob I feared I'd have to fake was so real and overpowering that I gasped my final lines and wondered for an instant if I'd ever be able to recover from the grief. As I lay in the center of the stage, the curtain dropped, the distance between its hem and the stage floor illuminated by the rising houselights. The grand drape reopened and I rose and joined hands with the rest of the cast so that we might bow in unison. The capacity audience filled the room with their applause, then leaped to their feet to further express their gratitude. Our human chain moved forward and bowed once again, then we snaked into the wings and one by one released one another until eight women stood alone.

"Congratulations!"

"I could use a drink."

"Who'd a thought they'd be applauding this lousy play?"

We were giddy, jubilant, and a little punch-drunk. I passed out hugs like they were pennies for refugees and gratefully became part of the group, recounting those moments we knew went well and those which hadn't, though the audience wasn't likely to know. Family and friends drifted backstage, some with flowers, others with Brownie cameras slung around their necks. We exchanged introductions and received mixed accolades that made it apparent that most of the audience, while enjoying themselves, still hadn't a clue what they'd just seen.

"Rosie!" Jayne breezed into the room and wrapped her arms about my waist. Before I could acknowledge her, she swung me around, then dropped me indelicately back to the earth.

"What did you think?" I asked.

She leaned in close and I could smell her intermission martini. "You were divine—absolutely. You broke my heart during that last scene." She offered red eyes and a makeup-smeared handkerchief as evidence of my talent. "I don't know what they'll make of the show, but if you don't get a paragraph of praise, I'll eat my hat."

"Rosie." Tony B., red-faced and clad in a chalk-striped suit, emerged from behind Jayne. "You were marvelous. Absolutely. I had no idea you could act." Though the words were intended for me, he couldn't take his eyes off my pal. He may have been a louse—and one of Mangano's louses at that—but he loved her, that was plain to see.

I let him capture my hand in his oversized paws. "Thanks, Tony, it's good to see you again." Behind Tony hovered Al, looking like a lost child hoping to spy his parents in the crowd.

"Look who's here," I said. "Does this mean you're speaking to us now?"

Al talked to the floor. "Jayne needed a favor."

You had to appreciate his honesty. "What did you think of the play?"

His head turned in my direction, but still he didn't meet my eyes. He was too busy trying not to look like he was watching Jayne's every move. "Interesting. Ain't never seen a play before."

"And did this one make you want to see another one?"

He shrugged and fidgeted like a man in desperate need of a cigarette.

"So," I said to the three of them. "Anything unusual happen during the show?"

They exchanged looks and silently appointed Jayne as spokeswoman. "Not a thing," she whispered.

"Did anyone leave early?" I asked.

"It was awfully crowded, Rosie, but I think I might've seen Ruby sneak in halfway through the first act."

So Ruby was safe and sound. Good news, I guessed, though now I was completely mystified as to what she'd been up to. "Any idea where she went?"

"Nope," said Jayne, "but a fin says she shows up again before the evening's over."

An hour after the show the crowd dispersed with instructions to head to John Kelly's, where a light reception was being served. While I was talking to Jayne, the rest of the cast shed their costumes and changed into their party dresses. By the time I was ready to do the same, the place was almost empty.

"Should I wait?" asked Jayne.

"I wouldn't. Go on ahead and stake out a drink for me. I'll be over in ten." I started to leave, then stopped myself. "Jayne."

She hummed a response.

"I know this is going to sound crazy, but I don't think Raymond Fielding is dead."

"You're right, that does sound crazy."

"Even so, keep an eye out for him, would you? If he was clever enough to fake his death and masquerade as Detmire, he could be pretending to be anyone tonight."

"At this point," said Jayne. "Nothing would surprise me."

The dressing room was dark when I made it upstairs. I felt for the overhead light's pull chain and flooded the room. A huge floral arrangement sat at my dressing table. I plucked a daisy from the display, closed my eyes, and took a deep whiff.

"Do you like them?"

I opened my eyes and found Peter's reflection watching me from the mirror. I returned the flower—worse for wear—to the vase. "They're beautiful, but it wasn't necessary."

"After your performance tonight it most certainly was. You were wonderful."

I turned away from the vanity and met him in real life. His suit seemed cleaner, his manner confident. "You know how potent fear is—it has the power to transform."

"Give yourself more credit than that. You impressed a lot of people tonight."

"Ruby won't be too happy to hear that." I sat on my dressing table stool and pulled the pins from my hair. "I understand she was here."

The lines of Peter's face turned vertical. "Who did you hear that from?"

"My girlfriend saw her during the show."

"Well, if she was here, she didn't make it known to me." His hands flattened against his thighs and rubbed his trousers.

I brushed my hair until it lay loose and soft about my shoulders. "I guess the good news is she's all right. I can't for the life of me understand why she wouldn't have done the show, especially since you two left on good terms last night."

He glanced out the door and returned his gaze to me. "Do you know much about Ruby's background?"

"Not really. Why?"

He sat on the stool beside me. "I mentioned before that we'd worked together on another Fielding play?" I nodded. "She was very young and had this incredible raw talent. Fielding was in the habit then of talking to all the actors in his plays, usually by telephone or letter, although in one or two rare instances he met them in person. He and Ruby apparently became quite close—so much so that he became a benefactor for her during her first few months in New York. Then, right before the play was to open, Ruby was offered a bigger, better part in a much more commercial piece, one she had pursued without telling anyone. She dropped out of Fielding's show with almost no notice and appeared in a big show with a big part that was a big flop. Meanwhile, Fielding's show also floundered. It was a good piece, but the actress who stepped in lacked the naturalism Raymond wanted. Critics savaged the production because of her, which Fielding considered inexcusable. The actors, after all, shouldn't have even been noticed. Needless to say, he was very displeased with Ruby and the way she so easily swept aside his play for a piece he considered theatrical garbage. He implied on more than one occasion that he would find a way to repay her self-interest. She took on a stage name to avoid his retaliation, though naturally he was able to track her down."

"Wow. So the missing play . . . Ruby believed it was about her?" My mind flashed back to Jim's office. He'd mentioned a woman in his case notes, the broad with nice gams and a bad attitude. He couldn't have described Ruby better if he'd included her 8 x 10.

"Yes, she's convinced Fielding's play will be her ruin. She even confided in me that she'd received letters to that effect. For months now someone has been writing her missives that hint at scenes that depict Ruby not as a young, desperate performer but as a calculating woman who would stoop to anything—the lowest of casting couches— to guarantee her personal success."

So that was why she took the job with Eloise. It had nothing to do with Bentley. She was trying to find the play for herself. "But what has that got to do with tonight?"

His face changed and something in it told me he'd fixed the whole thing.

"You forced Ruby out of the show," I said.

He took a deep breath. "She left because I asked her to."

"Why?"

He sighed and left his seat. "She betrayed Fielding. Since he was my mentor, I owed it to him never to work with her again, even if I wasn't willing to drag her name through the mud as he may have wished. As I've said, the board pressured me to put her in the role, and from day one I found her weak and unconvincing. If this show was to succeed despite its script, I needed talent more than a name, especially a name Raymond himself would've reviled. I knew you'd do a better job, that you'd help maintain the spirit of what it was Raymond wanted. I also knew the board would never agree to it unless they believed Ruby had abandoned us. I'm sorry for lying to you this afternoon, but I didn't want to make you complicit."

He was pandering to my vanity, but that didn't mean I didn't like it. "How did you get Ruby to leave?"

He tilted his head and smiled at me the way parents do when their children say precious things. "As I said, Ruby was convinced the missing play presented her in an ugly light. Last night I told her you knew who had it, but you had refused to tell anyone the script's whereabouts unless you could take over her role."

"You did what?"

"I'm sorry I dragged you into this, Rosie. It was selfish of me especially since . . . well there's no telling what her intentions were coming back tonight."

Was I supposed to be scared of Ruby? The idea was preposterous, and yet I couldn't disagree with what Peter was telling me. Was her career so important that she would be willing to kill for it?

"Don't worry about this right now." He put his hand under my chin and tipped my face upward. "You need to celebrate your achievement tonight. You were magnetic onstage. Heartbreaking. Vivid. And that was in a lousy play. You're going to get a tremendous amount of work from this."

I knew better than to believe the castle in the sky stories so many directors and producers wove for actors, but I gave myself over to Peter's fantasy. "Did you really think so?"

"Absolutely."

I pushed Ruby out of my mind and relived my final moments onstage. "It's funny—tonight's the first night I really felt like an actress. The whole time I was up there, all that mattered to me was playing the part, not because it was a job but because it was my duty." I winced. "That probably doesn't make any sense."

"I think I understand what you mean." He put his hand on my shoulder. "We make a good team, you and I. As I said before, I would love to work with you again."

"Under more legitimate circumstances?"

His second hand joined his first. "You have proven yourself tenfold. I won't have to deceive anyone to use you in the future." He combed his fingers through my hair and plucked out the remaining pins. "We must be cautious about our next project. The audience may be willing to forgive this play because we took care to rise above the material, but next time they may not be so willing. Instead of being a great actress who was accidentally trapped in poor material, they'll start to see you as someone who habitually chooses to be part of something awful. They'll blame you for choosing badly, for even promoting bad theater, and, eventually, they'll stop coming to see you."

"Slow down, Peter. I just had my first victory. Don't go ruining my entire career yet."

He smiled. "I'm protecting my investment, Rosie. That's all. I want to make sure you choose the right path."

I stopped his hand with my own. "Is that what I am, your investment?"

His eyes met mine in the mirror. "Is that what you want to be?"

I couldn't answer.

"Who is he, Rosie?"

"Who's who?"

"The reason you hesitate."

"I'm not . . ." What wasn't I? Hesitating? Over Jack? Ready to move on? "There's nobody."

"I'm glad to hear that." He kissed the top of my head and the warmth traveled the length of my spine. "We could go far together. I'd like to think that my directing had something to do with your success tonight. Of course, if you go on to do brilliantly without me, my case will be much weaker."

I tipped my head backward until I could see the real him. "I'll tell every reporter that I learned the ropes from you. I'd never forget the little people. How could I when they're there every time I look down?"

His smile disappeared.

"I'm joking, Peter. I'd give my eyeteeth to work with you again." I turned back toward him. "So what should our next project be?"

He stretched his arms wide. "How about Raymond Fielding's missing play?"

35 Dr. Faustus

I LAUGHED AND ROSE FROM the stool. "Nice recall, Peter. First rule of comedy: big jokes are the result of accumulated little jokes."

He again took hold of my shoulders, forcing me back into my seat. "I'm serious, Rosie. You said you have a good lead on where the play is and I think we'd be fools if we didn't take advantage of it. This is a career maker."

I rested my hands in the nooks of his elbows. "I hate to be the one to tell you this, but there is no play. There never was."

"But you said—"

"You were drunk and I was worried. I'm sorry."

I expected disappointment, maybe grief, but what I got was a grip on my arms so tight my blood stopped circulating. "Don't be preposterous. There has to be a play. McCain was hired to look for it."

I tried to shrug free, but he tightened his grip. "How do you know about Jim?"

Peter released me and stepped away. "Why does it matter?"

"Because he's dead, that's why." I stood up from the stool and walked the line of the dressing table. "Did you kill him?"

He started to speak, then stopped himself. He clasped his hands and brought them to his mouth. "He wouldn't cooperate."

The words froze me. "Let me guess: Fielding told you the play was missing and that he'd hired a dick to find it. You tracked Jim down and tried to find out what he knew, only Jim wouldn't give you what you wanted, probably because he couldn't find it and didn't have the guts to admit it. You were convinced he was lying and tried to force it out of him, but things went wrong and you ended up with no play and a dead man on your hands. Maybe Jim ran at the mouth about the actress who worked for him, so you hunted me down and invited me to your audition, hoping you could woo me into telling you everything you wanted to know."

"It wasn't like that, Rosie."

I pursued him, wagging my finger in his face like a small-town schoolmarm. "You killed him, you son of a bitch. Over a play. A play, Peter! And not even one you're named in, but one you're desperate to direct. How sick is that?"

He brushed aside my attempt to be physically intimidating and moved toward me until my remonstrating finger hit his chest. "It was an accident. I didn't mean to kill him. Things got rough on both our parts. You know how Jim was."

"No, but I'm starting to know how you are."

His arms again claimed mine. "You don't understand, Rosie. I need that play. We both do. A piece like that would be dynamite in this town. Every career has a defining moment when it leaves ordinary and becomes extraordinary. This could be ours."

"Did you kill Fielding, too?"

He released me as though he recognized that defending himself was much more difficult when he was threatening me. "Of course not. How can you say that? I adored Raymond."

"Him? Sure, but what about his son?"

He put his fingers to his temples. "He wasn't his real son. He didn't care about Raymond's work, only his own reputation. If he or his mother had found the play, they would've destroyed it."

"How did you know they had the files?"

He didn't respond.

"You were eavesdropping the day I called Jayne and told her Agnes had the files, weren't you? You probably tried to get them yourself, but Edgar got there first. You broke into his apartment, filched the files, and got rid of the witness."

"The play was promised to me," said Peter.

"How so?"

He dropped his arms limply to his sides. "It just was."

"How? What were Fielding's exact words?"

He shook his head as if he were trying to jog the memory loose from the ether around him. "Raymond told me he'd created something extraordinary. Something that was going to change the face of drama and he wanted to make sure I was a part of it. He said I was the only director he wanted to come near it."

I laughed. I couldn't help it. Everything was so obvious now.

Peter frowned at what he took as my mocking. "He meant it, Rosie. He shared my enthusiasm. He wanted to help me make a career. He hated directors—did you know that? He believed they spoiled plays by imposing their own meaning on a script. He said a good writer gave actors all they needed and that directors only muddied up the process with their egos. He told me that, and yet he insisted he was creating a play just for me. Can you imagine?"

"There is no play, Peter," I whispered.

"Stop saying that."

I backed away until I made contact with the dressing table. "Fielding invented a play and planted the idea that not only could it ruin lives and make careers, but it was missing. We're the characters, finding the play is our objective, and our obstacles are one another. Our tactic is to eliminate one another until the last person standing does so empty-handed. You were supposed to be that person, Peter. You rubbed out Jim and Edgar. Fielding expected you'd kill others to get your hands on the play. He didn't value you. You're a pawn, like me. He was trying to prove theater was its own organic beast, that drama didn't need actors, directors, buildings, or even a script to exist. It just needed a central conflict to propel the action forward. I'm sorry."

His head tilted toward the floor. "This can't be true. Of course there's a play."

I brushed the air before him with my hands. "Think about it: No one's seen it. Everyone who'd heard about it had a very different understanding of what it was about. He fed on ego and paranoia to make a point about his work being important. He even left someone behind to record all of this. I've met him. He's the one who admitted the truth about what's going on."

Peter stood in silence, slowly taking in all that I'd told him. As recognition sunk beneath the surface, anger bubbled upward until the cords in his neck grew prominent. His peepers left the floor and searched out the room for something at which to direct his anger. He picked up the vase of flowers and flung it into the mirror, shattering both objects. As debris flew through the air, I ducked and crawled toward the door.

The air grew taut with the distinct sound of a rod being cocked. "I didn't want to make this ugly, Rosie. I hoped you'd be cooperative."

I turned and found a gun aimed at me. "Be rational. Why would I lie about this?"

He gestured me to the dressing table stool and put his back to the door. "I don't know the answer to that. I only know what makes sense. Tell me where the play is."

"I just did."

He straightened his arm to ready himself for the gun's kick. "You have ten seconds. What's more important: the play or your life?"

Before I could comment on the irony of that statement, Jayne threw open the door. It slammed into Peter's back, knocking him off his feet and sending the gun skittering across the floor. As it reached the middle of the room, Peter's head slammed into the ground.

"Oops," said Jayne. She took in the broken vase and the rod in the middle of the room.

"Nice timing," I said.

"Is he out?"

"If he were any more chilled, we'd be sending his ma our condolences." I smiled at her like a simpleton. "Would you mind getting the gun?"

"That won't be necessary," said a voice. I turned and found Alan Detmire in the dressing room doorway, his own rod pointed at my heart.

I cleared my throat. "Nice to see you, Mr. Fielding. It is Raymond Fielding, isn't it?"

"You're smarter than I thought, Miss Winter."

"Don't be too impressed—your disguise didn't have a leg to stand on. Did you get to see the show?"

"I'm afraid not. It was sold out."

"Had you mentioned my name, the girl at the door would've gotten you in."

"I wish I had thought of that. I heard you were very good."

"Thanks. I never get tired of hearing that."

He gestured me over to where Jayne was standing. She remained unfazed, which only rattled me more. "If memory serves, I told you two to let things play out. Nothing good comes from interfering."

"I understand," I said, "but I got a little jittery when my own death became a part of the plot."

"We must be willing to sacrifice for art, Miss Winter."

"Couldn't my first sacrifice be on a smaller scale, like, say, a goat or a lamb?"

Peter groaned and his eyelids flickered.

"Step away from Mr. Sherwood, please," said Fielding.

Jayne and I did as he instructed, our bodies growing closer the farther we moved from him. "With all due respect," I said, "isn't this a little too deus ex machina for you?" Jayne tossed me a confused look. I told her with a wave that I'd explain it later. "I mean, how can a plot progress normally if you're strutting in here directing the action?"

"A necessary evil, Miss Winter. Had Miss Hamilton stayed away, I would have happily remained uninvolved. By the way, I made sure the theater doors are locked, just to make sure we don't have any further unscripted interruptions. Naturally, things will have to change now. The good thing is I think two murders are much more interesting than one. They certainly will help to speed things up. Wouldn't you agree?"

"Not really, no."

He nudged the body on the floor with his foot. "Alas, it's not your decision, it's Mr. Sherwood's. Isn't that right, Peter?"

Peter groaned again and Fielding backed away to make sure he was in full view when Peter came around. "Peter? Peter?" he called out. Peter's eyes fluttered as he fought to focus. "Peter," Fielding said again, the word no longer a name but a taunt. "Wake up. The show isn't over yet." Peter's eyes finally opened and remained that way. Slowly he sat up, one hand steadying his body while the other massaged the growing goose egg on his head. "That's a good boy," said Fielding. "Do you know where you are?"

"The theater," said Peter.

Fielding smiled. "And do you know what's happened?"

Peter scanned the room, taking in Fielding, Jayne, me, the broken vase. They made the trip a second time before settling on the old man with the gun. His gaze widened, his mouth moved noiselessly, and the hand intended to diminish the pain in his noggin left his body and pointed at Fielding. "Who are you?"

Fielding clucked his tongue. "I'm disappointed, Peter. For a man who claimed to worship me, you haven't done your research."

Peter rubbed his eyes to confirm the vision was real. "You're dead."

"Shhh . . . ," said Fielding.

Peter shook his head, then winced as the activity worsened his agony. "How can it be? Raymond Fielding's dead. I went to his wake."

"It was a setup," I said. "Nobody had seen Fielding for years, so he knocked off a fellow named Alan Detmire and pretended it was him."

"That can't be right," said Peter. "Why would you do such a thing?"

I stepped forward and tried to find in Peter a shred of the person I'd known for the past month. "It's like I told you: There was no play. The whole idea of this controversial, life-altering script was invented by Fielding as an experiment to test the concept of theater. Detmire probably disapproved of his methods and Fielding recognized he needed something to keep the action moving before people's interest waned. So he killed his lover, made it look like it was himself, and planted the idea that the death was over the missing play."

Peter moved his focus back to Fielding. "Is it true?"

Fielding stepped toward him and bent at the waist. "Miss Winter has a very active imagination. I have not killed anybody. I didn't have to."

"Eloise?" squeaked Jayne.

"Close, Miss Hamilton. My dear, dear Eloise couldn't stand the thought of our little secret getting out. She'd killed for lesser things in the past, and I had no doubt that she would be willing to do it again to protect her money and her reputation. I was wrong, though. She sent her son to do her dirty work. I will confess that I engineered things. I let her know that I was going to bed early one night and was planning on taking a sleeping tablet. Pity Edgar had never met me, so he wasn't able to verify who the man in my bed was."

"That's it?" I said. "No tears for a man you supposedly loved?"

"Alan was a character like everyone else, Miss Winter. It was his time to exit in order to help me further the story. Had he a choice in the matter, I'm sure he would have gladly given up his life for me."

Conveniently, we'd never hear what Alan had to say on the matter.

"So you see, Peter, you can't believe anything Miss Winter says. Just as I didn't kill Alan, there is a play. Rosie just doesn't want you to have it. She had it herself, and while you were unconscious, I took it away from her. And now if you agree to help me out, I'm going to give it to you, its rightful bearer."

I tried to step forward, but Jayne grabbed my arm and held me back. "Don't listen to him, Peter. He's a murderer and a liar!"

Fielding kept his eyes focused on Peter, who was as unaware that I'd spoken as an ant is that a tax hike is in progress. "That's right, Peter: the play is yours, with a few caveats. I know you killed Jim and Edgar. I have sufficient evidence to prove it. And judging from Miss Winter's comments, she knows, too. You also know I'm alive. If you keep my secret for me, I'll do the same for you. We will be bound to each other. Understand?"

Peter nodded his agreement. Fielding sighed and waved the gun toward Jayne and me. "The problem, of course, is these two. Neither is trustworthy; nor do they have anything invested in seeing that our secrets remain such. Therefore, in order for me to give you what you so desperately want, you must eliminate them. Once that's done, I'll hand you the script and help you plant evidence that proves this whole incident was at the hands of any number of people who have spoken up against Miss Winter. Are we agreed?"

Peter stared at the floor, contemplating his options. "I want to see the script."

Fielding straightened and his smile grew so wide I expected it to spill off his face. "I thought you might say that." He reached into his coat and pulled out a thick packet of paper bound with brass brads. "The play is right here." Peter's hands reached into the air. Fielding drew the script back into his chest. "As soon as the deed is done, it's yours to do with as you please."

"Don't believe him," I said. "That's a decoy. There is no play. This is all a game."

Fielding rested the script in the nook of his arm and aimed the gun at my chest. "Do shut up, Miss Winter. While I'd like to give Peter the satisfaction of killing you both, I'm not against doing it myself." He nodded at Peter, his previously calm demeanor rippling with impatience. "Have you made your decision, Mr. Sherwood? It shouldn't be a hard one. Not only will my play make you a star, but the circumstances of your lead actress's death will fill the papers for months. Peter Sherwood is going to be a household name."

Peter struggled to his feet and went to Fielding's side. He held out his hand and Raymond gently placed the gun in his palm. "Move," Peter told us. He motioned the two of us toward the corner of the room farthest from the door. Jayne gripped my hand and I closed my eyes and prayed that whatever was about to happen happened quickly. Off in the night a whippoorwill sang its sad song, and I tried to list all the plays I knew where a bird was a portent of death. And what the heck was a whippoorwill doing in the city anyway? A shot rang out, so loud my ears grew incapable of recognizing any other sound. I let out a sob and clutched Jayne's hand more tightly. Metal squirted again and

Jayne's body fell into mine. We tumbled to the ground and I opened my eyes just in time to see Fielding crumple to the floor.

"Everything's all right, Rosie," said Al. "They're both down."

Peter moaned from the floor, a geyser of blood shooting from his shoulder and staining his dress shirt a startling ruby. Fielding lay motionless by the door, his artificial leg splayed at an angle a showgirl would've killed for. Al straddled the distance between them like Gulliver among the Lilliputians. "Where's Jayne?" I asked.

"I'm right here, you dope." She stood above me, offering me her hand. "What took you so long?" she asked Al.

He shrugged and replaced his rod in a shoulder holster concealed by his coat. "The doors were locked. I had to find a hairpin."

"Did you call the cops?" she asked.

"Tony's on it," said Al. "You two scram and let me clean this up."

"Are you going to kill them?" I asked.

"Naw," said Al. "I ain't killing anyone. I'm just going to encourage them to be honest and forthright. I can be very convincing."

36 Out of a Blue Sky

LATER THAT NIGHT, I GOT the details of what went down. After Jayne left the theater, she ran into Ruby lurking outside the backstage door. She was mad and had been drinking to boot. Jayne played at being a sympathetic ear, and Ruby raged about how I'd found the script and was plotting with Peter to ruin her. Once Jayne realized this was the reason Ruby had disappeared, she understood something was afoot.

"So you assumed Peter believed I had the play and I was in danger?" I asked.

Jayne shrugged. "The idea wasn't quite that developed. I assumed Peter would try to get you to tell him where the script was, you'd tell him there was no play, and he'd get angry."

"Did you share this theory with Ruby?"

Jayne smiled. "Nope. I told her if you did have the play odds were you'd left it back at the Shaw House for safekeeping. I figured the last thing we needed was her hanging around."

That was good thinking on Jayne's part. I almost didn't mind the mess Ruby made while ransacking our room.

After Ruby left, Jayne decided to go back to the theater, but before doing so, she told Tony and Al what she thought was going on. They formed a plan whereby Jayne would track me down and five minutes later Al would go in and verify that everything was silk. If anything seemed wrong, Al was to signal to Tony, who would then ready himself at the nearest pay phone, where he'd buzz the cops as soon as he heard Al's birdcall.

"Why wouldn't Tony be part of the action?" I asked. "Calling the coppers doesn't seem his style."

"Tony's reforming," said Jayne. "I don't want blood on his hands, real or imaginary."

After our rescue, Al stayed back with a bleeding Peter and an unconscious Raymond Fielding.

"What did you say to Peter?" I asked him.

"I explained that if he sang, there was a good chance the cops would view him more favorably. I told him I was able to avoid a three spot at Riker's Island after turning on someone."

I frowned. "Really?"

"Of course not, you dumb bunny. I was lying, see?"

I put an arm on Al's shoulders. "No, you were acting. Welcome to the world of theater." Al must've been a pretty convincing actor, for when Lieutenant Schmidt and his boys arrived, Peter did as Al had instructed: confessing his own crimes while squealing about what the still-unconscious Raymond Fielding had been up to. Rather than congratulating him on his honesty, Schmidt put him in bracelets and loaded him into a meat wagon bound for the prison hospital.

I caught up with Ruby the next morning and thanked her for opening up to Jayne. Like it or not, I owed my life to her big mouth.

"It was nothing really." She flipped that dark, glossy hair of hers until it whipped me in the face. "I'm just glad nobody got hurt. Aside from your acting career, of course."

I tried to match her hair toss but instead wrenched my neck. "What do you mean?"

She leaned in close, feigning confidence, though her tone was clearly intended for anyone in a five-mile radius. "I mean if I were you I'd strike *In the Dark* from my résumé and change my name. That show is going to follow you like a bad stink." She checked her face in the mirror and headed to the foyer. "I'd love to catch up more, but I have a lunch date. Toodles."

"Toodles." At the wall of portraits I paused before her picture. A wad of gum was stuck beneath it and I pulled it off and pressed it firmly on her nose. If I had a mark on me, she was going to have one, too.

Both Fielding and Sherwood recovered from their gunshot wounds. Schmidt arrested Fielding for fraud for impersonating Detmire and faking his own death but wasn't able to charge him with anything else. Eloise got the wrap for conspiracy to murder. Peter was brought up on first-degree murder charges for the deaths of Jim McCain and Edgar Fielding. The story immediately supplanted any mention of *In the Dark*'s opening night success. Instead, the papers tracked Fielding's bizarre attempt at experimental theater, Eloise McCain's obsession with a play that didn't exist, Peter Sherwood's desperation to follow wherever his mentor led him, and, of course, Lieutenant Schmidt's clever unraveling of the whole sordid affair. I was mentioned once, though my name was misspelled and my role was reduced to the "lucky understudy whose big break came about because of murder." The AP picked up the story and for weeks the developments flooded the papers and radios, guaranteeing that anyone else who might have been embroiled in Fielding's play knew the truth about the piece. Then some folks in Warsaw decided they weren't content with ghetto life and public interest in the case faded.

People's Theatre opted to discontinue *In the Dark* and instead ran a series of short films about conditions in Japanese relocation camps. The production's halt meant Ruby's schedule was once again freed up. Since Lawrence had committed to using Jayne as his romantic lead, he rewrote his script to include a Polish nurse who comes to America on the eve of Jayne's wedding and engages in a two-page monologue describing how miserable her life had been since her GI boyfriend left her to marry another woman. Although Jayne's character got the guy in the end, Ruby's eight minutes onstage, convincing Polish accent, and tour de force performance led many critics to declare that she deserved a Drama League Award.

Two weeks after opening night my life was back to normal. I'd been to four auditions, I was contemplating a war plant job to get me

318 KATHRYN MILLER HAINES

through the lean times, and I'd written nine letters to Jack, none of which I'd mailed.

"Hiya," said Jayne from her post on the bed. She and Churchill lounged before a box of chocolates that still bore the card Tony had sent with them. Jayne had restricted her dining to the left side of the box, letting Churchill do what he pleased with the right. "How's tricks?"

"Fine," I said. Her casualness seemed forced, her question an attempt to stall. "Why?"

"No reason. By the way, you have mail." She raised an eyebrow. "V-mail."

I snatched the letter from her bed and nicked a chocolate from her side of the box. It was filled with coconut. Yuck.

"Aren't you going to read it?"

"I'm thinking about it." I held the letter to the light and tried to guess at its contents.

Jayne grabbed my arm. "If you don't open it, I will."

"Hold your horses already." I sat on my bed and delicately tore the fold. With a dramatic huff, I unfurled the page and showed Jayne my back.

"Well?"

I peered at the unfamiliar scrawl reduced to fit on the tiny page. "It's not from him. It's from someone in his platoon, an M. Harrington."

"That's a hell of a thing to do—breaking up with a girl and then passing around her picture." She tried to take the letter from me, but I waved her off.

He made me promise that if something were to happen to him, I would contact you. "He's MIA."

"Missing in action?" asked Jayne. I couldn't answer. I let go of the letter and let it flutter to my lap. She snatched it up and read the words I'd already committed to memory. "Jack?"

I nodded. *If something were to happen to him.* "It's a joke, right? Some kind of cruel gag he's pulling to teach me a lesson?" Jayne put her hand on mine and squeezed. "Missing's not dead, right? It's not even wounded. It's just . . . not there."

"Sure," said Jayne. "Absolutely. He'll come back."

Jayne was right: Jack was fine. He had to be. Nothing bad could ever happen to him. And yet an ache in my bones told me otherwise. I collapsed against my best pal and held her tight. Churchill pressed close against the other side of me as though he too wanted to participate in the embrace. I longed to cry, but for once the tears wouldn't come. I'd left them onstage.

Fake plays and egotistical directors were unbelievable and strange, but there was a war on, much as I hated to admit it, and that aced everything. Jack had become a phantom to me, a memory that faded the longer he stayed away. I might not have known what I wanted from him anymore, but I still loved him. And I knew that if something were missing, I would have to look for it even if it had never been there in the first place.

Acknowledgments

Rosie would never have seen the light of day without the work, research, support, and input of a number of fabulous people, among them: my wonderful agent, Paul Fedorko, who knows just what to say and when to say it; Erin Brown, the editor who first ushered this project into HarperCollins; and Sarah Durand, who did a wonderful job taking over the project after Erin moved on.

If you want to learn how to write, you surround yourself with talented writers. I did just that when I found the inestimable members of SPEC, and the Fiction Critique Group Without a Name (we really should call it something, guys), especially Paula Martinac and Ralph Scherder, who were never afraid to tell me that just because I could call it jawing, chinning, and bumping gums doesn't mean I should.

I am forever indebted to my dear friend and first reader, David L. White, who has never told me he was too busy to read just one more draft of anything, and his wife, Allison Trimarco, who was happy to apply her status as a lifelong New Yorker to whatever bizarre trivia question I hurled her way.

I am also grateful for the support of my sister, Pamela Nicholson, who cheered me on from across an ocean.

And of course, I must acknowledge my canine companions Mr. Rizzo, Chonka, and Violet. I could write without dogs, but why would I want to?

BOOKS BY KATHRYN MILLER HAINES

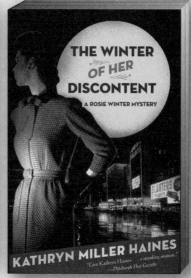

THE WAR AGAINST MISS WINTER
A Novel

ISBN 978-0-06-113978-9 (paperback)

Evocative, entertaining, and wonderfully original, Kathryn Miller Haines's *The War Against Miss Winter* introduces not only an unforgettable new sleuth, but also an exciting new voice in the mystery genre, with a fast-paced tale of murder and deception set during World War II.

"Perfectly captures the feel, sights, and sounds of New York in the 1940s."

—Rhys Bowen

THE WINTER OF HER DISCONTENT
A Rosie Winter Mystery

ISBN 978-0-06-113980-2 (paperback)

The second suspenseful and atmospheric World War II mystery starring aspiring actress Rosie Winter, from the author whose "pitch-perfect rendering of the early '40s brings wartime New York City beautifully to life." (*Kirkus Reviews*)

"Give Kathryn Haines . . . a standing ovation."

—*Pittsburgh Post-Gazette*